PLAIN TALES FROM THE HILLS

Rudyard Joseph Kipling was born in Bombay in 1865. His father, John Lockwood Kipling, was the author and illustrator of *Beast and Man in India* and his mother, Alice, was the sister of Lady Burne-Jones. In 1871 Kipling was brought home from India and spent five unhappy years with a foster family in Southsea, an experience he later drew on in *The Light That Failed* (1890). The years he spent at the United Services College, a school for officers' children, are depicted in *Stalky and Co.* (1899) and the character of Beetle is something of a self-portrait. It was during his time at the college that he began writing poetry and *Schoolboy Lyrics* was published privately in 1881. In the following year he started work as a journalist in India, and while there produced a body of work, stories, sketches and poems – notably *Plain Tales from the Hills* (1888) – which made him an instant literary celebrity when he returned to England in 1889. *Barrack Room Ballads* (1892) contains some of his most popular pieces, including 'Mandalay', 'Gunga Din' and 'Danny Deever'. In this collection Kipling experimented with form and dialect, notably the cockney accent of the soldier poems, but the influence of hymns, music-hall songs, ballads and public poetry can be found throughout his verse.

In 1892 he married an American, Caroline Balestier, and from 1892 to 1896 they lived in Vermont, where Kipling wrote *The Jungle Book*, published in 1894. In 1901 came *Kim* and in 1902 the *Just So Stories*. Tales of every kind – including historical and science fiction – continued to flow from his pen, but *Kim* is generally thought to be his greatest long work, putting him high among the chroniclers of British expansion.

From 1902 Kipling made his home in Sussex, but he continued to travel widely and caught his first glimpse of warfare in South Africa, where he wrote some excellent reportage on the Boer War. However, many of the views he expressed were rejected by anti-imperialists who accused him of jingoism and love of violence. Though rich and successful, he never again enjoyed the literary esteem of his early years. With the onset of the Great War his work became a great deal more sombre. The stories he subsequently wrote, *A Diversity of Creatures* (1917), *Debits and Credits* (1926) and *Limits and Renewals* (1932) are now thought by many to contain some of his finest writing. The death of his only son in 1915 also contributed to a new inwardness of vision.

Kipling refused to accept the role of Poet Laureate and other civil honours, but he was the first English writer to be awarded the Nobel Prize, in 1907. He died in 1936 and his autobiographical fragment *Something of Myself* was published the following year.

Mr H. R. Woudhuysen and David Trotter are Lecturers in English at University College, London. David Trotter's previous publications include *The Poetry of Abraham Cowley* and *The Making of the Reader: Language and Subjectivity in Modern American, English and Irish Poetry*.

Rudyard Kipling

PLAIN TALES
FROM THE HILLS

EDITED

BY H. R. WOUDHUYSEN

WITH AN INTRODUCTION AND NOTES

BY DAVID TROTTER

PENGUIN BOOKS

Penguin Books Ltd, Harmondsworth, Middlesex, England
Viking Penguin Inc., 40 West 23rd Street, New York, New York 10010, U.S.A.
Penguin Books Australia Ltd, Ringwood, Victoria, Australia
Penguin Books Canada Ltd, 2801 John Street, Markham, Ontario, Canada L3R 1B4
Penguin Books (N.Z.) Ltd, 182–190 Wairau Road, Auckland 10, New Zealand

First published by Macmillan 1890
Published in Penguin Books 1987

Introduction and notes copyright © David Trotter, 1987
All rights reserved

Made and printed in Great Britain by
Richard Clay Ltd, Bungay, Suffolk
Typeset in Lasercomp Ehrhardt

Contents

Introduction

There are more plains than hills in *Plain Tales from the Hills*. Kipling's title promises stories about life at Simla, the small town in the Himalayas where the Government of India settled during the hot season. These he certainly delivers. But it is the plain tales from the plains and from the cities, tales of heat and bewilderment and wasted effort and broken faith, which we are likely to remember: Trejago's meetings with his 15-year-old lover, Bisesa; the capture of Lungtungpen; the dust-storm during which Saumarez proposes to the wrong woman; Lieutenant Golightly's arrival at Amritzar, 'nearly hysterical with rage and the chill and the mistake and the handcuffs and the headache that the cut on his forehead had given him'. For the scope of Kipling's plainness, in this first volume of stories, is remarkable.

Kipling returned to India in 1882, at the age of 16. He had spent eleven years in England and he was coming back to a job which his parents had secured for him, as Assistant Editor on the Lahore *Civil and Military Gazette*. Much of his editorial work was routine, but in 1884 he began to write more extensively for the journal: special reports, feature articles, social notes, book reviews, comic sketches. (Some of this material has been collected by Thomas Pinney and reprinted as *Kipling's India*.) Then, in 1886, his friend Kay Robinson arrived to take over as editor of the *Gazette*. Robinson wanted to liven the paper up, and promptly put Kipling's talents to work. He introduced a new feature, 'turnovers', which began on the first page and continued on to the second. They soon became very popular with readers. Thirty-nine of the stories later published as *Plain Tales from the Hills* appeared in that form between November 1886 and June 1887, under the same title.

In his autobiography, *Something of Myself*, Kipling conceived his early life as a story of exile and return. He represented India as a land of imaginative and emotional stimulus, England as a

7

land of exile where he learnt (through deprivation) the advantages of self-discipline and reserve. Arriving back in India at the age of 16 to take up his post on the *Civil and Military Gazette*, he knew at once that his original responsiveness had survived intact: 'I found myself at Bombay where I was born, moving among sights and smells that made me deliver the vernacular sentences whose meaning I knew not … my English years fell away, nor ever, I think, came back in full strength.' The English years did persist at Lahore, in the shape of a tyrannical editor who kept him hard at work on routine matters. But he benefited from the discipline; and the productive sights and smells of India were never far away.

Kipling's biographers and critics have used this story of exile and return, of English years and Indian years, to distinguish between constraint and imaginative sympathy in the man and in the work. Anglo–Indian children (the children of British people living in India) were sent home in order to be reminded of their duty to Empire and to stoicism. In Kipling's case, we are told, stoicism and Empire had to contend with an inclination to wander and absorb, an energetic responsiveness. It was the Indian rather than the English years which gave him his first subject, his most important territory, and that breadth of imagination found above all in *Kim*.

There is much truth in this view, and even more convenience. For one thing, it allows us to overlook Kipling's politics. We can say that the imagination stimulated by the Indian years made the political assumptions or enthusiasms of the English years a metaphor for more fundamental trials of spirit; or that the uncertain outcome of the tales undoes the colonizing assurance of the teller. However, the sketches and reports Kipling wrote for the *CMG* demonstrate that his view of 'the Indian scene' was mediated by English standards and fictions. These standards and fictions made him aware of his own distance from India, and thus enabled him to see both it and himself for the first time. They formed the repertoire out of which he was to make the *Plain Tales*.

Kipling proved himself as a reporter while covering the Viceroy's visit to Patiala, a native state 200 miles south-east of

Lahore, in 1884. One of the four pieces he wrote there begins as an account of the copiousness and variety of the Maharajah's Palace, and turns into a self-dramatization. Wandering through a maze of corridors, he comes across five ancient counsellors seated on Persian rugs in a small chamber:

As soon as they recognized the presence of a Sahib among them, they rose *en masse*, and, with the greatest gravity, proceeded to 'shoo' me out of their presence as one might 'shoo' a strayed fowl. It seems that I had trespassed too close to the ladies, and as none of the five elders understood English, they had adopted this course in order to let me understand that it was as well to withdraw. I took the hint, and managed to rejoin modern civilization in the shape of the barouche kindly placed at my service by the authorities in the great outer square.

The recognition of Kipling as a Sahib generates in the narrative the stylistic markers of cultural difference: the French idiom, the inverted commas, the simile, the dapper acknowledgement of trespass, the expansive double-edged irony of 'modern civilization'. Kipling discovers himself and India in relation to English (or European) standards. He discovers himself as a writer: learns what a writer does, how a writer gains some sort of purchase on his material. This plunge into the Indian scene kindles small ironies rather than large sympathies. A rhetorical distance establishes and holds the distance between cultures; the writer himself is held by that distance.

A year later Kipling investigated the milk supply of Lahore, thought to be a source of typhoid. He took his English standards and fictions with him. His report imitated the narratives of the English sanitary reformers who had written about the slums of Manchester and London. (One of his jobs on the *Civil and Military Gazette* was to epitomize Blue Books: according to his editor, Kay Robinson, he did his best to convert them into 'interesting and picturesque narratives'.) The reports and essays of the English reformers tended to follow a pattern: departure from a police station, descent into the slums, a chronicle of filth and rot and miasma. They all dramatized the distinctness of the investigator.

Kipling's is no exception: 'An Englishman parading the bye-ways of a native town, in company with a policeman, is an object of the liveliest curiosity, not to say suspicion.' As the Englishman descends into the native town, his narrative descends into the vernacular: 'Within three feet of the rank was located a *hulwaie*'s shop, and the proprietor thereof, wrapped up in his *rezai*, sat upon the shop-board waiting the morning supply of milk which the *gowalla* was even then drawing.' Among the exotic milkmaids he finds what his English narrative had led him to expect: filth, rot, miasma: 'The second room – stall, stable, or cess-pit – was pitch dark, and the unwary explorer sank over ankle deep into the foul compost that lay thick on the floor, and was nearly suffocated by the fetid stench inside.' The filth belongs to Lahore, the modes of description and self-dramatization to an English (or at least a European) narrative. Eventually the explorer staggers out into the fresh air and into the French language: 'The details have been sketched as lightly as possible; but any one who knows the manners and customs of the Punjabi will be able to fill them in *à discretion*.' They have the manners and customs, we have the discretion.

Kipling was later to write in the same terms of the slums of Calcutta, in 'City of Dreadful Night'. Forming an 'amateur sanitary commission' of one, he explores 'just such mysterious, conspiring tenements as Dickens would have loved'. The narratives of sanitary reform had produced a knowledge of the slums by asserting at every step the difference between us and them, rulers and ruled, colonizers and colonized: they make mysteries, we make choices. At once political and literary, Benthamite and Dickensian, these narratives helped Kipling to imagine 'the Indian scene', and his own place in it.

There were other narratives, of course. Kipling often represented himself as an innocent abroad: a role studied from Dickens's *Sketches by Boz*, perhaps, or the early journalism of Mark Twain. The spectacle of military discipline or military technology, for example, always provoked attacks of acute innocence: 'How it's done, the civilian's mind cannot tell.' On such occasions, Kipling appears as a 'mere outsider' or an 'unprofessional observer'. The role makes his presence felt, while at the same time enlarging our perception of the prowess of Empire. Thus he will play the Twainian loafer in order to register the efficiency and dedication of Englishmen repairing a railway line; or the Twainian 'country cousin' in order to compare the miseries of travel by *dak gharri* with the miseries of travel by stage-coach in the American West. Like the sanitary reformer, the innocent abroad is a self-dramatization to be tested in and against 'the Indian scene'.

Kipling developed as a reporter and as a writer not by transcending these strategies, but by discarding the ones which didn't work and adapting the ones which did. Innocence would not run an Empire, and there were good political reasons why he should set a limit to his unwariness. In the *Plain Tales* he chose to be wary, to rely on the kind of knowingness he had begun to develop as a journalist. In 1886, posing as an Enthusiastic Excursionist, he visited the 'evil-smelling enclosures' of the Lahore horse-market and interviewed a shady dealer. Whereas Twain's innocence of horse-flesh had led to the purchase of an unmanageable Genuine Mexican Plug, Kipling was not going to allow himself to be fooled by an Afghan bandit; he didn't buy. Too great an unwariness would only encourage mystery and conspiracy. Too many Enthusiastic Excursionists, and there would be no more Empire. So he dropped the role. When the market and the dealer reappear in *Kim*, one is merely 'turbulent', the other a British spy.

Much as Kipling admired Twain, he could not afford the levelling devices of 'Western' humour. In his early sketches Twain created the figure of the Unreliable, a yobbish news-paperman who turns up at parties looking 'hungry and vicious' and intending to commit bad behaviour. The Unreliable eats and drinks a lot, insults people and dances a quadrille with eight inches of codfish sticking out of his pocket. Twain can enjoy this disruption of the fragile gentility of Carson City without being held responsible for it; he simply observes. In 'A Friend's Friend', published in the *Civil and Military Gazette* in 1887, a similar figure performs similar feats and then bursts into tears for good measure. But Kipling's narrator is not amused. He regards the whole performance as an insult to himself and takes an elaborate revenge. The Anglo-Indian Unreliable is plastered with meringue, rolled up in sixty feet of cloth and tossed into a passing bullock-cart. Kipling was determined to protect the fragile gentility of Lahore against carnival. If there is any carnival here, it is in the vengeance, not in the disruption.

Kipling the Reliable protected English standards by acknowledging and reproducing the special skills and vocabularies which embodied colonial authority. Writing about Amritzar Fair, he displays a sudden familiarity with horseflesh: 'Badly formed weak hocks, ditto feet, and a want of bone below the knee – the old established faults of the Indian horse – were visible everywhere.' The knowingness creates a (faintly ludicrous) narrative presence; it also seems to ensure the safety of the various English buyers 'walled up' by the dense crowds. Kipling may have learnt the political and rhetorical value of expertise from the members of his Club: 'In that Club and elsewhere I met none except picked men at their definite work – Civilians, Army, Education, Canals, Forestry, Engineering, Irrigation, Railways, Doctors, and Lawyers – samples of each branch and each talking his own shop.' The definiteness of such talk enhanced the definiteness of the work and of the men. Kipling, an unenthusiastic rider, chose to be reliably definite about horses.

In *Plain Tales from the Hills*, these notations of expertise supersede the innocent abroad. They establish what George Moore identified as Kipling's major anxiety: 'not to be taken in'. The stories dispense with the services of a narrator whose sentimental and veterinary education would dramatize growth and assimilation. Their narrator is consistently and at times absurdly knowing, with a perfect command both of horse-talk and of book-talk. He is at once more comprehensive in his view of Anglo-Indian life and more detailed in his familiarity with specialized activities than those he tells us about. He is not to be seen admiring a half-lame horse or rattling about inside a *ticca gharri*. He holds off, observing events coolly, only becoming involved when his particular expertise seems to demand it.

The sense of detachment was if anything reinforced by the publication of the stories in book form, first in Calcutta and then in London. The *Plain Tales* were written with a very specific audience in mind: the readers of a provincial newspaper. When Kipling came to publish them in book form, he revised them for a more general Anglo-Indian readership, and then for a British readership. The revisions he made show him turning to face a different audience, an audience unfamiliar with India. So, 'anna' became 'penny' (p. 64). In the *Gazette* version of 'Pig', Kipling records that Nafferton 'hounded Pinecoffin from Mithankot to Jagadhri, and from Gurgaon to Abottabad'; which is to say, he adds in 1888, 'up and across the Punjab, a large Province, and in places remarkably dry' (p. 197). What he could assume in the readers of the *Gazette* – 'You know of course that . . .' – he has to tell British readers: 'Nearly every household in India knows that Doctors are very helpless in typhoid' (p. 266).

Such revisions induced a small but significant change in the relationship between story and reader. The same stories that confirmed what readers of the *Gazette* already knew, recording common pleasures and miseries, presented to British readers an almost inconceivably remote world. Where the book speaks of 'India', the *Gazette* has 'this country' or 'out here'. 'This' and 'here' are specifying agents which indicate the object referred to without identifying it. It is up to the reader to recognize which country the writer has in mind; we perform the work of identification ourselves, and thus become implicated in the creation of a world; we show solidarity by completing the reference. In the 1888 text, we are presented with a world which we do not belong to, which we are observing from the outside: the writer himself supplies the reference. His knowingness is not now a kind of *camaraderie*. Rather, it secures the authority of a frank and at times even polemical presentation of the hardships of Empire.

Kipling dismantled the journalistic format of the *Gazette* turnovers. 'You will say that all this story is . . . made up,' he observes in 'The Bisara of Pooree' (p. 229) – 'to fill a column and a half,' the *Gazette* version adds. He also elevated their language. In the 1888 edition, for example, 'swore' became 'vowed', 'got on' became 'succeeded', 'went with' became 'accompanied', 'tried' became 'strove', 'later on' became 'in after seasons', 'got up off' became 'rose from', 'speak to' became 'confer with', and so on. Whole phrases and sentences reappeared in formal dress: 'stood round him' became 'grouped themselves picturesquely around him, (p. 140); 'But they would have been wrong' became 'But this verdict would have been incorrect' (p. 64). Sometimes

Kipling also added the trade-marks of literariness. The neutral statement 'Here he lied' acquired an allusion to Swift, and became 'Here he spoke the thing which was not' (p. 39). The description of Aurelian McGoggin – 'Something had wiped his lips of speech ...' – acquired a simile: '... as a mother wipes the milky lips of her child' (p. 121). Elevated language helped to make a place for Kipling in the London literary world, among the picked men at their definite work of writing; and it dignified his portrait of Anglo-India.

'Mr Kipling, the Anglo-Indian,' wrote T. S. Eliot in 1919, 'had frontier welfare, and rebellions, and Khartoum, and he produced the Empire.' Twenty years before, similar expectations had characterized the critical reception of Kipling's early poems and stories. Andrew Lang, for example, argued that *Plain Tales from the Hills* would 'teach more of India, of our task there, of the various peoples whom we try to rule, than many Blue Books'. Kipling in India had deployed English standards and fictions in order to explain the Imperial task. The knowingness of *Plain Tales* was such a fiction, producing Empire out of frontier welfare. If we are to appreciate its reasons and its qualities, we must examine the English standards to which it answered.

'We seem, as it were, to have conquered and peopled half the world in a fit of absence of mind.' So said Sir John Seeley, Professor of Modern History at Cambridge, during the course of a series of lectures published in 1883 as *The Expansion of England*. 'While we were doing it, that is in the eighteenth century, we did not allow it to affect our imaginations or in any degree to change our ways of thinking; nor have we even now ceased to think of ourselves as simply a race inhabiting an island off the northern coast of the Continent of Europe.' The destiny of England had been shaped by expansion, but the English didn't want to know; they didn't much care about the vast territories acquired in their name. The purpose of militant Imperialists like Seeley was to make the English change their ways of thinking, to make them care about power and dominion.

By 1850, the Empire consisted of Canada, Australia, India, the British West Indies and the South African settlements. Some people thought it not worth the trouble. Others thought parts of it – the parts containing unruly subject races – not worth the trouble. But it went on growing anyway, under Tory and Liberal governments alike, throughout an era of acquisition. Independent states became spheres of influence, spheres of influence became governed territories. During the thirty years after 1850, the Empire incorporated more and more non-European peoples into an increasingly formal structure. Conquest and government brought a new sense of the pride of dominion; episodes like the 'Indian Mutiny' of 1857 and the 'Jamaican Revolt' of 1865 brought a new sense of its dangers.

In a speech at the Crystal Palace on 24 June 1872, Benjamin Disraeli presented himself as the defender of an Empire which the Liberals had been trying to dismantle for forty years. He concluded by telling his listeners that they would soon have to decide 'whether you will be content to be a comfortable England, modelled and moulded upon continental principles and meeting in due course an inevitable fate, or whether you will be a great country, a country where your sons when they rise, rise to paramount positions, and obtain not merely the esteem of your countrymen but command the respect of the world.' English men and women were being asked to imagine their country as an Empire, rather than as a wealthy and progressive democracy; and to imagine their children as the agents of Empire. The respect of the world should be the only measure of their achievement.

Imperialism was Disraeli's response to a period of economic distress and social tension, and to pressure for electoral reform. In 1866 it did seem possible that the ruling class might be overwhelmed by a new working-class electorate, or by the violence of its insurrectionary and criminal elements. The Conservative government tried to submerge class divisions in a renewed sense of nationhood. It insisted that the Queen come out of seclusion, and began to pursue a far more aggressive foreign policy. The Empire would focus the energies of all classes and direct them away from domestic problems; it would become the symbol of national unity and national purpose.

The success of this policy remains a matter of controversy. But we can perhaps say that it either provoked or contributed to the emergence of a working-class culture which was impervious to middle-class evangelism and yet politically docile. The 'Two Nations' had not become one. But the non-political working classes did join with their rulers in a general feeling for the glamour of Empire, and in specific celebrations such as Mafeking Night.

From one point of view, then, Imperialism could be seen as a solution to class-conflict, an exporting of resentment and aggression. It served to displace and to revalue an intransigence which could neither be transformed nor swept away. Here Kipling does seem to have played a part. His poems and stories about the life of the private soldier emphasize both the harshness and the intransigence of that life, and its ultimate dedication to national purposes. There are four such stories in *Plain Tales*.

Kipling's privates – Mulvaney, Learoyd and Ortheris – speak a virtually impenetrable mixture of dialect and Anglo-Indian slang; their speech closes off the world they inhabit from the middle-class narrator and his middle-class readers. Their behaviour is resolutely unaccommodating to middle-class pieties and aspirations. Yet they remain loyal to Queen and Country. Their aggression is directed either at Liberal critics of Empire, or at Burmese dacoits and wily Pathans. When writing about the three privates, Kipling reproduces the patterns of behaviour projected on to the working class by Imperial ideology.

The sign of this is the relative passivity or neutrality of the narrator. Conscious of being a privileged guest, of hearing about events he could never take part in, of glimpsing a world whose customs and codes he could never live by, he just buys the drinks and stands with notebook open while the soldiers talk. 'I can't give dialects properly,' he says in the *Gazette* version of 'The Three Musketeers', thus acknowledging that he will always remain an outsider (see note 7). Indeed, Kipling did find it hard to get the dialects right, making many minor revisions. His aim seems to have been to reproduce as accurately as possible the tone of working-class intransigence, to revalue it by finding a place for it within literature and within ideology.

The narrator plays a far more active role in the stories about middle-class men and women. Empire had also, of course, to mean something to the people who administered and engineered and policed it, often under harsh and demoralizing conditions. The answer was to present those conditions as a test of character, a rite of passage which turned boys into men, which made you a tougher and more responsible person than you would have become had you stayed at home. These individual regenerations validated the system which had made them necessary in the first place; they demonstrated its moral utility. An empire founded on individual regenerations was clearly preferable to one founded on greed.

British Imperialism, as Kipling might have learnt from G. O. Trevelyan's *Competition Wallah*, which he read on the boat out, represented service in India as a rite of passage:

The real education of a civil servant consists in the responsibility that devolves on him at an early age, which brings out whatever good there is in a man; the obligation to do nothing that can reflect dishonour on the service; the varied and attractive character of his duties; and the example and precept of his superiors, who regard him rather as a younger brother than as a subordinate official.

The conditions of service on the frontier of Empire bring out whatever good there is in a person; they reveal the true self hidden beneath the artifice of habit and mannerism. Sir Richard Temple, who had served in India for nearly thirty years, enthused about the rites of passage awaiting the young administrator whose duties would involve a six-month tour of his district:

After some weeks or some months of marching and touring, during which time he has seldom heard the English language spoken, he returns to his headquarters with his physical frame invigorated, his mind refreshed, his imagination stored with new ideas and his will braced with fresh resolves. Many of the beneficent plans, which he then conceived, he proceeds to carry out, as he once more sits in his central office during the long hours of the summer days [*India in 1880*, 1881].

According to this view, the duties of the administrator will regenerate him physically, mentally and morally. Rites of passage will transform innocence into experience, and so demonstrate the moral utility of the frontier and its intimate connection with the homeland.

Kipling was less sanguine. His early stories show innocence broken rather than transformed, and Britain separated from the British in India by irreconcilable differences of perception. In 'Thrown Away', for example, a young subaltern's education in England renders him incapable of adjusting to conditions in India: 'There was a Boy once who had been brought up under the "sheltered life" theory; and the theory killed him dead . . . He was beautifully taught in all that wins marks by a private tutor, and carried the extra weight of "never having given his parents an hour's anxiety in his life" ' (pp. 42–3). The Boy's duties do not bring out whatever good there is in him. They do not reveal the true self obscured by the wrong kind of education. Rather, his bloody suicide dramatizes the gap between innocence and experience, between the theories of home and the realities of abroad.

Brooding over that gap, the narrator's knowingness comes into its own: 'It was pitiful to watch The Boy knocking himself to pieces, as an over-handled colt falls down and cuts himself when he gets away from his groom' (p. 44). His comments imply a knowledge of life – yet it is only a knowledge of horses, and does not touch directly on The Boy's dilemma. His expertise does not educate; it simply dramatizes the gaps which education cannot bridge, including the gap between a knowledge of horses and a knowledge of oneself. He is called upon to write a letter to The Boy's parents, covering up the suicide: 'In due course I made the draft to my satisfaction, setting forth how The Boy was the pattern of all virtues, beloved by his Regiment, with every promise of a great career before him, and so on; how we had helped him through the sickness – it was no time for little lies, you will understand – and how he had died without pain' (p. 47). The special skills of the writer have served to conceal the reality of incurable innocence, and of the Indian frontier, from those at home: they have reinforced the gap between innocence and experience, between home and abroad, just like that other lie, told by Marlow to Kurz's fiancée in Conrad's *Heart of Darkness*.

The innocence deplored here is not just that of the Enthusiastic Excursionist, but that of Imperial ideology. The fact of literal or metaphoric distance has taken so strong a grip on Kipling's imagination that he seems to have lost all regard for pieties. Whereas in the working-class stories rites of passage function smoothly – Mulvaney is good at initiating raw recruits into the mysteries of army discipline and army beer – in the middle-class stories they always fail. There the aim had been to assimilate the dangerously intransigent; here it is to show the strain under which the already assimilated must live and work. There the narrator had merely observed; here he steps in to emphasize, even to reinforce, separation.

Literal or metaphoric distance is certainly the theme of the stories about relationships between men and women. Difference of gender often serves to emphasize the difference between innocence and experience or the difference between home and abroad. In 'The Rescue of Pluffles', the mature and experienced Mrs Hauksbee guides a callow young man away from danger: 'She began to talk to Pluffles after the manner of a mother, and as if there had been three hundred years, instead of fifteen, between them' (p. 78). The drama lies in the distance between what she knows about the world and what he knows, between innocence and experience. In '"Yoked with an Unbeliever"' and 'In the Pride of His Youth', young men go abroad, leaving the women they love behind them. The failure of both relationships is caused by, and serves to reinforce, the failure of people at home to understand the reality of life in India.

But the misunderstanding of men by women, and of women by men, can perfectly well stand alone, as it does in 'False Dawn' and 'Bitters Neat':

In India, where life goes quicker than at Home, things are more obviously tangled, and therefore more pitiful to look at. Men speak the truth as they understand it, and women as they think men would like to understand it; and then they all act lies which would deceive Solomon, and the result is a heart-rending muddle that half-a-dozen open words would put straight [p. 57].

In Kipling's stories, the open words are never spoken. Men lie to women, women lie to men, just as the narrator must lie to The Boy's parents. There are and must be limits to all knowledge, just as there are and must be limits to class and personality. Kipling's subject is the pathos of those limits, the pathos of distance.

Introduction

The most potent of all limits was that set between the races, between black and white. Necessary to the maintenance of power, it also became a habit of mind and the subject of many of Kipling's stories. 'The Anglo-Indian has a very fine eye for colour,' wrote George Aberigh-Mackay in *Twenty-One Days in India* (1881):

> He will mark down 'one anna in the rupee' with unerring certainty; he will suspect smaller coin. He will tell you how he can detect an adulterated European by his knuckles, his nails, his eyebrows, his pronunciation of the vowels, and his conception of propriety in dress, manners, and conduct.

Racial discrimination has become a habit of mind, almost an aesthetic. It seeks out signs of difference, pretending to measure even the consistency of blood. 'The amount of native blood in an Eurasian is expressed by so many annas in a rupee; thus, there being sixteen annas in a rupee, a half-breed would be styled "eight annas in the rupee", and so on' (H.S., *The Young Soldier in India*, 1889). Discrimination identifies both the observer and the observed; *they* have the manners and customs, *we* have the ability to measure and to grade. That we should do so in terms of their language and their currency makes it even more of an expression of power. The British in India appropriated the vernacular not in order to listen, but in order to make themselves heard: to show that they could enforce meanings as well as laws.

Some of Kipling's stories endorse this habit of mind. In 'Kidnapped', for example, Peythroppe's friends prevent him from marrying Miss Castries, whose fingernails reveal her mixed blood 'as plainly as print' (p. 134). And they are clearly right to do so. For the narrator has already characterized him as a man liable to be taken in, a perpetual innocent: 'How can a man who has never married, who cannot be trusted to pick up at sight a moderately sound horse, whose head is hot and upset with visions of domestic felicity, go about the choosing of a wife?' (p. 133). The narrator belongs among the experts, Hindu as well as Anglo-Indian, who know that the races should not mix. Peythroppe himself does not have sufficient presence in the story to provide an alternative point of view. We can only conclude that his friends are right to kidnap him and beat him up, rather than let him marry a contaminated European. The narrator's knowingness reproduces an Anglo-Indian habit.

In 'His Chance in Life', a Eurasian clerk takes command during a riot because the panic-stricken Police Inspector, 'obeying the old race-instinct which recognizes a drop of White blood as far as it can be diluted, said, "What orders does the Sahib give?"' (p. 94). The form of address settles it, making the clerk an honorary white man, giving him a white man's courage. It seems that this might be a story about the dependence of authority on symbolism: 'Never forget that unless the outward and visible signs of Our Authority are always before a native he is as incapable as a child of understanding what authority means, or where is the danger of disobeying it' (p. 93). But the only explanations offered by the story rely less on an analysis of outward and visible signs than on the old race-instinct itself. After the riot, the Assistant Collector arrives: 'in the presence of this young Englishman, Michele felt himself slipping back more and more into the native' pp. 95). He bursts into tears: 'It was the White drop in Michele's veins dying out, though he did not know it' (p. 95). The outward and visible signs of white authority are not arbitrary, but based on racial differences. Kipling meant, I think, to indicate the depth of the division between the races. But the terms in which he did so were those of white power. The detachment of the narrative merely reproduces, without examination, the detachment of white rulers from their black subjects.

Kipling's revisions strengthened the absoluteness of the division between the races. In the *C M G* version the Assistant Collector had arrived, with due circumspection, to 'talk to the men of' Tibasu: a bit too liberal, evidently, since in the final version he comes to 'quell' them (p. 95). In the *CMG* version of 'Kidnapped' Miss Castries possesses what 'they' call a 'Spanish complexion'; in the final version this senti-mentality is attributed to 'innocent people': people at home who will never understand the depth of the division between black and white, and the necessity to measure annas in the rupee (p. 134).

The division between black and white was an effect of, and served to reinforce, social and political structure. Kipling had a vivid sense of the constraints imposed by structure, and tried to imagine a way out, a crossing of the boundary which separated black from white. Like many Romantic writers before him, he dramatized his hostility to structure by taking the point of view of children or marginals. The only people likely to cross over are those who have not yet found their place within the system, or those who have found it and then chosen to abandon it.

Anglo-Indian children fell into the first category. Surrounded by native servants whose language and attitudes they were eager to absorb, they had not yet learnt their place in Empire and in stoicism. Kipling mythologized this precocious fluidity in *Kim*, in *Something of Myself*, and in 'Tods' Amendment': 'Tods was the idol of some eighty *jhampanis*, and half as many *saises*. He saluted them all as "O Brother"' (p. 180). Tods crosses and recrosses a boundary whose existence he is unaware of (and will remain unaware of until he is sent into exile in England). He knows more about native opinion and native anxieties than the Viceroy's Council, who amend a Bill in order to accommodate his knowledge. Kipling clearly found this fluidity, this freedom from set habits and views, very attractive. It is Kim's main virtue.

Adults seem more reluctant to cross boundaries. Only those who live on the edges of social structure – the marginals, the drifters and loafers – will risk it. McIntosh Jellaludin has, jettisoning his Oxford education and his status as a sahib in the process: 'When a man begins to sink in India, and is not sent Home by his friends as soon as may be, he falls very low from a respectable point of view. By the time that he changes his creed, as did McIntosh, he is past redemption' (p. 271). Kipling obviously found this bohemian loafer attractive. But not attractive enough, perhaps. He never completed his novel of low-life in India (see 'To be Filed for Reference', note 9).

McIntosh is contemptuous of another marginal, the policeman Strickland, whose characterization makes one doubt the extent of Kipling's commitment to marginality. Strickland, an expert in disguise, has accumulated an immense knowledge of native life, a knowledge which the conventionally minded resent or deplore: 'He was perpetually "going Fantee" among natives, which, of course, no man with any sense believes in' (p. 51). The irony aligns us with the marginal rather than with the men of sense, the occupants of social structure. But it is a rather precarious alignment. For Strickland goes Fantee either in order to woo the woman he loves, or in order to gather information: either, that is, to secure his own place within the social structure, or to protect it through more efficient policing. Strickland does not transgress the codes of British rule so much as extend and reinforce them.

Neither Tods nor Jellaludin nor Strickland has much vitality. At this point in his career, Kipling's commitment to structure and to limits was both ideological and imaginative. He imagined boundaries more effectively than he imagined crossings, detachment more effectively than integration. The writing reproduces hierarchy and separation, then begins to feed on them with unideological abandon, until finally it differentiates even where ideology would prefer to reconcile. Two of his best stories, 'Lispeth' and 'Beyond the Pale', dramatize racial difference without either exploiting or transcending it.

In 'Kidnapped' and 'His Chance in Life', the behaviour of the whites is natural and self-evident: no need to explain why Peythroppe's friends think it better to capture him and beat him up rather than allow him to marry a Eurasian; no need to explain the grounds of the Assistant Collector's authority. The behaviour of non-whites, on the other hand, appears to have been made rather than given, produced by specific cultural codes which are susceptible of analysis. But in the best stories the ironic detachment of the narrator reveals white behaviour too as the product of specific cultural codes: it too is made rather than given.

'Beyond the Pale' is a story about division: 'A man should, whatever happens, keep to his own caste, race, and breed. Let the White go to the White and the Black to the Black' (p. 162). Trejago falls in love with Bisesa and crosses the boundary between races. But in this story the boundary is relative, not absolute. It has been built out of cultural codes, out of what people choose to believe: '"You are an Englishman. I am only a black girl" – she was fairer than bar-gold in the Mint – "and the widow of a black man"' (p. 166). The narrator intervenes to point out that colour exists in the mind, not in the veins. Trejago is as white, and Bisesa as black, as their respective cultures have made them. But the codes are none the less powerful for their arbitrariness, as the conclusion to the story demonstrates.

The narrator is thoroughly knowing, thoroughly in control of the tale he has to tell. He also shares Trejago's 'instinctive' and dangerous knowledge of native customs. His most striking intervention, cited above, comes in the form of a simile. Yet his literary and cultural self-possession get him nowhere. More precisely, they confirm his opening remarks about the need for the races to remain separate. White will never meet Black in 'the City where each man's house is as guarded and as unknowable as the grave' (p. 167). The knowing narrator re-inscribes the boundary, even as he exposes its arbitrariness.

One obvious way to reveal the coding of attitudes is to put them into the mouth of a character who thereby becomes their representative. Thus in 'Lispeth' the Chaplain's wife voices Anglo-Indian contempt for native credulity: '"She is but a child, you know, and, I fear, at heart a heathen," said the Chaplain's wife' (p. 36). Another way is to cordon off such attitudes with inverted commas, even when they occur in third-person narrative: 'It gave her comfort, and the Chaplain's wife finding her happier thought that she was getting over her "barbarous and most indelicate folly"' (p. 36). This nicety is delivered by the narrator, but clearly belongs to the Chaplain's wife. That he should speak it indicates its pervasiveness, its rootedness in the Anglo-Indian world: it cannot be confined to the vicarage. At the same time it must not be allowed to seem natural, self-evident. Inverted commas identify it as the product of cultural coding.

A third way is to remove the inverted commas and hope that irony will quarantine the problematic attitudes: 'Being a savage by birth, she took no trouble to hide her feelings, and the Englishman was amused' (p. 35). The casual swagger of the explanation sweeps across those feelings and delivers us to the Englishman's amusement. But as we read on and encounter the Chaplain's wife, we realize that the term 'savage' belongs to a specific idiom, a code which the narrative has isolated and cordoned off. We must learn not to be taken in, not to be carried away by the apparently obvious. In the *CMG* the Chaplain's wife points out that 'it was "wrong and improper" of Lispeth to think of marriage with an Englishman, who was of quite a different clay' (p. 36). The inverted commas alert us to danger. But in the 1890 edition Kipling removed them, leaving us to spot the irony; in 1889 he had changed 'different' to 'superior', thus making it all the more critical that we should be able to do so, because what is at issue now is the representation of power. Removal of inverted commas was the most frequent revision Kipling made to the *CMG* 'Tales'. It is up to us to be alert to idiom, to irony.

However, ironic detachment from the attitudes of the white community does not bring us any closer to the black community. For the sophistication and detachment required to see through prejudice – through the coding of attitudes and perceptions – is something which the Indian and Eurasian characters in these stories conspicuously lack. Unable either to ignore or to overcome distance, Kipling dwells on its pathos. That in the end is what the *Plain Tales* speak most plainly about.

Suggested Further Reading

Louis L. Cornell, *Kipling in India*, Macmillan, London, 1966

Roger Lancelyn Green (ed.), *Kipling: The Critical Heritage*, Routledge & Kegan Paul, London, 1971

John A. McClure, *Kipling and Conrad: The Colonial Fiction*, Harvard University Press, Cambridge, Massachusetts, 1981

Harold Orel (ed.), *Kipling: Interviews and Recollections*, 2 vols., Macmillan, London, 1983

Thomas Pinney (ed.), *Kipling's India: Uncollected Sketches 1884–1888*, Macmillan, London, 1986

Angus Wilson, *The Strange Ride of Rudyard Kipling*, Secker & Warburg, London, 1977

Note on the Text

Between November 1886 and June 1887, 39 stories appeared at irregular intervals in the Lahore *Civil and Military Gazette* under the heading of 'Plain Tales from the Hills'. Their authorship was unattributed, and at least one of the stories was contributed by Kipling's sister, Alice. Kipling collected 29 of these stories with 11 more for publication as *Plain Tales from the Hills* at Calcutta in 1888. Of the 11, three – 'The Gate of the Hundred Sorrows', 'In the House of Suddhoo' and 'The Story of Muhammad Din' – had appeared in print in the *Civil and Military Gazette* shortly before the 'Plain Tales' series had begun. The remaining eight stories were new.

Kipling revised the texts of the stories as they appeared in the *Gazette* quite heavily for the first Indian edition and again, but more lightly, for the second Indian edition, published at Calcutta in 1889. For the first English edition issued by Macmillan in 1890, Kipling again revised the text to make its Indian background more accessible for English readers. The text was lightly revised for the Uniform edition of 1899, for the Bombay edition of 1913, and finally for the Sussex edition of 1937, which was the last new edition of the stories to appear during Kipling's lifetime. (Kipling's corrected first proofs for the *Tales*, which were the first volume of the Sussex edition, survive in the Macmillan Archive in the British Library: Additional Manuscript 55852.) As well as revising the text for the Sussex edition Kipling added two stories – 'Bitters Neat' and 'Haunted Subalterns' – to the collection. These had first appeared in the *Civil and Military Gazette* as part of the original series of *Tales*, but had only been republished once before in the American and English editions of the collected works which came out in 1897.

The text reprinted here is of the 42 stories comprising the Sussex edition, which incorporates Kipling's final revisions.

Note on the Text

Earlier readings, additions and deletions which are of critical interest have been included in the Notes. A few minor typographical changes in presentation have been silently made.

PLAIN TALES
FROM THE HILLS

To

THE WITTIEST WOMAN IN INDIA

I dedicate this Book

Preface

Eight-and-twenty of these tales appeared originally in the *Civil and Military Gazette*. I am indebted to the kindness of the Proprietors of that paper for permission to reprint them. The remaining tales are, more or less, new.

RUDYARD KIPLING

⁅ Lispeth ⁆

Look, you have cast out Love! What Gods are these
    You bid me please?
The Three in One, the One in Three? Not so!
    To my own gods I go.
It may be they shall give me greater ease
Than your cold Christ and tangled Trinities.

The Convert

She was the daughter of Sonoo, a Hill-man of the Himalayas, and Jadéh his wife. One year their maize failed, and two bears spent the night in their only opium poppy-field just above the Sutlej Valley on the Kotgarh side; so, next season, they turned Christian, and brought their baby to the Mission to be baptized. The Kotgarh Chaplain christened her Elizabeth, and 'Lispeth' is the Hill or *pahari* pronunciation.

Later, cholera came into the Kotgarh Valley and carried off Sonoo and Jadéh, and Lispeth became half servant, half companion, to the wife of the then Chaplain of Kotgarh. This was after the reign of the Moravian missionaries[1] in that place, but before Kotgarh had quite forgotten her title of 'Mistress of the Northern Hills'.

Whether Christianity improved Lispeth, or whether the Gods of her own people would have done as much for her under any circumstances, I do not know; but she grew very lovely. When a Hill-girl grows lovely, she is worth travelling fifty miles over bad ground to look upon. Lispeth had a Greek face – one of those faces people paint so often, and see so seldom. She was of a pale, ivory colour, and, for her race, extremely tall. Also, she possessed eyes that were wonderful; and, had she not been dressed in the abominable print-cloths affected by Missions, you would, meeting her on the hillside unexpectedly, have thought her the original Diana[2] of the Romans going out to slay.

33

Lispeth took to Christianity readily, and did not abandon it when she reached womanhood, as do some Hill-girls. Her own people hated her because she had, they said, become a white woman and washed herself daily; and the Chaplain's wife did not know what to do with her. One cannot ask a stately goddess, five feet ten in her shoes, to clean plates and dishes. She played with the Chaplain's children and took classes in the Sunday School, and read all the books in the house, and grew more and more beautiful, like the Princesses in fairy tales. The Chaplain's wife said that the girl ought to take service in Simla as a nurse or something 'genteel'. But Lispeth did not want to take service. She was very happy where she was.

When travellers – there were not many in those years – came in to Kotgarh, Lispeth used to lock herself into her own room for fear they might take her away to Simla, or out into the unknown world.

One day, a few months after she was seventeen years old, Lispeth went out for a walk. She did not walk in the manner of English ladies – a mile and a half out, with a carriage-ride back again. She covered between twenty and thirty miles in her little constitutionals, all about and about, between Kotgarh and Narkanda. This time she came back at full dusk, stepping down the breakneck descent into Kotgarh with something heavy in her arms. The Chaplain's wife was dozing in the drawing-room when Lispeth came in breathing heavily and very exhausted with her burden. Lispeth put it down on the sofa, and said simply, 'This is my husband. I found him on the Bagi Road. He has hurt himself. We will nurse him, and when he is well your husband shall marry him to me.'

This was the first mention Lispeth had ever made of her matrimonial views, and the Chaplain's wife shrieked with horror. However, the man on the sofa needed attention first. He was a young Englishman, and his head had been cut to the bone by something jagged. Lispeth said she had found him down the hillside, and had brought him in. He was breathing queerly and was unconscious.

He was put to bed and tended by the Chaplain, who knew something of medicine, and Lispeth waited outside the door in case she could be useful. She explained to the Chaplain that this was the man she meant to marry, and the Chaplain and his wife lectured her severely on the impropriety of her conduct. Lispeth listened quietly, and repeated her first proposition. It takes a great deal of Christianity to wipe out uncivilized Eastern instincts, such as falling in love at first sight. Lispeth, having found the man she worshipped, did not see why she should keep silent as to her choice. She had no intention of being sent away, either. She was going to nurse that Englishman until he was well enough to marry her. That was her programme.

After a fortnight of slight fever and inflammation, the Englishman recovered coherence and thanked the Chaplain and his wife, and Lispeth – especially Lispeth – for their kindness. He was a traveller in the East, he said – they never talked about 'globe-trotters'[3] in those days, when the P. & O. fleet was young and small – and had come from Dehra Dun to hunt for plants and butterflies among the Simla hills. No one at Simla, therefore, knew anything about him. He fancied that he must have fallen over the cliff while reaching out for a fern on a rotten tree-trunk, and that his coolies must have stolen his baggage and fled. He thought he would go back to Simla when he was a little stronger. He desired no more mountaineering.

He made small haste to go away, and recovered his strength slowly. Lispeth objected to being advised either by the Chaplain or his wife. Therefore the latter spoke to the Englishman, and told him how matters stood in Lispeth's heart. He laughed a good deal, and said it was very pretty and romantic, but, as he was engaged to a girl at Home, he fancied that nothing would happen. Certainly he would behave with discretion. He did that. Still, he found it very pleasant to talk to Lispeth, and walk with Lispeth, and say nice things to her, and call her pet names while he was getting strong enough to go away. It meant nothing at all to him, and everything in the world to Lispeth. She was very happy while the fortnight lasted, because she had found a man to love.

Being a savage by birth, she took no trouble to hide her feelings, and the Englishman was amused. When he went away, Lispeth walked with him up the Hill as far as Narkanda, very troubled and very miserable. The Chaplain's wife, being a good Christian

and disliking anything in the shape of fuss or scandal – Lispeth
was beyond her management entirely – had told the Englishman
to tell Lispeth that he was coming back to marry her. 'She is but
a child, you know, and, I fear, at heart a heathen,' said the
Chaplain's wife. So all the twelve miles up the Hill the Englishman, with his arm round Lispeth's waist, was assuring the girl
that he would come back and marry her; and Lispeth made him
promise over and over again. She wept on the Narkanda Ridge
till he had passed out of sight along the Muttiani path.

Then she dried her tears and went in to Kotgarh again, and
said to the Chaplain's wife, 'He will come back and marry me.
He has gone to his own people to tell them so.' And the Chaplain's
wife soothed Lispeth and said, 'He will come back.' At the end
of two months Lispeth grew impatient, and was told that the
Englishman had gone over the seas to England. She knew where
England was, because she had read little geography primers; but,
of course, she had no conception of the nature of the sea, being a
Hill-girl. There was an old puzzle-map of the World in the house.
Lispeth had played with it when she was a child. She unearthed
it again, and put it together of evenings, and cried to herself, and
tried to imagine where her Englishman was. As she had no ideas
of distance or steamboats her notions were somewhat wild. It
would not have made the least difference had she been perfectly
correct, for the Englishman had no intention of coming back to
marry a Hill-girl. He forgot all about her by the time he was
butterfly-hunting in Assam. He wrote a book on the East afterwards. Lispeth's name did not appear there.

At the end of three months Lispeth made daily pilgrimage to
Narkanda to see if her Englishman was coming along the road.
It gave her comfort, and the Chaplain's wife finding her happier
thought that she was getting over her 'barbarous and most
indelicate folly'. A little later the walks ceased to help Lispeth,
and her temper grew very bad. The Chaplain's wife thought this
a profitable time to let her know the real state of affairs – that the
Englishman had only promised his love to keep her quiet – that
he had never meant anything, and that it was wrong and improper
of Lispeth to think of marriage with an Englishman, who was of
a superior clay, besides being promised in marriage to a girl of

his own people. Lispeth said that all this was clearly impossible because he had said he loved her, and the Chaplain's wife had, with her own lips, asserted that the Englishman was coming back.

'How can what he and you said be untrue?' asked Lispeth.

'We said it as an excuse to keep you quiet, child,' said the Chaplain's wife.

'Then you have lied to me,' said Lispeth, 'you and he?'

The Chaplain's wife bowed her head, and said nothing. Lispeth was silent too for a little time; then she went out down the valley, and returned in the dress of a Hill-girl – infamously dirty, but without the nose-stud and ear-rings. She had her hair braided into the long pigtail, helped out with black thread, that Hill-women wear

'I am going back to my own people,' said she. 'You have killed Lispeth. There is only left old Jadéh's daughter – the daughter of a *pahari* and the servant of Tarka Devi.[4] You are all liars, you English.'

By the time that the Chaplain's wife had recovered from the shock of the announcement that Lispeth had 'verted to her mother's Gods the girl had gone; and she never came back.

She took to her own unclean people savagely, as if to make up the arrears of the life she had stepped out of; and, in a little time, she married a wood-cutter who beat her after the manner of *paharis*, and her beauty faded soon.

'There is no law whereby you can account for the vagaries of the heathen,' said the Chaplain's wife, 'and I believe that Lispeth was always at heart an infidel.' Seeing she had been taken into the Church of England at the mature age of five weeks, this statement does not do credit to the Chaplain's wife.

Lispeth was a very old woman when she died. She had always a perfect command of English, and when she was sufficiently drunk could sometimes be induced to tell the story of her first love-affair.

It was hard then to realize that the bleared, wrinkled creature, exactly like a wisp of charred rag, could ever have been 'Lispeth of the Kotgarh Mission'.

⟨ Three and – an Extra ⟩

When halter and heel-ropes are slipped, do not give chase with sticks
but with *gram*.[1]

Punjabi Proverb

After marriage arrives a reaction, sometimes a big, sometimes a
little one; but it comes sooner or later, and must be tided over by
both parties if they desire the rest of their lives to go with the
current.

In the case of the Cusack-Bremmils this reaction did not set
in till the third year after the wedding. Bremmil was hard to hold
at the best of times; but he was a beautiful husband until the baby
died and Mrs Bremmil wore black, and grew thin, and mourned
as though the bottom of the Universe had fallen out. Perhaps
Bremmil ought to have comforted her. He tried to do so, but
the more he comforted, the more Mrs Bremmil grieved, and,
consequently, the more uncomfortable grew Bremmil. The fact
was that they both needed a tonic. And they got it. Mrs Bremmil
can afford to laugh now, but it was no laughing matter to her at
the time.

Mrs Hauksbee appeared on the horizon; and where she existed
was fair chance of trouble. At Simla her by-name was 'the Stormy
Petrel'.[2] She had won that title five times to my own certain
knowledge. She was a little, brown, thin, almost skinny, woman,
with big, rolling, violet-blue eyes, and the sweetest manners in
the world. You had only to mention her name at afternoon teas
for every woman in the room to rise up and call her not blessed.
She was clever, witty, brilliant, and sparkling beyond most of her
kind; but possessed of many devils of malice and mischievousness.
She could be nice, though, even to her own sex. But that is another
story.

Bremmil went off at score[3] after the baby's death and the

38

general discomfort that followed, and Mrs Hauksbee annexed him. She took no pleasure in hiding her captives. She annexed him publicly, and saw that the world saw it. He rode with her, and walked with her, and talked with her, and picnicked with her, and tiffined at Peliti's with her, till people put up their eyebrows and said, 'Shocking!' Mrs Bremmil stayed at home, turning over the dead baby's frocks and crying into the empty cradle. She did not care to do anything else. But some eight dear, affectionate lady-friends explained the situation at length to her in case she should miss the cream of it. Mrs Bremmil listened quietly, and thanked them for their good offices. She was not as clever as Mrs Hauksbee, but she was no fool. She kept her own counsel, and did not speak to Bremmil of what she had heard. This is worth remembering. Speaking to or crying over a husband never did any good yet.

When Bremmil was at home, which was not often, he was more affectionate than usual; and that showed his hand. The affection was forced, partly to soothe his own conscience and partly to soothe Mrs Bremmil. It failed in both regards.

Then 'the A.D.C. in Waiting was commanded by Their Excellencies, Lord and Lady Lytton, to invite Mr and Mrs Cusack-Bremmil to Peterhof on July 26 [4] at 9.30 p.m.' – 'Dancing' in the bottom left-hand corner.

'I can't go,' said Mrs Bremmil. 'It is too soon after poor little Florrie . . . But it needn't stop you, Tom.'

She meant what she said then, and Bremmil said that he would go just to put in an appearance. Here he spoke the thing which was not;[5] and Mrs Bremmil knew it. She guessed – a woman's guess is much more accurate than a man's certainty – that he had meant to go from the first, and with Mrs Hauksbee. She sat down to think, and the outcome of her thoughts was that the memory of a dead child was worth considerably less than the affections of a living husband. She made her plan and staked her all upon it. In that hour she discovered that she knew Tom Bremmil thoroughly, and this knowledge she acted on.

'Tom,' said she, 'I shall be dining out at the Longmores' on the evening of the 26th. You'd better dine at the Club.'

This saved Bremmil from making an excuse to get away and

dine with Mrs Hauksbee, so he was grateful, and felt small and mean at the same time – which was wholesome. Bremmil left the house at five for a ride. About half-past five in the evening a large leather-covered basket came in from Phelps's for Mrs Bremmil. She was a woman who knew how to dress; and she had not spent a week on designing that dress and having it gored, and hemmed, and herring-boned, and tucked and rucked (or whatever the terms are), for nothing. It was a gorgeous dress – slight mourning. I can't describe it, but it was what *The Queen*[6] calls 'a creation' – a thing that hit you straight between the eyes and made you gasp. She had not much heart for what she was going to do; but as she glanced at the long mirror she had the satisfaction of knowing that she had never looked so well in her life. She was a large blonde and, when she chose, carried herself superbly.

After the dinner at the Longmores' she went on to the dance – a little late – and encountered Bremmil with Mrs Hauksbee on his arm. That made her flush, and as the men crowded round her for dances she looked magnificent. She filled up all her dances except three, and those she left blank. Mrs Hauksbee caught her eye once, and knew it was war – real war – between them. She started handicapped in the struggle, for she had ordered Bremmil about just the least little bit in the world too much, and he was beginning to resent it. Moreover, he had never seen his wife look so lovely. He stared at her from doorways, and glared at her from passages as she went about with her partners; and the more he stared, the more taken was he. He could scarcely believe that this was the woman with the red eyes and the black stuff gown who used to weep over the eggs at breakfast.

Mrs Hauksbee did her best to hold him in play, but, after two dances, he crossed over to his wife and asked for a dance.

'I'm afraid you've come too late, *Mister* Bremmil,' she said, with her eyes twinkling.

Then he begged her to give him a dance, and, as a great favour, she allowed him the fifth waltz. Luckily Five stood vacant on his programme. They danced it together, and there was a little flutter round the room. Bremmil had a sort of a notion that his wife could dance, but he never knew she danced so divinely. At the end of that waltz he asked for another – as a favour, not as a right;

and Mrs Bremmil said, 'Show me your programme, dear!' He showed it as a naughty little schoolboy hands up contraband sweets to a master. There was a fair sprinkling of 'H's on it, besides 'H' at supper. Mrs Bremmil said nothing, but she smiled contemptuously, ran her pencil through Seven and Nine – two 'H's – and returned the card with her own name written above – a pet name that only she and her husband used. Then she shook her finger at him, and said, laughing 'Oh, you silly, *silly* boy!'

Mrs Hauksbee heard that, and – she owned as much – felt she had the worst of it. Bremmil accepted Seven and Nine gratefully. They danced Seven, and sat out Nine in one of the little tents. What Bremmil said and what Mrs Bremmil did is no concern of any one.

When the band struck up 'The Roast Beef of Old England',[7] the two went out into the veranda, and Bremmil began looking for his wife's dandy[8] (this was before 'rickshaw days) while she went into the cloak-room. Mrs Hauksbee came up and said, 'You take me in to supper, I think, Mr Bremmil?' Bremmil turned red and looked foolish, 'Ah – h'm! I'm going home with my wife, Mrs Hauksbee. I think there has been a little mistake.' Being a man, he spoke as though Mrs Hauksbee were entirely responsible.

Mrs Bremmil came out of the cloak-room in a swansdown cloak with a white 'cloud' round her head. She looked radiant; and she had a right to.

The couple went off into the darkness together, Bremmil riding very close to the dandy.

Then said Mrs Hauksbee to me – she looked a trifle faded and jaded in the lamplight: 'Take my word for it, the silliest woman can manage a clever man; but it needs a very clever woman to manage a fool.'

Then we went into supper.

⚡ Thrown Away ⚡

And some are sulky, while some will plunge.
  (*So ho! Steady! Stand still, you!*)
Some you must gentle, and some you must lunge.[1]
  (*There! There! Who wants to kill you?*)
Some – there are losses in every trade –
Will break their hearts ere bitted and made,
Will fight like fiends as the rope cuts hard,
And die dumb-mad in the breaking-yard.

Toolungala Stockyard Chorus

To rear a boy under what parents call the 'sheltered life' system is, if the boy must go into the world and fend for himself, not wise. Unless he be one in a thousand he has certainly to pass through many unnecessary troubles; and may, possibly, come to extreme grief simply from ignorance of the proper proportions of things.

Let a puppy eat the soap in the bath-room or chew a newly-blacked boot. He chews and chuckles until, by and by, he finds out that blacking and Old Brown Windsor make him very sick. So he argues that soap and boots are not wholesome. Any old dog about the house will soon show him the unwisdom of biting big dogs' ears. Being young, he remembers, and goes abroad, at six months, a well-mannered little beast with a chastened appetite. If he had been kept away from boots, and soap, and big dogs till he came to the trinity full-grown and with developed teeth, consider how fearfully sick and thrashed he would be! Apply that notion to the 'sheltered life', and see how it works. It does not sound pretty, but it is the better of two evils.

There was a Boy once who had been brought up under the 'sheltered life' theory; and the theory killed him dead. He stayed with his people all his days, from the hour he was born till the hour he went into Sandhurst nearly at the top of the list. He was beautifully taught in all that wins marks by a private tutor, and carried the extra weight of 'never having given his parents an hour's anxiety in his life'. What he learnt at Sandhurst beyond the regular routine is of no great consequence. He looked about him, and he found soap and blacking, so to speak, very good. He ate a little, and came out of Sandhurst not so high as he went in. Then there was an interval and a scene with his people, who expected much from him. Next a year of living unspotted from the world in a third-rate depôt battalion where all the juniors were children and all the seniors old women; and lastly, he came out to India, where he was cut off from the support of his parents, and had no one to fall back on in time of trouble except himself.

Now India is a place beyond all others where one must not take things too seriously – the mid-day sun always excepted. Too much work and too much energy kill a man just as effectively as too much assorted vice or too much drink. Flirtation does not matter, because every one is being transferred, and either you or she leave the station and never return. Good work does not matter, because a man is judged by his worst output, and another man takes all the credit of his best as a rule. Bad work does not matter, because other men do worse, and incompetents hang on longer in India than anywhere else. Amusements do not matter, because you must repeat them as soon as you have accomplished them once, and most amusements only mean trying to win another person's money. Sickness does not matter, because it's all in the day's work, and if you die, another man takes over your place and your office in the eight hours between your death and burial. Nothing matters except Home-furlough and acting allowances, and these only because they are scarce. It is a slack country, where all men work with imperfect instruments, and the wisest thing is to escape as soon as ever you can to some place where amusement is amusement and a reputation worth the having.

But this Boy – the tale is as old as the Hills – came out, and took all things seriously. He was pretty and was petted. He took the pettings seriously, and fretted over women not worth saddling a pony to call upon. He found his new free life in India very good. It *does* look attractive in the beginning, from a subaltern's point of view – all ponies, partners, dancing, and so on. He tasted it as the puppy tastes the soap. Only he came late to the eating, with a grown set of teeth. He had no sense of balance – just like the puppy – and could not understand why he was not treated with the consideration he received under his father's roof. That hurt his feelings.

He quarrelled with other boys and, being sensitive to the marrow, remembered these quarrels, and they excited him. He found whist, and gymkhanas, and things of that kind (meant to amuse one after office) good; but he took them seriously too, just as seriously as he took the 'head' that followed after drink. He lost his money over whist and gymkhanas because they were new to him.[2]

He took his losses seriously, and wasted as much energy and interest over a two-goldmohur race for maiden *ekka*-ponies with their manes hogged,[3] as if it had been the Derby. One-half of this came from inexperience – much as the puppy squabbles with the corner of the hearthrug – and the other half from the dizziness bred by stumbling out of his quiet life into the glare and excitement of a livelier one. No one told him about the soap and the blacking, because an average man takes it for granted that an average man is ordinarily careful in regard to them. It was pitiful to watch The Boy knocking himself to pieces, as an over-handled colt falls down and cuts himself when he gets away from his groom.

This unbridled licence in amusements not worth the trouble of breaking line for, much less rioting over, endured for six months – all through one cold weather – and then we thought that the heat and the knowledge of having lost his money and health and lamed his horses would sober The Boy down, and he would stand steady. In ninety-nine cases out of a hundred this would have happened. You can see the principle working in any Indian station. But this particular case fell through because The Boy was sensitive and took things seriously – as I may have said some seven times before. Of course, we could not tell how his excesses struck him personally. They were nothing very heartbreaking or above the average. He might be crippled for life financially, and want a little nursing. Still, the memory of his performances would wither away in one hot weather, and the bankers would help him to tide over the money-troubles. But he must have taken another view altogether, and have believed himself ruined beyond redemption. His Colonel talked to him severely when the cold weather ended. That made him more wretched than ever; and it was only an ordinary 'Colonel's wigging'![4]

What follows is a curious instance of the fashion in which we are all linked together and made responsible for one another. *The* thing that kicked the beam in The Boy's mind was a remark that a woman made when he was talking to her. There is no use in repeating it, for it was only a cruel little sentence, rapped out before thinking, that made him flush to the roots of his hair. He kept himself to himself for three days, and then put in for two days' leave to go shooting near a Canal Engineer's Rest House about thirty miles out. He got his leave, and that night at Mess was noisier and more offensive than ever. He said that he was 'going to shoot big game', and left at half-past ten o'clock in an *ekka*. Partridge – which was the only thing a man could get near the Rest House – is not big game; so every one laughed.

Next morning one of the Majors came in from short leave, and heard that The Boy had gone out to shoot 'big game'. The Major had taken an interest in The Boy, and had, more than once, tried to check him. The Major put up his eyebrows when he heard of the expedition, and went to The Boy's rooms, where he rummaged.

Presently he came out and found me leaving cards on the Mess. There was no one else in the ante-room.

He said, 'The Boy has gone out shooting. *Does* a man shoot partridge with a revolver and writing-case?'

I said, 'Nonsense, Major!' for I saw what was in his mind.

He said, 'Nonsense or no nonsense, I'm going to the Canal now – at once. I don't feel easy.'

Then he thought for a minute, and said, 'Can you lie?'

'You know best,' I answered. 'It's my profession.'

'Very well,' said the Major, 'you come out with me now – at once – in an *ekka* to the Canal to shoot black-buck. Go and put on *shikar*-kit[5] – *quick* – and drive here with a gun.'

The Major was a masterful man, and I knew that he would not

give orders for nothing. So I obeyed, and on return found the Major packed up in an *ekka* – gun-cases and food slung below – all ready for a shooting-trip.

He dismissed the driver and drove himself. We jogged along quietly while in the station; but, as soon as we got to the dusty road across the plains, he made that pony fly. A country-bred can do nearly anything at a pinch. We covered the thirty miles in under three hours, but the poor brute was nearly dead.

Once I said, 'What's the blazing hurry, Major?'

He said quietly, 'The Boy has been alone, by himself for – one, two, five, – fourteen hours now! I tell you, I don't feel easy.'

This uneasiness spread itself to me, and I helped to beat the pony.

When we came to the Canal Engineer's Rest House the Major called for The Boy's servant; but there was no answer. Then we went up to the house, calling for The Boy by name; but there was no answer.

'Oh, he's out shooting,' said I.

Just then I saw through one of the windows a little hurricane-lamp burning. This was at four in the afternoon. We both stopped dead in the veranda, holding our breath to catch every sound; and we heard, inside the room, the '*brr – brr – brr*' of a multitude of flies. The Major said nothing, but he took off his helmet and we entered very softly.

The Boy was dead on the bed in the centre of the bare, lime-washed room. He had shot his head nearly to pieces with his revolver. The gun-cases were still strapped, so was the bedding, and on the table lay The Boy's writing-case with photographs. He had gone away to die like a poisoned rat!

The Major said to himself softly, 'Poor Boy! Poor, *poor* devil!' Then he turned away from the bed and said, 'I want your help in this business.'

Knowing The Boy was dead by his own hand, I saw exactly what that help would be, so I passed over to the table, took a chair, lit a cheroot, and began to go through the writing-case; the Major looking over my shoulder and repeating to himself, 'We came too late! – Like a rat in a hole! – Poor, *poor* devil!'

The Boy must have spent half the night in writing to his people, to his Colonel, and to a girl at Home; and as soon as he had finished, must have shot himself, for he had been dead a long time when we came in.

I read all that he had written, and passed over each sheet to the Major as I finished it.

We saw from his accounts how very seriously he had taken everything. He wrote about 'disgrace which he was unable to bear' – 'indelible shame' – 'criminal folly' – 'wasted life', and so on; besides a lot of private things to his father and mother much too sacred to put into print. The letter to the girl at Home was the most pitiful of all, and I choked as I read it. The Major made no attempt to keep dry-eyed. I respected him for that. He read and rocked himself to and fro, and simply cried like a woman without caring to hide it. The letters were so dreary and hopeless and touching. We forgot all about The Boy's follies, and only thought of the poor Thing on the bed and the scrawled sheets in our hands. It was utterly impossible to let the letters go Home. They would have broken his father's heart and killed his mother after killing her belief in her son.

At last the Major dried his eyes openly, and said, 'Nice sort of thing to spring on an English family! What shall we do?'

I said, knowing what the Major had brought me out for, 'The Boy died of cholera. We were with him at the time. We can't commit ourselves to half-measures. Come along.'

Then began one of the most grimly comic scenes I have ever taken part in – the concoction of a big, written lie, bolstered with evidence to soothe The Boy's people at Home. I began the rough draft of the letter, the Major throwing in hints here and there while he gathered up all the stuff that The Boy had written and burnt it in the fireplace. It was a hot, still evening when we began, and the lamp burned very badly. In due course I made the draft to my satisfaction, setting forth how The Boy was the pattern of all virtues, beloved by his Regiment, with every promise of a great career before him, and so on; how we had helped him through the sickness – it was no time for little lies, you will understand – and how he had died without pain. I choked while I was putting down these things and thinking of the poor people who would read them. Then I laughed at the grotesqueness of

47

the affair, and the laughter mixed itself up with the choke – and the Major said that we both wanted drinks.

I am afraid to say how much whisky we drank before the letter was finished. It had not the least effect on us. Then we took off The Boy's watch, locket, and ring.[6]

Lastly, the Major said, 'We must send a lock of hair too. A woman values that.'

But there were reasons why we could not find a lock fit to send. The Boy was black-haired, and so was the Major, luckily. I cut off a piece of the Major's hair above the temple with a knife, and put it into the packet we were making. The laughing-fit and the chokes got hold of me again, and I had to stop. The Major was nearly as bad; and we both knew that the worst part of the work was to come.

We sealed up the packet, photographs, locket, seals, ring, letter, and lock of hair with The Boy's sealing-wax and The Boy's seal.

Then the Major said, 'For God's sake, let's get outside – away from the room – and think!'

We went outside, and walked on the banks of the Canal for an hour, eating and drinking what we had with us, until the moon rose. I know now exactly how a murderer feels. Finally, we forced ourselves back to the room with the lamp and the Other Thing in it, and began to take up the next piece of work. I am not going to write about this. It was too horrible. We burned the bedstead and dropped the ashes into the Canal; we took up the matting of the room and treated that in the same way. I went off to a village and borrowed two big hoes, – I did not want the villagers to help, – while the Major arranged – the other matters. It took us four hours' hard work to make the grave. As we worked, we argued out whether it was right to say as much as we remembered of the Burial of the Dead. We compromised things by saying the Lord's Prayer with a private unofficial prayer for the peace of the soul of The Boy. Then we filled in the grave and went into the veranda – not the house – to lie down to sleep. We were dead tired.

When we woke the Major said wearily, 'We can't go back till to-morrow. We must give him a decent time to die in. He died early *this* morning, remember. That seems more natural.' So the Major must have been lying awake all the time, thinking.

I said, 'Then why didn't we bring the body back to cantonments?'

The Major thought for a minute. 'Because the people bolted when they heard of the cholera. And the *ekka* has gone!'

That was strictly true. We had forgotten all about the *ekka*-pony, and he had gone home.

So we were left there alone, all that stifling day, in the Canal Rest House, testing and re-testing our story of The Boy's death to see if it was weak in any point. A native appeared in the afternoon, but we said that a Sahib was dead of cholera, and he ran away. As the dusk gathered, the Major told me all his fears about The Boy, and awful stories of suicide or nearly-carried-out suicide – tales that made one's hair crisp. He said that he himself had once gone into the same Valley of the Shadow[7] as The Boy, when he was young and new to the country; so he understood how things fought together in The Boy's poor jumbled head. He also said that youngsters, in their repentant moments, consider their sins much more serious and ineffaceable than they really are. We talked together all through the evening and rehearsed the story of the death of The Boy. As soon as the moon was up, and The Boy, theoretically, just buried, we struck across country for the Station. We walked from eight till six o'clock in the morning; but though we were dead tired, we did not forget to go to The Boy's rooms and put away his revolver with the proper amount of cartridges in the pouch. Also to set his writing-case on the table. We found the Colonel and reported the death, feeling more like murderers than ever. Then we went to bed and slept the clock round, for there was no more in us.

The tale had credence as long as was necessary; for every one forgot about The Boy before a fortnight was over. Many people, however, found time to say that the Major had behaved scandalously in not bringing in the body for a Regimental funeral. The saddest thing of all was the letter from The Boy's mother to the Major and me – with big inky blisters all over the sheet. She wrote the sweetest possible things about our great kindness, and the obligation she would be under to us as long as she lived.

All things considered, she was under an obligation, but not exactly as she meant.

⦃ Miss Youghal's *Sais*[1] ⦄

When Man and Woman are agreed, what can the Kazi[2] do?
Proverb

Some people say that there is no romance in India. Those people are wrong. Our lives hold quite as much romance as is good for us. Sometimes more.

Strickland was in the Police, and people did not understand him. So they said he was a doubtful sort of man and passed by on the other side. Strickland had himself to thank for this. He held the extraordinary theory that a Policeman in India should try to know as much about the natives as the natives themselves. Now, in the whole of Upper India, there is only one man who can pass for Hindu or Mahommedan, hide-dresser or priest, as he pleases. He is feared and respected by the natives from the Ghor Kathri to the Jamma Musjid;[3] and he is supposed to have the gift of invisibility and executive control over many Devils. But this has done him no good in the eyes of the Indian Government.[4]

Strickland was foolish enough to take that man for his model; and, following out his absurd theory, dabbled in unsavoury places which no respectable man would think of exploring – all among the native riff-raff. He educated himself in this peculiar way for seven years, and people could not appreciate it. He was perpetually 'going Fantee' among natives, which, of course, no man with any sense believes in. He was initiated into the *Sat Bhai* at Allahabad once, when he was on leave. He knew the Lizard-Song of the Sansis, and the *Hálli-Hukk* dance, which is a religious can-can of a startling kind. When a man knows who dance the *Hálli-Hukk*, and how, and when, and where, he knows something to be proud of. He has gone deeper than the skin. But Strickland was not proud, though he had helped once, at Jagadhri, at the Painting

51

of the Death Bull, which no Englishman must even look upon; had mastered the thieves'-patter of the *chángars*; had taken a Yusufzai horse-thief alone near Attock; and had stood under the sounding-board of a Border mosque and conducted service in the manner of a Sunni Mullah.

His crowning achievement was spending eleven days as a *fakir* or priest in the gardens of Baba Atal at Amritzar, and there picking up the threads of the great Nasiban Murder Case.[5] But people said, justly enough, 'Why on earth can't Strickland sit in his office and write up his diary, and recruit, and keep quiet, instead of showing up the incapacity of his seniors?' So the Nasiban Murder Case did him no good Departmentally; but, after his first feeling of wrath, he returned to his outlandish custom of prying into native life. When a man once acquires a taste for this particular amusement, it abides with him all his days. It is the most fascinating thing in the world – Love not excepted. Where other men took ten days to the Hills, Strickland took leave for what he called *shikar*, put on the disguise that appealed to him at the time, stepped down into the brown crowd, and was swallowed up for a while. He was a quiet, dark young fellow – spare, black-eyed – and, when he was not thinking of something else, a very interesting companion. Strickland on Native Progress as he had seen it was worth hearing. Natives hated Strickland; but they were afraid of him. He knew too much.

When the Youghals came into the station, Strickland – very gravely, as he did everything – fell in love with Miss Youghal; and she, after a while, fell in love with him because she could not understand him. Then Strickland told her parents; but Mrs Youghal said she was not going to throw her daughter into the worst-paid Department in the Empire, and old Youghal said, in so many words, that he mistrusted Strickland's ways and works, and would thank him not to speak or write to his daughter any more. 'Very well,' said Strickland, for he did not wish to make his lady-love's life a burden. After one long talk with Miss Youghal he dropped the business entirely.

The Youghals went up to Simla in April.

In July Strickland secured three months' leave on 'urgent private affairs'. He locked up his house – though not a native in the Province would wittingly have touched 'Estreekin Sahib's' gear for the world – and went down to see a friend of his, an old dyer, at Tarn Taran.

Here all trace of him was lost, until a *sais* or groom met me on the Simla Mall with this extraordinary note:

Dear Old Man,
 Please give bearer a box of cheroots – Supers, No. 1, for preference. They are freshest at the Club. I'll repay when I reappear; but at present I'm out of society.
 Yours,
  E. Strickland.

I ordered two boxes, and handed them over to the *sais* with my love. That *sais* was Strickland, and he was in old Youghal's employ, attached to Miss Youghal's Arab. The poor fellow was suffering for an English smoke, and knew that, whatever happened, I should hold my tongue till the business was over.

Later on, Mrs Youghal, who was wrapped up in her servants, began talking at houses where she called of her paragon among *saises* – the man who was never too busy to get up in the morning and pick flowers for the breakfast-table, and who blacked – actually *blacked* – the hoofs of his horse like a London coachman! The turn-out of Miss Youghal's Arab was a wonder and a delight. Strickland – Dulloo, I mean – found his reward in the pretty things that Miss Youghal said to him when she went out riding. Her parents were pleased to find she had forgotten all her foolishness for young Strickland, and said she was a good girl.

Strickland vows that the two months of his service were the most rigid mental discipline he has ever gone through. Quite apart from the little fact that the wife of one of his fellow-*saises* fell in love with him and then tried to poison him with arsenic because he would have nothing to do with her, he had to school himself into keeping quiet when Miss Youghal went out riding with some man who tried to flirt with her, and he was forced to trot behind carrying the blanket and hearing every word! Also, he had to keep his temper when he was slanged in the theatre porch by a policeman – especially once when he was abused by a Naik he had himself recruited from Isser Jang village – or, worse

53

still, when a young subaltern called him a pig for not making way quickly enough.

But the life had its compensations. He obtained great insight into the ways and thefts of *saises* – enough, he says, to have summarily convicted half the population of the Punjab if he had been on business. He became one of the leading players at knuckle-bones, which all *jhampanis* and many *saises* play while they are waiting outside the Government House or the Gaiety Theatre of nights; he learned to smoke tobacco that was three-fourths cow-dung; and he heard the wisdom of the grizzled Jemadar[6] of the Government House grooms. Whose words are valuable. He saw many things which amused him; and he states, on honour, that no man can appreciate Simla properly till he has seen it from the *sais*'s point of view. He also says that, if he chose to write all he saw, his head would be broken in several places.

Strickland's account of the agony he endured on wet nights, hearing the music and seeing the lights in Benmore,[7] with his toes tingling for a waltz and his head in a horse-blanket, is rather amusing. One of these days Strickland is going to write a little book on his experiences. That book will be worth buying, and even more worth suppressing.

Thus he served faithfully as Jacob served for Rachel;[8] and his leave was nearly at an end when the explosion came. He had really done his best to keep his temper in the hearing of the flirtations I have mentioned; but he broke down at last. An old and very distinguished General took Miss Youghal for a ride, and began that specially offensive 'you're-only-a-little-girl' sort of flirtation – most difficult for a woman to turn aside deftly, and most maddening to listen to. Miss Youghal was shaking with fear at the things he said in the hearing of her *sais*. Dulloo – Strickland – stood it as long as he could. Then he caught hold of the General's bridle, and, in most fluent English, invited him to step off and be flung over the cliff. Next minute Miss Youghal began to cry, and Strickland saw that he had hopelessly given himself away, and everything was over.

The General nearly had a fit, while Miss Youghal was sobbing out the story of the disguise and the engagement that was not recognized by the parents. Strickland was furiously angry with himself, and more angry with the General for forcing his hand; so he said nothing, but held the horse's head and prepared to thrash the General as some sort of satisfaction. But when the General had thoroughly grasped the story, and knew who Strickland was, he began to puff and blow in the saddle, and nearly rolled off with laughing. He said Strickland deserved a V.C., if it were only for putting on a *sais*'s blanket. Then he called himself names, and vowed that he deserved a thrashing, but he was too old to take it from Strickland. Then he complimented Miss Youghal on her lover. The scandal of the business never struck him; for he was a nice old man, with a weakness for flirtations. Then he laughed again, and said that old Youghal was a fool. Strickland let go of the cob's head, and suggested that the General had better help them if that was his opinion. Strickland knew Youghal's weakness for men with titles and letters after their names and high official position. 'It's rather like a forty-minute farce,' said the General, 'but, begad, I *will* help, if it's only to escape that tremendous thrashing I deserve. Go along to your home, my *sais*-Policeman, and change into decent kit, and I'll attack Mr Youghal. Miss Youghal, may I ask you to canter home and wait?'

About seven minutes later there was a wild hurroosh at the Club. A *sais*, with blanket and head-rope, was asking all the men he knew: 'For Heaven's sake, lend me decent clothes!' As the men did not recognize him, there were some peculiar scenes before Strickland could get a hot bath, with soda in it, in one room, a shirt here, a collar there, a pair of trousers elsewhere, and so on. He galloped off, with half the Club wardrobe on his back, and an utter stranger's pony under him, to the house of old Youghal. The General, arrayed in purple and fine linen,[9] was before him. What the General had said Strickland never knew, but Youghal received Strickland with moderate civility; and Mrs Youghal, touched by the devotion of the transformed Dulloo, was almost kind. The General beamed and chuckled, and Miss Youghal came in, and, almost before old Youghal knew where he was, the parental consent had been wrenched out, and Strickland had departed with Miss Youghal to the Telegraph Office to wire for his European kit. The final embarrassment was when a stranger attacked him on the Mall and asked for the stolen pony.

In the end, Strickland and Miss Youghal were married, on the strict understanding that Strickland should drop his old ways, and stick to Departmental routine, which pays best and leads to Simla. Strickland was far too fond of his wife, just then, to break his word, but it was a sore trial to him; for the streets and the bazars, and the sounds in them, were full of meaning to Strickland, and these called to him to come back and take up his wanderings and his discoveries. Some day I will tell you how he broke his promise to help a friend. That was long since, and he has, by this time, been nearly spoilt for what he would call *shikar*. He is forgetting the slang, and the beggar's cant, and the marks, and the signs, and the drift of the under-currents, which, if a man would master, he must always continue to learn.

But he fills in his Department returns beautifully.

⟨ Bitters Neat ⟩

The oldest trouble in the world comes from want of understanding. And it is entirely the fault of the Woman. Somehow, she is built incapable of speaking the truth, even to herself. She only finds it out about four months later, when the man is dead, or has been transferred. Then she says she never was so happy in her life, and marries some one else, who again touched some woman's heart elsewhere, and did not know it, but was mixed up with another man's wife, who only used him to pique a third man. And so round again – all criss-cross.

In India, where life goes quicker than at Home, things are more obviously tangled, and therefore more pitiful to look at. Men speak the truth as they understand it, and women as they think men would like to understand it; and then they all act lies which would deceive Solomon, and the result is a heart-rending muddle that half-a-dozen open words would put straight.

This particular muddle did not differ from any other muddle you may see, if you are not busy playing cross-purposes yourself, going on in a big station any cold season. Its only merit was that it did not come all right in the end; as muddles are made to do in the third volume.

I've forgotten what the man was – he was an ordinary sort of man –' man you meet any day at the A.D.C.s' end of the table, and go away and forget about. His name was Surrey; but whether he was in the Army, or the P.W.D., or the Commissariat, or the Police, or a factory, I don't remember. He wasn't a Civilian.[1] He was just an ordinary man, of the light-coloured variety, with a fair moustache and with the average amount of pay that comes between twenty-seven and thirty-two – from six to nine hundred a month.

He didn't dance, and he did what little riding he wanted to do by himself, and was busy in his office all day, and never bothered his head about women. No man ever dreamed he would. He was of the type that doesn't marry, just because it doesn't think about marriage. He was one of the plain cards, whose only use is to make up the pack, and furnish background to put the Court cards against.

Then there was a girl – ordinary girl – the dark-coloured variety – daughter of a man in the Army, who played a little, sang a little, talked a little, and furnished the background, exactly as Surrey did. She had been sent out here to get married if she could, because there were many sisters at home, and Colonels' allowances aren't elastic. She lived with an aunt. She was a Miss Tallaght, and men spelt her name 'Tart' on the programmes when they couldn't catch what the introducer said.

Surrey and she were thrown together in the same station one cold weather; and the particular Devil who looks after muddles prompted Miss Tallaght to fall in love with Surrey. He had spoken to her perhaps twenty times – certainly not more – but she fell as unreasoningly in love with him as if she had been Elaine and he Lancelot.

She, of course, kept her own counsel; and, equally of course, her manner to Surrey, who never noticed manner or style or dress any more than he noticed a sunset, was icy, not to say repellent. The deadly dullness of Surrey struck her as reserve of force, and she grew to believe he was wonderfully clever in some secret and mysterious sort of line. She did not know in what line; but she believed, and that was enough. No one suspected anything of any kind, for the simple reason that no one took any deep interest in Miss Tallaght except her Aunt; who wanted to get the girl off her hands.

This went on for some months, till a man suddenly woke up to the fact that Miss Tallaght was the one woman in the world for him, and told her so. She *jawabed*[2] him – without rhyme or reason; and that night there followed one of those awful bedroom conferences that men know nothing about. Miss Tallaght's Aunt, querulous, indignant, and merciless, with her mouth full of hair-pins, and her hands full of false hair-plaits, set herself to find out by cross-examination what in the name of everything wise, prudent, religious, and dutiful, Miss Tallaght meant by *jawabing* her suitor. The conference lasted for an hour and a half, with question on question, insult and reminders of poverty – appeals to Providence, then a fresh mouthful of hair-pins – then all the questions over again, beginning with: 'But *what* do you see to dislike in Mr —?' then a vicious tug at what was left of the mane; then impressive warnings, and more appeals to Heaven; and then the collapse of poor Miss Tallaght, a rumpled, crumpled, tear-stained arrangement in white on the couch at the foot of the bed, and, between sobs and gasps, the whole absurd little story of her love for Surrey.

Now, in all the forty-five years' experience of Miss Tallaght's Aunt, she had never heard of a girl throwing over a real genuine lover with an appointment, for a problematical, hypothetical lover to whom she had spoken merely in the course of the ordinary social visiting rounds. So Miss Tallaght's Aunt was struck dumb, and, merely praying that Heaven might direct Miss Tallaght into a better frame of mind, dismissed the *ayah*, and went to bed; leaving Miss Tallaght to sob and moan herself to sleep.

Understand clearly, I don't for a moment defend Miss Tallaght. She was wrong – absurdly wrong – but attachments like hers *must* sprout by the law of averages, just to remind people that Love is as nakedly unreasoning as when Venus first gave him his kit and told him to run away and play.

Surrey must be held innocent – innocent as his own pony. Could he guess that, when Miss Tallaght was as curt and as unpleasing as she knew how, she would have risen up and followed him from Colombo to Dadar[3] at a word? He didn't know anything, or care anything, about Miss Tallaght. He had his work to do.

Miss Tallaght's Aunt might have respected her niece's secret. But she didn't. What we call 'talking rank scandal', she called 'seeking advice'; and she sought advice, on the case of Miss Tallaght, from the Judge's wife, 'in strict confidence, my dear', who told the Commissioner's wife, 'of course you won't repeat it, my dear', who told the Deputy-Commissioner's wife, 'you understand it is to go no further, my dear', who told the newest bride, who was so delighted at being in possession of a secret concerning real grown-up men and women, that she told any one and every one who called on her. So the tale went all over the station, and from being no one in particular, Miss Tallaght came to take precedence of the last interesting squabble between the Judge's wife and the Civil Engineer's wife. Then began a really interesting system of persecution worked by women — soft and sympathetic and intangible, but calculated to drive a girl off her head. They were all *so* sorry for Miss Tallaght, and they cooed together and were exaggeratedly kind and sweet in their manner to her, as those who said: 'You may confide in *us*, my stricken deer!'[4]

Miss Tallaght was a woman and sensitive. It took her less than one evening at the Bandstand to find that her poor little, precious little secret, that had been wrenched from her on the rack, was known as widely as if it had been written on her hat. I don't know what she went through. Women don't speak of these things, and men ought not to guess; but it must have been some specially refined torture, for she told her Aunt she would go Home and die as a governess sooner than stay in this hateful — hateful — place. Her Aunt said she was a rebellious girl, and sent her Home to her people after a couple of months; and said no one knew what the pains of a chaperon's life were.

Poor Miss Tallaght had one pleasure just at the last. Half-way down the line, she caught a glimpse of Surrey, who had gone down on duty, and was then in the up-train. And he took off his hat to her. She went Home, and if she is not dead by this time must be living still.

Months afterwards, there was a lively dinner at the Club for the Races. Surrey was mooning about as usual, and there was a good deal of idle talk flying every way. Finally, one man, who had taken more than was good for him, said, apropos of something about Surrey's reserved ways: 'Ah, you old fraud. It's all very well for you to pretend. I know a girl who was awf'ly mashed on you — once. Dead nuts she was on old Surrey. What had you been doing, eh?'

Surrey expected some sort of sell, and said with a laugh: 'Who was she?'

Before any one could kick the man, he plumped out with the name; and the Honorary Secretary tactfully upset the half of a big brew of shandy-gaff all over the table. After the mopping up, the men went out to the Lotteries.

But Surrey sat on, and, after ten minutes, said very humbly to the only other man in the deserted dining-room: 'On your honour, was there a word of truth in what the drunken fool said?'

Then the man who is writing this story, who had known of the thing from the beginning, and now felt all the hopelessness and tangle of it – the waste and the muddle – said, a good deal more energetically than he meant:

'Truth! Oh, man, man, couldn't you *see* it?'

Surrey said nothing, but sat still, smoking and smoking and thinking, while the Lottery tent babbled outside, and the *khitmutgars* turned down the lamps.

To the best of my knowledge and belief that was the first thing Surrey ever knew about love. But his awakening did not seem to delight him. It must have been rather unpleasant, to judge by the look on his face. He looked like a man who had missed a train and had been half stunned at the same time.

When the men came in from the Lotteries, Surrey went out. He wasn't in the mood for bones[5] and 'horse' talk. He went to his tent, and the last thing he said, quite aloud to himself, was: 'I didn't see. I didn't see. If I had *only* known!'

Even if he had known I don't believe . . .

But these things are *Kismet*, and we only find out all about them just when any knowledge is too late.

⦃ 'Yoked with an Unbeliever'[1] ⦄

I am dying for you, and you are dying for another.
Punjabi Proverb

When the Gravesend tender left the P. & O. steamer for Bombay
and went back to catch the train to Town, there were many people
in it crying. But the one who wept most, and most openly, was
Miss Agnes Laiter. She had reason to cry, because the only man
she ever loved – or ever could love, so she said – was going out
to India; and India, as every one knows, is divided equally
between jungle, tigers, cobras, cholera, and sepoys.

Phil Garron, leaning over the side of the steamer in the rain,
felt very unhappy too; but he did not cry. He was sent out to 'tea'.
What 'tea' meant he had not the vaguest idea, but fancied that he
would have to ride on a prancing horse over hills covered with
tea-vines, and draw a sumptuous salary for doing so; and he was
very grateful to his uncle for getting him the berth. He was really
going to reform all his slack, shiftless ways, save a large proportion
of his magnificent salary yearly, and in a very short time return
to marry Agnes Laiter. Phil Garron had been lying loose on his
friends' hands for three years, and, as he had nothing to do, he
naturally fell in love. He was very nice; but he was not strong in
his views and opinions and principles, and though he never came
to actual grief, his friends were thankful when he said good-bye,
and went out to this mysterious 'tea' business near Darjeeling.
They said, 'God bless you, dear boy! Let us never see your face
again,' – or at least that was what Phil was given to understand.

When he sailed, he was very full of a great plan to prove himself
several hundred times better than any one had given him credit
for – to work like a horse, and triumphantly marry Agnes Laiter.
He had many good points besides his good looks; his only fault
being that he was weak – the least little bit in the world weak. He

62

had as much notion of economy as the Morning Sun; and yet you could not lay your hand on any one item, and say, 'Herein Phil Garron is extravagant or reckless.' Nor could you point out any particular vice in his character; but he was 'unsatisfactory' and as workable as putty.

Agnes Laiter went about her duties at home – her family objected to the engagement – with red eyes, while Phil was sailing to Darjeeling – a 'port on the Bengal Ocean', as his mother used to tell her friends. He was popular enough on board ship, made many acquaintances and a moderately large liquor-bill, and sent off huge letters to Agnes Laiter at each port. Then he fell to work on his plantation, somewhere between Darjeeling and Kangra, and, though the salary and the horse and the work were not quite all he had fancied, he succeeded fairly well, and gave himself much unnecessary credit for his perseverance.

In the course of time, as he settled more into collar, and his work grew fixed before him, the face of Agnes Laiter went out of his mind and only came when he was at leisure, which was not often. He would forget all about her for a fortnight, and remember her with a start, like a schoolboy who has forgotten to learn his lesson. She did not forget Phil, because she was of the kind that never forgets. Only, another man – a really desirable young man – presented himself before Mrs Laiter; and the chance of a marriage with Phil was as far off as ever; and his letters were so unsatisfactory; and there was a certain amount of domestic pressure brought to bear on the girl; and the young man really was an eligible person as incomes go; and the end of all things was that Agnes married him, and wrote a tempestuous whirlwind of a letter to Phil in the wilds of Darjeeling, and said she should never know a happy moment all the rest of her life. Which was a true prophecy.

Phil received that letter, and held himself ill-treated. This was two years after he had come out; but by dint of thinking fixedly of Agnes Laiter, and looking at her photograph, and patting himself on the back for being one of the most constant lovers in history, and warming to the work as he went on, he really fancied that he had been very hardly used. He sat down and wrote one final letter – a really pathetic 'world without end, amen', epistle; explaining how he would be true to Eternity, and that all women were very much alike, and he would hide his broken heart, etc. etc.; but if, at any future time, etc. etc., he could afford to wait, etc. etc., unchanged affections, etc. etc., return to her old love, etc. etc., for eight closely-written pages. From an artistic point of view it was very neat work, but an ordinary Philistine who knew the state of Phil's real feelings – not the ones he rose to as he went on writing – would have called it the thoroughly mean and selfish work of a thoroughly mean and selfish weak man. But this verdict would have been incorrect. Phil paid for the postage, and felt every word he had written for at least two days and a half. It was the last flicker before the light went out.

That letter made Agnes Laiter very unhappy, and she cried and put it away in her desk, and became Mrs Somebody Else for the good of her family. Which is the first duty of every Christian maid.

Phil went his ways, and thought no more of his letter, except as an artist thinks of a neatly touched-in sketch. His ways were not bad, but they were not altogether good until they brought him across Dunmaya, the daughter of a Rajput ex-Subadar-Major² of our Native Army. The girl had a strain of Hill blood in her and, like the Hill-women, was not a *purdah-nashin* or woman who lives behind the veil. Where Phil met her, or how he heard of her, does not matter. She was a good girl and handsome, and, in her way, very clever and shrewd; though, of course, a little hard. It is to be remembered that Phil was living very comfortably, denying himself no small luxury, never putting by a penny, very satisfied with himself and his good intentions, was dropping all his English correspondents one by one, and beginning more and more to look upon India as his home. Some men fall this way, and they are of no use afterwards. The climate where he was stationed was good, and it really did not seem to him that there was any reason to return to England.

He did what many planters have done before him – that is to say, he made up his mind to marry a Hill-girl and settle down. He was seven-and-twenty then, with a long life before him, but no spirit to go through with it. So he married Dunmaya by the forms of the English Church, and some fellow-planters said he was a fool, and some said he was a wise man. Dunmaya was a thoroughly honest girl, and, in spite of her reverence for an Englishman, had a reasonable estimate of her husband's weaknesses. She managed him tenderly, and became, in less than a year, a very passable imitation of an English lady in dress and carriage. It is curious to think that a Hill-man after a lifetime's education is a Hill-man still; but a Hill-woman can in six months master most of the ways of her English sisters. There was a cooliewoman once ... But that is another story. Dunmaya dressed by preference in black and yellow, and looked well.

Meanwhile Phil's letter lay in Agnes Laiter's desk, and now and again she would think of poor, resolute, hard-working Phil among the cobras and tigers of Darjeeling, toiling in the vain hope that she might come back to him. Her husband was worth ten Phils, except that he had rheumatism of the heart. Three years after he was married, – and after he had tried Nice and Algeria for his complaint, – he went to Bombay, where he died, and set Agnes free. Being a devout woman, she looked on his death and the place of it as a direct interposition of Providence, and when she had recovered from the shock, she took out and re-read Phil's letter with the 'etc. etc.', and the big dashes, and the little dashes, and kissed it several times. No one knew her in Bombay; she had her husband's income, which was a large one, and Phil was close at hand. It was wrong and improper, of course, but she decided, as heroines do in novels, to find her old lover, to offer him her hand and her gold, and with him spend the rest of her life in some spot far from unsympathetic souls. She sat for two months, alone in Watson's Hotel, elaborating this decision, and the picture was a pretty one. Then she set out in search of Phil Garron, assistant on a tea plantation with a more than usually unpronounceable name.

She found him. She spent a month over it, for his plantation was not in the Darjeeling district at all, but nearer Kangra. Phil was very little altered, and Dunmaya was very nice to her.

Now the particular sin and shame of the whole business is that Phil, who really is not worth thinking of twice, was and is loved by Dunmaya, and more than loved by Agnes, the whole of whose life he seems to have spoilt.

Worst of all, Dunmaya is making a decent man of him; and he will ultimately be saved from perdition through her training.

Which is manifestly unfair.

{ False Dawn }

To-night, God knows what thing shall tide,
    The Earth is racked and fain –
Expectant, sleepless, open-eyed;
And we, who from the Earth were made,
    Thrill with our Mother's pain.

In Durance

No man will ever know the exact truth of this story; though women may sometimes whisper it to one another after a dance, when they are putting up their hair for the night and comparing lists of victims. A man, of course, cannot assist at these functions. So the tale must be told from the outside – in the dark – all wrong.

Never praise a sister to a sister, in the hope of your compliments reaching the proper ears, and so preparing the way for you later on. Sisters are women first, and sisters afterwards; and you will find that you do yourself harm.

Saumarez knew this when he made up his mind to propose to the elder Miss Copleigh. Saumarez was a strange man, with few merits so far as men could see, though he was popular with women, and carried enough conceit to stock a Viceroy's Council and leave a little over for the Commander-in-Chief's Staff. He was a Civilian.[1] Very many women took an interest in Saumarez, perhaps because his manner to them was offensive. If you hit a pony over the nose at the outset of your acquaintance, he may not love you, but he will take a deep interest in your movements ever afterwards. The elder Miss Copleigh was nice, plump, winning, and pretty. The younger was not so pretty, and, from men disregarding the hint set forth above, her style was repellent and unattractive. Both girls had, practically, the same figure, and there was a strong likeness between them in look and voice; though no one could doubt for an instant which was the nicer of the two.

Saumarez made up his mind, as soon as they came into the station from Behar, to marry the elder one. At least, we all made sure that he would, which comes to the same thing. She was two-and-twenty, and he was thirty-three, with pay and allowances of nearly fourteen hundred rupees a month. So the match, as we arranged it, was in every way a good one. Saumarez was his name, and summary was his nature, as a man once said. Having drafted his Resolution, he formed a Select Committee of One to sit upon it, and resolved to take his time. In our unpleasant slang, the Copleigh girls 'hunted in couples'. That is to say, you could do nothing with one without the other. They were very loving sisters; but their mutual affection was sometimes inconvenient. Saumarez held the balance hair-true between them, and none but himself could have said to which side his heart inclined, though every one guessed. He rode with them a good deal and danced with them, but he never succeeded in detaching them from each other for any length of time.

Women said that the two girls kept together through deep mistrust, each fearing that the other would steal a march on her. But that has nothing to do with a man. Saumarez was silent for good or bad, and as business-likely attentive as he could be, having due regard to his work and his polo. Beyond doubt both girls were fond of him.

As the hot weather drew nearer and Saumarez made no sign, women said that you could see their trouble in the eyes of the girls – that they were looking strained, anxious, and irritable. Men are quite blind in these matters unless they have more of the woman than the man in their composition; in which case it does not matter what they say or think. I maintain it was the hot April days that took the colour out of the Copleigh girls' cheeks. They should have been sent to the Hills early. No one – man or woman – feels an angel when the hot weather is approaching. The younger sister grew more cynical, not to say acid, in her ways; and the winningness of the elder wore thin. There was effort in it.

The station wherein all these things happened was, though not a little one, off the line of rail, and suffered through want of attention. There were no Gardens or bands or amusements worth

speaking of, and it was nearly a day's journey to come into Lahore
for a dance. People were grateful for small things to interest them.

About the beginning of May, and just before the final exodus
of Hill-goers, when the weather was very hot and there were
not more than twenty people in the station, Saumarez gave a
moonlight riding-picnic at an old tomb, six miles away, near the
bed of the river. It was a 'Noah's Ark' picnic; and there was to
be the usual arrangement of quarter-mile intervals between each
couple on account of the dust. Six couples came altogether,
including chaperons. Moonlight picnics are useful just at the very
end of the season, before all the girls go away to the Hills. They
lead to understandings, and should be encouraged by chaperons,
especially those whose girls look sweetest in riding-habits. I knew
a case once … But that is another story. That picnic was called
the 'Great Pop Picnic', because every one knew Saumarez would
propose then to the elder Miss Copleigh; and, besides his affair,
there was another which might possibly come to happiness. The
social atmosphere was heavily charged and wanted clearing.

We met at the parade-ground at ten. The night was fearfully
hot. The horses sweated even at walking-pace, but anything was
better than sitting still in our own dark houses. When we moved
off[2] under the full moon we were four couples, one triplet, and
Me. Saumarez rode with the Copleigh girls, and I loitered at the
tail of the procession wondering with whom Saumarez would
ride home. Every one was happy and contented; but we all felt
that things were going to happen. We rode slowly; and it was
nearly midnight before we reached the old tomb, facing the ruined
tank, in the decayed gardens where we were going to eat and
drink. I was late in coming up; and, before I went into the garden,
I saw that the horizon to the north carried a faint, dun-coloured
feather. But no one would have thanked me for spoiling so well-
managed an entertainment as this picnic – and a dust-storm,
more or less, does no great harm.

We gathered by the tank. Some one had brought out a banjo –
which is a most sentimental instrument – and three or four of us
sang. You must not laugh at this. Our amusements in out-of-the-
way stations are very few indeed. Then we talked in groups or
together, lying under the trees, with the sun-baked roses

dropping their petals on our feet, until supper was ready. It was a beautiful supper, as cold and as iced as you could wish; and we stayed long over it.

I had felt that the air was growing hotter and hotter; but nobody seemed to notice it until the moon went out and a burning hot wind began lashing the orange-trees with a sound like the noise of the sea. Before we knew where we were the dust-storm was on us, and everything was roaring, whirling darkness. The supper-table was blown bodily into the tank. We were afraid of staying anywhere near the old tomb for fear it might be blown down. So we felt our way to the orange-trees where the horses were picketed and waited for the storm to blow over. Then the little light that was left vanished, and you could not see your hand before your face. The air was heavy with dust and sand from the bed of the river, that filled boots and pockets, and drifted down necks, and coated eyebrows and moustaches. It was one of the worst dust-storms of the year. We were all huddled together close to the trembling horses, with the thunder chattering overhead, and the lightning spurting like water from a sluice, all ways at once. There was no danger, of course, unless the horses broke loose. I was standing with my head down wind and my hands over my mouth, hearing the trees thrashing each other. I could not see who was next me till the flashes came. Then I found that I was packed near Saumarez and the elder Miss Copleigh, with my own horse just in front of me. I recognized the elder Miss Copleigh, because she had a *pagri*[3] round her helmet, and the younger had not. All the electricity in the air had gone into my body, and I was quivering and tingling from head to foot – exactly as a corn shoots and tingles before rain. It was a grand storm. The wind seemed to be picking up the earth and pitching it to leeward in great heaps, and the heat beat up from the ground like the heat of the Day of Judgment.

The storm lulled slightly after the first half-hour, and I heard a despairing little voice close to my ear, saying to itself, quietly and softly, as if some lost soul were flying about with the wind, 'Oh, my God!' Then the younger Miss Copleigh stumbled into my arms, saying, 'Where is my horse? Get my horse. I want to go home. I want to go home. Take me home.'

I thought that the lightning and the black darkness had frightened her. So I said there was no danger, but she must wait till the storm blew over. She answered, 'It is not that! I want to go home! Oh, take me away from here!'

I said that she could not go till the light came; but I felt her brush past me and go away. It was too dark to see where. Then the whole sky was split open with one tremendous flash, as if the end of the world were coming, and all the women shrieked.

Almost directly after this I felt a man's hand on my shoulder, and heard Saumarez bellowing in my ear. Through the rattling of the trees and howling of the wind I did not catch his words at once, but at last I heard him say, 'I've proposed to the wrong one! What shall I do?' Saumarez had no occasion to make this confidence to me. I was never a friend of his, nor am I now; but I fancy neither of us were ourselves just then. He was shaking as he stood with excitement, and I was feeling queer all over with the electricity. I could not think of anything to say except, 'More fool you for proposing in a dust-storm.' But I did not see how that would improve the mistake.

Then he shouted, 'Where's Edith – Edith Copleigh?' Edith was the younger sister. I answered out of my astonishment, 'What do you want with *her*?' For the next two minutes he and I were shouting at each other like maniacs, – he vowing that it was the younger sister he had meant to propose to all along, and I telling him, till my throat was hoarse, that he must have made a mistake! I cannot account for this except, again, by the fact that we were neither of us ourselves. Everything seemed to me like a bad dream – from the stamping of the horses in the darkness to Saumarez telling me the story of his loving Edith Copleigh from the first. He was still clawing my shoulder and begging me to tell him where Edith Copleigh was, when another lull came and brought light with it, and we saw the dust-cloud forming on the plain in front of us. So we knew the worst was over. The moon was low down, and there was just the glimmer of the false dawn that comes about an hour before the real one. But the light was very faint, and the dun cloud roared like a bull. I wondered where Edith Copleigh had gone; and as I was wondering I saw three things together: First, Maud Copleigh's face come smiling out of the darkness and move towards Saumarez who was standing by me. I heard the girl whisper, 'George,' and slide her arm through the arm that was not clawing my shoulder, and I saw that look on her face which only comes once or twice in a lifetime – when a woman is perfectly happy and the air is full of trumpets and gorgeously-coloured fire, and the Earth turns into cloud because she loves and is loved. At the same time, I saw Saumarez's face as he heard Maud Copleigh's voice, and, fifty yards away from the clump of orange-trees, I saw a brown holland habit getting upon a horse.

It must have been my state of over-excitement that made me so ready to meddle with what did not concern me. Saumarez was moving off to the habit; but I pushed him back and said, 'Stop here and explain. I'll fetch her back!' And I ran out to get at my own horse. I had a perfectly unnecessary notion that everything must be done decently and in order, and that Saumarez's first care was to wipe the happy look out of Maud Copleigh's face. All the time I was linking up the curb-chain I wondered how he would do it.

I cantered after Edith Copleigh, thinking to bring her back slowly on some pretence or another. But she galloped away as soon as she saw me, and I was forced to ride after her in earnest. She called back over her shoulder, 'Go away! I'm going home. Oh, go away!' two or three times; but my business was to catch her first, and argue later. The ride fitted in with the rest of the evil dream. The ground was very rough, and now and again we rushed through the whirling, choking 'dust-devils' in the skirts of the flying storm. There was a burning hot wind blowing that brought up a stench of stale brick-kilns with it; and through the half-light and through the dust-devils, across that desolate plain, flickered the brown holland habit on the grey horse. She headed for the station at first. Then she wheeled round and set off for the river through beds of burnt-down jungle-grass, bad even to ride pig over. In cold blood I should never have dreamed of going over such a country at night, but it seemed quite right and natural with the lightning crackling overhead, and a reek like the smell of the Pit in my nostrils. I rode and shouted, and she bent forward and lashed her horse, and the aftermath of the dust-storm came up, and caught us both, and drove us down wind like pieces of paper.

I don't know how far we rode; but the drumming of the horse-hoofs and the roar of the wind and the race of the faint blood-red moon through the yellow mist seemed to have gone on for years and years, and I was literally drenched with sweat from my helmet to my gaiters when the grey stumbled, recovered himself, and pulled up dead lame. My brute was used up altogether. Edith Copleigh was bareheaded, plastered with dust, and crying bitterly. 'Why can't you let me alone?' she said. 'I only wanted to get away and go home. Oh, *please* let me go!'

'You have got to come back with me, Miss Copleigh. Saumarez has something to say to you.'

It was a foolish way of putting it; but I hardly knew Miss Copleigh, and, though I was playing Providence at the cost of my horse, I could not tell her in as many words what Saumarez had told me. I thought he could do that better himself. All her pretence about being tired and wanting to go home broke down, and she rocked herself to and fro in the saddle as she sobbed, and the hot wind blew her black hair to leeward. I am not going to repeat what she said, because she was utterly unstrung.

This was the cynical Miss Copleigh, and I, almost an utter stranger to her, was trying to tell her that Saumarez loved her, and she was to come back to hear him say so. I believe I made myself understood, for she gathered the grey together and made him hobble somehow, and we set off for the tomb, while the storm went thundering down to Umballa and a few big drops of warm rain fell. I found out that she had been standing close to Saumarez when he proposed to her sister, and had wanted to go home to cry in peace, as an English girl should. She dabbed her eyes with her pocket-handkerchief as we went along, and babbled to me out of sheer lightness of heart and hysteria. That was perfectly unnatural; and yet it seemed all right at the time and in the place. All the world was only the two Copleigh girls, Saumarez, and I, ringed in with the lightning and the dark; and the guidance of this misguided world seemed to lie in my hands.

When we returned to the tomb in the deep, dead stillness that followed the storm, the dawn was just breaking and nobody had gone away. They were waiting for our return. Saumarez most of all. His face was white and drawn. As Miss Copleigh and I limped up, he came forward to meet us, and, when he helped her down from her saddle, he kissed her before all the picnic. It was like a scene in a theatre, and the likeness was heightened by all the dust-white, ghostly-looking men and women under the orange-trees clapping their hands – as if they were watching a play – at Saumarez's choice. I never knew anything so un-English in my life.

Lastly, Saumarez said we must all go home or the station would come out to look for us, and would I be good enough to ride home with Maud Copleigh? Nothing would give me greater pleasure, I said.

So we formed up, six couples in all, and went back two by two; Saumarez walking at the side of Edith Copleigh, who was riding his horse. Maud Copleigh did not talk to me at any length.

The air was cleared; and, little by little, as the sun rose, I felt we were all dropping back again into ordinary men and women, and that the 'Great Pop Picnic' was a thing altogether apart and out of the world – never to happen again. It had gone with the dust-storm and the tingle in the hot air.

I felt tired and limp, and a good deal ashamed of myself, as I went in for a bath and some sleep.

There is a woman's version of this story, but it will never be written ... unless Maud Copleigh cares to try.

⸨ The Rescue of Pluffles ⸩

Thus, for a season, they fought it fair –
   She and his cousin May –
Tactful, talented, debonnair,
   Decorous foes were they;
But never can battle of man compare
   With merciless feminine fray.
                              Two and One

Mrs Hauksbee was sometimes nice to her own sex. Here is a story to prove this; and you can believe just as much as ever you please.

Pluffles was a subaltern in the 'Unmentionables'. He was callow, even for a subaltern. He was callow all over – like a canary that had not finished fledging itself. The worst of it was that he had three times as much money as was good for him; Pluffles' Papa being a rich man, and Pluffles being the only son. Pluffles' Mamma adored him. She was only a little less callow than Pluffles, and she believed everything he said.

Pluffles' weakness was not believing what people said. He preferred what he called trusting to his own judgment. He had as much judgment as he had seat or hands, and this preference tumbled him into trouble once or twice. But the biggest trouble Pluffles ever manufactured came about at Simla – some years ago, when he was four-and-twenty.

He began by trusting to his own judgment as usual, and the result was that, after a time, he was bound hand and foot to Mrs Reiver's 'rickshaw wheels.

There was nothing good about Mrs Riever, unless it was her dress. She was bad from her hair – which started life on a Brittany girl's head – to her boot-heels, which were two and three-eighths inches high. She was not honestly mischievous like Mrs Hauksbee. She was wicked in a business-like way.

75

There was never any scandal – she had not generous impulses enough for that. She was the exception which proved the rule that Anglo–Indian ladies are in every way as nice as their sisters at Home. She spent her life in proving that rule.

Mrs Hauksbee and she hated each other fervently. They hated far too much to clash; but the things they said of each other were startling – not to say original. Mrs Hauksbee was honest – honest as her own front teeth – and, but for her love of mischief, would have been a woman's woman. There was no honesty about Mrs Reiver; nothing but selfishness. And at the beginning of the season poor little Pluffles fell a prey to her. She laid herself out to that end, and who was Pluffles to resist? He trusted to his judgment, and he got judged.

I have seen Captain Hayes[1] argue with a tough horse – I have seen a tonga-driver coerce a stubborn pony – I have seen a riotous setter broken to gun by a hard keeper – but the breaking-in of Pluffles of the 'Unmentionables' was beyond all these. He learned to fetch and carry like a dog, and to wait like one, too, for a word from Mrs Reiver. He learned to keep appointments which Mrs Reiver had no intention of keeping. He learned to take thankfully dances which Mrs Reiver had no intention of giving him. He learned to shiver for an hour and a quarter on the windward side of Elysium[2] while Mrs Reiver was making up her mind to come for a ride. He learned to hunt for a 'rickshaw, in a light dress-suit under pelting rain, and to walk by the side of that 'rickshaw when he had found it. He learned what it was to be spoken to like a coolie and ordered about like a cook. He learned all this and many other things besides. And he paid for his schooling.

Perhaps, in some hazy way, he fancied that it was fine and impressive, that it gave him a status among men, and was altogether the thing to do. It was nobody's business to warn Pluffles that he was unwise. The pace that season was too good to inquire; and meddling with another man's folly is always thankless work. Pluffles' Colonel should have ordered him back to his Regiment when he heard how things were going. But Pluffles had got himself engaged to a girl in England the last time he went Home; and, if there was one thing more than another that the Colonel detested, it was a married subaltern. He chuckled when he heard of the education of Pluffles, and said it was good training for the boy. But it was not good training in the least. It led him into spending money beyond his means, which were good; above that, the education spoilt an average boy and made it a tenth-rate man of an objectionable kind. He wandered into a bad set, and his little bill at the jewellers' was a thing to wonder at.

Then Mrs Hauksbee rose to the occasion. She played her game alone, knowing what people would say of her; and she played it for the sake of a girl she had never seen. Pluffles' *fiancée* was to come out, under chaperonage of an aunt, in October, to be married to Pluffles.

At the beginning of August Mrs Hauksbee discovered that it was time to interfere. A man who rides much knows exactly what a horse is going to do next before he does it.[3] In the same way, a woman of Mrs Hauksbee's experience knows accurately how a boy will behave under certain circumstances – notably when he is infatuated with one of Mrs Reiver's stamp. She said that, sooner or later, little Pluffles would break off that engagement for nothing at all – simply to gratify Mrs Reiver, who, in return, would keep him at her feet and in her service just so long as she found it worth her while. She said she knew the signs of these things. If she did not no one else could.

Then she went forth to capture Pluffles under the guns of the enemy; just as Mrs Cusack-Bremmil carried away Bremmil under Mrs Hauksbee's eyes.

This particular engagement lasted seven weeks – we called it the Seven Weeks' War – and was fought out inch by inch on both sides. A detailed account would fill a book, and would be incomplete then. Any one who knows about these things can fit in the details for himself. It was a superb fight – there will never be another like it as long as Jakko Hill stands – and Pluffles was the prize of victory. People said shameful things about Mrs Hauksbee. They did not know what she was playing for. Mrs Reiver fought partly because Pluffles was useful to her, but mainly because she hated Mrs Hauksbee, and the matter was a trial of strength between them. No one knows what Pluffles thought. He had not many ideas at the best of times, and the few he possessed made him conceited. Mrs Hauksbee said, 'The boy must be caught; and the only way of catching him is by treating him well.'

So she treated him as a man of the world and of experience so long as the issue was doubtful. Little by little Pluffles fell away from his old allegiance and came over to the enemy, by whom he was made much of. He was never sent on outpost duty after 'rickshaws any more, nor was he given dances which never came off, nor were the drains on his purse continued. Mrs Hauksbee held him on the snaffle;[4] and, after his treatment at Mrs Reiver's hands, he appreciated the change.

Mrs Reiver had broken him of talking about himself, and made him talk about her own merits. Mrs Hauksbee acted otherwise, and won his confidence, till he mentioned his engagement to the girl at Home, speaking of it in a high and mighty way as a piece of boyish folly. This was when he was taking tea with her one afternoon, and discoursing in what he considered a gay and fascinating style. Mrs Hauksbee had seen an earlier generation of his stamp bud and blossom, and decay into fat Captains and tubby Majors.

At a moderate estimate there were about three-and-twenty sides to that lady's character. Some men say more. She began to talk to Pluffles after the manner of a mother, and as if there had been three hundred years, instead of fifteen, between them. She spoke with a sort of throaty quaver in her voice which had a soothing effect, though what she said was anything but soothing. She pointed out the exceeding folly, not to say meanness, of Pluffles' conduct, and the smallness of his views. Then he stammered something about 'trusting to his own judgment as a man of the world'; and this paved the way for what she wanted to say next. It would have withered up Pluffles had it come from any other woman; but, in the soft cooing style in which Mrs Hauksbee put it, it only made him feel limp and repentant – as if he had been in some superior kind of church. Little by little, very softly and pleasantly, she began taking the conceit out of Pluffles, as they take the ribs out of an umbrella before re-covering it. She told him what she thought of him and his judgment and his knowledge of the world; and how his performance had made him ridiculous to other people; and how it was his intention to make love to herself if she gave him the chance. Then she said that marriage would be the making of him; and drew a pretty little picture – all rose and opal – of the Mrs Pluffles of the future going through life relying on the judgment and knowledge of the world of a husband who had nothing to reproach himself with. How she reconciled these two statements she alone knew. But they did not strike Pluffles as conflicting.

Hers was a perfect little homily – much better than any clergyman could have given – and it ended with touching allusions to Pluffles' Mamma and Papa, and the wisdom of taking his bride Home.

Then she sent Pluffles out for a walk, to think over what she had said. Pluffles left, blowing his nose very hard and holding himself very straight. Mrs Hauksbee laughed.

What Pluffles had intended to do in the matter of the engagement only Mrs Reiver knew, and she kept her own counsel to her death. She would have liked it spoiled as a compliment, I fancy.

Pluffles enjoyed many talks with Mrs Hauksbee during the next few days. They were all to the same end, and they helped Pluffles in the path of Virtue.

Mrs Hauksbee wanted to keep him under her wing to the last. Therefore she discountenanced his going down to Bombay to get married. 'Goodness only knows what might happen by the way!' she said. 'Pluffles is cursed with the curse of Reuben,[5] and India is no fit place for him!'

In the end the *fiancée* arrived with her aunt; and Pluffles, having reduced his affairs to some sort of order – here again Mrs Hauksbee helped him – was married.

Mrs Hauksbee gave a sigh of relief when both the 'I wills' had been said, and went her way.

Pluffles took her advice about going Home. He left the Service and is now raising speckled cattle inside green-painted fences somewhere in England. I believe he does this very judiciously. He would have come to extreme grief in India.

For these reasons, if any one says anything more than usually nasty about Mrs Hauksbee, tell him the story of the Rescue of Pluffles.

⟩ Cupid's Arrow ⟨

Pit where the buffalo cooled his hide,
By the hot sun emptied, and blistered and dried;
Log in the plume-grass, hidden and lone;
Bund where the earth-rat's mounds are strown;
Cave in the bank where the sly stream steals;
Aloe that stabs at the belly and heels,
Jump if you dare on a steed untried —
Safer it is to go wide — go wide!
Hark, from in front where the best men ride:—
'*Pull to the off, boys! Wide! Go wide!*'

The Peora Hunt

Once upon a time there lived at Simla a very pretty girl, the daughter of a poor but honest District and Sessions Judge. She was a good girl, but could not help knowing her power and using it. Her Mamma was very anxious about her daughter's future, as all good Mammas should be.

When a man is a Commissioner and a bachelor, and has the right of wearing open-work jam-tart jewels in gold and enamel on his clothes, and of going through a door before every one except a Member of Council, a Lieutenant-Governor, or a Viceroy, he is worth marrying. At least, that is what ladies say. There was a Commissioner in Simla, in those days, who was, and wore, and did all I have said. He was a plain man – an ugly man – the ugliest man in Asia, with two exceptions. His was a face to dream about and try to carve on a pipe-head afterwards. His name was Saggott – Barr-Saggott – Anthony Barr-Saggott and six letters to follow. Departmentally, he was one of the best men the Government of India owned. Socially, he was like unto a blandishing gorilla.

When he turned his attentions to Miss Beighton, I believe that Mrs Beighton wept with delight at the reward Providence had sent her in her old age.

80

Mr Beighton held his tongue. He was an easy-going man.

A Commissioner is very rich. His pay is beyond the Dreams of Avarice – is so enormous that he can afford to save and scrape in a way that would almost discredit a Member of Council. Most Commissioners are mean; but Barr-Saggott was an exception. He entertained royally; he horsed himself well; he gave dances; he was a power in the land; and he behaved as such.

Consider that everything I am writing of took place in an almost prehistoric era in the history of British India. Some folk may remember the years before lawn-tennis[1] was born, when we all played croquet. There were seasons before that, if you will believe me, when even croquet had not been invented, and archery – which was revived in England in 1844 – was as great a pest as lawn-tennis is now. People talked learnedly about 'holding' and 'loosing', 'steles', 'reflexed bows', '56-pound bows', 'backed' or 'self-yew'[2] bows, as we talk about 'rallies', 'volleys', 'smashes', 'returns', and '16-ounce rackets'.

Miss Beighton shot divinely over ladies' distance – 60 yards that is – and was acknowledged the best lady archer in Simla. Men called her 'Diana of Tara-Devi'.

Barr-Saggott paid her great attention; and, as I have said, the heart of her mother was uplifted in consequence. Kitty Beighton took matters more calmly. It was pleasant to be singled out by a Commissioner with letters after his name, and to fill the hearts of other girls with bad feelings. But there was no denying the fact that Barr-Saggott was phenomenally ugly; and all his attempts to adorn himself only made him more grotesque. He was not christened 'The *Langur*' – which means grey ape – for nothing. It was pleasant, Kitty thought, to have him at her feet, but it was better to escape from him and ride with the graceless Cubbon – the man in a Dragoon Regiment at Umballa – the boy with a handsome face and no prospects. Kitty liked Cubbon more than a little. He never pretended for a moment that he was anything less than head over heels in love with her, for he was an honest boy. So Kitty fled, now and again, from the stately wooings of Barr-Saggott to the company of young Cubbon, and was scolded by her Mamma in consequence. 'But, Mother,' she said, 'Mr Saggott is such – such a – is so *fearfully* ugly, you know!'

'My dear,' said Mrs Beighton piously, 'we cannot be other than an all-ruling Providence has made us. Besides, you will take precedence of your own Mother, you know! Think of that and be reasonable.'

Then Kitty put up her little chin and said irreverent things about precedence, and Commissioners, and matrimony. Mr Beighton rubbed the top of his head; for he was an easy-going man.

Late in the season, when he judged that the time was ripe, Barr-Saggott developed a plan which did great credit to his administrative powers. He arranged an archery-tournament for ladies, with a most sumptuous diamond-studded bracelet as prize. He drew up his terms skilfully, and every one saw that the bracelet was a gift to Miss Beighton; the acceptance carrying with it the hand and the heart of Commissioner Barr-Saggott. The terms were a St Leonard's Round – thirty-six shots at sixty yards – under the rules of the Simla Toxophilite Society.

All Simla was invited. There were beautifully arranged tea-tables under the deodars at Annandale, where the Grand Stand is now; and, alone in its glory, winking in the sun, sat the diamond bracelet in a blue velvet case. Miss Beighton was anxious – almost too anxious – to compete. On the appointed afternoon all Simla rode down to Annandale to witness the Judgment of Paris turned upside-down. Kitty rode with young Cubbon, and it was easy to see that the boy was troubled in his mind. He must be held innocent of everything that followed. Kitty was pale and nervous, and looked long at the bracelet. Barr-Saggott was gorgeously dressed, even more nervous than Kitty, and more hideous than ever.

Mrs Beighton smiled condescendingly, as befitted the mother of a potential Commissioneress, and the shooting began; all the world standing in a semicircle as the ladies came out one after the other.

Nothing is so tedious as an archery competition. They shot, and they shot, and they kept on shooting, till the sun left the valley, and little breezes got up in the deodars, and people waited for Miss Beighton to shoot and win. Cubbon was at one horn of the semicircle round the shooters, and Barr-Saggott at the other.

Miss Beighton was last on the list. The scoring had been weak, and the bracelet, with Commissioner Barr-Saggott, was hers to a certainty.

The Commissioner strung her bow with his own sacred hands. She stepped forward, looked at the bracelet, and her first arrow went true to a hair – full into the heart of the 'gold' – counting nine points.

Young Cubbon on the left turned white, and his Devil prompted Barr-Saggott to smile. Now, horses used to shy when Barr-Saggott smiled. Kitty saw that smile. She looked to her left-front, gave an almost imperceptible nod to Cubbon, and went on shooting.

I wish I could describe the scene that followed. It was out of the ordinary and most improper. Miss Kitty fitted her arrows with immense deliberation, so that every one might see what she was doing. She was a perfect shot, and her 46-pound bow suited her to a nicety. She pinned the wooden legs of the target with great care four successive times. She pinned the wooden top of the target once, and all the ladies looked at each other. Then she began some fancy shooting at the white, which if you hit it, counts exactly one point. She put five arrows into the white. It was wonderful archery; but, seeing that her business was to make 'golds' and win the bracelet, Barr-Saggott turned a delicate green, like young water-grass. Next, she shot over the target twice, then wide to the left twice – always with the same deliberation – while a chilly hush fell over the company, and Mrs Beighton took out her handkerchief. Then Kitty shot at the ground in front of the target, and split several arrows. Then she made a red – or seven points – just to show what she could do if she liked, and she finished up her amazing performance with some more fancy shooting at the target supports. Here is her score as it was pricked off:

	Gold.	Red.	Blue.	Black.	White.	Total Hits.	Total Score.
Miss Beighton	1	1	0	0	5	7	21

Barr-Saggott looked as if the last few arrow-heads had been

driven into his legs instead of the target's, and the deep stillness was broken by a little snubby, mottled, half-grown girl saying in a shrill voice of triumph, 'Then *I*'ve won!'

Mrs Beighton did her best to bear up; but she wept in the presence of the people. No training could help her through such a disappointment. Kitty unstrung her bow with a vicious jerk, and went back to her place, while Barr-Saggott was trying to pretend that he enjoyed snapping the bracelet on the snubby girl's raw, red wrist. It was an awkward scene – most awkward. Every one tried to depart in a body and leave Kitty to the mercy of her Mamma.

But Cubbon took her away instead, and – the rest isn't worth printing.

⟨ The Three Musketeers ⟩

An' when the war began, we chased the bold Afghan,
An' we made the bloomin' Ghazi for to flee, boys, O!
An' we marched into Kabul, an' we tuk the Balar 'Issar,[1]
An' we taught 'em to respec' the British Soldier.

Barrack-Room Ballad

Mulvaney, Ortheris, and Learoyd are Privates in B Company of
a Line Regiment, and personal friends of mine. Collectively, I
think, but am not certain, they are the worst men in the Regiment
so far as genial blackguardism goes.

They told me this story in the Umballa Refreshment Room
while we were waiting for an up-train. I supplied the beer. The
tale was cheap at a gallon and a half.

All men know Lord Benira Trig. He is a Duke, or an Earl, or
something unofficial; also a Peer;[2] also a Globe-trotter. On all
three counts, as Ortheris says, ''e didn't deserve no consideration.'
He was out in India for three months collecting materials for a
book on 'Our Eastern Impedimenta', and quartering himself
upon everybody, like a Cossack in evening-dress.

His particular vice – because he was a Radical, men said – was
having garrisons turned out for his inspection. He would then
dine with the Officer Commanding, and insult him, across the
Mess table, about the appearance of the troops. That was Benira's
way.

He turned out troops once too often. He came to Helanthami[3]
Cantonment on a Tuesday. He wished to go shopping in the
bazar on Wednesday, and he 'desired' the troops to be turned out
on a Thursday. *On – a – Thursday!* The Officer Commanding
could not well refuse; for Benira was a Lord. There was an
indignation meeting of subalterns in the ante-room, to call the
Colonel pet names.

'But the rale dimonstrashin,' said Mulvaney, 'was in B Comp'ny barrick; we three headin' ut.'

Mulvaney climbed on to the refreshment-bar, settled himself comfortably by the beer, and went on, 'Whin the row was at uts foinest an' B Comp'ny was fur goin' out to murther this man Thrigg on the p'rade-groun', Learoyd here takes up his helmut an' sez – fwhat was ut ye said?'

'Ah said,' said Learoyd, 'gie us t' brass. Tak oop a subscripshun, lads, for to put off t' p'rade, an' if t' p'rade's not put off, Ah'll gie t' brass back agean. Thot's wot Ah said. All B Coomp'ny knawed me. Ah took oop a big subscripshun – fower rupees eight annas 'twere – an' Ah went oot to turn t' job ovver. Mulvaney an' Orth'ris coom with me.'

'We three raises the Divil in couples gin'rally,' explained Mulvaney.

Here Ortheris interrupted. ''Ave you read the papers?' said he.

'Sometimes,' I said.

'We 'ad read the papers, an' we put hup a faked decoity,[4] a – a sedukshun.'

'*Ab*dukshin, ye cockney,' said Mulvaney.

'*Ab*dukshun or *se*dukshun – no great odds. Any'ow, we arranged to take an' put Mister Benhira out o' the way till Thursday was over, or 'e too busy to rux 'isself about p'raids. *Hi* was the man wot said, "We'll make a few rupees off o' the business."'

'We hild a Council av War,' continued Mulvaney, 'walkin' roun' by the Artill'ry Lines. I was Prisidint, Learoyd was Minister av Finance, an' little Orth'ris here was –'

'A bloomin' Bismarck! *Hi* made the 'ole show pay.'

'This interferin' bit av a Benira man,' said Mulvaney, 'did the thrick for us himsilf; for, on me sowl, we hadn't a notion av what was to come afther the next minut'. He was shoppin' in the bazar on fut. 'Twas dhrawin' dusk thin, an' we stud watchin' the little man hoppin' in an' out av the shops, thryin' to injuce the naygurs to *mallum* his *bat*. Prisintly, he sthrolls up, his arrums full av thruck, an' he sez in a consiquinshal way, shticking out his little belly, "Me good men," sez he, "have ye seen the Colonel's

b'roosh?" – "B'roosh?" says Learoyd. "There's no b'roosh here –
nobbut a *hekka*." – "Fwhat's that?" sez Thrigg. Learoyd shows
him wan down the sthreet, an' he sez, "How thruly Orientil! I
will ride on a *hekka*." I saw thin that our Rig'mintil Saint was
for givin' Thrigg over to us neck an' brisket. I purshued a *ekka*,
an' I sez to the dhriver-divil, I sez, "Ye black limb, there's a
Sahib comin' for this *ekka*. He wants to go *jildi* to the Padsahi
Jhil" – 'twas about tu moiles away – "to shoot snipe – *chirria*.
You dhrive *Jehannum ke marfik, mallum* – like Hell! 'Tis no
manner av use *bukkin*' to the Sahib, bekaze he doesn't *samjao*
your talk. Av he *bolos* anything, just you *choop* and *chel. Dekker?*
Go *arsty* for the first *arder*-mile fron cantonmints. Thin *chel,
Shaitan ke marfik*; an' the *chooper* you *choops* an' the *jildier* you
chels the better *kooshy* will that Sahib be; an' here's a rupee for
ye!'

'The *ekka*-man knew there was somethin' out av the common
in the air. He grinned an' sez, "*Bote achee!*⁵ I goin' damn fast."
I prayed the Colonel's b'roosh wudn't arrive till me darlin' Benira
by the grace av God was undher weigh. The little man puts his
thruck into the *ekka* an' scuttles in like a fat guinea-pig; niver
offerin' us the price av a dhrink for our services in helpin' him
home. "He's off to the Padsahi Jhil," sez I to the others.'

Ortheris took up the tale:

'Jist then, little Buldoo kim up, 'oo was the son of one of the
Artillery grooms – 'e would 'av made a 'evinly newspaper-boy in
London, bein' sharp an' fly to all manner o' games. 'E 'ad bin
watchin' us puttin' Mister Benhira into 'is temp'ry baroosh, an'
'e sez, "Wot '*ave* you been a-doin' of, Sahib?" sez 'e. Learoyd 'e
caught 'im by the ear an 'e sez –'

'Ah says,' went on Learoyd, '"Young mon, that mon's gooin'
to have t' goons out o' Thursday – to-morrow – an' thot's more
work for you, young mon. Now, sitha, tak' a *tat* an' a *lookri*,⁶ an'
ride tha domdest to t' Padsahi Jhil. Cotch thot there *hekka*, and
tell t' driver iv your lingo thot you've coom to tak' his place. T'
Sahib doesn't speak t' *bat*, an' he's a little mon. Drive t' *hekka*
into t' Padsahi Jhil into t' watter. Leave t' Sahib theer an' roon
hoam; an' here's a rupee for tha."'''

Then Mulvaney and Ortheris spoke together in alternate

fragments: Mulvaney leading (You must pick out the speakers as best you can):[7] – 'He was a knowin' little divil was Bhuldoo – 'e sez *bote achee* an' cuts – wid a wink in his oi – but *Hi* sez there's money to be made – an' I wanted to see the ind av the campaign – so *Hi* sez we'll double hout to the Padsahi Jhil – an' save the little man from bein' dacoited by the murtherin' Bhuldoo – an' turn hup like reskooers in a Victoria[8] Melodramma – so we doubled for the *jhil*, an' prisintly there was the divil av a hurroosh behind us an' three bhoys on grasscuts' ponies come by, poundin' along for the dear life – s'elp me Bob, if Buldoo 'adn't raised a rig'lar *harmy* of decoits – to do the job in shtile. An' we ran, an' they ran, shplittin' with laughin', till we gets near the *jhil* – and 'ears sounds of distress floatin' molloncolly on the hevenin' hair.' (Orthcris was growing poetical under the influence of the beer. The duet recommenced: Mulvaney leading again.)

'Thin we heard Bhuldoo, the dacoit, shoutin' to the *ekka*-man, an' wan of the young divils brought his stick down on the top av the *ekka*-cover, an' Benira Thrigg inside howled "Murther an' Death." Bhuldoo takes the reins and dhrives like mad for the *jhil*, havin' dishpersed the *ekka*-dhriver – 'oo cum up to us an' 'e sez, sez 'e, "That Sahib's nigh mad with funk! Wot devil's work 'ave you led me into?" – "Hall right," sez we, "you catch that there pony an' come along. This Sahib's been decoited, an' we're going to resky 'im!" Sez the driver, "Decoits! Wot decoits? That's Buldoo the *budmash*"[9] – "Bhuldoo be shot!" sez we. "'Tis a woild dissolute Paythan frum the hills. There's about eight av thim coercin' the Sahib. You remimber that an' you'll get another rupee!" Thin we heard the *whop-whop-whop* av the *ekka* turnin' over, an' a splash av wather, an' the voice av Benira Thrigg callin' upon God to forgive his sins – an' Buldoo an' 'is friends squatterin' in the water like boys in the Serpentine.'

Here the Three Musketeers retired simultaneously into the beer.

'Well? What came next?' said I.

'Fwhat nex'?' answered Mulvaney, wiping his mouth. 'Wud ye let three bould sodger-bhoys lave the ornamint av the House av Lords to be dhrowned an' dacoited in a *jhil*? We formed line av quarther-column an' we discinded upon the inimy. For the better part av tin minut's you cud not hear yersilf spake. The *tattoo* was screamin' in chune wid Benira Thrigg an' Bhuldoo's army, an' the shticks was whistlin' roun' the *ekka* an' Orth'ris was beatin' the *ekka*-cover wid his fistes, an' Learoyd yellin', "Look out for their knives!" an' me cuttin' into the dhark, right an' lef', dishpersin' arrmy corps av Paythans. Holy Mother av Moses! 'Twas more disp'rit than Ahmid Kheyl wid Maiwand[10] thrown in. Afther a while Bhuldoo an' his bhoys flees. Have ye iver seen a rale live Lord thryin' to hide his nobility undher a fut an' half av brown swamp-wather? 'Tis the livin' image av a wather-carrier's goatskin wid the shivers. It tuk toime to pershuade me frind Benira he was not disimbowilled: an' more toime to get out the *ekka*. The dhriver come up afther the battle, swearin' he tuk a hand in repulsin' the inimy. Benira was sick wid the fear. We escorted him back, very slow, to cantonmints, for that an' the chill to soak into him. It suk! Glory be to the Rig'mintil Saint, but it suk to the marrow av Lord Benira Thrigg!'

Here Ortheris, slowly, with immense pride: ''E sez, "You har my noble preservers," sez'e. "You har a *honour* to the British Harmy," sez 'e. With that 'e describes the hawful band of decoits wot set on 'im. There was about forty of 'em an' 'e was hoverpowered by numbers, so 'e was; but 'e never lorst 'is presence of mind, so 'e didn't. 'E guv the *hekka*-driver five rupees for 'is noble assistance, an' 'e said 'e would see to us after 'e 'ad spoken to the Colonel. For we was a *honour* to the Regiment, we was.'

'An' we three,' said Mulvaney, with a seraphic smile, 'have dhrawn the par-ti-cu-lar attinshin av Bobs Bahadur[11] more than wanst. But he's a rale good little man is Bobs. Go on, Orth'ris, me son.'

'Then we leaves 'im at the Colonel's 'ouse, werry sick, an' we cuts hover to B Comp'ny barrick an' we sez we 'ave saved Benira from a bloody doom, an' the chances was agin there bein' p'raid on Thursday. About ten minutes later come three envelicks, one for each of us. S'elp me Bob, if the old bloke 'adn't guv us a fiver apiece – sixty-four rupees in the bazar! On Thursday 'e was in 'orspital recoverin' from 'is sanguinary encounter with a gang of Paythans, an' B Comp'ny was drinkin' 'emselves into Clink by squads. So there never was no Thursday p'raid. But the Colonel, when 'e 'eard of our galliant conduck, 'e sez, "Hi know there's been some devilry somewheres," sez 'e, "but I can't bring it 'ome to you three."'

'An' my privit imprisshin is,' said Mulvaney, getting off the bar and turning his glass upside-down, 'that, av they had known they wudn't have brought ut home. 'Tis flyin' in the face, firstly av Natur', secon' av the Rig'lations, an' third the will av Terence Mulvaney, to huld p'rades av Thursdays.'

'Good, ma son!' said Learoyd; 'but, young mon, what's t' notebook for?'

'Let be,' said Mulvaney; 'this toime next month we're in the *Sherapis*.[12] 'Tis immortial fame the gentleman's goin' to give us. But kape it dhark till we're out av the range av me little frind Bobs Bahadur.'

And I have obeyed Mulvaney's order!

‡ His Chance in Life ‡

Then a pile of heads he laid –
    Thirty thousands heaped on high –
All to please the Kafir maid,
    Where the Oxus ripples by.
Grimly spake Atulla Khan:–
    'Love hath made this thing a Man.'
                    Oatta's Story

If you go straight away from Levées and Government House Lists, past Trades' Balls – far beyond everything and everybody you ever knew in your respectable life – you cross, in time, the Borderline where the last drop of White blood ends and the full tide of Black sets in. It would be easier to talk to a new-made Duchess on the spur of the moment than to the Borderline folk without violating some of their conventions or hurting their feelings. The Black and the White mix very quaintly in their ways. Sometimes the White shows in spurts of fierce, childish pride – which is Pride of Race run crooked – and sometimes the Black in still fiercer abasement and humility, half-heathenish customs and strange, unaccountable impulses to crime. One of these days, this people – understand they are far lower than the class whence Derozio,[1] the man who imitated Byron, sprung – will turn out a writer or a poet; and then we shall know how they live and what they feel. In the meantime, any stories about them cannot be absolutely correct in fact or inference.

Miss Vezzis came from across the Borderline to look after some children who belonged to a lady until a regularly ordained nurse could come out. The lady said Miss Vezzis was a bad, dirty nurse and inattentive. It never struck her that Miss Vezzis had her own life to lead and her own affairs to worry over; or that these affairs were the most important things in the world to Miss Vezzis. Very few mistresses admit this sort of reasoning. Miss Vezzis was as black as a boot, and, to our standard of taste, hideously ugly. She wore cotton-print gowns and bulgy shoes; and when she lost her temper with the children, she abused them in the language of the Borderline – which is part English, part Portuguese, and part Native. She was not attractive; but she had her pride, and she preferred being called 'Miss Vezzis'.

Every Sunday she dressed herself wonderfully and went to see her Mamma, who lived, for the most part, on an old cane chair in a greasy tussore-silk² dressing-gown and a big rabbit-warren of a house full of Vezzises, Pereiras, Ribieras, Lisboas, and Gonsalveses, and a floating population of loafers; besides fragments of the day's market, garlic, stale incense, clothes thrown on the floor, petticoats hung on strings for screens, old bottles, pewter crucifixes, dried *immortelles*, pariah puppies, plaster images of the Virgin, and hats without crowns. Miss Vezzis drew twenty rupees a month for acting as nurse, and she squabbled weekly with her Mamma as to the percentage to be given towards housekeeping. When the quarrel was over, Michele D'Cruze used to shamble across the low mud wall of the compound and make love to Miss Vezzis after the fashion of the Borderline, which is hedged about with much ceremony. Michele was a poor, sickly weed and very black; but he had his pride. He would not be seen smoking a hookah for anything; and he looked down on natives as only a man with seven-eighths native blood in his veins can. The Vezzis family had their pride too. They traced their descent from a mythical platelayer who had worked on the Sone Bridge when railways were new in India, and they valued their English origin. Michele was a Telegraph Signaller on Rs.35 a month. The fact that he was in Government employ made Mrs Vezzis lenient to the shortcomings of his ancestors.

There was a compromising legend – Dom Anna the tailor brought it from Poonani – that a black Jew of Cochin had once married into the D'Cruze family; while it was an open secret that an uncle of Mrs D'Cruze was, at that very time, doing menial work, connected with cooking, for a Club in Southern India! He sent Mrs D'Cruze seven rupees eight annas a month; but she felt the disgrace to the family very keenly all the same.

However, in the course of a few Sundays, Mrs Vezzis brought

herself to overlook these blemishes, and gave her consent to the marriage of her daughter with Michele, on condition that Michele should have at least fifty rupees a month to start married life upon. This wonderful prudence must have been a lingering touch of the mythical platelayer's Yorkshire blood; for across the Borderline people take a pride in marrying when they please – not when they can.

Having regard to his Departmental prospects, Mrs Vezzis might as well have asked Michele to go away and come back with the moon in his pocket. But Michele was deeply in love with Miss Vezzis, and that helped him to endure. He accompanied Miss Vezzis to Mass one Sunday, and after Mass, walking home through the hot stale dust with her hand in his, he swore by several Saints, whose names would not interest you, never to forget Miss Vezzis; and she swore by her Honour and the Saints – the oath runs rather curiously; '*In nomine Sanctissimae* –' (whatever the name of the she-Saint is) and so forth, ending with a kiss on the forehead, a kiss on the left cheek, and a kiss on the mouth – never to forget Michele.

Next week Michele was transferred, and Miss Vezzis dropped tears upon the window-sash of the 'Intermediate' compartment as he left the station.

If you look at the telegraph-map of India you will see a long line skirting the coast from Backergunge[3] to Madras. Michele was ordered to Tibasu, a little Sub-office one-third down this line, to send messages on from Berhampur to Chicacola, and to think of Miss Vezzis and his chances of getting fifty rupees a month out of office-hours. He had the noise of the Bay of Bengal and a Bengali Babu for company. Nothing more. He sent foolish letters, with crosses tucked inside the flaps of the envelopes, to Miss Vezzis.

When he had been at Tibasu for nearly three weeks his chance came.

Never forget that unless the outward and visible signs of Our Authority are always before a native he is as incapable as a child of understanding what authority means, or where is the danger of disobeying it. Tibasu was a forgotten little place with a few Orissa Mahommedans in it. These, hearing nothing of the

Collector-Sahib for some time, and heartily despising the Hindu Sub-Judge, arranged to start a little Mohurrum[4] riot of their own. But the Hindus turned out and broke their heads; when, finding lawlessness pleasant, Hindus and Mahommedans together raised an aimless sort of Donnybrook just to see how far they could go. They looted each other's shops, and paid off private grudges in the regular way. It was a nasty little riot, but not worth putting in the newspapers.

Michele was working in his office when he heard the sound that a man never forgets all his life – the '*ah-yah*' of an angry crowd. (When that sound drops about three tones, and changes to a thick, droning *ut*, the man who hears it had better go away if he is alone.) The Native Police Inspector ran in and told Michele that the town was in an uproar and coming to wreck the Telegraph Office. The Babu put on his cap and quietly dropped out of the window; while the Police Inspector, afraid, but obeying the old race-instinct which recognizes a drop of White blood as far as it can be diluted, said, 'What orders does the Sahib give?'

The 'Sahib' decided Michele. Though horribly frightened, he felt that, for the hour, he, the man with the Cochin Jew and the menial uncle in his pedigree, was the only representative of English authority in the place. Then he thought of Miss Vezzis and the fifty rupees, and took the situation on himself. There were seven native policemen in Tibasu, and four crazy smooth-bore muskets among them. All the men were grey with fear, but not beyond leading. Michele dropped the key of the telegraph instrument, and went out, at the head of his army, to meet the mob. As the shouting crew came round a corner of the road, he dropped and fired; the men behind him loosing off instinctively at the same time.

The whole crowd – curs to the backbone – yelled and ran, leaving one man dead and another dying in the road. Michele was sweating with fear; but he kept his weakness under, and went down into the town, past the house where the Sub-Judge had barricaded himself. The streets were empty. Tibasu was more frightened than Michele, for the mob had been taken at the right time.

Michele returned to the Telegraph Office, and sent a message to Chicacola asking for help. Before an answer came, he received a deputation of the elders of Tibasu, telling him that the Sub-Judge said his actions generally were 'unconstitutional', and trying to bully him. But the heart of Michele D'Cruze was large and white in his breast, because of his love for Miss Vezzis, the nurse-girl, and because he had tasted for the first time Responsibility and Success. Those two make an intoxicating drink, and have ruined more men than ever has Whisky. Michele answered that the Sub-Judge might say what he pleased, but, until the Assistant Collector came, he, the Telegraph Signaller, was the Government of India in Tibasu, and the elders of the town would be held accountable for further rioting. Then they bowed their heads and said, 'Show mercy!' or words to that effect, and went back in great fear; each accusing the other of having begun the rioting.

Early in the dawn, after a night's patrol with his seven policemen, Michele went down the road, musket in hand, to meet the Assistant Collector who had ridden in to quell Tibasu. But, in the presence of this young Englishman, Michele felt himself slipping back more and more into the native; and the tale of the Tibasu Riots ended, with the strain on the teller, in an hysterical outburst of tears, bred by sorrow that he had killed a man, shame that he could not feel as uplifted as he had felt through the night, and childish anger that his tongue could not do justice to his great deeds. It was the White drop in Michele's veins dying out, though he did not know it.

But the Englishman understood; and, after he had schooled those men of Tibasu, and had conferred with the Sub-Judge till that excellent official turned green, he found time to draft an official letter describing the conduct of Michele. Which letter filtered through the Proper Channels, and ended in the transfer of Michele up-country once more, on the Imperial salary of sixty-six rupees a month.

So he and Miss Vezzis were married with great state and ancientry; and now there are several little D'Cruzes sprawling about the verandas of the Central Telegraph Office.

But, if the whole revenue of the Department he serves were to be his reward, Michele could never, never repeat what he did at Tibasu for the sake of Miss Vezzis the nurse-girl.

Which proves that, when a man does good work out of all proportion to his pay, in seven cases out of nine there is a woman at the back of the virtue.

The two exceptions must have suffered from sunstroke.

⟨ Watches of the Night ⟩

> What is in the Brahmin's books, that is in the Brahmin's heart.
> Neither you nor I knew there was so much evil in the world.
>
> *Hindu Proverb*

This began in a practical joke; but it has gone far enough now, and is getting serious.

Platte, the Subaltern, being poor, had a Waterbury watch and a plain leather guard.

The Colonel had a Waterbury watch also, and, for guard, the lip-strap[1] of a curb-chain. Lip-straps make the best watch-guards. They are strong and short. Between a lip-strap and an ordinary leather-guard there is no great difference. Between one Waterbury watch and another none at all. Every one in the Station knew the Colonel's lip-strap. He was not a horsy man, but he liked people to believe he had been one once; and he wove fantastic stories of the hunting-bridle to which this particular lip-strap had belonged. Otherwise he was painfully religious.

Platte and the Colonel were dressing at the Club – both late for their engagements, and both in a hurry. That was *Kismet*.[2] The two watches were on a shelf below the looking-glass – guards hanging down. That was carelessness. Platte changed first, snatched a watch, looked in the glass, settled his tie, and ran. Forty seconds later the Colonel did exactly the same thing, each man taking the other's watch.

You may have noticed that many religious people are deeply suspicious. They seem – for purely religious purposes, of course – to know more about iniquity than the unregenerate. Perhaps they were specially bad before they became converted! At any rate, in the imputation of things evil, and in putting the worst construction on things innocent, a certain type of good people may be trusted to surpass all others. The Colonel and his Wife were of that type.

But the Colonel's Wife was the worst. She manufactured the station scandal, and – talked to her *ayah*! Nothing more need be said. The Colonel's Wife broke up the Laplaces' home. The Colonel's Wife stopped the Ferris-Haughtrey engagement. The Colonel's Wife induced young Buxton to keep his wife down in the Plains through the first year of the marriage. Wherefore little Mrs Buxton died, and the baby with her. These things will be remembered against the Colonel's Wife so long as there is a regiment in the country.

But to come back to the Colonel and Platte. They went their several ways from the dressing-room. The Colonel dined with two Chaplains, while Platte went to a bachelor party, and whist to follow.

Mark how things happen! If Platte's groom had put the new saddle-pad on the mare, the butts of the territs[3] would not have worked through the worn leather and the old pad into the mare's withers, when she was coming home at two o'clock in the morning. She would not have reared, bolted, fallen into a ditch, upset the cart, and sent Platte flying over an aloe-hedge on to Mrs Larkyn's well-kept lawn; and this tale would never have been written. But the mare did all these things, and while Platte was rolling over and over on the turf, like a shot rabbit, the watch and guard flew from his waistcoat – as an Infantry Major's sword hops out of the scabbard when they are firing a *feu-de-joie*[4] – and rolled and rolled in the moonlight, till it stopped under a window.

Platte stuffed his handkerchief under the pad, put the cart straight, and went home.

Mark again how *Kismet* works! This would not arrive once in a hundred years. Towards the end of his dinner with the two Chaplains, the Colonel let out his waistcoat and leaned over the table to look at some Mission Reports. The bar of the watch-guard worked through the button-hole, and the watch – Platte's watch – slid quietly on to the carpet; where the bearer found it next morning and kept it.

Then the Colonel went home to the wife of his bosom; but the driver of the carriage was drunk and lost his way. So the Colonel returned at an unseemly hour and his excuses were not accepted. If the Colonel's Wife had been an ordinary Vessel of Wrath[5] appointed for destruction, she would have known that when a man stays away on purpose, his excuse is always sound and original. The very baldness of the Colonel's explanation proved its truth.

See once more the workings of *Kismet*! The Colonel's watch which came with Platte hurriedly on to Mrs Larkyn's lawn, chose to stop just under Mrs Larkyn's window, where she saw it early in the morning, recognized it, and picked it up. She had heard the crash of Platte's cart at two o'clock that morning, and his voice calling the mare names. She knew Platte and liked him. That day she showed him the watch and heard his story. He put his head on one side, winked and said, 'How disgusting! Shocking old man! With his religious training, too! I should send the watch to the Colonel's Wife and ask for explanations.'

Mrs Larkyn thought for a minute of the Laplaces – whom she had known when Laplace and his wife believed in each other – and answered, 'I will send it. I think it will do her good. But, remember, we must *never* tell her the truth.'

Platte guessed that his own watch was in the Colonel's possession, and thought that the return of the lip-strapped Waterbury with a soothing note from Mrs Larkyn would merely create a small trouble for a few minutes. Mrs Larkyn knew better. She knew that any poison dropped would find good holding-ground in the heart of the Colonel's Wife.

The packet, and a note containing a few remarks on the Colonel's calling-hours, were sent over to the Colonel's Wife, who wept in her own room and took counsel with herself.

If there was one woman under heaven whom the Colonel's Wife hated with holy fervour, it was Mrs Larkyn. Mrs Larkyn was a frivolous lady, and called the Colonel's Wife 'old cat'. The Colonel's Wife said that somebody in Revelation was remarkably like Mrs Larkyn. She mentioned other Scripture people as well: from the Old Testament. But the Colonel's Wife was the only person who cared or dared to say anything against Mrs Larkyn. Every one else accepted her as an amusing, honest little body.[6] Wherefore, to believe that her husband had been shedding watches under that 'Thing's' window at ungodly hours, coupled with the fact of his late arrival on the previous night, was . . .

At this point she rose up and sought her husband. He denied everything except the ownership of the watch. She besought him, for his Soul's sake to speak the truth. He denied afresh, with two bad words. Then a stony silence held the Colonel's Wife, while a man could draw his breath five times.

The speech that followed is no affair of mine or yours. It was made up of wifely and womanly jealousy; knowledge of old age and sunk cheeks; deep mistrust born of the text that says even little babies' hearts[7] are as bad as they make them; rancorous hatred of Mrs Larkyn, and the tenets of the creed of the Colonel's Wife's upbringing.

Over and above all was the damning lip-strapped Waterbury, ticking away in the palm of her shaking, withered hand. At that hour, I think, the Colonel's Wife realized a little of the restless suspicion she had injected into old Laplace's mind; a little of poor Miss Haughtrey's misery; and some of the canker that ate into Buxton's heart as he watched his wife dying before his eyes. The Colonel stammered and tried to explain. Then he remembered that his watch had disappeared; and the mystery grew greater. The Colonel's Wife talked and prayed by turns till she was tired, and went away to devise means for chastening the stubborn heart of her husband. Which, translated, means, in our slang, 'tail-twisting'.

Being deeply impressed with the doctrine of Original Sin, she could not believe in the face of appearances. She knew too much, and jumped to the wildest conclusions.

But it was good for her. It spoilt her life, as she had spoilt the life of the Laplaces. She had lost her faith in the Colonel, and – here the creed-suspicion came in – he might, she argued, have erred many times, before a merciful Providence, at the hands of so unworthy an instrument as Mrs Larkyn, had established his guilt. He was a bad, wicked, grey-haired profligate. This may sound too sudden a revulsion for a long-wedded wife; but it is a venerable fact that, if a man or woman makes a practice of, and takes a delight in, believing and spreading evil of people indifferent to him or her, he or she will end in believing evil of folk very near and dear. You may think, also, that the mere incident of the watch was too small and trivial to raise this misunderstanding. It is another aged fact that, in life as well as racing, all the worst accidents happen at little ditches and cut-down fences. In the same way, you sometimes see a woman who would have made a Joan of Arc in another century and climate, threshing herself to pieces over all the mean worry of housekeeping ... But that is another story.

Her belief only made the Colonel's Wife more wretched, because it insisted so strongly on the villainy of men. Remembering what she had done, it was pleasant to watch her unhappiness, and the penny-farthing attempts she made to hide it from the station. But the station knew and laughed heartlessly; for they had heard the story of the watch, with much dramatic gesture, from Mrs Larkyn's lips.

Once or twice Platte said to Mrs Larkyn, seeing that the Colonel had not cleared himself, 'This thing has gone far enough. I move we tell the Colonel's Wife how it happened.' Mrs Larkyn shut her lips and shook her head, and vowed that the Colonel's Wife must bear her punishment as best she could. Now Mrs Larkyn was a frivolous woman, in whom none would have suspected deep hate. So Platte took no action, and came to believe gradually, from the Colonel's silence, that the Colonel must have run off the line somewhere that night, and, therefore, preferred to stand sentence on the lesser count of rambling into other people's compounds out of calling-hours. Platte forgot about the watch business after a while, and moved down-country with his Regiment. Mrs Larkyn went Home when her husband's tour of Indian service expired. She never forgot.

But Platte was quite right when he said that the joke had gone too far. The mistrust and the tragedy of it – which we outsiders cannot see and do not believe in – are killing the Colonel's Wife, and are making the Colonel wretched. If either of them read this story, they can depend upon its being a fairly true account of the case, and can kiss and make friends.

Shakespeare alludes[8] to the pleasure of watching an Engineer being shelled by his own Battery. Now this shows that poets should not write about what they do not understand. Any one could have told him that Sappers and Gunners are perfectly different branches of the Service.

But, if you correct the sentence, and substitute Gunner for Sapper, the moral comes just the same.

⟨ The Other Man ⟩

When the Earth was sick and the skies were grey
    And the woods were rotted with rain,
The Dead Man rode through the autumn day
    To visit his love again.

Old Ballad

Far back in the 'seventies, before they had built any Public Offices at Simla, when the broad road round Jakko lived in a pigeon-hole in the P. W. D.¹ hovels, her parents made Miss Gaurey marry Colonel Schreiderling. He could not have been much more than thirty-five years her senior; and, as he lived on two hundred rupees a month and had money of his own, he was well off. He belonged to good people, and suffered in the cold weather from lung-complaints. In the hot weather he dangled on the brink of heat-apoplexy; but it never quite killed him.

Understand, I do not blame Schreiderling. He was a good husband according to his lights, and his temper only failed him when he was being nursed: which was some seventeen days in each month. He was almost generous to his wife about money matters, and that, for him, was a concession. Still Mrs Schreiderling was not happy. They married her when she was this side of twenty and had given all her poor little heart to another man. I have forgotten his name, but we will call him the Other Man. He had no money and no prospects. He was not even good-looking; and I think he was in the Commissariat or Transport. But, in spite of all these things, she loved him very badly; and there was some sort of an engagement between the two when Schreiderling appeared and told Mrs Gaurey that he wished to marry her daughter. Then the other engagement was broken off – washed away by Mrs Gaurey's tears, for that lady governed her house by weeping over disobedience to her authority and the lack of reverence she received in her old age. The daughter did not take after her mother. She never cried. Not even at the wedding.

The Other Man bore his loss quietly, and was transferred to as bad a station as he could find. Perhaps the climate consoled him. He suffered from intermittent fever, and that may have distracted him from his other trouble. He was weak about the heart also. Both ways. One of the valves was affected, and the fever made it worse. This showed itself later on.

Then many months passed, and Mrs Schreiderling took to being ill. She did not pine away like people in story-books, but she seemed to pick up every form of illness that went about a station, from simple fever upwards. She was never more than ordinarily pretty at the best of times; and the illnesses made her ugly. Schreiderling said so. He prided himself on speaking his mind.

When she ceased being pretty, he left her to her own devices, and went back to the lairs of his bachelordom. She used to trot up and down Simla Mall in a forlorn sort of way, with a grey terai[2] hat well on the back of her head, and a shocking bad saddle under her. Schreiderling's generosity stopped at the horse. He said that any saddle would do for a woman as nervous as Mrs Schreiderling. She never was asked to dance, because she did not dance well; and she was so dull and uninteresting that her box very seldom had any cards in it. Schreiderling said that if he had known she was going to be such a scarecrow after her marriage he would never have married her. He always prided himself on speaking his mind, did Schreiderling.

He left her at Simla one August, and went down to his Regiment. Then she revived a little, but she never recovered her looks. I found out at the Club that the Other Man was coming up sick – very sick – on an off chance of recovery. The fever and the heart-valve had nearly killed him. She knew that too, and she knew – what I had no interest in knowing – when he was coming up. I suppose he wrote to tell her. They had not seen each other since a month before the wedding. And here comes the unpleasant part of the story.

A late call kept me down at the Dovedell Hotel till dusk one evening. Mrs Schreiderling had been flitting up and down the

Mall all the afternoon in the rain. Coming up along the Cart-Road a tonga passed me, and my pony, tired with standing so long, set off at a canter. Just by the road down to the Tonga Office Mrs Schreiderling, dripping from head to foot, was waiting for the tonga. I turned uphill as the tonga was no affair of mine, and just then she began to shriek. I went back at once and saw, under the Tonga Office lamps, Mrs Schreiderling kneeling in the wet road by the back seat of the newly-arrived tonga, screaming hideously. Then she fell face-down in the dirt as I came up.

Sitting in the back seat, very square and firm, with one hand on the awning-stanchion and the wet pouring off his hat and moustache, was the Other Man – dead. The sixty-mile uphill jolt had been too much for his valves, I suppose. The tonga-driver said, 'This Sahib died two stages out of Solon. Therefore, I tied him with a rope, lest he should fall out by the way, and so came to Simla. Will the Sahib give me *bukshish*?[3] *It*,' pointing to the Other Man, 'should have given me one rupee.'

The Other Man sat with a grin on his face, as if he enjoyed the joke of his arrival; and Mrs Schreiderling, in the mud, began to groan. There was no one except us four in the office, and it was raining heavily. The first thing was to take Mrs Schreiderling home, and the second was to prevent her name from being mixed up with the affair. The tonga-driver received five rupees to find a bazar 'rickshaw for Mrs Schreiderling. He was to tell the Tonga Babu[4] afterwards of the Other Man, and the Babu was to make such arrangements as seemed best.

Mrs Schreiderling was carried into the shed out of the rain, and for three-quarters of an hour we two waited for the 'rickshaw. The Other Man was left exactly as he had arrived. Mrs Schreiderling would do everything but cry, which might have helped her. She tried to scream as soon as her senses came back, and then she began praying for the Other Man's soul. Had she not been as honest as the day, she would have prayed for her own soul too. I waited to hear her do this, but she did not. Then I tried to get some of the mud off her habit. Lastly, the 'rickshaw came, and I got her away – partly by force. It was a terrible business from beginning to end; but most of all when the 'rickshaw had to squeeze between the wall and the tonga, and she saw by the lamp-light that thin, yellow hand grasping the awning-stanchion.

She was taken home just as every one was going to a dance at Viceregal Lodge – 'Peterhof' it was then – and the doctor found out that she had fallen from her horse, that I had picked her up at the back of Jakko, and really deserved great credit for the prompt manner in which I had secured medical aid. She did not die – men of Schreiderling's stamp marry women who don't die easily. They live and grow ugly.

She never told of her one meeting, since her marriage, with the Other Man; and, when the chill and cough following the exposure of that evening allowed her abroad, she never by word or sign alluded to having met me by the Tonga Office. Perhaps she never knew.

She used to trot up and down the Mall, on that shocking bad saddle, looking as if she expected to meet someone round the corner every minute. Two years afterwards she went Home, and died – at Bournemouth, I think.

Schreiderling, when he grew maudlin at Mess, used to talk about 'my poor dear wife'. He always set great store on speaking his mind, did Schreiderling.

⚒ Haunted Subalterns ⚒

So long as the 'Inextinguishables' confined themselves to running picnics, gymkhanas, flirtations, and innocences of that kind, no one said anything. But when they ran ghosts, people put up their eyebrows. 'Man can't feel comfy with a Regiment that entertains ghosts on its establishment. It is against General Orders. The 'Inextinguishables' said that the ghosts were private and not Regimental property. They referred you to Tesser for particulars; and Tesser told you to go to – the hottest Cantonment of all. He said that it was bad enough to have men making hay of his bedding and breaking his banjo-strings when he was out, without being chaffed afterwards; and he would thank you to keep your remarks on ghosts to yourself. This was before the 'Inextinguishables' had sworn by their several lady-loves that they were innocent of any intrusion into Tesser's quarters. Then Horrocks mentioned casually at Mess that a couple of white figures had been bounding about his room the night before, and he didn't approve of it. The 'Inextinguishables' denied, energetically, that they had had any hand in the manifestations, and advised Horrocks to consult Tesser.

I don't suppose that a subaltern believes in anything except his chances of a Company; but Horrocks and Tesser were exceptions. They came to believe in their ghosts. They had reason.

Horrocks used to find himself, at about three o'clock in the morning, staring wide-awake, watching two white Things hopping about his room and jumping up to the ceiling. Horrocks was of a placid turn of mind. After a week or so spent in watching his servants, and lying in wait for strangers, and trying to keep awake all night, he came to the conclusion that he was haunted, and that, consequently, he need not bother. He wasn't going to encourage these ghosts by being frightened of them. Therefore when he woke – as usual – with a start and saw these Things jumping like kangaroos, he only murmured: 'Go on! Don't mind me!' and went to sleep again.

Tesser said, 'It's all very well for you to make fun of *your* show. You can *see* your ghosts. Now I can't see mine, and I don't half like it.'

Tesser used to come into his room of nights, and find the whole of his bedding neatly stripped, as if it had been done with one sweep of the hand, from the top right-hand corner of his cot to the bottom left-hand corner. Also his lamp used to lie weltering on the floor, and generally his pet screw-head, inlaid, nickel-plated banjo was lying on the cot, with all its strings broken. Tesser took away the strings, on the occasion of the third manifestation, and the next night a man complimented him on his playing the best music ever got out of a banjo, for half an hour.

'Which half-hour?' said Tesser.

'Between nine and ten,' said the man. Tesser had gone out to dinner at 7.30 and had returned at midnight.

He talked to his bearer and threatened him with unspeakable things. The bearer was grey with fear. 'I'm a poor man,' said he. 'If the Sahib is haunted by a Devil, what can I do?'

'Who says I'm haunted by a Devil?' howled Tesser, for he was angry.

'I have seen It,' said the bearer, 'at night, walking round and round your bed; and that is why everything is *ulta-pulta*¹ in your room. I am a poor man, but I never go into your room alone. The *bhisti* comes with me.'

Tesser was thoroughly savage at this, and he spoke to Horrocks, and the two laid traps to catch that Devil, and threatened their servants with dog-whips if any more '*Shaitan-ke*-hanky-panky' took place. But the servants were soaked with fear, and it was no use adding to their tortures. When Tesser went out at night, four of his men, as a rule, slept in the veranda of his quarters, until the banjo without the strings struck up, and then they fled.

One day, Tesser had to put in a month at a Fort with a detachment of 'Inextinguishables'. The Fort might have been Govindghar, Jumrood, or Phillour; but it wasn't. He left cantonments rejoicing, for his Devil was preying on his mind; and with

him went another Subaltern, a junior. But the Devil came too.
After Tesser had been in the Fort about ten days he went out to
dinner. When he came back he found his Subaltern doing sentry
on a banquette[2] across the Fort Ditch, as far removed as might
be from the Officers' Quarters.

'What's wrong?' said Tesser.

The Subaltern said, 'Listen!' and the two, standing under the
stars, heard from the Officers' Quarters, high up in the wall of
the Fort, the '*strumty. tumty tumty*' of the banjo, which seemed to
have an oratorio on hand.

'That performance,' said the Subaltern, 'has been going on for
three mortal hours. I never wished to desert before, but I do now.
I say, Tesser, old man, you are the best of good fellows, I'm sure,
but ... I say ... look here, now, you are quite unfit to live with.
'Tisn't in my Commission, you know, that I'm to serve under a
... a ... man with Devils.'

'Isn't it?' said Tesser. 'If you make an ass of yourself I'll put
you under arrest ... and *in my room*!'

'You can put me where you please, but I'm not going to assist
at these infernal concerts. 'Tisn't right. 'Tisn't natural. Look
here, I don't want to hurt your feelings, but – try to think now –
haven't you done something – committed some – murder that
has slipped your memory – or forged something ... ?'

'Well! For an all-round, double-shotted, half-baked fool you
are the ...'

'I daresay I am,' said the Subaltern. 'But you don't expect me
to keep my wits with that row going on, do you?'

The banjo was rattling away as if it had twenty strings. Tesser
sent up a stone, and a shower of broken window-pane fell into
the Fort Ditch; but the banjo kept on. Tesser hauled the other
Subaltern up to the quarters, and found his room in frightful
confusion – lamp upset, bedding all over the floor, chairs over-
turned and table tilted sideways. He took stock of the wreck and
said despairing, 'Oh, this *is* lovely!'

The Subaltern was peeping in at the door.

'I'm glad you think so,' he said. ''Tisn't lovely enough for me.
I *locked up* your room directly after you had gone out. See here,
I think you'd better apply for Horrocks to come out in my place.

He's troubled with your complaint, and this business will make me a jabbering idiot if it goes on.'

Tesser went to bed amid the wreckage, very angry, and next morning he rode into cantonments and asked Horrocks to arrange to relieve 'that fool with me now'.

'You've got 'em again, have you?' said Horrocks. 'So've I. *Three* white figures this time. We'll worry through the entertainment together.'

So Horrocks and Tesser settled down in the Fort together, and the 'Inextinguishables' said pleasant things about 'seven other Devils'.[3] Tesser didn't see where the joke came in. His room was thrown upside-down three nights out of the seven. Horrocks was not troubled in any way, so his ghosts must have been purely local ones. Tesser, on the other hand, was personally haunted; for his Devil had moved with him from cantonments to the Fort. Those two boys spent three parts of their time trying to find out *who* was responsible for the riot in Tesser's rooms. At the end of a fortnight they tried to find out *what* was responsible; and seven days later they gave it up as a bad job. Whatever It was, It refused to be caught; even when Tesser went out of the Fort ostentatiously, and Horrocks lay under Tesser's charpoy with a revolver. The servants were afraid – more afraid than ever – and all the evidence showed that they had been playing no tricks. As Tesser said to Horrocks: 'A haunted Subaltern is a joke, but s'pose this keeps on. Just think what a haunted Colonel would be! And, look here – s'pose I marry! D'you s'pose a girl would live a week with me *and* this Devil?'

'I don't know,' said Horrocks. 'I haven't married often, but I knew a woman once who lived with her husband when he had D.T. He's dead now and I daresay *she* would marry you if you asked her. She isn't exactly a girl, though, but she has a large experience of the *other* devils – the blue variety. She's a Government pensioner now, and you might write, y'know. Personally, if I hadn't suffered from ghosts of my own, I should rather avoid you.'

'That's just the point,' said Tesser. 'This Devil thing will end in getting me *budnamed*,[4] and you know I've lived on lemon-squashes and gone to bed at ten for weeks past.'

''Tisn't that sort of Devil,' said Horrocks. 'It's either a first-class fraud for which some one ought to be killed or else you've offended one of these Indian Devils. It stands to reason that such a beastly country should be full of fiends of all sorts.'

'But why should the creature fix on *me*?' said Tesser. 'And why won't he show himself and have it out like a – like a Devil?'

They were talking outside the Mess after dark, and, even as they spoke, they heard the banjo begin to play in Tesser's room, about twenty yards off.

Horrocks ran to his own quarters for a shot-gun and a revolver, and Tesser and he crept up quietly, the banjo still playing, to Tesser's door.

'Now we've got It!' said Horrocks as he threw the door open and let fly with the twelve-bore; Tesser squibbing off all six barrels into the dark, as hard as he could pull trigger.

The furniture was ruined, and the whole Fort was awake; but that was all. No one had been killed, and the banjo was lying on the dishevelled bed-clothes as usual.

Then Tesser sat down in the veranda, and used language that would have qualified him for the companionship of unlimited Devils. Horrocks said things too; but Tesser said the worst.

When the month in the Fort came to an end, both Horrocks and Tesser were glad. They held a final council of war, but came to no conclusion.

'Seems to me, your best plan would be to make your Devil stretch himself. Go down to Bombay with the time-expired men,' said Horrocks. 'If he really *is* a Devil, he'll come in the train with you.'

''Tisn't good enough,' said Tesser. 'Bombay's no fit place to live in at this time of the year. But I'll put in for Depôt duty at the Hills.' And he did.

Now here the tale rests. The Devil stayed below, and Tesser went up and was free. If I had invented this story, I should have put in a satisfactory ending – explained the manifestations as somebody's practical joke. My business being to keep to facts, I can only say what I have said. The Devil may have been a hoax. If so, it was one of the best ever arranged. If it was not a hoax . . . But you must settle that for yourselves.

{ Consequences }

Rosicrucian subtleties
In the Orient had rise;
Ye may find their teachers still
Under Jacatâlâ's Hill.
Seek ye Bombast Paracelsus,
Read what Flood [1] the Seeker tells us
Of the Dominant that runs
Through the Cycles of the Suns –
Read my story last, and see
Luna at her apogee.

There are yearly appointments, and two-yearly appointments, and five-yearly appointments at Simla, and there are, or used to be, permanent appointments, whereon you stayed up for the term of your natural life, and secured red cheeks and a nice income. Of course, you could descend in the cold weather; for Simla is rather dull then.

Tarrion came from goodness knows where – all away and away in some forsaken part of Central India, where they call Pachmari [2] a Sanitarium, and drive behind trotting-bullocks, I believe. He belonged to a Regiment; but what he really wanted to do was to escape from his Regiment and live in Simla for ever and ever. He had no preference for anything in particular, beyond a good horse and a nice partner. He thought he could do everything well; which is a beautiful belief when you hold it with all your heart. He was clever in many ways, and good to look at, and always made people round him comfortable – even in Central India.

So he went up to Simla, and, because he was clever and amusing, he gravitated naturally to Mrs Hauksbee, who could forgive everything but stupidity. Once he did her great service by changing the date on an invitation-card for a big dance which Mrs Hauksbee wished to attend, but couldn't, because she had quarrelled with the A.D.C., who took care, being a mean man, to invite her to a small dance on the 6th instead of the big Ball of the 26th. It was a very clever piece of forgery; and when Mrs Hauksbee showed the A.D.C. her invitation-card, and chaffed him mildly for not better managing his vendettas, he really thought that he had made a mistake; and – which was wise – realized that it was no use to fight with Mrs Hauksbee. She was grateful to Tarrion, and asked what she could do for him. He said simply, 'I'm a Freelance up here on leave, on the look-out for what I can loot. I haven't a square inch of interest in all Simla. My name isn't known to any man with an appointment in his gift, and I want an appointment – a good, sound one. I believe you can do anything you turn yourself to. Will you help me?' Mrs Hauksbee thought for a minute, and passed the lash of her riding-whip through her lips, as was her custom when thinking. Then her eyes sparkled and she said, 'I will'; and she shook hands on it. Tarrion, having perfect confidence in this great woman, took no further thought of the business at all, except to wonder what sort of an appointment he would win.

Mrs Hauksbee began calculating the prices of all the Heads of Departments and Members of Council she knew, and the more she thought the more she laughed, because her heart was in the game and it amused her. Then she took a Civil List and ran over a few of the appointments. (There are some beautiful appointments in the Civil List.) Eventually, she decided that, though Tarrion was too good for the Political Department, she had better begin by trying to place him there. Her own plans to this end do not matter in the least, for Luck or Fate played into her hands, and she had nothing to do but to watch the course of events and take the credit of them.

All Viceroys, when they first come out, pass through the Diplomatic Secrecy craze. It wears off in time; but they all catch it in the beginning, because they are new to the country. The particular Viceroy who was suffering from the complaint just then – this was a long time ago, before Lord Dufferin ever came from Canada, or Lord Ripon[3] from the bosom of the English Church – had it very badly; and the result was that men who were new to keeping official secrets went about looking unhappy; and the Viceroy plumed himself on the way in which he had instilled notions of reticence into his Staff.

Now, the Supreme Government have a careless custom of committing what they do to printed papers. These papers deal with all sorts of things – from the payment of Rs. 200 to a 'Secret Service' native, up to rebukes administered to Vakils and Motamids of Native States, and rather brusque letters to Native Princes, telling them to put their houses in order, to refrain from kidnapping women, or filling offenders with pounded red pepper,[4] and eccentricities of that kind. Of course, these things could never be made public, because Native Princes never err officially, and their States are officially as well administered as Our territories. Also, the private allowances to various queer people are not exactly matters to put into newspapers, though they give quaint reading sometimes. When the Supreme Government is at Simla these papers are prepared there, and go round to the people who ought to see them in office-boxes or by post. The principle of secrecy was to that Viceroy quite as important as the practice; and he held that a benevolent despotism like Ours should never allow even little things, such as appointments of subordinate clerks, to leak out till the proper time. He was always remarkable for his principles.

There was a very important batch of papers in preparation at that time. It had to travel from one end of Simla to the other by hand. It was not put into an official envelope, but a large, square, pale pink one; the matter being in M S. on soft crinkly paper. It was addressed to 'The Head Clerk, etc. etc.' Now, between 'The Head Clerk, etc. etc.' and 'Mrs Hauksbee' and a flourish, is no very great difference, if the address be written in a very bad hand, as this was. The orderly who took the envelope was not more of an idiot than most orderlies. He merely forgot where this most unofficial cover was to be delivered, and so asked the first Englishman he met, who happened to be a man riding down to Annandale in a great hurry. The Englishman hardly looked at it, said, 'Mrs Hauksbee,' and went on. So did the orderly, because that letter was the last in stock and he wanted to get his work over. There was no book to sign; he thrust the letter into Mrs Hauksbee's bearer's hands and went off to smoke with a friend.

Mrs Hauksbee was expecting some cut-out pattern things in flimsy paper from a friend. As soon as she got the big square packet, therefore, she said, 'Oh, the dear creature!' and tore it open with a paper-knife, and all the M S. enclosures tumbled out on the floor.

Mrs Hauksbee began reading. I have said the batch was rather important. That is quite enough for you to know. It referred to some correspondence, two measures, a peremptory order to a native chief, and two dozen other things. Mrs Hauksbee gasped as she read, for the first glimpse of the naked machinery of the Great Indian Government, stripped of its casings, and lacquer, and paint, and guard-rails, impresses even the most stupid man. And Mrs Hauksbee was a clever woman. She was a little afraid at first, and felt as if she had taken hold of a lightning-flash by the tail, and did not quite know what to do with it. There were remarks and initials at the side of the papers; and some of the remarks were rather more severe than the papers. The initials belonged to men who are all dead or gone now; but they were great in their day. Mrs Hauksbee read on and thought calmly as she read. Then the value of her trove struck her, and she cast about for the best method of using it. Then Tarrion dropped in, and they read through all the papers together, and Tarrion, not knowing how she had come by them, vowed that Mrs Hauksbee was the greatest woman on earth. Which I believe was true or nearly so.

'The honest course is always the best,' said Tarrion, after an hour and a half of study and conversation. 'All things considered, the Intelligence Branch is about my form. Either that or the Foreign Office. I go to lay siege to the High Gods in their Temples.'

He did not seek a little man, or a little big man, or a weak Head of a strong Department, but he called on the biggest and strongest man that the Government owned, and explained that he wanted an appointment at Simla on a good salary. The compound insolence of this amused the Strong Man, and, as he had nothing to do for the moment, he listened to the proposals of the audacious Tarrion. 'You have, I presume, some special qualifications, besides the gift of self-assertion, for the claims you put forward?'

said the Strong Man. 'That, sir,' said Tarrion, 'is for you to judge.' Then he began, for he had a good memory, quoting a few of the more important notes in the papers – slowly and one by one as a man drops chlorodyne[5] into a glass. When he had reached the peremptory order – and it was a very peremptory order – the Strong Man was troubled. Tarrion wound up: 'And I fancy that special knowledge of this kind is at least as valuable for, let us say, a berth in the Foreign Office, as the fact of being the nephew of a distinguished officer's wife.' That hit the Strong Man hard, for the last appointment to the Foreign Office had been by black favour, and he knew it.

'I'll see what I can do for you,' said the Strong Man.

'Many thanks,' said Tarrion. Then he left, and the Strong Man departed to see how the appointment was to be blocked.[6]

Followed a pause of eleven days; with thunders and lightnings and much telegraphing. The appointment was not a very important one, carrying only between Rs. 500 and Rs. 700 a month; but, as the Viceroy said, it was the principle of diplomatic secrecy that had to be maintained, and it was more than likely that a boy so well supplied with special information would be worth translating. So they translated Tarrion. They must have suspected him, though he protested that his information was due to singular talents of his own. Now, much of this story, including the after-history of the missing envelope, you must fill in for yourself, because there are reasons why it cannot be written. If you do not know about things Up Above, you won't understand how to fill in, and you will say it is impossible.

What the Viceroy said[7] when Tarrion was introduced to him was: 'This is the boy who "rushed" the Government of India, is it? Recollect, sir, that is not done twice.' So he must have known something.

What Tarrion said when he saw his appointment gazetted was: 'If Mrs Hauksbee were twenty years younger, and I her husband, I should be Viceroy of India in fifteen years.'

What Mrs Hauksbee said, when Tarrion thanked her, almost with tears in his eyes, was first: 'I told you so!' and next, to herself: 'What fools men are!'

The Conversion of Aurelian McGoggin

Ride with an idle whip, ride with an unused heel,
But, once in a way, there will come a day
When the colt must be taught to feel
The lash that falls, and the curb that galls, and the sting of the rowelled steel.
Life's Handicap

This is not a tale exactly. This is a Tract; and I am immensely proud of it. Making a Tract is a Feat.

Every man is entitled to his own religious opinions; but no man – least of all a junior – has a right to thrust these down other men's throats. The Government sends out weird Civilians now and again; but McGoggin was the queerest exported for a long time. He was clever – brilliantly clever – but his cleverness worked the wrong way. Instead of keeping to the study of the vernaculars, he had read some books written by a man called Comte, I think, and a man called Spencer.[1] (You will find these books in the Library.) They deal with people's insides from the point of view of men who have no stomachs. There was no order against his reading them; but his Mamma should have smacked him. They fermented in his head, and he came out to India with a rarefied religion over and above his work. It was not much of a creed. It only proved that men had no souls, and there was no God and no hereafter, and that you must worry along somehow for the good of Humanity.

One of its minor tenets seemed to be that the one thing more sinful than giving an order was obeying it. At least, that was what McGoggin said; but I suspect he had misread his primers.

I do not say a word against this creed. It was made up in Town where there is nothing but machinery and asphalt and building – all shut in by the fog. Naturally, a man grows to think that there is no one higher than himself, and that the Metropolitan Board

117

of Works made everything. But in India, where you really see humanity – raw, brown, naked humanity – with nothing between it and the blazing sky, and only the used-up, over-handled earth underfoot, the notion somehow dies away, and most folk come back to simpler theories. Life, in India, is not long enough to waste in proving that there is no one in particular at the head of affairs. For this reason. The Deputy is above the Assistant, the Commissioner above the Deputy, the Lieutenant-Governor above the Commissioner, and the Viceroy above all four, under the orders of the Secretary of State, who is responsible to the Empress. If the Empress be not responsible to her Maker – if there is no Maker for her to be responsible to – the entire system of Our administration must be wrong. Which is manifestly impossible. At Home men are to be excused. They are stalled up a good deal and get intellectually 'beany'. When you take a gross, 'beany' horse to exercise, he slavers and slobbers over the bit till you can't see the horns. But the bit is there just the same. Men do not get 'beany' in India. The climate and the work are against playing bricks with words.

If McGoggin had kept his creed, with the capital letters and the endings in 'ism', to himself, no one would have cared; but his grandfathers on both sides had been Wesleyan preachers, and the preaching strain came out in his mind. He wanted every one at the Club to see that they had no souls too, and to help him to eliminate his Creator. As a good many men told him, *he* undoubtedly had no soul, because he was so young, but it did not follow that his seniors were equally undeveloped; and, whether there was another world or not, a man still wanted to read his papers in this. 'But that is not the point – that is not the point!' Aurelian used to say. Then men threw sofa-cushions at him and told him to go to any particular place he might believe in. They christened him 'The Blastoderm',[2] – he said he came from a family of that name somewhere, in the prehistoric ages, – and by insult and laughter strove to choke him dumb, for he was an unmitigated nuisance at the Club, besides being an offence to the older men. His Deputy Commissioner, who was working on the Frontier when Aurelian was rolling on a bed-quilt, told him that, for a clever boy, Aurelian was a very big idiot. And, if he had gone on with his work, he would have been caught up to the Secretariat in a few years. He was of the type that goes there – all head, no physique and a hundred theories. Not a soul was interested in McGoggin's soul. He might have had two, or none, or somebody else's. His business was to obey orders and keep abreast of his files, instead of devastating the Club with 'isms'.

He worked brilliantly; but he could not accept any order without trying to better it. That was the fault of his creed. It made men too responsible and left too much to their honour. You can sometimes ride an old horse in a halter, but never a colt. McGoggin took more trouble over his cases than any of the men of his year. He may have fancied that thirty-page judgments on fifty-rupee cases – both sides perjured to the gullet – advanced the cause of Humanity. At any rate, he worked too much, and worried and fretted over the rebukes he received, and lectured away on his ridiculous creed out of office, till the Doctor had to warn him that he was overdoing it. No man can toil eighteen annas in the rupee in June without suffering. But McGoggin was still intellectually 'beany' and proud of himself and his powers, and he would take no hint. He worked nine hours a day steadily.

'Very well,' said the Doctor, 'you'll break down, because you are over-engined for your beam.' McGoggin was a little man.

One day the collapse came – as dramatically as if it had been meant to embellish a Tract.

It was just before the Rains. We were sitting in the veranda in the dead, hot, close air, gasping and praying that the black-blue clouds would let down and bring the cool. Very, very far away, there was a faint whisper, which was the roar of the Rains breaking over the river. One of the men heard it, got out of his chair, listened and said, naturally enough, 'Thank God!'

Then The Blastoderm turned in his place and said, 'Why? I assure you it's only the result of perfectly natural causes – atmospheric phenomena of the simplest kind. Why you should, therefore, return thanks to a Being, who never did exist – who is only a figment –'

'Blastoderm,' grunted the man in the next chair, 'dry up and throw me over the *Pioneer*. We know all about your figments.' The Blastoderm reached out to the table, took up one paper, and jumped as if something had stung him. Then he handed the paper.

'As I was saying,' he went on slowly and with an effort, 'due to perfectly natural causes – perfectly natural causes. I mean –'

'Hi! Blastoderm, you've given me the *Calcutta Mercantile Advertiser.*'

The dust got up in little whorls, while the tree-tops rocked and the kites whistled. But no one was looking at the coming of the Rains. We were all staring at The Blastoderm, who had risen from his chair and was fighting with his speech. Then he said, still more slowly:

'Perfectly conceivable – dictionary – red oak – amenable – cause – retaining – shuttle-cock – alone.'

'Blastoderm's drunk,' said one man. But The Blastoderm was not drunk. He looked at us in a dazed sort of way, and began motioning with his hands in the half-light as the clouds closed overhead. Then – with a scream –

'What is it? – Can't – reserve – attainable – market – obscure –'

But his speech seemed to freeze in him, and – just as the lightning shot two tongues that cut the whole sky into three pieces and the rain fell in quivering sheets – The Blastoderm was struck dumb. He stood pawing and champing like a hard-held horse, and his eyes were full of terror.

The Doctor came over in three minutes, and heard the story. 'It's aphasia,' he said. 'Take him to his room. I knew the smash would come.' We carried The Blastoderm across in the pouring rain to his quarters, and the Doctor gave him bromide of potassium to make him sleep.

Then the Doctor came back to us and told us that aphasia was like all the arrears of 'Punjab Head' falling in a lump; and that only once before – in the case of a sepoy – had he met with so complete a case. I have seen mild aphasia in an overworked man, but this sudden dumbness was uncanny – though, as The Blastoderm himself might have said, 'due to perfectly natural causes'.

'He'll have to take leave after this,' said the Doctor. 'He won't be fit for work for another three months. No; it isn't insanity or anything like it. It's only complete loss of control over the speech and memory. I fancy it will keep The Blastoderm quiet, though.'

Two days later The Blastoderm found his tongue again. The first question he asked was: 'What was it?' The Doctor enlightened him. 'But I can't understand it!' said The Blastoderm. 'I'm quite sane; but I can't be sure of my mind, it seems – my *own* memory – can I?'

'Go up into the Hills for three months, and don't think about it,' said the Doctor.

'But I can't understand it,' repeated The Blastoderm. 'It was my *own* mind and memory.'

'I can't help it,' said the Doctor. 'There are a good many things you can't understand; and, by the time you have put in my length of service, you'll know exactly how much a man dare call his own in this world.'

The stroke cowed The Blastoderm. He could not understand it. He went into the Hills in fear and trembling, wondering whether he would be permitted to reach the end of any sentence he began.

This gave him a wholesome feeling of mistrust. The legitimate explanation, that he had been overworking himself, failed to satisfy him. Something had wiped his lips of speech, as a mother wipes the milky lips of her child, and he was afraid – horribly afraid.

So the Club had rest when he returned; and if ever you come across Aurelian McGoggin laying down the law on things Human – he doesn't seem to know as much as he used to about things Divine – put your forefinger to your lip for a moment, and see what happens.

Don't blame me if he throws a glass at your head.

The Taking of Lungtungpen

So we loosed a bloomin' volley,
    An' we made the beggars cut,
An' when our pouch was emptied out,
    We used the bloomin' butt.
        Ho! My!
        Don't yer come anigh,
When Tommy is a-playin' with the baynit an' the butt.

Barrack-Room Ballad

My friend Private Mulvaney told me this, sitting on the parapet of the road to Dagshai,[1] when we were hunting butterflies together. He had theories about the Army, and coloured clay pipes perfectly. He said that the young soldier is the best to work with, 'on account av the surpassin' innocince av the choild'.

'Now listen!' said Mulvaney, throwing himself full length on the wall in the sun. 'I'm a born scutt[2] av the barrick-room! The Army's mate an' dhrink to me, bekaze I'm wan av the few that can't quit ut. I've put in sivinteen years, an' the pipeclay's in the marrow av me. Av I cud have kept out av wan big dhrink a month, I wud have been a Hon'ry Lift'nint by this time – a nuisance to my betthers, a laughin'-shtock to my aquils, an' a curse to mesilf. Bein' fwhat I am, I'm Privit Mulvaney, wid no good-conduc' pay an' a devourin' thirst. Always barrin' me little frind Bobs Bahadur, I know as much about the Army as most men.'

I said something here.

'Wolseley[3] be shot! Betune you an' me an' that butterfly net, he's a ramblin', incoherint sort av a divil, wid wan eye on the Quane an' the Coort, an' the other on his blessed silf – everlastin'ly playin' Saysar and Alexandrier rowled into a lump. Now Bobs is a sinsible little man. Wid Bobs an' a few three-year-oulds, I'd swape any army av the earth into a towel, an' throw ut away afthardwards. Faith, I'm not jokin'! 'Tis the bhoys – the raw

122

bhoys – that don't know fhwat a bullut manes, an' wudn't care av they did – that do the work. They're crammed wid bull-mate till they fairly *ramps*[4] wid good livin'; and thin, av they don't fight, they blow each other's hids off. 'Tis the trut' I'm tellin' you. They shud be kept on wather an' rice in the hot weather; but there'd be a mut'ny av 'twas done.

'Did ye iver hear how Privit Mulvaney tuk the town av Lungtungpen? I thought not! 'Twas the Lift'nint got the credit; but 'twas me planned the schame. A little before I was inviladed from Burma, me an' four-an'-twinty young wans undher a Lift'nint Brazenose, was ruinin' our dijeshins thryin' to catch dacoits. An' such double-inded divils I niver knew! 'Tis only a *dah* an' a Snider[5] that makes a dacoit. Widout thim, he's a paceful cultivator, an' felony for to shoot. We hunted, an' we hunted, an' tuk fever an' elephints now an' again; but no dacoits. Evenshually, we *puckarowed*[6] wan man. "Trate him tinderly," sez the Lift'nint. So I tuk him away into the jungle, wid the Burmese Interprut'r an' my clanin'-rod. Sez I to the man, "My paceful squireen," sez I, "you shquot on your hunkers an' dimonstrate to *my* frind here, where *your* frinds are whin they're at home" Wid that I introjuced him to the clanin'-rod, an' he comminst to jabber; the Interprut'r interprutin' in betweens, an' me helpin' the Intilligince Department wid my clanin'-rod whin the man misremimbered.

'Prisintly, I learn that, acrost the river, about nine miles away, was a town dhrippin' wid *dahs*, an' bohs an' arrows, an' dacoits, an' elephints, an' *jingles*.[7] "Good!" sez I; "this office will now close!"

'That night I wint to the Lift'nint an' communicates my informashin. I niver thought much av Lift'nint Brazenose till that night. He was shtiff wid books an' the-ouries, an' all manner av thrimmin's no manner av use. "Town, did ye say?" sez he. "Accordin' to the the-ouries av War, we shud wait for reinforcemints." – "Faith!" thinks I, "we'd betther dig our graves thin"; for the nearest throops was up to their shtocks in the marshes out Mimbu way. "But," sez the Lift'nint, "since 'tis a speshil case, I'll make an excepshin. We'll visit this Lungtungpen to-night."

'The bhoys was fairly woild wid deloight whin I tould 'em;

123

an', by this an' that, they wint through the jungle like buck-rabbits. About midnight we come to the shtrame which I had clane forgot to minshin to my orf'cer. I was on, ahead, wid four bhoys, an' I thought that the Lift'nint might want to the-ourise. "Shtrip bhoys!" sez I. "Shtrip to the buff, an' shwim in where glory waits!" – "But I *can't* shwim!" sez two av thim. "To think I shuld live to hear that from a bhoy wid a board-school edukashin!" sez I. "Take a lump av timbher, an' me an' Conolly here will ferry ye over, ye young ladies!"

'We got an ould tree-trunk, an' pushed off wid the kits an' the rifles on ut. The night was chokin' dhark, an' just as we was fairly embarked, I heard the Lift'nint behind av me callin' out. "There's a bit av a nullah[8] here, sorr," sez I, "but I can feel the bottom already." So I cud, for I was not a yard from the bank.

'"Bit av a nullah! Bit av an eshtury!" sez the Lift'nint. "Go on, ye mad Irishman! Shtrip, bhoys!" I heard him laugh; an' the bhoys begun shtrippin' an' rowlin' a log into the wather to put their kits on. So me an' Conolly shtruck out through the warm water wid our log, an' the rest come on behind.

'That shtrame was miles woide! Orth'ris, on the rear-rank log, whispers we had got into the Thames below Sheerness by mistake. "Kape on shwimmin', ye little blayguard," sez I, "an' don't go pokin' your dirty jokes at the Irriwaddy." – "Silence, men!" sings out the Lift'nint. So we shwum on into the black dhark, wid our chests on the logs, trustin' in the Saints an' the luck av the British Army.

'Evenshually, we hit ground – a bit av sand – an' a man. I put my heel on the back av him. He screeched an' ran.

'"*Now* we've done ut!" sez Lift'nint Brazenose. "Where the Divil *is* Lungtungpen?" There was about a minut' and a half to wait. The bhoys laid a hoult av their rifles an' some thried to put their belts on; we was marchin' wid fixed baynits av coorse. Thin we knew where Lungtungpen was; for we had hit the river-wall av ut in the dhark, an' the whole town blazed wid thim messin' *jingles* an' Sniders like a cat's back on a frosty night. They was firin' all ways at wanst; but over our hids into the shtrame.

'"Have you got your rifles?" sez Brazenose. "Got 'em!" sez Orth'ris. "I've got that thafe Mulvaney's for all my back-pay, an' she'll kick my heart sick wid that blunderin' long shtock av hers." – "Go on!" yells Brazenose, whippin' his sword out. "Go on an' take the town! An' the Lord have mercy on our sowls!"'

'Thin the bhoys gave wan devastatin' howl, an' pranced into the dhark, feelin' for the town, an' blindin' an' stiffin' like Cavalry Ridin'-Masters whin the grass pricked their bare legs. I hammered wid the butt at some bamboo-thing that felt wake, an' the rest come an' hammered contagious, while the *jingles* was jinglin', an' feroshus yells from inside was shplittin' our ears. We was too close undher the wall for thim to hurt us.

'Evenshually, the thing, whatever ut was, bruk; an' the six-and-twinty av us tumbled, wan afther the other, nakid as we was borrun, in to the town av Lungtungpen. There was a *melly* av a sumpshus kind for a whoile; but whether they tuk us, all white an' wet, for a new breed av divil, or a new kind av dacoit, I don't know. They ran as though we was both, an' we wint into thim, baynit an' butt, shriekin' wid laughin'. There was torches in the shtreets, an' I saw little Orth'ris rubbin' his shoulther ivry time he loosed my long-shtock Martini; an' Brazenose walkin' into the gang wid his sword, like Diarmid[9] av the Gowlden Collar – barrin' he hadn't a stitch av clothin' on him. We diskivered eliphints wid dacoits undher their bellies, an', fwhat wid wan thing an' another, we was busy till mornin' takin' possession av the town of Lungtungpen.

'Thin we halted an' formed up, the women howlin' in the houses an' Lift'nint Brazenose blushin' pink in the light av the mornin' sun. 'Twas the most ondasint p'rade I iver tuk hand in. Foive-and-twinty privits an' an orf'cer av the Line in review ordher, an' not as much as wud dust a fife betune 'em all in the way av clothin'! Eight av us had their belts an' pouches on; but the rest had gone in wid a handful av cartridges an' the skin God gave thim. *They* was as nakid as Vanus!

'"Number off from the right!" sez the Lift'nint. "Odd numbers fall out to dress; even numbers pathrol the town till relieved by the dressing party." Let me tell you, pathrollin' a town wid nothing on is an ex*pay*rience. I pathrolled for tin minut's, an' begad, before 'twas over, I blushed. The women laughed so. I niver blushed before or since; but I blushed all over my carkiss thin. Orth'ris didn't pathrol. He sez only, "Portsmith Barricks an' the 'Ard av a Sunday!" Thin he lay down an' rowled any ways wid laughin'.

'Whin we was all dhressed we counted the dead – sivinty-foive dacoits besides wounded. We tuk foive elephints, a hundher' an' sivinty Sniders, two hundher' *dahs*, and a lot av other burglarious thruck. Not a man av us was hurt – excep' maybe the Lift'nint, an' him from the shock to his dasincy.

'The Headman av Lungtungpen, who surrindered himsilf, asked the Interprut'r: "Av the English fight like that wid their clo'es off, what in the wurruld do they do wid their clo'es on?" Orth'ris began rowlin' his eyes an' crackin' his fingers an' dancin' a step-dance for to impress the Headman. He ran to his house; an' we spint the rest av the day carryin' the Lift'nint on our shoulthers round the town, an' playin' wid the Burmese babies – fat little, brown little divils, as pretty as pictur's.

'Whin I was invilided for the dysent'ry to India, I sez to the Lift'nint, "Sorr," sez I, "you've the makin's in you av a great man; but, av you'll let an ould sodger spake, you're too fond av the-ourisin'." He shuk hands wid me and sez, "Hit high, hit low, there's no plasin' you, Mulvaney. You've seen me waltzin' through Lungtungpen like a Red Injin widout the war-paint, an' you say I'm too fond av the-ourisin'?" – "Sorr," sez I, for I loved the bhoy, "I wud waltz wid you in that condishin through Hell, an' so wud the rest av the men!" Thin I wint down-shtrame in the flat an' left him my blessin'. May the Saints carry ut where ut shud go, for he was a fine upstandin' young orf'cer.

'To reshume. Fwhat I've said jist shows the use av three-year-olds. Wud fifty seasoned sodgers have taken Lungtungpen in the dhark that way? No! They'd know the risk av fever and chill; let alone the shootin'. Two hundher' might have done ut. But the three-year-olds know little an' care less; an' where there's no fear there's no danger. Catch thim young, feed thim high, an' by the honour av that great Little Man Bobs, behind a good orf'cer, 'tisn't only dacoits they'd smash wid their clo'es off: 'tis Con-ti-nental Ar-r-r-mies! They tuk Lungtungpen nakid; an' they'd take St Pethersburg in their dhrawers! Begad, they wud that!

'Here's your pipe, sorr. Shmoke her tinderly wid honey-dew,

afther letting the reek av the Canteen plug die away. But 'tis no good, thanks to you all the same, fillin' my pouch wid your chopped hay. Canteen baccy's like the Army. Ut shpoils a man's taste for moilder things.'

So saying, Mulvaney took up his butterfly-net, and returned to barracks.

A Germ-Destroyer

Pleasant it is for the Little Tin Gods
   When great Jove nods;
But Little Tin Gods make their little mistakes
In missing the hour when great Jove wakes.

As a general rule, it is inexpedient to meddle with questions of State in a land where men are highly paid to work them out for you. This tale is a justifiable exception.

Once in every five years, as you know, we indent for a new Viceroy; and each Viceroy imports, with the rest of his baggage, a Private Secretary, who may or may not be the real Viceroy, just as Fate ordains. Fate looks after the Indian Empire because it is so big and so helpless.

There was a Viceroy once who brought out with him a turbulent Private Secretary – a hard man with a soft manner and a morbid passion for work. This Secretary was called Wonder – John Fennil Wonder. The Viceroy possessed no name – nothing but a string of counties and two-thirds of the alphabet after them. He said, in confidence, that he was the electro-plated figure-head of a golden administration, and he watched in a dreamy, amused way Wonder's attempts to draw matters which were entirely outside his province into his own hands. 'When we are all cherubim together,' said His Excellency once, 'my dear, good friend Wonder will head the conspiracy for plucking out Gabriel's tail-feathers or stealing Peter's keys. *Then* I shall report him.'

But, though the Viceroy did nothing to check Wonder's officiousness, other people said unpleasant things. Maybe the Members of Council began it; but, finally, all Simla agreed that there was 'too much Wonder and too little Viceroy' in that rule. Wonder was always quoting 'His Excellency'. It was 'His Excellency this,' 'His Excellency that', 'In the opinion of His

Excellency', and so on. The Viceroy smiled; but he did not heed.
He said that, so long as his old men squabbled with his 'dear,
good Wonder', they might be induced to leave the Immemorial
East in peace.

'No wise man has a Policy,' said the Viceroy. 'A Policy is
blackmail levied on the Fool by the Unforeseen. I am not the
former, and I do not believe in the latter.'

I do not quite see what this means, unless it refers to an
Insurance Policy. Perhaps it was the Viceroy's way of saying, 'Lie
low.'

That season came up to Simla one of those crazy people with
only a single idea. These are the men who make things move; but
they are not nice to talk to. This man's name was Mellish, and
he had lived for fifteen years on land of his own, in Lower Bengal,
studying cholera. He held that cholera was a germ that propagated
itself as it flew through a muggy atmosphere, and stuck in the
branches of trees like a wool-flake. The germ could be rendered
sterile, he said, by 'Mellish's Own Invincible Fumigatory' – a
heavy violet-black powder – 'the result of fifteen years' scientific
investigation, sir!'

Inventors seem very much alike as a caste. They talk loudly,
especially about 'conspiracies of monopolists'; they beat upon the
table with their fists; and they secrete fragments of their inventions
about their persons.

Mellish said that there was a Medical 'Ring' at Simla, headed
by the Surgeon-General, who was in league, apparently, with all
the Hospital Assistants in the Empire. I forget exactly how he
proved it, but it had something to do with 'skulking up to the
Hills'; and what Mellish wanted was the independent evidence
of the Viceroy – 'Steward of our Most Gracious Majesty the
Queen, sir.' So Mellish went up to Simla, with eighty-four pounds
of Fumigatory in his trunk, to speak to the Viceroy and to show
him the merits of the invention.

But it is easier to see a Viceroy than to talk to him, unless you
chance to be as important as Mellishe of Madras. He was a six-
thousand-rupee man, so great that his daughters never 'married'.
They 'contracted alliances'. He himself was not paid. He 'received
emoluments', and his journeys about the country were 'tours of

observation'. His business was to stir up the people in Madras with a long pole – as you stir up tench in a pond – and the people had to come up out of their comfortable old ways and gasp: 'This is Enlightenment and Progress. Isn't it fine!' Then they gave Mellishe statues and jasmine garlands, in the hope of getting rid of him.

Mellishe came up to Simla 'to confer with the Viceroy'. That was one of his perquisites. The Viceroy knew nothing of Mellishe except that he was 'one of those middle-class deities who seem necessary to the spiritual comfort of this Paradise of the Middle-classes', and that, in all probability, he had 'suggested, designed, founded, and endowed all the public institutions in Madras'. Which proves that His Excellency, though dreamy, had experience of the ways of six-thousand-rupee men.

Mellishe's name was E. Mellishe, and Mellish's was E. S. Mellish, and they were both staying at the same hotel, and the Fate that looks after the Indian Empire ordained that Wonder should blunder and drop the final '*e*'; that the orderly should help him, and that the note which ran:

Dear Mr Mellish,

Can you set aside your other engagements, and lunch with us at two to-morrow? His Excellency has an hour at your disposal then,

should be given to Mellish with the Fumigatory. He nearly wept with pride and delight, and at the appointed hour cantered to Peterhof, a big paperbag full of the Fumigatory in his coat-tail pockets. He had his chance, and he meant to make the most of it. Mellishe of Madras had been so portentously solemn about his 'conference' that Wonder had arranged for a private tiffin,[1] – no A.D.C.s, no Wonder, no one but the Viceroy, who said plaintively that he feared being left alone with unmuzzled autocrats like the great Mellishe of Madras.

But his guest did not bore the Viceroy. On the contrary, he amused him. Mellish was nervously anxious to go straight to his Fumigatory, and talked at random until tiffin was over and His Excellency asked him to smoke. The Viceroy was pleased with Mellish because he did not talk 'shop'.

As soon as the cheroots were lit, Mellish spoke like a man; beginning with his cholera-theory, reviewing his fifteen years' 'scientific labours', the machinations of the 'Simla Ring', and the excellence of his Fumigatory, while the Viceroy watched him between half-shut eyes and thought, 'Evidently this is the wrong tiger; but it is an original animal.' Mellish's hair was standing on end with excitement, and he stammered. He began groping in his coat-tails and, before the Viceroy knew what was about to happen, he had tipped a bagful of his powder into the big silver ash-tray.

'J-j-judge for yourself, sir,' said Mellish. 'Y' Excellency shall judge for yourself! Absolutely infallible, on my honour.'

He plunged the lighted end of his cigar into the powder, which began to smoke like a volcano, and send up fat, greasy wreaths of copper-coloured smoke. In five seconds the room was filled with a most pungent and sickening stench – a reek that took fierce hold of the trap of your windpipe and shut it. The powder hissed and fizzed, and sent out blue and green sparks, and the smoke rose till you could neither see, nor breathe, nor gasp. Mellish, however, was used to it.

'Nitrate of strontia,' he shouted; 'baryta, bone-meal, etcetera! Thousand cubic feet smoke per cubic inch. Not a germ could live – not a germ, Y' Excellency!'

But His Excellency had fled, and was coughing at the foot of the stairs, while all Peterhof hummed like a hive. Red Lancers came in, and the Head *Chaprassi* who speaks English came in, and mace-bearers came in, and ladies ran downstairs screaming, 'Fire'; for the smoke was drifting through the house and oozing out of the windows, and bellying along the verandas, and wreathing and writhing across the gardens. No one could enter the room where Mellish was lecturing on his Fumigatory till that unspeakable powder had burned itself out.

Then an Aide-de-Camp, who desired the V.C., rushed through the rolling clouds and hauled Mellish into the hall. The Viceroy was prostrate with laughter, and could only waggle his hands feebly at Mellish, who was shaking a fresh bagful of powder at him.

'Glorious! Glorious!' sobbed His Excellency. 'Not a germ, as you justly observe, could exist! I can swear it. A magnificent success!'

Then he laughed till the tears came, and Wonder, who had caught the real Mellishe snorting on the Mall, entered and was deeply shocked at the scene. But the Viceroy was delighted, because he saw that Wonder would presently depart. Mellish with the Fumigatory was also pleased, for he felt that he had smashed the Simla Medical 'Ring'.

Few men could tell a story like His Excellency when he took the trouble, and his account of 'my dear, good Wonder's friend with the powder' went the round of Simla, and flippant folk made Wonder unhappy by their remarks.

But His Excellency told the tale once too often – for Wonder. As he meant to do. It was at a Seepee[2] Picnic. Wonder was sitting just behind the Viceroy.

'And I really thought for a moment,' wound up His Excellency, 'that my dear, good Wonder had hired an assassin to clear his way to the throne!'

Everyone laughed; but there was a delicate sub-tinkle in the Viceroy's tone which Wonder understood.[3] He found that his health was giving way; and the Viceroy allowed him to go, and presented him with a flaming 'character' for use at Home among big people.

'My fault entirely,' said His Excellency, in after seasons, with a twinkle in his eye. 'My inconsistency must always have been distasteful to such a masterly man.'

⦃ Kidnapped ⦄

There is a tide in the affairs of men
Which, taken any way you please, is bad,
And strands them in forsaken guts and creeks
No decent soul would think of visiting.
You cannot stop the tide; but, now and then,
You may arrest some rash adventurer,
Who – h'm – will hardly thank you for your pains.
Vibart's Moralities

We are a high-caste and enlightened race, and infant-marriage is very shocking, and the consequences are sometimes peculiar; but, nevertheless, the Hindu notion – which is the Continental notion, which is the aboriginal notion – of arranging marriages irrespective of the personal inclinations of the married is sound. Think for a minute, and you will see that it must be so; unless, of course, you believe in 'affinities'. In which case you had better not read this tale. How can a man who has never married, who cannot be trusted to pick up at sight a moderately sound horse, whose head is hot and upset with visions of domestic felicity, go about the choosing of a wife? He cannot see straight or think straight if he tries; and the same disadvantages exist in the case of a girl's fancies.[1] But when mature, married, and discreet people arrange a match between a boy and a girl, they do it sensibly, with a view to the future, and the young couple live happily ever afterwards. As everybody knows.

Properly speaking, Government should establish a Matrimonial Department, efficiently officered, with a Jury of Matrons, a Judge of the Chief Court, a Senior Chaplain, and an Awful Warning, in the shape of a love-match that has gone wrong, chained to the trees in the courtyard. All marriages should be made through the Department, which might be subordinate to the Educational Department, under the same penalty as that attaching to the transfer of land without a stamped document. But Government won't take suggestions. It pretends that it is too busy. However, I will put my notion on record, and explain the example that illustrates the theory.

Once upon a time there was a good young man – a first-class officer in his own Department – a man with a career before him and, possibly, a K.C.I.E.[2] at the end of it. All his superiors spoke well of him, because he knew how to hold his tongue and his pen at the proper times. There are, to-day, only eleven men in India who possess this secret; and they have all, with one exception, attained great honour and enormous incomes.

This good young man was quiet and self-contained – too old for his years by far. Which always carries its own punishment. Had a Subaltern, or a Tea-Planter's Assistant, or anybody who enjoys life and has no thought for to-morrow, done what he tried to do, not a soul would have cared. But when Peythroppe – the estimable, virtuous, economical, quiet, hard-working, young Peythroppe – fell, there was a flutter through five Departments.

The manner of his fall was in this way. He met a Miss Castries – D'Castries it was originally, but the family dropped the D' for administrative reasons – and he fell in love with her even more energetically than he worked. Understand clearly that there was not a breath of a word to be said against Miss Castries – not a shadow of a breath. She was good and very lovely – possessed what innocent people at Home[3] call a 'Spanish' complexion, with thick blue-black hair growing low down on the forehead, into a 'widow's peak', and big violet eyes under eyebrows as black and as straight as the borders of a *Gazette Extraordinary* when a big man dies. But – but – but – Well, she was a *very* sweet girl and very pious, but for many reasons she was 'impossible'. Quite so. All good Mammas know what 'impossible' means. It was obviously absurd that Peythroppe should marry her. The little opal-tinted onyx at the base of her finger-nails[4] said this as plainly as print. Further, marriage with Miss Castries meant marriage with several other Castries – Honorary Lieutenant Castries her Papa, Mrs Eulalie Castries her Mamma, and all the ramifications of the Castries family, on incomes ranging from Rs. 175 to Rs. 470 a month, and *their* wives and connections again.

Kidnapped

It would have been cheaper for Peythroppe to have assaulted a Commissioner with a dog-whip, or to have burned the records of a Deputy-Commissioner's office, than to have contracted an alliance with the Castries. It would have weighted his after-career less – even under a Government which never forgets and *never* forgives. Everybody saw this but Peythroppe. He was going to marry Miss Castries, he was – being of age and drawing a good income – and woe betide the house that would not afterwards receive Mrs Virginie Saulez Peythroppe with the deference due to her husband's rank. That was Peythroppe's ultimatum, and any remonstrance drove him frantic.

These sudden madnesses most afflict the sanest men. There was a case once . . . But I will tell you of that later on. You cannot account for the mania except under a theory directly contradicting the one about the Place wherein marriages are made. Peythroppe was burningly anxious to put a millstone round his neck at the outset of his career, and argument had not the least effect on him. He was going to marry Miss Castries, and the business was his own business. He would thank you to keep your advice to yourself. With a man in his condition mere words only fix him in his purpose. Of course he cannot see that marriage in India does not concern the individual but the Government he serves.

Do you remember Mrs Hauksbee – the most wonderful woman in India? She saved Pluffles from Mrs Reiver, won Tarrion his appointment in the Foreign Office, and was defeated in open field by Mrs Cusack-Bremmil. She heard of the lamentable condition of Peythroppe, and her brain struck out the plan that saved him. She had the wisdom of the Serpent,[5] the logical coherence of the Man, the fearlessness of the Child, and the triple intuition of the Woman. Never – no, never – as long as a tonga buckets down the Solon dip, or the couples go a-riding at the back of Summer Hill,[6] will there be such a genius as Mrs Hauksbee! She attended the consultation of Three Men on Peythroppe's case; and she stood up with the lash of her riding-whip between her lips and spake.

Three weeks later, Peythroppe dined with the Three Men, and the *Gazette of India* came in. Peythroppe found to his surprise that he had been gazetted a month's leave. Don't ask me how this was managed. I believe firmly that, if Mrs Hauksbee gave the order, the whole Great Indian Administration would stand on its head. The Three Men had also a month's leave each. Peythroppe put the *Gazette* down and said bad words. Then there came from the compound the soft 'pad-pad' of camels – 'thieves' camels', the Bikanir breed that don't bubble and howl when they sit down and get up.

After that, I don't know what happened. This much is certain. Peythroppe disappeared – vanished like smoke – and the long foot-rest chair in the house of the Three Men was broken to splinters. Also a bedstead departed from one of the bedrooms.

Mrs Hauksbee said that Mr Peythroppe was shooting in Rajputana with the Three Men; so we were compelled to believe her.

At the end of the month Peythroppe was gazetted twenty days' extension of leave; but there was wrath and lamentation in the house of Castries. The marriage-day had been fixed, but the bridegroom never came; and the D'Silvas, Pereiras, and Ducketts lifted their voices and mocked Honorary Lieutenant Castries as one who had been basely imposed on. Mrs Hauksbee went to the wedding, and was much astonished when Peythroppe did not appear. After seven weeks Peythroppe and the Three Men returned from Rajputana. Peythroppe was in hard, tough condition, rather white, and more self-contained than ever.

One of the Three Men had a cut on his nose, caused by the kick of a gun. Twelve-bores kick rather curiously.

Then came Honorary Lieutenant Castries, seeking for the blood of his perfidious son-in-law to be. He said things – vulgar and 'impossible' things which showed the raw, rough 'ranker' below the 'Honorary', and I fancy Peythroppe's eyes were opened. Anyhow, he held his peace till the end, when he spoke briefly. Honorary Lieutenant Castries asked for a 'peg'[7] before he went away to die or bring a suit for breach of promise.

Miss Castries was a *very* good girl. She said that she would have no breach of promise suits. She said that, if she was not a lady, she was refined enough to know that ladies kept their broken hearts to themselves; and, as she ruled her parents, nothing happened. Later on, she married a most respectable and gentle-manly person. He travelled for an enterprising firm in Calcutta, and was all that a good husband should be.

So Peythroppe came to his right mind again, and did much good work, and was honoured by all who knew him. One of these days he will marry; but he will marry a sweet pink-and-white maiden, on the Government House List, with a little money and some influential connections, as every wise man should. And he will never, all his life, tell her what happened during the seven weeks of his shooting-tour in Rajputana.

But just think how much trouble and expense – for camel-hire is not cheap, and those Bikanir brutes had to be fed like humans – might have been saved by a properly conducted Matrimonial Department, under the control of the Director-General of Education, but corresponding direct with the Viceroy!

The Arrest of Lieutenant Golightly

'I've forgotten the countersign,' sez 'e.

'Oh! You 'ave, 'ave you?' sez I.

'But I'm the Colonel,' sez 'e.

'Oh! You are, are you?' sez I. 'Colonel nor no Colonel, you waits 'ere till I'm relieved, an' the Sarjint reports on your ugly old mug. *Choop!*' sez I.

An' swelp me soul, 'twas the Colonel after all! But I was a recruity then

The Unedited Autobiography of Private Ortheris

If there was one thing on which Golightly prided himself more than another, it was looking like 'an Officer and a Gentleman'. He said it was for the honour of the Service that he attired himself so elaborately; but those who knew him best said that it was just personal vanity. There was no harm about Golightly – not an ounce. He recognized a horse when he saw one, and could do more than fill a saddle. He played a very fair game at billiards, and was a sound man at the whist-table. Every one liked him; and nobody ever dreamed of seeing him handcuffed on a station platform as a deserter. But this sad thing happened.

He was going down from Dalhousie, at the end of his leave – riding down. He had run his leave as fine as he dared, and wanted to come down in a hurry.

It was fairly warm at Dalhousie, and, knowing what to expect below, he descended in a new khaki suit – tight-fitting – of a delicate olive-green; a peacock-blue tie, white collar, and a snowy white *solah* helmet. He prided himself on looking neat even when he was riding post.[1] He *did* look neat, and he was so deeply concerned about his appearance before he started that he quite forgot to take anything but some small change with him. He left all his notes at the hotel. His servants had gone down the road before him, to be ready in waiting at Pathânkot with a change of gear. That was what he called travelling in 'light marching-order'. He was proud of his faculty of organization – what we call *bundobust*.

Twenty-two miles out of Dalhousie it began to rain – not a mere Hill-shower, but a good, tepid, monsoonish downpour. Golightly bustled on, wishing that he had brought an umbrella. The dust on the roads turned into mud, and the pony mired a good deal. So did Golightly's khaki gaiters. But he kept on steadily and tried to think how pleasant the coolth was.

His next pony was rather a brute at starting, and, Golightly's hands being slippery with the rain, contrived to get rid of Golightly at a corner. He chased the animal, caught it, and went ahead briskly. The spill had not improved his clothes or his temper, and he had lost one spur. He kept the other one employed. By the time that stage was ended the pony had had as much exercise as he wanted, and, in spite of the rain, Golightly was sweating freely. At the end of another miserable half hour Golightly found the world disappear before his eyes in clammy pulp. The rain had turned the pith of his huge and snowy *solah-topee* into an evil-smelling dough, and it had closed on his head like a half-opened mushroom. Also, the green lining was beginning to run.

Golightly did not say anything worth recording here. He tore off and squeezed up as much of the brim as was in his eyes and ploughed on. The back of the helmet was flapping on his neck, and the sides stuck to his ears, but the leather band and green lining kept things roughly together, so that the hat did not actually melt away where it flapped.

Presently, the pulp and the green stuff made a sort of slimy mildew which ran over Golightly in several directions – down his back and bosom for choice. The khaki colour ran too – it was really shocking bad dye – and sections of Golightly were brown, and patches were violet, and contours were ochre, and streaks were brick-red, and blotches were nearly white, according to the nature and peculiarities of the dye. When he took out his handkerchief to wipe his face, and the green of the hat-lining and the purple stuff that had soaked through on to his neck from the tie became thoroughly mixed, the effect was amazing.

Near Dhar the rain stopped and the evening sun came out and dried him up slightly. It fixed the colours, too. Three miles from Pathânkot the last pony fell dead lame, and Golightly was forced to walk. He pushed on into Pathânkot to find his servants. He did not know then that his *khitmutgar*[2] had stopped by the roadside to get drunk, and would come on the next day saying that he had sprained his ankle. When he got into Pathânkot he couldn't find his servants, his boots were stiff and ropy with mud, and there were large quantities of dust about his body. The blue tie had run as much as the khaki. So he took it off with the collar and threw it away. Then he said something about servants generally and tried to get a peg. He paid eight annas for the drink, and this revealed to him that he had only six annas more in his pocket – or in the world as he stood at that hour.

He went to the Stationmaster to negotiate for a first-class ticket to Khasa, where he was stationed. The booking-clerk said something to the Stationmaster, the Stationmaster said something to the telegraph-clerk, and the three looked at him with curiosity. They asked him to wait for half an hour, while they telegraphed to Amritzar for authority. So he waited and four constables came and grouped themselves picturesquely round him. Just as he was preparing to ask them to go away, the Stationmaster said that he would give the Sahib a ticket to Amritzar, if the Sahib would kindly come inside the booking-office. Golightly stepped inside, and the next thing he knew was that a constable was attached to each of his legs and arms, while the Stationmaster was trying to cram a mail-bag over his head.

There was a very fair scuffle all round the booking-office, and Golightly took a nasty cut over his eye through falling against a table. But the constables were too much for him, and they and the Stationmaster handcuffed him securely. As soon as the mail-bag was slipped, he began expressing his opinions, and the head constable said, 'Without doubt this is the soldier-Englishman we required. Listen to the abuse!' Then Golightly asked the Stationmaster what the this and the that the proceedings meant. The Stationmaster told him he was 'Private John Binkle of the — Regiment, 5 ft. 9 in., fair hair, grey eyes, and a dissipated appearance, no marks on the body,' who had deserted a fortnight ago. Golightly began explaining at great length; and the more he explained the less the Stationmaster believed him. He said that no Lieutenant could look such a ruffian as did Golightly, and that his instructions were to send his capture under proper escort to Amritzar. Golightly was feeling very damp and uncomfortable, and the language he used was not fit for publication, even in an expurgated form. The four constables saw him safe to Amritzar in an 'Intermediate' compartment, and he spent the four-hour journey in abusing them as fluently as his knowledge of the vernaculars allowed.

At Amritzar he was bundled out on the platform into the arms of a Corporal and two men of the — Regiment. Golightly drew himself up and tried to carry off matters jauntily. He did not feel too jaunty in handcuffs, with four constables behind him, and the blood from the cut on his forehead stiffening on his left cheek. The Corporal was not jocular either. Golightly got as far as: 'This is a very absurd mistake, my men,' when the Corporal told him to 'stow his lip' and come along. Golightly did not want to come along. He desired to stop and explain. He explained very well indeed, until the Corporal cut in with: '*You* a orficer! It's the like o' *you* as brings disgrace on the likes of *us*. Bloomin' fine orficer you are! I know your regiment. The Rogue's March is the quickstep where you come from. You're a black shame to the Service.'

Golightly kept his temper, and began explaining all over again from the beginning. Then he was marched out of the rain into the refreshment-room, and told not to make a qualified fool of himself. The men were going to run him up to Fort Govindghar. And 'running up' is a performance almost as undignified as the Frog March.

Golightly was nearly hysterical with rage and the chill and the mistake and the handcuffs and the headache that the cut on his forehead had given him. He really laid himself out to express what was in his mind. When he had quite finished and his throat was feeling dry, one of the men said, 'I've 'eard a few beggars in the Clink blind, stiff, and crack on a bit; but I've never 'eard any one to touch this 'ere "orficer".' They were not angry with him. They rather admired him. They had some beer at the refreshment-room, and offered Golightly some too, because he had 'swore won'erful'. They asked him to tell them all about the adventures of Private John Binkle while he was loose on the countryside; and that made Golightly wilder than ever. If he had kept his wits about him he would have been quiet until an officer came; but he attempted to run.

Now the butt of a Martini in the small of your back hurts a great deal, and rotten, rain-soaked khaki tears easily when two men are yerking at your collar.

Golightly rose from the floor feeling very sick and giddy, with his shirt ripped open all down his breast and nearly all down his back. He yielded to his luck, and at that point the down-train from Lahore came in, carrying one of Golightly's Majors.

This is the Major's evidence in full:

'There was the sound of a scuffle in the second-class refreshment-room, so I went in and saw the most villainous loafer that I ever set eyes on. His boots and breeches were plastered with mud and beer-stains. He wore a muddy-white dunghill sort of thing on his head, and it hung down in slips on his shoulders, which were a good deal scratched. He was half in and half out of a shirt as nearly in two pieces as it could be, and he was begging the guard to look at the name on the tail of it. As he had rucked the shirt all over his head, I couldn't at first see who he was, but I fancied that he was a man in the first stage of D.T.[3] from the way he swore while he wrestled with his rags. When he turned round, and I had made allowances for a lump as big as a pork-pie over one eye, and some green war-paint on the face, and some violet stripes round the neck, I saw that it was Golightly. He was very glad to see me,' said the Major, 'and he hoped I would not tell the Mess about it. *I* didn't, but you can, if you like, now that Golightly has gone Home.'

Golightly spent the greater part of that summer in trying to get the Corporal and the two soldiers tried by Court-Martial for arresting an 'Officer and a Gentleman'. They were, of course, very sorry for their error. But the tale leaked into the regimental Canteen, and thence ran about the Province.

In the House of Suddhoo

> A stone's throw out on either hand
> From that well-ordered road we tread,
>   And all the world is wild and strange:
> *Churel* and ghoul and *Djinn*[1] and sprite
> Shall bear us company to-night,
> For we have reached the Oldest Land
>   Wherein the Powers of Darkness range.
>
>   *From the Dusk to the Dawn*

The house of Suddhoo, near the Taksali Gate,[2] is two-storeyed, with four carved windows of old brown wood, and a flat roof. You may recognize it by five red hand-prints arranged like the Five of Diamonds on the whitewash between the upper windows. Bhagwan Dass the grocer and a man who says he gets his living by seal-cutting live in the lower storey with a troop of wives, servants, friends, and retainers. The two upper rooms used to be occupied by Janoo and Azizun, and a little black-and-tan terrier that was stolen from an Englishman's house and given to Janoo by a soldier. To-day, only Janoo lives in the upper rooms. Suddhoo sleeps on the roof generally, except when he sleeps in the street. He used to go to Peshawur in the cold weather to visit his son who sells curiosities near the Edwardes' Gate, and then he slept under a real mud roof. Suddhoo is a great friend of mine, because his cousin had a son who secured, thanks to my recommendation, the post of head-messenger to a big firm in the station. Suddhoo says that God will make me a Lieutenant-Governor one of these days. I daresay his prophecy will come true. He is very, very old, with white hair and no teeth worth showing, and he has outlived his wits – outlived nearly everything except his fondness for his son at Peshawur. Janoo and Azizun are Kashmiris, Ladies of the City, and theirs was an ancient and more or less honourable profession; but Azizun has since married

143

a medical student from the North-West and has settled down to a most respectable life somewhere near Bareilly. Bhagwan Dass is an extortioner and an adulterator. He is very rich. The man who is supposed to get his living by seal-cutting pretends to be poor. This lets you know as much as is necessary of the four principal tenants in the house of Suddhoo. Then there is Me, of course; but I am only the chorus that comes in at the end to explain things. So I do not count.

Suddhoo was not clever. The man who pretended to cut seals was the cleverest of them all – Bhagwan Dass only knew how to lie – except Janoo. She was also beautiful, but that was her own affair.

Suddhoo's son at Peshawur was attacked by pleurisy, and old Suddhoo was troubled. The seal-cutter man heard of Suddhoo's anxiety and made capital out of it. He was abreast of the times. He got a friend in Peshawur to telegraph daily accounts of the son's health. And here the story begins.

Suddhoo's cousin's son told me, one evening, that Suddhoo wanted to see me; that he was too old and feeble to come personally, and that I should be conferring an everlasting honour on the House of Suddhoo if I went to him. I went; but I think, seeing how well off Suddhoo was then, that he might have sent something better than an *ekka*, which jolted fearfully, to haul out a future Lieutenant-Governor to the City on a muggy April evening. The *ekka* did not run quickly. It was full dark when we pulled up opposite the door of Ranjit Singh's Tomb near the main gate of the Fort. Here was Suddhoo, and he said that by reason of my condescension, it was absolutely certain that I should become a Lieutenant-Governor while my hair was yet black. Then we talked about the weather and the state of my health, and the wheat crops, for fifteen minutes, in the Huzuri Bagh,[3] under the stars.

Suddhoo came to the point at last. He said that Janoo had told him that there was an order of the Sirkar[4] against magic, because it was feared that magic might one day kill the Empress of India. I didn't know anything about the state of the law; but I fancied that something interesting was going to happen. I said that so far from magic being discouraged by the Government, it was highly commended. The greatest officials of the State practised it themselves. (If the Financial Statement isn't magic, I don't know what is.) Then, to encourage him further, I said that, if there was any *jadoo* afoot, I had not the least objection to giving it my countenance and sanction, and to seeing that it was clean *jadoo* – white magic, as distinguished from the unclean *jadoo* which kills folk. It took a long time before Suddhoo admitted that this was just what he had asked me to come for. Then he told me, in jerks and quavers, that the man who said he cut seals was a sorcerer of the cleanest kind; that every day he gave Suddhoo news of the sick son in Peshawur more quickly than the lightning could fly, and that this news was always corroborated by the letters. Further, that he had told Suddhoo how a great danger was threatening his son, which could be removed by clean *jadoo*; and, of course, heavy payment. I began to see exactly how the land lay, and told Suddhoo that I also understood a little *jadoo* in the Western line, and would go to his house to see that everything was done decently and in order. We set off together; and on the way Suddhoo told me that he had paid the seal-cutter between one hundred and two hundred rupees already; and the *jadoo* of that night would cost two hundred more. Which was cheap, he said, considering the greatness of his son's danger; but I do not think he meant it.

The lights were all cloaked in the front of the house when we arrived. I could hear awful noises from behind the seal-cutter's shop-front, as if some one were groaning his soul out. Suddhoo shook all over, and while we groped our way upstairs told me that the *jadoo* had begun. Janoo and Azizun met us at the stair-head, and told us that the *jadoo*-work was coming off in their rooms, because there was more space there. Janoo is a lady of a free-thinking turn of mind. She whispered that the *jadoo* was an invention to get money out of Suddhoo, and that the seal-cutter would go to a hot place when he died. Suddhoo was nearly crying with fear and old age. He kept walking up and down the room in the half-light, repeating his son's name over and over again, and asking Azizun if the seal-cutter ought not to make a reduction in the case of his own landlord. Janoo pulled me over to the shadow in the recess of the carved bow-windows. The boards were up, and the rooms were only lit by one tiny oil-lamp. There was no chance of my being seen if I stayed still.

Presently, the groans below ceased, and we heard steps on the staircase. That was the seal-cutter. He stopped outside the door as the terrier barked and Azizun fumbled at the chain, and he told Suddhoo to blow out the lamp. This left the place in jet darkness, except for the red glow from the two hookahs that belonged to Janoo and Azizun. The seal-cutter came in, and I heard Suddhoo throw himself down on the floor and groan. Azizun caught her breath, and Janoo backed on to one of the beds with a shudder. There was a clink of something metallic, and then shot up a pale blue-green flame near the ground. The light was just enough to show Azizun, pressed against one corner of the room with the terrier between her knees; Janoo, with her hands clasped, leaning forward as she sat on the bed; Suddhoo, face-down, quivering, and the seal-cutter.

I hope I may never see another man like that seal-cutter. He was stripped to the waist, with a wreath of white jasmine as thick as my wrist round his forehead, a salmon-coloured loin-cloth round his middle, and a steel bangle on each ankle. This was not awe-inspiring. It was blue-grey in the first place. In the second, the eyes were rolled back till you could see the whites of them; and, in the third, the face was the face of a demon – a ghoul – anything you please except of the sleek, oily old ruffian who sat in the daytime over his turning-lathe downstairs. He was lying on his stomach with his arms turned and crossed behind him, as if he had been thrown down pinioned. His head and neck were the only parts of him off the floor. They were nearly at right angles to the body, like the head of a cobra at spring. It was ghastly. In the centre of the room, on the bare earth floor, stood a big, deep, brass basin, with a pale blue-green light floating in the centre like a night-light. Round that basin the man on the floor wriggled himself three times. How he did it I do not know. I could see the muscles ripple along his spine and fall smooth again; but I could not see any other motion. The head seemed the only thing alive about him, except that slow curl and uncurl of the labouring back-muscles. Janoo from the bed was breathing seventy to the minute; Azizun held her hands before her eyes; and old Suddhoo, fingering at the dirt that had got into his white beard, was crying to himself. The horror of it was that the creeping, crawly thing made no sound – only crawled! And, remember, this lasted for ten minutes, while the terrier whined, and Azizun shuddered, and Janoo gasped, and Suddhoo cried!

I felt the hair lift at the back of my head, and my heart thump like a thermantidote-paddle.[5] Luckily, the seal-cutter betrayed himself by his most impressive trick and made me calm again. After he had finished that unspeakable triple crawl, he stretched his head away from the floor as high as he could, and sent out a jet of fire from his nostrils. Now, I knew how fire-spouting is done – I can do it myself – so I felt at ease. The business was a fraud. If he had only kept to that crawl without trying to raise the effect, goodness knows what I might not have thought. Both the girls shrieked at the jet of fire, and the head dropped, chin down on the floor, with a thud; the whole body lying there like a corpse with its arms trussed. There was a pause of five full minutes after this, and the blue-green flame died down. Janoo stooped to settle one of her anklets, while Azizun turned her face to the wall and took the terrier in her arms. Suddhoo put out an arm mechanically to Janoo's hookah, and she slid it across the floor with her foot. Directly above the body and on the wall were a couple of flaming portraits, in stamped-paper frames, of the Queen and the Prince of Wales. They looked down on the performance, and, to my thinking, seemed to heighten the grotesqueness of it all.

Just when the silence was getting unendurable, the body turned over and rolled away from the basin to the side of the room, where it lay stomach-up. There was a faint 'plop' from the basin – exactly like the noise a fish makes when it takes a fly – and the green light in the centre revived.

I looked at the basin, and saw, bobbing in the water, the dried, shrivelled, black head of a native baby – open eyes, open mouth, and shaved scalp. It was worse, being so very sudden, than the crawling exhibition. We had no time to say anything before it began to speak.

Read Poe's account[6] of the voice that came from the mesmerized dying man, and you will realize less than one-half of the horror of that head's voice.

There was an interval of a second or two between each word, and a sort of 'ring, ring, ring', in the note of the voice, like the timbre of a bell. It pealed slowly, as if talking to itself, for several minutes before I got rid of my cold sweat. Then the blessed solution struck me. I looked at the body lying near the doorway, and saw, just where the hollow of the throat joins on the shoulders, a muscle that had nothing to do with any man's regular breathing twitching away steadily. The whole thing was a careful reproduction of the Egyptian teraphim [7] that one reads about sometimes; and the voice was as clever and as appalling a piece of ventriloquism as one could wish to hear. All this time the head was 'lip-lip-lapping' against the side of the basin, and speaking. It told Suddhoo, on his face again whining, of his son's illness and of the state of the illness up to the evening of that very night. I always shall respect the seal-cutter for keeping so faithfully to the time of the Peshawur telegrams. It went on to say that skilled doctors were night and day watching over the man's life; and that he would eventually recover if the fee to the potent sorcerer, whose servant was the head in the basin, were doubled.

Here the mistake from the artistic point of view came in. To ask for twice your stipulated fee in a voice that Lazarus might have used when he rose from the dead, is absurd. Janoo, who is really a woman of masculine intellect, saw this as quickly as I did. I heard her say, '*Asli nahin! Fareib!*'[8] scornfully under her breath; and just as she said so, the light in the basin died out, the head stopped talking, and we heard the room door creak on its hinges. Then Janoo struck a match, lit the lamp, and we saw that the head, basin, and seal-cutter were gone. Suddhoo was wringing his hands, and explaining to anyone who cared to listen that, if his chances of eternal salvation depended on it, he could not raise another two hundred rupees. Azizun was nearly in hysterics in the corner; while Janoo sat down composedly on one of his beds to discuss the probabilities of the whole thing being a *bunao*, or 'make-up'.

I explained as much as I knew of the seal-cutter's way of *jadoo*; but her argument was much more simple. 'The magic that is always demanding gifts is no true magic,' said she. 'My mother told me that the only potent love-spells are those which are told you for love. This seal-cutter man is a liar and a devil. I dare not tell, do anything, or get anything done, because I am in debt to Bhagwan Dass the *bunnia*⁹ for two gold rings and a heavy anklet. I must get my food from his shop. The seal-cutter is the friend of Bhagwan Dass, and he would poison my food. A fool's *jadoo* has been going on for ten days, and has cost Suddhoo many rupees each night. The seal-cutter used black hens and lemons and charms before. He never showed us anything like this till to-night. Azizun is a fool, and will be a *purdahnashin*¹⁰ soon. Suddhoo has lost his strength and lost his wits. See now! I had hoped to get from Suddhoo many rupees while he lived, and many more after his death; and behold, he is spending everything on that offspring of a devil and a she-ass, the seal-cutter!'

Here I said, 'But what induced Suddhoo to drag *me* into the business? Of course I can speak to the seal-cutter, and he shall refund. The whole thing is child's talk – shame – and senseless.'

'Suddhoo *is* an old child,' said Janoo. 'He has lived on the roofs these seventy years and is as senseless as a milch-goat. He brought you here to assure himself that he was not breaking any law of the Sirkar, whose salt he ate many years ago. He worships the dust off the feet of the seal-cutter, and that cow-devourer has forbidden him to go and see his son. What does Suddhoo know of your laws or the lightning-post? *I* have to watch his money going day by day to that lying beast below.'

Janoo stamped her foot on the floor and nearly cried with vexation; while Suddhoo was whimpering under a blanket in the corner, and Azizun was trying to guide the pipe-stem to his foolish old mouth.

Now, the case stands thus. Unthinkingly, I have laid myself open to the charge of aiding and abetting the seal-cutter in obtaining money under false pretences, which is forbidden by Section 420 of the Indian Penal Code. I am helpless in the matter for these reasons. I cannot inform the Police. What witnesses would support my statements? Janoo refuses flatly, and Azizun is a married woman somewhere near Bareilly – lost in this big India of ours. I dare not again take the law into my own hands, and speak to the seal-cutter; for certain am I that, not only would

Suddhoo disbelieve me, but this step would end in the poisoning of Janoo, who is bound hand and foot by her debt to the *bunnia*. Suddhoo is an old dotard; and whenever we meet mumbles my idiotic joke that the Sirkar rather patronizes the Black Art than otherwise. His son is well now; but Suddhoo is completely under the influence of the seal-cutter, by whose advice he regulates the affairs of his life. Janoo watches daily the money that she hoped to wheedle out of Suddhoo taken by the seal-cutter and becomes daily more furious and sullen.

She will never tell, because she dare not; but, unless something happens to prevent her, I am afraid that the seal-cutter will die of cholera – the white arsenic kind – about the middle of May. And thus I shall be privy to a murder in the House of Suddhoo!

⟨ His Wedded Wife ⟩

Cry 'Murder!' in the market-place, and each
Will turn upon his neighbour anxious eyes
That ask: 'Art thou the man?' We hunted Cain,
Some centuries ago, across the world.
That bred the fear our own misdeeds maintain
To-day.

Vibart's Moralities

Shakespeare says something[1] about worms, or it may be giants
or beetles, turning if you tread on them too severely. The safest
plan is never to tread on a worm – not even on the last new
subaltern from Home, with his buttons hardly out of their tissue-
paper, and the red of sappy English beef in his cheeks. This is a
story of the worm that turned. For the sake of brevity, we will
call Henry Augustus Ramsay Faizanne 'The Worm', though he
really was an exceedingly pretty boy, without a hair on his face,
and with a waist like a girl's, when he came out to the Second
'Shikarris' and was made unhappy in several ways. The
'Shikarris'[2] are a high-caste regiment, and you must be able to
do things well – play a banjo, or ride more than a little, or sing,
or act – to get on with them.

The Worm did nothing except fall off his pony, and knock
chips out of the gate-posts with his trap. Even that became
monotonous after a time. He objected to whist, cut the cloth at
billiards, sang out of tune, kept very much to himself, and wrote
to his Mamma and sisters at Home. Four of these five things were
vices which the 'Shikarris' objected to and set themselves to
eradicate. Every one knows how subalterns are, by brother
subalterns, softened and not permitted to be ferocious. It is good
and wholesome, and does no one any harm, unless tempers are
lost; and then there is trouble. There was a man once –

The 'Shikarris' *shikarred* The Worm very much, and he bore

everything without winking. He was so good and so anxious to learn, and flushed so pink, that his education was cut short, and he was left to his own devices by every one except the Senior Subaltern, who continued to make life a burden to The Worm. The Senior Subaltern meant no harm; but his chaff was coarse and he didn't quite understand where to stop. He had been waiting too long for his Company; and that always sours a man. Also he was in love, which made him worse.

One day, after he had borrowed The Worm's trap for a lady who never existed, had used it himself all the afternoon, had sent a note to The Worm, purporting to come from the lady, and was telling the Mess all about it, The Worm rose in his place and said, in his quiet, lady-like voice: 'That was a very pretty sell; but I'll lay you a month's pay to a month's pay when you get your step, that I work a sell on you that you'll remember for the rest of your days, and the Regiment after you when you're dead or broke.' The Worm wasn't angry in the least, and the rest of the Mess shouted. Then the Senior Subaltern looked at The Worm from the boots upwards, and down again, and said, 'Done, Baby.' The Worm held the rest of the Mess to witness that the bet had been taken, and retired into a book with a sweet smile.

Two months passed, and the Senior Subaltern still educated The Worm, who began to move about a little more as the hot weather came on. I have said that the Senior Subaltern was in love. The curious thing is that a girl was in love with the Senior Subaltern. Though the Colonel said awful things, and the Majors snorted, and the married Captains looked unutterable wisdom, and the juniors scoffed, those two were engaged.

The Senior Subaltern was so pleased with getting his Company and his acceptance at the same time that he forgot to worry The Worm. The girl was a pretty girl, and had money of her own. She does not come into this story at all.

One night, at the beginning of the hot weather, all the Mess, except The Worm, who had gone to his own room to write Home letters, were sitting on the platform outside the Mess House. The Band had finished playing, but no one wanted to go in. And the Captains' wives were there also. The folly of a man in love is unlimited. The Senior Subaltern had been holding forth on the merits of the girl he was engaged to, and the ladies were purring approval while the men yawned, when there was a rustle of skirts in the dark, and a tired, faint voice lifted itself.

'Where's my husband?'

I do not wish in the least to reflect on the morality of the 'Shikarris'; but it is on record that four men jumped up as if they had been shot. Three of them were married men. Perhaps they were afraid that their wives had come from Home unbeknownst. The fourth said that he had acted on the impulse of the moment. He explained this afterwards.

Then the voice cried, 'Oh, Lionel!' Lionel was the Senior Subaltern's name. A woman came into the little circle of light by the candles on the peg-tables, stretching out her hands to the dark where the Senior Subaltern was, and sobbing. We rose to our feet, feeling that things were going to happen and ready to believe the worst. In this bad, small world of ours, one knows so little of the life of the next man – which, after all, is entirely his own concern – that one is not surprised when a crash comes. Anything might turn up any day for any one. Perhaps the Senior Subaltern had been trapped in his youth. Men are crippled that way occasionally. We didn't know. We wanted to hear; and the Captains' wives were as anxious as we. If he had been trapped, he was to be excused; for the woman from nowhere, in the dusty shoes and grey travelling-dress, was very lovely, with black hair and great eyes full of tears. She was tall with a fine figure, and her voice had a running sob in it pitiful to hear. As soon as the Senior Subaltern stood up, she threw her arms around his neck, and called him 'my darling', and said she could not bear waiting alone in England, and his letters were so short and cold, and she was his to the end of the world, and would he forgive her? This did not sound quite like a lady's way of speaking. It was too demonstrative.

Things seemed black indeed, and the Captains' wives peered under their eyebrows at the Senior Subaltern, and the Colonel's face set like the Day of Judgment framed in grey bristles, and no one spoke for a while.

Next the Colonel said, very shortly, 'Well, sir?' and the woman sobbed afresh. The Senior Subaltern was half choked with the arms round his neck, but he gasped out: 'It's a damned lie! I never had a wife in my life!' – 'Don't swear,' said the Colonel. 'Come into the Mess. We must sift this clear somehow.' And he sighed to himself, for he believed in his 'Shikarris', did the Colonel.

We trooped into the ante-room, under the full lights, and there we saw how beautiful the woman was. She stood up in the middle of us all, sometimes choking with crying, then hard and proud, and then holding her arms to the Senior Subaltern. It was like the fourth act of a tragedy. She told us how the Senior Subaltern had married her when he was Home on leave eighteen months before; and she seemed to know all that we knew, and more too, of his people and his past life. He was white and ashy-grey, trying now and again to break into the torrent of her words; and we, seeing how lovely she was and what a criminal he looked, esteemed him a beast of the worst kind. We felt sorry for him, though.

I shall never forget the indictment of the Senior Subaltern by his wife. Nor will he. It was so sudden, rushing out of the dark, unannounced, into our dull lives. The Captains' wives stood back; but their eyes were alight, and you could see that they had already convicted and sentenced the Senior Subaltern. The Colonel seemed five years older. One Major was shading his eyes with his hand and watching the woman from underneath it. Another was chewing his moustache and smiling quietly as if he were witnessing a play. Full in the open space in the centre, by the whist-tables, the Senior Subaltern's terrier was hunting fleas. I remember all this as clearly as though a photograph were in my hand. I remember the look of horror on the Senior Subaltern's face. It was rather like seeing a man hanged, but much more interesting. Finally, the woman wound up by saying that the Senior Subaltern carried a double F. M. in tattoo on his left shoulder. We all knew that, and to our innocent minds it seemed to clinch the matter. But one of the bachelor Majors said very politely, 'I presume that your marriage-certificate would be more to the purpose.'

That roused the woman. She stood up and sneered at the Senior Subaltern for a cur, and abused the Major and the Colonel and all the rest. Then she wept, and then she pulled a paper from

her breast, saying imperially, 'Take that! And let my husband –
my lawfully-wedded husband – read it aloud – if he dare!'

There was a hush, and the men looked into each other's eyes
as the Senior Subaltern came forward in a dazed and dizzy way,
and took the paper. We were wondering, as we stared, whether
there was anything against any one of us that might turn up later
on. The Senior Subaltern's throat was dry; but, as he ran his eye
over the paper, he broke out into a hoarse cackle of relief, and
said to the woman, 'You young blackguard!' But the woman had
fled through a door, and on the paper was written, 'This is to
certify that I, The Worm, have paid in full my debts to the Senior
Subaltern, and, further, that the Senior Subaltern is my debtor,
by agreement on the 23rd of February, as by the Mess attested,
to the extent of one month's Captain's pay, in the lawful currency
of the Indian Empire.'

Then a deputation set off for The Worm's quarters, and found
him, betwixt and between, unlacing his stays, with the hat, wig,
and serge dress, on the bed. He came over as he was, and the
'Shikarris' shouted till the Gunners' Mess sent over to know if
they might have a share of the fun. I think we were all, except
the Colonel and the Senior Subaltern, a little disappointed that
the scandal had come to nothing. But that is human nature. There
could be no two words about The Worm's acting. It leaned as
near to a nasty tragedy as anything this side of a joke can. When
most of the Subalterns sat upon him with sofa-cushions to find
out why he had not said that acting was his strong point, he
answered very quietly, 'I don't think you ever asked me. I used
to act at Home with my sisters.' But no acting with girls could
account for The Worm's display that night. Personally, I think
it was in bad taste; besides being dangerous. There is no sort of
use in playing with fire, even for fun.

The 'Shikarris' made him President of the Regimental Dramatic Club; and, when the Senior Subaltern paid up his debt,
which he did at once, The Worm sank the money in scenery and
dresses. He was a good Worm and the 'Shikarris' are proud of
him. The only drawback is that he has been christened 'Mrs
Senior Subaltern'; and, as there are now two Mrs Senior Subalterns in the station, this is sometimes confusing to strangers.

Later on, I will tell you of a case something like this, but with all the jest left out and nothing in it but real trouble.

The Broken-Link Handicap

While the snaffle holds, or the long-neck stings,
While the big beam tilts, or the last bell rings,
While horses are horses to train and to race,
Then women and wine take a second place
    For me – for me –
    While a short 'ten-three'
Has a field to squander or fence to face!
                  Song of the G. R.[1]

There are more ways of running a horse to suit your book than pulling his head off in the straight. Some men forget this. Understand clearly that all racing is rotten – as everything connected with losing money must be. In India, in addition to its inherent rottenness, it has the merit of being two-thirds sham; looking pretty on paper only. Every one knows every one else far too well for business purposes. How on earth can you rack and harry and post a man for his losings, when you are fond of his wife, and live in the same station with him? He says, 'on the Monday following,' 'I can't settle just yet.' You say, 'All right, old man,' and think yourself lucky if you pull off nine hundred out of a two-thousand-rupee debt. Any way you look at it, Indian racing is immoral, and expensively immoral. Which is much worse.[2] If a man wants your money he ought to ask for it, or send round a subscription-list, instead of juggling about the country with an Australian larrikin, a 'brumby', with as much breed as the boy, a brace of *chumars* in gold-laced caps, three or four *ekka*-ponies with hogged manes, and a switch-tailed demirep of a mare called Arab because she has a kink in her flag. Racing leads to the money-lender quicker than anything else. But if you have no conscience and no sentiments, and good hands, and some knowledge of pace, and ten years' experience of horses, and several

157

thousand rupees a month, I believe that you can occasionally contrive to pay your shoeing-bills.[3]

Did you ever know Shackles – b. w. g.,[4] 15. 1⅜ – coarse, loose, mule-like ears – barrel as long as a gate-post – tough as a telegraph-wire – and the queerest brute that ever looked through a bridle? He was of no brand, being one of an ear-nicked mob taken into the *Bucephalus* at £4 10s. a head to make up freight, and sold raw and out of condition at Calcutta for Rs.275. People who lost money on him called him a 'brumby'; but if ever any horse had Harpoon's shoulders and The Gin's temper, Shackles was that horse. Two miles was his own particular distance. He trained himself, ran himself, and rode himself; and, if his jockey insulted him by giving him hints, he shut up at once and bucked the boy off. He objected to dictation. Two or three of his owners did not understand this, and lost money in consequence. At last he was bought by a man who discovered that, if a race was to be won, Shackles and Shackles only, would win it in his own way, so long as his jockey sat still. This man had a riding-boy called Brunt – a lad from Perth, West Australia – and he taught Brunt, with a trainer's whip, the hardest thing a jock can learn – to sit still, and keep on sitting still. When Brunt fairly grasped this truth, Shackles devastated the country. No weight could stop him at his own distance; and the fame of Shackles spread from Ajmir in the South, to Chedputter in the North. There was no horse like Shackles, so long as he was allowed to do his work in his own way. But he was beaten in the end; and the story of his fall is enough to make angels weep.

At the lower end of Chedputter racecourse, just before the turn into the straight, the track passes close to a couple of old brick-mounds enclosing a funnel-shaped hollow. The big end of the funnel is not six feet from the railings on the off side. The astounding peculiarity of the course is that, if you stand at one particular place, about half a mile away, inside the course, and speak at ordinary pitch, your voice just hits the funnel of the brick-mounds and makes a curious whining echo there. A man discovered this one morning by accident while out training with a friend. He marked the place to stand and speak from with a couple of bricks, and he kept his knowledge to himself. *Every*

peculiarity of a course is worth remembering in a country where
rats play mischief with the elephant-litter, and Stewards build
jumps to suit their own stables. This man ran a very fairish
country-bred, a long, racking high mare with the temper of a
fiend, and the paces of an airy wandering seraph – a drifty, glidy
stretch. The mare was, as a delicate tribute to Mrs Reiver, called
'The Lady Regula Baddun' – or for short, Regula Baddun.

Shackles' jockey, Brunt, was a quite well-behaved boy, but his
nerve had been shaken. He began his career by riding jump-races
in Melbourne, where a few Stewards want lynching, and was one
of the jockeys who came through the awful butchery – perhaps
you will recollect it – of the Maribyrnong Plate. The walls were
colonial ramparts – logs of *jarrah*[5] spiked into masonry – with
wings as strong as church buttresses. Once in his stride, a horse
had to jump or fall. He couldn't run out. In the Maribyrnong
Plate twelve horses were jammed at the second wall. Red Hat,
leading, fell this side, and threw out The Gled, and the ruck came
up behind, and the space between wing and wing was one
struggling, screaming, kicking shambles. Four jockeys were taken
out dead; three were very badly hurt, and Brunt was among the
three. He told the story of the Maribyrnong Plate sometimes; and
when he described how Whalley on Red Hat said, as the mare
fell under him, 'God ha' mercy, I'm done for!' and how, next
instant, Sithee There and White Otter had crushed the life out
of poor Whalley, and the dust hid a small hell of men and
horses, no one marvelled that Brunt had dropped jump-races and
Australia together. Regula Baddun's owner knew that story by
heart. Brunt never varied it in the telling. He had no education.

Shackles came to the Chedputter Autumn races one year, and
his owner walked about insulting the sportsmen of Chedputter
generally, till they went to the Honorary Secretary in a body and
said, 'Appoint handicappers, and arrange a race which shall break
Shackles and humble the pride of his owner.' The Districts rose
against Shackles and sent up of their best: Ousel, who was
supposed to be able to do his mile in 1.53; Petard, the stud-bred,
trained by a cavalry regiment who knew how to train; Gringalet,
the ewe-lamb of the 75th; Bobolink, the pride of Peshawur; and
many others.

They called that race The Broken-Link Handicap, because it was to smash Shackles; and the Handicappers piled on the weights, and the Fund gave eight hundred rupees, and the distance was 'round the course for all horses'. Shackles' owner said, 'You can arrange the race with regard to Shackles only. So long as you don't bury him under weight-cloths, I don't mind.' Regula Baddun's owner said, 'I throw in my mare to fret Ousel. Six furlongs is Regula's distance, and she will then lie down and die. So also will Ousel, for his jockey doesn't understand a waiting race.' Now, this was a lie, for Regula had been in work for two months at Dehra, and her chances were good, always supposing that Shackles broke a blood-vessel – or Brunt moved on him.

The plunging in the lotteries was fine. They filled eight thousand-rupee lotteries on the Broken-Link Handicap, and the account in the *Pioneer* said that 'favouritism was divided'. In plain English, the various contingents were wild on their respective horses; for the Handicappers had done their work well. The Honorary Secretary shouted himself hoarse through the din; and the smoke of the cheroots was like the smoke, and the rattling of the dice-boxes like the rattle, of small-arm fire.

Ten horses started – very level– and Regula Baddun's owner cantered out on his hack to a place inside the circle of the course, where two bricks had been thrown. He faced towards the brick-mounds at the lower end of the course and waited.

The story of the running is in the *Pioneer*. At the end of the first mile, Shackles crept out of the ruck, well on the outside, ready to get round the turn, lay hold of the bit and spin up the straight before the others knew he had got away. Brunt was sitting still, perfectly happy, listening to the 'drum-drum-drum' of the hoofs behind, and knowing that, in about twenty strides, Shackles would draw one deep breath and go up the last half-mile like the Flying Dutchman. As Shackles went short to take the turn and came abreast of the brick-mound, Brunt heard, above the noise of the wind in his ears, a whining, wailing voice on the off side, saying, 'God ha' mercy, I'm done for!' In one stride, Brunt saw the whole seething smash of the Maribyrnong Plate before him, started in his saddle, and gave a yell of terror. The start brought the heels into Shackles' side, and the scream hurt Shackles' feelings. He couldn't stop dead; but he put out his feet and slid along for fifty yards, and then, very gravely and judicially, bucked off Brunt — a shaking, terror-stricken lump — while Regula Baddun made a neck-and-neck race with Bobolink up the straight, and won by a short head — Petard a bad third. Shackles' owner, in the Stand, tried to think that his field-glasses had gone wrong. Regula Baddun's owner, waiting by the two bricks, gave one deep sigh of relief, and cantered back to the Stand. He had won, in lotteries and bets, about fifteen thousand.

It was a Broken-Link Handicap with a vengeance. It broke nearly all the men concerned, and nearly broke the heart of Shackles' owner. He went down to interview Brunt. The boy lay, livid and gasping with fright, where he had tumbled off. The sin of losing the race never seemed to strike him. All he knew was that Whalley had 'called' him, that the 'call' was a warning; and, were he cut in two for it, he would never get up again. His nerve had gone altogether, and he only asked his master to give him a good thrashing, and let him go. He was fit for nothing, he said. He got his dismissal, and crept up to the paddock, white as chalk, with blue lips, his knees giving way under him. People said nasty things in the paddock; but Brunt never heeded. He changed into tweeds, took his stick and went down the road, still shaking with fright, and muttering over and over again, 'God ha' mercy, I'm done for!' To the best of my knowledge and belief, he spoke the truth.

So now you know how the Broken-Link Handicap was run and won. Of course you don't believe it. You would credit anything about Russia's designs on India, or the recommendations of the Currency Commission; but a little bit of sober fact is more than you can stand.

⟨ Beyond the Pale ⟩

Love heeds not caste nor sleep a broken bed. I went in search of love
and lost myself.

Hindu Proverb

A man should, whatever happens, keep to his own caste, race and
breed. Let the White go the White and the Black to the Black.
Then whatever trouble falls is in the ordinary course of things –
neither sudden, alien, nor unexpected.

This is the story of a man who wilfully stepped beyond the safe
limits of decent everyday society, and paid for it heavily.

He knew too much in the first instance; and he saw too much in
the second. He took too deep an interest in native life; but he
will never do so again.

Deep away in the heart of the City, behind Jitha Megji's
bustee,¹ lies Amir Nath's Gully, which ends in a dead-wall pierced
by one grated window. At the head of the Gully is a big cow-
byre, and the walls on either side of the Gully are without
windows. Neither Suchet Singh nor Gaur Chand approve of their
women-folk looking into the world. If Durga Charan had been
of their opinion he would have been a happier man to-day, and
little Bisesa would have been able to knead her own bread. Her
room looked out through the grated window into the narrow
dark Gully where the sun never came and where the buffaloes
wallowed in the blue slime. She was a widow, about fifteen years
old, and she prayed the Gods, day and night, to send her a lover;
for she did not approve of living alone.

One day, the man – Trejago his name was – came into Amir
Nath's Gully on an aimless wandering; and, after he had passed
the buffaloes, stumbled over a big heap of cattle-food.

Then he saw that the Gully ended in a trap, and heard a little
laugh from behind the grated window. It was a pretty little laugh,

and Trejago, knowing that, for all practical purposes, the old *Arabian Nights* are good guides, went forward to the window, and whispered that verse of 'The Love Song of Har Dyal' which begins:

Can a man stand upright in the face of the naked Sun; or a lover in the Presence of his Beloved?
If my feet fail me, O Heart of my Heart, am I to blame, being blinded by the glimpse of your beauty?

There came the faint *tchink* of a woman's bracelets from behind the grating, and a little voice went on with the song at the fifth verse:

Alas! alas! Can the Moon tell the Lotus of her love when the Gate of Heaven is shut and the clouds gather for the Rains?
They have taken my Beloved, and driven her with the pack-horses to the North.
There are iron chains on the feet that were set on my heart.
Call to the bowmen to make ready –

The voice stopped suddenly, and Trejago walked out of Amir Nath's Gully, wondering who in the world could have capped 'The Love Song of Har Dyal' so neatly.

Next morning, as he was driving to office, an old woman threw a packet into his dogcart. In the packet was the half of a broken glass bangle, one flower of the blood-red *dhak*, a pinch of *bhusa* or cattle-food, and eleven cardamoms.[2] That packet was a letter – not a clumsy compromising letter, but an innocent, unintelligible lover's epistle.

Trejago knew far too much about these things, as I have said. No Englishman should be able to translate object-letters. But Trejago spread all the trifles on the lid of his office-box and began to puzzle them out.

A broken glass bangle stands for a Hindu widow all India over; because, when her husband dies, a woman's bracelets are broken on her wrists. Trejago saw the meaning of the little bit of glass. The flower of the *dhak* means diversely 'desire', 'come', 'write', or 'danger', according to the other things with it. One cardamom means 'jealousy'; but when any article is duplicated in an object-letter, it loses its symbolic meaning and stands merely for one of a number indicating time, or, if incense, curds, or saffron be sent also, place. The message ran then: 'A widow – *dhak* flower and *bhusa* – at eleven o'clock.' The pinch of *bhusa* enlightened Trejago. He saw – this kind of letter leaves much to instinctive knowledge – that the *bhusa* referred to the big heap of cattle-food over which he had fallen in Amir Nath's Gully, and that the message must come from the person behind the grating; she being a widow. So the message ran then: 'A widow, in the Gully in which is the heap of *bhusa*, desires you to come at eleven o'clock.'

Trejago threw all the rubbish into the fireplace and laughed. He knew that men in the East do not make love under windows at eleven in the forenoon, nor do women fix appointments a week in advance. So he went, that very night at eleven, into Amir Nath's Gully, clad in a *boorka*,[3] which cloaks a man as well as a woman. Directly the gongs of the City made the hour, the little voice behind the grating took up 'The Love Song of Har Dyal' at the verse where the Pathan girl calls upon Har Dyal to return. The song is really pretty in the vernacular. In English you miss the wail of it. It runs something like this:

> Alone upon the housetops, to the North
>   I turn and watch the lightnings in the sky, –
> The glamour of thy footsteps in the North.
>   *Come back to me, Beloved, or I die!*
>
> Below my feet the still bazar is laid –
>   Far, far below the weary camels lie, –
> The camels and the captives of thy raid.
>   *Come back to me, Beloved, or I die!*
>
> My father's wife is old and harsh with years,
>   And drudge of all my father's house am I. –
> My bread is sorrow and my drink is tears.
>   *Come back to me, Beloved, or I die!*

As the song stopped, Trejago stepped up under the grating and whispered, 'I am here.'

Bisesa was good to look upon.

That night was the beginning of many strange things, and of a double life so wild that Trejago to-day sometimes wonders if it

were not all a dream. Bisesa, or her old handmaiden who had
thrown the object-letter, had detached the heavy grating from
the brick-work of the wall; so that the window slid inside, leaving
only a square of raw masonry into which an active man might
climb.

In the daytime, Trejago drove through his routine of office
work, or put on his calling-clothes and called on the ladies of the
station, wondering how long they would know him if they knew
of poor little Bisesa. At night, when all the City was still, came
the walk under the evil-smelling *boorka*, the patrol through Jitha
Megji's *bustee*, the quick turn into Amir Nath's Gully between
the sleeping cattle and the dead walls, and then, last of all, Bisesa,
and the deep, even breathing of the old woman who slept outside
the door of the bare little room that Durga Charan allotted to his
sister's daughter. Who or what Durga Charan was, Trejago never
inquired; and why in the world he was not discovered and knifed
never occurred to him till his madness was over, and Bisesa ...
But this comes later.

Bisesa was an endless delight to Trejago. She was as ignorant
as a bird; and her distorted versions of the rumours from the
outside world that had reached her in her room, amused Trejago
almost as much as her lisping attempts to pronounce his name –
'Christopher'. The first syllable was always more than she could
manage, and she made funny little gestures with her roseleaf
hands, as one throwing the name away, and then, kneeling before
Trejago, asked him, exactly as an Englishwoman would do, if he
were sure he loved her. Trejago swore that he loved her more
than any one else in the world. Which was true.

After a month of this folly, the exigencies of his other life
compelled Trejago to be especially attentive to a lady of his
acquaintance. You may take it for a fact that anything of this kind
is not only noticed and discussed by a man's own race, but by
some hundred and fifty natives as well. Trejago had to walk with
this lady and talk to her at the Bandstand, and once or twice to
drive with her; never for an instant dreaming this would affect
his dearer, out-of-the-way life. But the news flew, in the usual
mysterious fashion, from mouth to mouth, till Bisesa's duenna
heard of it and told Bisesa. The child was so troubled that she

did the household work evilly, and was beaten by Durga Charan's wife in consequence.

A week later, Bisesa taxed Trejago with the flirtation. She understood no gradations and spoke openly. Trejago laughed, and Bisesa stamped her little feet – little feet, light as marigold flowers, that could lie in the palm of a man's one hand.

Much that is written about Oriental passion and impulsiveness is exaggerated and compiled at second hand; but a little of it is true, and when an Englishman finds that little, it is quite as startling as any passion in his own proper life. Bisesa raged and stormed, and finally threatened to kill herself if Trejago did not at once drop the alien Memsahib who had come between them. Trejago tried to explain, and to show her that she did not understand these things from a Western standpoint. Bisesa drew herself up, and said simply:

'I do not. I know only this – it is not good that I should have made you dearer than my own heart to me, Sahib. You are an Englishman. I am only a black girl' – she was fairer than bar-gold in the Mint – 'and the widow of a black man.'

Then she sobbed and said: 'But on my soul and my Mother's soul, I love you. There shall no harm come to you, whatever happens to me.'

Trejago argued with the child, and tried to soothe her, but she seemed quite unreasonably disturbed. Nothing would satisfy her save that all relations between them should end. He was to go away at once. And he went. As he dropped out of the window, she kissed his forehead twice, and he walked home wondering.

A week, and then three weeks, passed without a sign from Bisesa. Trejago, thinking that the rupture had lasted quite long enough, went down to Amir Nath's Gully for the fifth time in the three weeks, hoping that his rap at the sill of the shifting grating would be answered. He was not disappointed.

There was a young moon, and one stream of light fell down into Amir Nath's Gully, and struck the grating, which was drawn away as he knocked. From the black dark, Bisesa held out her arms into the moonlight. Both hands had been cut off at the wrists, and the stumps were nearly healed.

Then, as Bisesa bowed her head between her arms and sobbed,

some one in the room grunted like a wild beast, and something sharp – knife, sword, or spear – thrust at Trejago in his *boorka*. The stroke missed his body, but cut into one of the muscles of the groin, and he limped slightly from the wound for the rest of his days.

The grating went into its place. There was no sign whatever from inside the house – nothing but the moonlight strip on the high wall, and the blackness of Amir Nath's Gully behind.

The next thing Trejago remembers, after raging and shouting like a madman between those pitiless walls, is that he found himself near the river as the dawn was breaking, threw away his *boorka* and went home bareheaded.

What was the tragedy – whether Bisesa had, in a fit of causeless despair, told everything, or the intrigue had been discovered and she tortured to tell; whether Durga Charan knew his name, and what became of Bisesa – Trejago does not know to this day. Something horrible had happened, and the thought of what it must have been comes upon Trejago in the night now and again, and keeps him company till the morning. One special feature of the case is that he does not know where lies the front of Durga Charan's house. It may open on to a courtyard common to two or more houses, or it may lie behind any one of the gates of Jitha Megji's *bustee*. Trejago cannot tell. He cannot get Bisesa – poor little Bisesa – back again. He has lost her in the City where each man's house is as guarded and as unknowable as the grave; and the grating that opens into Amir Nath's Gully has been walled up.

But Trejago pays his calls regularly, and is reckoned a very decent sort of man.

There is nothing peculiar about him, except a slight stiffness, caused by a riding-strain, in the right leg.

⟨ In Error ⟩

They burnt a corpse upon the sand –
    The light shone out afar;
It guided home the plunging boats
    That beat from Zanzibar.
Spirit of Fire, where'er Thy altars rise,
Thou art the Light of Guidance to our eyes!
                            Salsette Boat-Song

There is hope for a man who gets publicly and riotously drunk
more often than he ought to do; but there is no hope for the man
who drinks secretly and alone in his own house – the man who is
never seen to drink.

This is a rule; so there must be an exception to prove it.
Moriarty's case was that exception.

He was a Civil Engineer, and the Government, very kindly,
put him quite by himself in an out-district, with nobody but
natives to talk to and a great deal of work to do. He did his work
well in the four years he was utterly alone; but he picked up the
vice of secret and solitary drinking, and came up out of the
wilderness more old and worn and haggard than the dead-alive
life had any right to make him. You know the saying that a man
who has been alone in the jungle for more than a year is never
quite sane all his life after. People credited Moriarty's queerness
of manner and moody ways to the solitude, and said that it showed
how Government spoilt the futures of its best men. Moriarty had
built himself the plinth of a very good reputation in the bridge-
dam-girder line. But he knew, every night of the week, that he
was taking steps to undermine that reputation with L. L. L. and
Christopher[1] and little nips of liqueurs, and filth of that kind. He
had a sound constitution and a great brain, or else he would have
broken down and died like a sick camel in the District; as better
men have done before him.

In Error

Government ordered him to Simla after he had come out of the desert; and he went up meaning to try for a post then vacant. That season, Mrs Reiver – perhaps you will remember her – was in the height of her power, and many men lay under her yoke. Everything bad that could be said has already been said about Mrs Reiver, in another tale. Moriarty was heavily-built and handsome, very quiet, and nervously anxious to please his neighbours when he wasn't sunk in a brown study. He started a good deal at sudden noises or if spoken to without warning; and, when you watched him drinking his glass of water at dinner, you could see the hand shake a little. But all this was put down to nervousness, and the quiet, steady, sip-sip-sip, fill and sip-sip-sip again that went on in his own room when he was by himself, was never known. Which was miraculous, seeing how everything in a man's private life is public property in India.

Moriarty was drawn, not into Mrs Reiver's set, because they were not his sort, but into the power of Mrs Reiver, and he fell down in front of her and made a goddess of her. This was due to his coming fresh out of the jungle to a big town. He could not scale things properly or see who was what.

Because Mrs Reiver was cold and hard he said she was stately and dignified. Because she had no brains, and could not talk cleverly, he said she was reserved and shy. Mrs Reiver shy! Because she was unworthy of honour or reverence from any one, he reverenced her from a distance and dowered her with all the virtues in the Bible and most of those in Shakespeare.

This big, dark, abstracted man who was so nervous when a pony cantered behind him, used to moon in the train of Mrs Reiver, blushing with pleasure when she threw a word or two his way. His admiration was strictly platonic. Even other women saw and admitted this. He did not move about in Simla, so he heard nothing against his idol: which was satisfactory. Mrs Reiver took no special notice of him, beyond seeing that he was added to her list of admirers, and going for a walk with him now and then, just to show that he was her property, claimable as such. Moriarty must have done most of the talking, for Mrs Reiver couldn't talk much to a man of his stamp; and the little she said could not have been profitable. What Moriarty believed in, as he had good reason to, was Mrs Reiver's influence over him, and, in that belief, he set himself seriously to try to do away with the vice that only he himself knew of.

His experiences while he was fighting with it must have been peculiar, but he never described them. Sometimes he would hold off from everything except water for a week. Then, on a rainy night, when no one had asked him out to dinner, and there was a nice fire in his room, and everything comfortable, he would sit down and make a wet night of it by adding little nip to little nip, planning schemes of reformation meanwhile, until he threw himself on his bed hopelessly drunk. He suffered next morning.

One night the big crash came. He was troubled in his own mind over his attempts to make himself 'worthy of the friend-ship' of Mrs Reiver. The past ten days had been very bad ones, and the end of it all was that he received the arrears of two and three-quarter years of sipping in one attack of *delirium tremens* of the subdued kind; beginning with suicidal depression, going on to fits and starts and hysteria, and ending with downright raving. As he sat in a chair in front of the fire, or walked up and down the room picking a handkerchief to pieces, you heard what poor Moriarty really thought of Mrs Reiver, for he raved about her and his own fall for the most part; though he ravelled some P. W. D. accounts into the same skein of thought. He talked and talked and talked in a low dry whisper to himself, and there was no stopping him. He seemed to know that there was something wrong, and twice tried to pull himself together and confer rationally with the Doctor; but his mind ran out of control at once, and he fell back to a whisper and the story of his troubles. It is terrible to hear a big man babbling like a child of all that a man usually locks up, and puts away in the deep of his heart. Moriarty read out his very soul for the benefit of any one who was in the room between ten-thirty that night and two-forty-five next morning.

From what he said, one gathered how immense an influence Mrs Reiver held over him, and how thoroughly he felt for his own lapse. His whisperings cannot, of course, be put down here; but they were very instructive – as showing the errors of his estimates.

*

In Error

When the trouble was over, and his few acquaintances were pitying him for the bad attack of jungle-fever that had so pulled him down, Moriarty swore a big oath to himself and went abroad again with Mrs Reiver till the end of the season, adoring her in a quiet and deferential way as an angel from Heaven. Later on, he took to riding – not hacking, but honest riding – which was good proof that he was improving, and you could slam doors behind him without his jumping to his feet with a gasp. That, again, was hopeful.

How he kept his oath, and what it cost him in the beginning, nobody knows. He certainly managed to compass the hardest thing that a man who has drunk heavily can do. He took his peg and wine at dinner; but he never drank alone, and he never let what he drank have the least hold on him.

Once he told a bosom-friend the story of his great trouble, and how the 'influence of a pure honest woman, and an angel as well', had saved him. When the man – startled at anything good being laid to Mrs Reiver's door – laughed, it cost him Moriarty's friendship. Moriarty, who is married now to a woman ten thousand times better than Mrs Reiver – a woman who believes that there is no man on earth as good and clever as her husband – will go down to his grave vowing and protesting that Mrs Reiver saved him from ruin in both worlds.

That she knew anything of Moriarty's weakness nobody believed for a moment. That she would have cut him dead, thrown him over, and acquainted all her friends with her discovery, if she had known of it, nobody who knew her doubted for an instant.

Moriarty thought her something she never was, and in that belief saved himself; which was just as good as though she had been everything that he had imagined.

But the question is, What claim will Mrs Reiver have to the credit of Moriarty's salvation, when her day of reckoning comes?

⟨ A Bank Fraud ⟩

He drank strong waters and his speech was coarse;
   He purchased raiment and forbore to pay;
He stuck a trusting junior with a horse,
   And won gymkhanas in a doubtful way.
Then, 'twixt a vice and folly, turned aside
To do good deeds – and straight to cloak them, lied.

The Mess-Room

If Reggie Burke were in India now he would resent this tale being
told; but as he is in Hong Kong and won't see it, the telling is
safe. He was the man who worked the big fraud on the Sind and
Sialkot Bank. He was manager of an up-country Branch, and a
sound practical man with a large experience of native loan and
insurance work. He could combine the frivolities of ordinary life
with his work, and yet do well. Reggie Burke rode anything that
would let him get up, danced as neatly as he rode, and was wanted
for every sort of amusement in the station.

As he said himself, and as many men found out rather to their
surprise, there were two Burkes, both very much at your service.
'Reggie Burke', between four and ten, ready for anything from a
hot-weather gymkhana to a riding-picnic, and, between ten and
four, 'Mr Reginald Burke, Manager of the Sind and Sialkot
Branch Bank'. You might play polo with him one afternoon and
hear him express his opinions when a man crossed; and you might
call on him next morning to raise a two-thousand-rupee loan
on a five-hundred-pound insurance policy, eighty pounds paid
in premiums. He would recognize you; but you might have some
trouble in recognizing him.

The Directors of the Bank – it had its headquarters in
Calcutta, and its General Manager's word carried weight with the
Government – picked their men well. They had tested Reggie
up to a fairly severe breaking-strain. They trusted him just as

172

much as Directors ever trust Managers. You must see for yourself whether their trust was misplaced.

Reggie's Branch was in a big station, and worked with the usual staff – one Manager, one Accountant, both English, a Cashier, and a horde of native clerks; besides the Police patrol at nights outside. The bulk of its work, for it was in a thriving district, was *hoondi*[1] and accommodation of all kinds. A fool has no grip of this sort of business; and a clever man who does not go about among his clients, and know more than a little of their affairs, is worse than a fool. Reggie was young-looking, clean-shaved, with a twinkle in his eye, and a head that nothing short of a gallon of the Gunners' Madeira could make any impression on.

One day, at a big dinner, he announced casually that the Directors had shifted on to him a Natural Curiosity, from England, in the Accountant line. He was perfectly correct. Mr Silas Riley, Accountant, was a most curious animal – a long, gawky, rawboned Yorkshireman, full of the savage self-conceit that blossoms only in the best county in England. Arrogance was a mild word for the mental attitude of Mr S. Riley. He had worked himself up, after seven years, to a Cashier's position in a Huddersfield Bank; and all his experience lay among the factories of the North. Perhaps he would have done better on the Bombay side, where they are happy with one-half per cent profits, and money is cheap. He was useless for Upper India and a wheat Province, where a man wants a large head and a touch of imagination if he is to turn out satisfactory balance sheets.

He was wonderfully narrow-minded in business, and, being new to the country, had no notion that Indian banking is totally distinct from Home work. Like most clever self-made men, he had much simplicity in his nature; and, somehow or other, had construed the ordinarily polite terms of his letter of engagement into a belief that the Directors had chosen him on account of his special and brilliant talents, and that they set great store by him. This notion grew and crystallized; thus adding to his natural North-country conceit. Further, he was delicate, suffered from some trouble in his chest, and was short in his temper.

You will admit that Reggie had reason to call his new Accountant a Natural Curiosity. The two men failed to hit it off at all.

Riley considered Reggie a wild, feather-headed idiot, given to Heaven only knew what dissipation in low places called 'Messes', and totally unfit for the serious and solemn vocation of banking. He could never get over Reggie's look of youth and 'you-be-damned' air; and he couldn't understand Reggie's friends – clean-built, careless men in the Army – who rode over to big Sunday breakfasts at the Bank, and told sultry stories till Riley got up and left the room. Riley was always showing Reggie how the business ought to be conducted, and Reggie had more than once to remind him that seven years' limited experience between Huddersfield and Beverley did not qualify a man to steer a big up-country business. Then Riley sulked, and referred to himself as a pillar of the Bank and a cherished friend of the Directors, and Reggie tore his hair. If a man's English subordinates fail him in India, he comes to a hard time indeed; for native help has strict limitations. In the winter Riley went sick for weeks at a time with his lung complaint, and this threw more work on Reggie. But he preferred it to the everlasting friction when Riley was well.

One of the Travelling Inspectors of the Bank discovered these collapses and reported them to the Directors. Now, Riley had been foisted on the Bank by an M.P., who wanted the support of Riley's father, who, again, was anxious to get his son out to a warmer climate because of those lungs. The M.P. had an interest in the Bank; but one of the Directors wanted to advance a nominee of his own; and, after Riley's father had died, he made the rest of the Board see that an Accountant who was sick for half the year had better give place to a healthy man. If Riley had known the real story of his appointment, he might have behaved better; but, knowing nothing, his stretches of sickness alternated with restless, persistent, meddling irritation of Reggie, and all the hundred ways in which conceit in a subordinate situation can find play. Reggie used to call him striking and hair-curling names behind his back as a relief to his own feelings; but he never abused him to his face, because he said, 'Riley is such a frail beast that half of his loathsome conceit is due to pains in the chest.'

Late one April, Riley went very sick indeed. The Doctor punched him and thumped him, and told him he would be better before long. Then the Doctor went to Reggie and said, 'Do you know how sick your Accountant is?' – 'No!' said Reggie; 'the worse the better, confound him! He's a clacking nuisance when he's well. I'll let you take away the Bank Safe if you can drug him silent for this hot weather.'

But the Doctor did not laugh. 'Man, I'm not joking,' he said. 'I'll give him another three months in his bed and a week or so more to die in. On my honour and reputation, that's all the grace he has in this world. Consumption has hold of him to the marrow.'

Reggie's face changed at once into the face of 'Mr Reginald Burke', and he answered, 'What can I do?' – 'Nothing,' said the Doctor; 'for all practical purposes the man is dead already. Keep him quiet and cheerful, and tell him he's going to recover. That's all. I'll look after him to the end, of course.'

The Doctor went away, and Reggie sat down to open the evening mail. His first letter was one from the Directors, intimating for his information that Mr Riley was to resign, under a month's notice, by the terms of his agreement, telling Reggie that their letter to Riley would follow, and advising Reggie of the coming of a new Accountant, a man whom Reggie knew and liked.

Reggie lit a cheroot, and, before he had finished smoking, he had sketched the outline of a fraud. He put away – burked[2] – the Directors' letter, and went in to talk to Riley, who was as ungracious as usual, and fretting himself over the way the Bank would run during his illness. He never thought of the extra work on Reggie's shoulders, but solely of the damage to his own prospects of advancement. Then Reggie assured him that everything would be well, and that he, Reggie, would confer with Riley daily on the management of the Bank. Riley was a little soothed, but he hinted in as many words that he did not think much of Reggie's business capacity. Reggie was humble. And he had letters in his desk from the Directors that a Gilbarte or a Hardie[3] might have been proud of!

The days passed in the big darkened house, and the Directors' letter of dismissal to Riley came and was put away by Reggie, who, every evening, brought the books to Riley's room, and showed him what had been going forward, while Riley snarled. Reggie did his best to make statements pleasing to Riley, but the

Accountant was sure that the Bank was going to rack and ruin without him. In June, as the lying in bed told on his spirit, he asked whether his absence had been noted by the Directors, and Reggie said that they had written most sympathetic letters, hoping that he would be able to resume his valuable services before long. He showed Riley the letters; and Riley said that the Directors ought to have written to him direct. A few days later, Reggie opened Riley's mail in the half-light of the room, and gave him the sheet – not the envelope – of a letter to Riley from the Directors. Riley said he would thank Reggie not to interfere with his private papers, especially as Reggie knew he was too weak to open his own letters. Reggie apologized.

Then Riley's mood changed, and he lectured Reggie on his evil ways: his horses and his bad friends. 'Of course, lying here, on my back, Mr Burke, I can't keep you straight; but when I'm well, I *do* hope you'll pay some heed to my words.' Reggie, who had dropped polo, and dinners, and tennis and all, to attend to Riley, said that he was penitent, and settled Riley's head on the pillow, and heard him fret and contradict in hard, dry, hacking whispers, without a sign of impatience. This, at the end of a heavy day's office work, doing double duty, in the latter half of June!

When the new Accountant came, Reggie told him the facts of the case, and announced to Riley that he had a guest staying with him. Riley said that he might have had more consideration than to entertain his 'doubtful friends' at such a time. Reggie made Carron, the new Accountant, sleep at the Club in consequence. Carron's arrival took some of the heavy work off his shoulders, and he had time to attend to Riley's exactions – to explain, soothe, invent, and settle and re-settle the poor wretch in bed, and to forge complimentary letters from Calcutta. At the end of the first month Riley wished to send some money home to his mother. Reggie sent the draft. At the end of the second month Riley's salary came in just the same. Reggie paid it out of his own pocket, and, with it, wrote Riley a beautiful letter from the Directors.

Riley was very ill indeed, but the flame of his life burnt unsteadily. Now and then he would be cheerful and confident about the future, sketching plans for going Home and seeing his mother. Reggie listened patiently when the office work was over, and encouraged him.

At other times Riley insisted on Reggie reading the Bible and grim 'Methody' tracts to him. Out of these tracts he pointed morals directed at his Manager. But he always found time to worry Reggie about the working of the Bank, and to show him where the weak points lay.

This indoor, sickroom life and constant strain wore Reggie down a good deal, and shook his nerves, and lowered his billiard-play by forty points. But the business of the Bank, and the business of the sickroom, had to go on, though the glass was 116° in the shade.

At the end of the third month Riley was sinking fast, and had begun to realize that he was very sick. But the conceit that made him worry Reggie kept him from believing the worst. 'He wants some sort of mental stimulant if he is to drag on,' said the Doctor. 'Keep him interested in life if you care about his living.' So Riley, contrary to all the laws of business and finance, received a 25-per-cent rise of salary from the Directors. The 'mental stimulant' succeeded beautifully. Riley was happy and cheerful, and, as is often the case in consumption, healthiest in mind when the body was weakest. He lingered for a full month, snarling and fretting about the Bank, talking of the future, hearing the Bible read, lecturing Reggie on sin, and wondering when he would be able to move abroad.

But at the end of September, one mercilessly hot evening, he rose up in his bed with a little gasp, and said quickly to Reggie: 'Mr Burke, I am going to die. I know it in myself. My chest is all hollow inside, and there's nothing to breathe with. To the best of my knowledge I have done nowt' – he was returning to the talk of his boyhood – 'to lie heavy on my conscience. God be thanked, I have been preserved from the grosser forms of sin; and I counsel *you*, Mr Burke . . .'

Here his voice died down, and Reggie stooped over him.

'Send my salary for September to my Mother . . . done great things with the Bank if I had been spared . . . mistaken policy . . . no fault of mine . . .'

Then he turned his face to the wall and died.

Reggie drew the sheet over Its face, and went out into the veranda with his last 'mental stimulant' – a letter of condolence and sympathy from the Directors – unused in his pocket.

'If I'd been only ten minutes earlier,' thought Reggie, 'I might have heartened him up to pull through another day.'

{ Tods' Amendment }

The World hath set its heavy yoke
Upon the old white-bearded folk
    Who strive to please the King.
God's mercy is upon the young,
God's wisdom in the baby tongue
    That fears not anything.
                The Parable of Chajju Bhagat[1]

Now Tods' Mamma was a singularly charming woman, and every
one in Simla knew Tods. Most men had saved him from death
on occasions. He was beyond his *ayah*'s control altogether, and
perilled his life daily to find out what[2] would happen if you pulled
a Mountain Battery mule's tail. He was an utterly fearless young
pagan, about six years old, and the only baby who ever broke the
holy calm of the Supreme Legislative Council.

It happened this way: Tods' pet kid got loose, and fled up the
hill, off the Boileaugunge road, Tods after it, until it burst in to
the Viceregal Lodge lawn, then attached to Peterhof. The Council
were sitting at the time, and the windows were open because it
was warm. The Red Lancer in the porch told Tods to go away;
but Tods knew the Red Lancer and most of the Members of
Council personally. Moreover, he had firm hold of the kid's collar,
and was being dragged all across the flower-beds. 'Give my *salaam*
to the long Councillor Sahib, and ask him to help me take Moti
back!' gasped Tods. The Council heard the noise through the
open windows; and, after an interval, was seen the shocking
spectacle of a Legal Member and a Lieutenant-Governor helping,
under the direct patronage of a Commander-in-Chief and a
Viceroy, one small and very dirty boy, in a sailor's suit and a
tangle of brown hair, to coerce a lively and rebellious kid. They
headed it off down the path to the Mall, and Tods went home in
triumph and told his Mamma that *all* the Councillor Sahibs had

been helping him to catch Moti. Whereat his Mamma smacked Tods for interfering with the administration of the Empire; but Tods met the Legal Member the next day, and told him in confidence that if the Legal Member ever wanted to catch a goat, he, Tods, would give him all the help in his power. 'Thank you, Tods,' said the Legal Member.

Tods was the idol of some eighty *jhampanis*, and half as many *saises*. He saluted them all as 'O Brother'. It had never entered his head that any living human being could disobey his orders; and he was the buffer between the servants and his Mamma's wrath. The working of that household turned on Tods, who was adored by every one from the *dhobi* to the dog-boy. Even Futteh Khan, the villainous loafer *khit*[3] from Mussoorie, shirked risking Tods' displeasure for fear his co-mates should look down on him.

So Tods had honour in the land from Boileaugunge to Chota Simla, and ruled justly according to his lights. Of course, he spoke Urdu, but he had also mastered many queer side-speeches like the *chotee bolee*[4] of the women, and held grave converse with shopkeepers and Hill-coolies alike. He was precocious for his age, and his mixing with natives had taught him some of the more bitter truths of life: the meanness and the sordidness of it. He used, over his bread and milk, to deliver solemn and serious aphorisms, translated from the vernacular into the English, that made his Mamma jump and vow that Tods *must* go Home next hot weather.

Just when Tods was in the bloom of his power, the Supreme Legislature were hacking out a Bill for the Sub-Montane Tracts,[5] a revision of the then Act, smaller than the Punjab Land Bill, but affecting a few hundred thousand people none the less. The Legal Member had built, and bolstered, and embroidered, and amended that Bill till it looked beautiful on paper. Then the Council began to settle what they called the 'minor details'. As if any Englishman legislating for natives knows enough to know which are the minor and which are the major points, from the native point of view, of any measure! That Bill was a triumph of 'safeguarding the interests of the tenant'. One clause provided that land should not be leased on longer terms than five years at a stretch; because, if the landlord had a tenant bound for, say, twenty years, he would squeeze the very life out of him. The notion was to keep up a stream of independent cultivators in the Sub-Montane Tracts; and ethnologically and politically the notion was correct. The only drawback was that it was altogether wrong. A native's life in India implies the life of his son. Wherefore, you cannot legislate for one generation at a time. You must consider the next from the native point of view. Curiously enough, the native now and then, and in Northern India more particularly, hates being over-protected against himself. There was a Naga village once, where they lived on dead *and* buried Commissariat mules . . . But that is another story.

For many reasons to be explained later, the people concerned objected to the Bill. The Native Member of Council knew as much about Punjabis as he knew about Charing Cross. He had said in Calcutta that 'the Bill was entirely in accord with the desires of that large and important class, the cultivators'; and so on, and so on. The Legal Member's knowledge of natives was limited to English-speaking Durbaris, and his own red *chaprassis*;[6] the Sub-Montane Tracts concerned no one in particular; the Deputy-Commissioners were a good deal too driven to make representations, and the measure was one which dealt with small landholders only. Nevertheless, the Legal Member prayed that it might be correct, for he was a nervously conscientious man. He did not know that no man can tell what natives think unless he mixes with them with the varnish off. And not always then. But he did the best he knew. So the measure came up to the Supreme Council for the final touches, while Tods patrolled the Burra Simla Bazar in his morning rides, and played with the monkey belonging to Ditta Mull, the *bunnia*, and listened, as a child listens, to all the stray talk about this new freak of the Lat[7] Sahib's.

One day there was a dinner-party at the house of Tods' Mamma, and the Legal Member came. Tods was in bed, but he kept awake till he heard the bursts of laughter from the men over the coffee. Then he paddled out in his little red flannel dressing-gown and his night-suit, and took refuge by the side of his father, knowing that he would not be sent back. 'See the miseries of having a family!' said Tods' father, giving Tods three prunes, some water in a glass that had been used for claret, and telling him to sit still. Tods sucked the prunes slowly, knowing that he would have to go when they were finished, and sipped the pink water like a man of the world, as he listened to the conversation. Presently, the Legal Member, talking 'shop' to the Head of a Department, mentioned his Bill by its full name – 'The Sub-Montane Tracts *Ryotwari*[8] Revised Enactment'. Tods caught the one native word, and lifting up his small voice said:

'Oh, I know *all* about that! Has it been *murramutted* yet, Councillor Sahib?'

'How much?' said the Legal Member.

'*Murramutted* – mended. – Put *theek*, you know – made nice to please Ditta Mull!'

The Legal Member left his place and moved up next to Tods.

'What do you know about *ryotwari*, little man?' he said.

'I'm not a little man – I'm Tods – and I know *all* about it. Ditta Mull, and Choga Lall, and Amir Nath, and – oh, *lakhs*[9] of my friends tell me about it in the bazars when I talk to them.'

'Oh, they do – do they? What do they say, Tods?'

Tods tucked his feet under his red flannel dressing-gown and said, 'I must *fink*.'

The Legal Member waited patiently. Then Tods, with infinite compassion:

'You don't speak my talk, do you, Councillor Sahib?'

'No; I am sorry to say I do not,' said the Legal Member.

'Very well,' said Tods, 'I must *fink* in English.'

He spent a minute putting his ideas in order, and began very slowly, translating in his mind from the vernacular to English, as many Anglo-Indian children do. You must remember that the Legal Member helped him on by questions when he halted, for Tods was not equal to the sustained flight of oratory that follows.

'Ditta Mull says, "This thing is the talk of a child, and was made up by fools." But *I* don't think you are a fool, Councillor Sahib,' said Tods hastily. 'You caught my goat. This is what Ditta Mull says: "I am not a fool, and why should the Sirkar say I am a child? *I* can see if the land is good and if the landlord is good. If I am a fool, the sin is upon my own head. For five years I take my ground for which I have saved money, and a wife I take too, and a little son is born." Ditta Mull has one daughter now, but he *says* he will have a son, soon. And he says, "At the end of five years, by this new *bundobust*, I must go. If I do not go, I must get fresh seals and *takkus*-stamps on the papers, perhaps in the middle of the harvest, and to go to the law-courts once is wisdom, but to go twice is *Jehannum*." That is *quite* true,' explained Tods gravely. 'All my friends say so. And Ditta Mull says, "Always fresh *takkus* and paying money to Vakils and *chaprassis* and law-courts every five years, or else the landlord makes me go. Why do I want to go? Am I a fool? If I am a fool and do not know, after forty years, good land when I see it, let me die! But if the new *bundobust*[10] says for *fifteen* years, that is good and wise. My little son is a man, and I am burnt, and he takes the ground, or another ground, paying only once for the *takkus*-stamps on the papers, and his little son is born, and at the end of fifteen years is a man too. But what profit is there in five years and fresh papers? Nothing but *dikh* – trouble – *dikh*. We are not young men who take these lands, but old ones – not farmers, but tradesmen with a little money – and for fifteen years we shall have peace. Nor are we children that the Sirkar should treat us so."'

Here Tods stopped short, for the whole table were listening. The Legal Member said to Tods, 'Is that all?'

'All I can remember,' said Tods. 'But you should see Ditta Mull's big monkey. It's just like a Councillor Sahib.'

'Tods! Go to bed,' said his father.

Tods gathered up his dressing-gown tail and departed.

The Legal Member brought his hand down on the table with a crash. 'By Jove!' said the Legal Member, 'I believe the boy is right. The short tenure *is* the weak point.'

He left early, thinking over what Tods had said. Now, it was obviously impossible for the Legal Member to play with a *bunnia*'s monkey, by way of getting understanding; but he did better. He made inquiries, always bearing in mind the fact that the real native – not the hybrid, University-trained mule – is as timid as a colt, and, little by little, he coaxed some of the men whom the measure concerned most intimately to give in their views, which squared very closely with Tods' evidence.

So the Bill was amended in that clause; and the Legal Member was filled with an uneasy suspicion that Native Members represent very little except the Orders they carry on their bosoms. But he put the thought from him as illiberal. He was a most Liberal man.

After a time, the news spread through the bazars that Tods had got the Bill recast in the tenure-clause, and if Tods' Mamma had not interfered, Tods would have made himself sick on the baskets of fruit and pistachio nuts and Kabuli grapes and almonds that crowded the veranda. Till he went Home, Tods ranked some few degrees before the Viceroy in popular estimation. But for the little life of him Tods could not understand why.

In the Legal Member's private-paper-box still lies the rough draft of the Sub-Montane Tracts *Ryotwari* Revised Enactment; and, opposite the twenty-second clause, pencilled in blue chalk, and signed by the Legal Member, are the words '*Tods' Amendment*'.

The Daughter of the Regiment

Jain 'Ardin' was a Sargint's wife,
    A Sargint's wife wus she.
She married of 'im in Orldershort
    An' comed acrost the sea.
(*Chorus*) 'Ave you never 'eard tell o' Jain 'Ardin'?
                        Jain 'Ardin'?
                        Jain 'Ardin'?
    'Ave you never 'eard tell o' Jain 'Ardin'?
The pride o' the Compan*ee*?

Old Barrack-Room Ballad

'A gentleman who doesn't know the Circassian Circle[1] ought not to stand up for it – puttin' everybody out.' That was what Miss McKenna said, and the Sergeant who was my *vis-à-vis* looked the same thing. I was afraid of Miss McKenna. She was six feet high, all yellow freckles and red hair, and was simply clad in white satin shoes, a pink muslin dress, an apple-green stuff sash, and black silk gloves, with yellow roses in her hair. Wherefore I fled from Miss McKenna and sought my friend Private Mulvaney, who was at the cant – refreshment-table.

'So you've been dancin' wid little Jhansi McKenna, sorr – she that's goin' to marry Corp'ril Slane? Whin you next conversh wid your lorruds an' your ladies, tell thim you've danced wid little Jhansi. 'Tis a thing to be proud av.'

But I wasn't proud. I was humble. I saw a story in Private Mulvaney's eye; and besides, if he stayed too long at the bar, he would, I knew, qualify for more pack-drill. Now to meet an esteemed friend doing pack-drill outside the guard-room is embarrassing, especially if you happen to be walking with his Commanding Officer.

'Come on to the parade-ground, Mulvaney, it's cooler there, and tell me about Miss McKenna. What is she, and who is she, and why is she called "Jhansi"?'

'D'ye mane to say you've niver heard av Ould Pummeloe's daughter? An' you thinkin' you know things! I'm wid ye in a minut' whin me poipe's lit.'

We came out under the stars. Mulvaney sat down on one of the artillery bridges, and began in the usual way: his pipe between his teeth, his big hands clasped and dropped between his knees, and his cap well on the back of his head:

'Whin Mrs Mulvaney that is, was Miss Shad that was, you were a dale younger than you are now, an' the Army was diff'rint in sev'ril e-senshuls. Bhoys have no call for to marry nowadays, an' that's why the Army has so few rale, good, honust, swearin', strapagin', tinder-hearted, heavy-futted wives as ut used to have whin I was a Corp'ril. I was rejuced afterwards – but no matther – I was a Corp'ril wanst. In thim times a man lived *an'* died wid his Rig'mint; an' by natur', he married whin he was a *man*. Whin I was Corp'ril – Mother av Hivin, how the Rig'mint has died an' been borrun since that day! – my Colour-Sargint was Ould McKenna, an' a married man tu. An' his woife – his first woife, for he married three times did McKenna – was Bridget McKenna, from Portarlington, like mesilf. I've misremimbered fwhat her first name was; but in B Comp'ny we called her "Ould Pummeloe",[2] by reason av her figure, which was entirely circum-fe-renshill. Like the big dhrum! Now that woman – God rock her sowl to rest in glory! – was for iverlastin' havin' childher; an' McKenna, whin the fifth or sixth come squallin' on to the musther-rowl, swore he wud number thim off in future. But Ould Pummeloe she prayed av him to christen them afther the names av the stations they was borrun in. So there was Colaba McKenna, an' Muttra McKenna, an' a whole Prisidincy av other McKennas, an' little Jhansi, dancin' over yondher. Whin the childher wasn't bornin', they was dyin'; for, av our childher die like sheep in these days, they died like flies thin. I lost me own little Shadd – but no matther. 'Tis long ago, and Mrs Mulvaney niver had another.

'I'm digresshin'. Wan divil's hot summer there come an ordher from some mad ijjit, whose name I misremimber, for the Rig'mint to go up-country. Maybe they wanted to know how the new rail carried throops. They knew! On me sowl, they knew before they was done! Ould Pummeloe had just buried Muttra McKenna;

an', the season bein' onwholesim, only little Jhansi McKenna, who was four year ould thin, was left on hand.

'Five childher gone in fourteen months. 'Twas harrd, wasn't ut?'

'So we wint up to our new station in that blazin' heat – may the curse av Saint Lawrence[3] conshume the man who gave the ordher! Will I iver forget that move? They gave us two wake thrains to the Rig'mint: an' we was eight hundher' and sivinty strong. There was A, B, C, an' D Comp'nies in the secon' thrain, wid twelve women, no orf'cers' ladies, an' thirteen childher. We was to go six hundher' miles, an' railways was new in thim days. Whin we had been a night in the belly av the thrain – the men ragin' in their shirts an' dhrinkin' anything they cud find, an' eatin' bad fruit-stuff whin they cud, for we cudn't stop 'em – I was a Corp'ril thin – the cholera bruk out wid the dawnin' av the day.

'Pray to the Saints you may niver see cholera in a throop-thrain! 'Tis like the judgmint av God hittin' down from the nakid sky! We run into a rest-camp – as ut might have been Ludianny, but not by any manes so comfortable. The Orf'cer Commandin' sent a telegrapt up the line, three hundher' mile up, askin' for help. Faith, we wanted ut, for ivry sowl av the followers ran for the dear life as soon as the thrain stopped; an' by the time that telegrapt was writ, there wasn't a naygur in the station exceptin' the telegrapt-clerk – an' he only bekaze he was held down to his chair by the scruff av his sneakin' black neck. Thin the day began wid the noise in the carr'ges, an' the rattle av the men on the platform fallin' over, arrums an' all, as they stud for to answer the Comp'ny musther-rowl before goin' over to the camp. 'Tisn't for me to say fwhat like the cholera was like. Maybe the Doctor cud ha' tould, av he hadn't dhropped on to the platform from the door av a carr'ge where he was takin' out the dead. He died wid the rest. Some bhoys had died in the night. We tuk out sivin, and twinty more was sickenin' as we tuk thim. The women was huddled up anyways, screamin' wid fear.

'Sez the Commandin' Orf'cer whose name I misremimber, "Take the women over to that tope[4] av trees yondher. Get thim out av the camp. 'Tis no place for thim."

'Ould Pummeloe was sittin' on her beddin'-rowl, thryin' to kape little Jhansi quiet. "Go off to that tope!" sez the orf'cer. "Get out av the men's way!"

'"Be damned av I do!" sez Ould Pummeloe, an' little Jhansi, squattin' by her mother's side, squeaks out, "Be damned av I do," tu. Thin Ould Pummeloe turns to the women an' she sez, "Are ye goin' to let the bhoys die while you're picnickin', ye sluts?" sez she. "'Tis wather they want. Come on an' help."

'Wid that, she turns up her sleeves an' steps out for a well behind the rest-camp – little Jhansi trottin' behind wid a *lotah*⁵ an' string, an' the other women followin' like lambs, wid horse-buckets an' cookin'-pots. Whin all the things was full, Ould Pummeloe marches back into camp – 'twas like a battlefield wid all the glory missin' – at the hid av the rig'mint av women.

'"McKenna, me man!" she sez, wid a voice on her like grand-roun's challenge, "tell the bhoys to be quiet. Ould Pummeloe's comin' to look afther thim – wid free dhrinks."

'Thin we cheered, an' the cheerin' in the lines was louder than the noise av the poor divils wid the sickness on thim. But not much.

'You see, we was a new an' raw Rig'mint in those days, an' we cud make neither head nor tail av the sickness; an' so we was useless. The men was goin' roun' an' about like dumb sheep, waitin' for the nex' man to fall over, an' sayin' undher their spache, "Fwhat is ut? In the name av God, *fwhat* is ut?" 'Twas horrible. But through ut all, up an' down, an' down an' up, wint Ould Pummeloe an' little Jhansi – all we cud see av the baby, undher a dead man's helmut wid the chin-strap swingin' about her little stummick – up an' down wid the wather an' fwhat brandy there was.

'Now an' thin Ould Pummeloe, the tears runnin' down her fat, red face, sez, "Me bhoys, me poor, dead, darlin' bhoys!" But, for the most, she was thryin' to put heart into the men an' kape thim stiddy; and little Jhansi was tellin' thim all they wud be "betther in the mornin'". 'Twas a thrick she'd picked up from hearin' Ould Pummeloe whin Muttra was burnin' out wid fever. In the mornin'! 'Twas the iverlastin' mornin' at St Pether's Gate was the mornin' for sivin-an'-twenty good men; an' twinty more was sick to the death in that bitter, burnin' sun. But the women worked like angils as I've said, an' the men like divils, till the two doctors come down from above, and we was rescued.

'But, just before that, Ould Pummeloe, on her knees over a bhoy in my squad – right-cot man to me he was in the barrick – tellin' him the wurrud av the Church that niver failed a man yet, sez, "Hould me up, bhoys! I'm feelin' bloody sick!" 'Twas the sun, not the cholera, did ut. She misremimbered that she was only wearin' her ould black bonnet, an' she died wid "McKenna, me man," houldin' her up, an' the bhoys howled whin they buried her.

'That night a big wind blew, an' blew, an' blew, an' blew the tents flat. But it blew the cholera away, an' niver another case there was all the while we was waitin' – ten days in quarintin'. Av you will belave me, the thrack av the sickness in the camp was for all the wurruld the thrack av a man walkin' four times in a figur'-av-eight through the tents. They say 'tis the Wandherin' Jew takes the cholera wid him. I believe ut.

'An' *that*,' said Mulvaney illogically, 'is the cause why little Jhansi McKenna is fwhat she is. She was brought up by the Quarthermaster-Sergint's wife whin McKenna died, but she b'longs to B Comp'ny; and this tale I'm tellin' you – *wid* a proper appreciashin av Jhansi McKenna – I've belted into ivry recruity av the Comp'ny as he was drafted. Faith, 'twas me belted Corp'ril Slane into askin' the girl!'

'Not really?'

'Man, I did! She's no beauty to look at, but she's Ould Pummeloe's daughter, an' 'tis my jooty to provide for her. Just before Slane got his promotion I sez to him, "Slane," sez I, "to-morrow 'twill be insubordinashin av me to chastise you; but, by the sowl av Ould Pummeloe, who is now in glory, av you don't give me your wurrud to ask Jhansi McKenna at wanst, I'll peel the flesh off yer bones wid a brass huk to-night. 'Tis a dishgrace to B Comp'ny she's been single so long!" sez I. Was I goin' to let a three-year-ould preshume to discoorse wid me – my will bein' set? No! Slane wint an' asked her. He's a good bhoy is Slane. Wan av these days he'll get into the Com'ssariat an' dhrive a buggy wid his – savin's. So I provided for Ould Pummeloe's daughter; an' now you go along an' dance agin wid her.'

And I did.

I felt a respect for Miss Jhansi McKenna; and I went to her wedding later on.

Perhaps I will tell you about that one of these days.

⦃ In the Pride of His Youth ⦄

'Stopped in the straight when the race was his own!
Look at him cutting it – cur to the bone!'
'Ask, ere the youngster be rated and chidden,
What did he carry and how was he ridden?
Maybe they used him too much at the start;
Maybe Fate's weight-cloths are breaking his heart.'
                                    Life's Handicap

When I was telling you of the joke that The Worm played off on the Senior Subaltern, I promised a somewhat similar tale, but with all the jest left out. This is that tale.

Dicky Hatt was kidnapped in his early, early youth – neither by landlady's daughter, housemaid, barmaid, nor cook, but by a girl so nearly of his own caste that only a woman could have seen she was just the least little bit in the world below it. This happened a month before he came out to India, and five days after his one-and-twentieth birthday. The girl was nineteen – six years older than Dicky in the things of this world, that is to say – and, for the time, twice as foolish as he.

Excepting, always, falling off a horse there is nothing more fatally easy than marriage before the Registrar. The ceremony costs less than fifty shillings, and is remarkably like walking into a pawn-shop. After the declarations of residence have been put in, four minutes will cover the rest of the proceedings – fees, attestation, and all. Then the Registrar slides the blotting-pad over the names, and says grimly, with his pen between his teeth, 'Now you're man and wife'; and the couple walk out into the street feeling as if something were horribly illegal somewhere.

But that ceremony holds and can drag a man to his undoing just as thoroughly as the 'long as ye both shall live' curse from the altar-rails, with the bridesmaids giggling behind, and 'The Voice that breathed o'er Eden' lifting the roof off. In this manner

191

was Dicky Hatt kidnapped, and he considered it vastly fine, for he had received an appointment in India which carried a magnificent salary from the Home point of view. The marriage was to be kept secret for a year. Then Mrs Dicky Hatt was to come out, and the rest of life was to be a glorious golden mist. That was how they sketched it under the Addison Road Station lamps; and, after one short month, came Gravesend and Dicky steaming out to his new life, and the girl crying in a thirty-shillings-a-week bed-and-living-room, in a back-street off Montpelier Square near the Knightsbridge Barracks.

But the country that Dicky came to was a hard land where men of twenty-one were reckoned very small boys indeed, and life was expensive. The salary that loomed so large six thousand miles away did not go far. Particularly when Dicky divided it by two, and remitted more than the fair half, at 1-6⅞,[1] to Montpelier Square. One hundred and thirty-five rupees out of three hundred and thirty is not much to live on; but it was absurd to suppose that Mrs Hatt could exist for ever on the £20 held back by Dicky from his outfit allowance. Dicky saw this and remitted at once; always remembering that Rs.700 were to be paid, twelve months later, for a first-class passage out for a lady. When you add to these trifling details the natural instincts of a boy beginning a new life in a new country and longing to go about and enjoy himself, and the necessity for grappling with strange work – which, properly speaking, should take up a boy's undivided attention – you will see that Dicky started handicapped. He saw it himself for a breath or two; but he did not guess the full beauty of his future.

As the hot weather began, the shackles settled on him and ate into his flesh. First would come letters – big, crossed, seven-sheet letters – from his wife, telling him how she longed to see him, and what a Heaven upon earth would be their property when they met. Then some boy of the chummery[2] wherein Dicky lodged would pound on the door of his bare little room, and tell him to come out to look at a pony – the very thing to suit him. Dicky could not afford ponies. He had to explain this. Dicky could not afford living in the chummery, modest as it was. He had to explain this before he moved to a single room next to the office where he worked all day. He kept house on a green oil-cloth table-cover, one chair, one bedstead, one photograph, one tooth-glass, very strong and thick, a seven-rupee eight-anna filter, and messing by contract at thirty-seven rupees a month. Which last item was extortion. He had no punkah, for a punkah costs fifteen rupees a month; but he slept on the roof of the office with all his wife's letters under his pillow. Now and again he was asked out to dinner, where he got both a punkah and an iced drink. But this was seldom, for people objected to recognizing a boy who had evidently the instincts of a Scotch tallow-chandler, and who lived in such a nasty fashion. Dicky could not subscribe to any amusement, so he found no amusement except the pleasure of turning over his Bank-book and reading what it said about 'loans on approved security'. That cost nothing. He remitted through a Bombay Bank, by the way, and the station knew nothing of his private affairs.

Every month he sent Home all he could possibly spare for his wife and for another reason which was expected to explain itself shortly, and would require more money.

About this time Dicky was overtaken with the nervous, haunting fear that besets married men when they are out of sorts. He had no pension to look to. What if he should die suddenly, and leave his wife unprovided for? The thought used to lay hold of him in the still, hot nights on the roof, till the shaking of his heart made him think that he was going to die then and there of heart disease. Now this is a frame of mind which no boy has a right to know. It is a strong man's trouble; but, coming when it did, it nearly drove poor punkah-less, perspiring Dicky Hatt mad. He could tell no one about it.

A certain amount of 'screw' is as necessary for a man as for a billiard-ball. It makes them both do wonderful things. Dicky needed money badly, and he worked for it like a horse. But, naturally, the men who owned him knew that a boy can live very comfortably on a certain income – pay in India is a matter of age, not merit, you see, and, if their particular boy wished to work like two boys, Business forbid that they should stop him. But Business forbid that they should give him an increase of pay at his present ridiculously immature age. So Dicky won certain rises of salary –

ample for a boy – not enough for a wife and child – certainly too little for the seven-hundred-rupee passage that he and Mrs Hatt had discussed so lightly once upon a time. And with this he was forced to be content.

Somehow, all his money seemed to fade away in Home drafts and the crushing Exchange, and the tone of the Home letters changed and grew querulous. Why wouldn't Dicky have his wife and the baby out? Surely he had a salary – a fine salary – and it was too bad of him to enjoy himself in India. But would he – could he – make the next draft a little more elastic? Here followed a list of baby's kit, as long as a Parsee's[3] bill. Then Dicky, whose heart yearned to his wife and the little son he had never seen – which, again, is a feeling no boy is entitled to – enlarged the draft, and wrote queer half-boy, half-man letters, saying that life was not so enjoyable after all, and would the little wife wait yet a little longer? But the little wife, however much she approved of money, objected to waiting, and there was a strange, hard sort of ring in her letters that Dicky didn't understand. How could he?

Later on still – just as Dicky had been told – apropos of another youngster who had 'made a fool of himself' as the saying is – that matrimony would not only ruin his further chances of advancement, but would lose him his present appointment – came the news that the baby, his own little, little son, had died and, behind this, forty lines of an angry woman's scrawl, saying the death might have been averted if certain things, all costing money, had been done, or if the mother and the baby had been with Dicky. The letter struck at Dicky's naked heart; but, not being officially entitled to a baby, he could show no sign of trouble.

How Dicky won through the next four months, and what hope he kept alight to force him into his work, no one dare say. He pounded on, the seven-hundred-rupee passage as far away as ever, and his style of living unchanged, except when he launched into a new filter. There was the strain of his office work, and the strain of his remittances, and the knowledge of his son's death, which touched the boy more, perhaps, than it would have touched a man; and, beyond all, the enduring strain of his daily life. Grey-headed seniors who approved of his thrift and his fashion of denying himself everything pleasant, reminded him of the old saw that says:

> 'If a youth would be distinguished in his art, art, art,
> He must keep the girls away from his heart, heart, heart.'

And Dicky, who fancied he had been through every trouble that a man is permitted to know, had to laugh and agree; with the last line of his balanced Bank-book jingling in his head day and night.

But he had one more sorrow to digest before the end. There arrived a letter from the little wife – the natural sequence of the others if Dicky had only known it – and the burden of that letter was 'gone with a handsomer man than you'.[4] It was a rather curious production, without stops, something like this – She was not going to wait for ever and the baby was dead and Dicky was only a boy and he would never set eyes on her again and why hadn't he waved his handkerchief to her when he left Gravesend[5] and God was her judge she was a wicked woman but Dicky was worse enjoying himself in India and this other man loved the ground she trod on and would Dicky ever forgive her for she would never forgive Dicky; and there was no address to write to.

Instead of thanking his stars that he was free, Dicky discovered exactly how an injured husband feels – again, not at all the knowledge to which a boy is entitled – for his mind went back to his wife as he remembered her in the thirty-shilling 'suite' in Montpelier Square, when the dawn of his last morning in England was breaking, and she was crying in the bed.[6] Whereat he rolled about on his bed and bit his fingers. He never stopped to think whether, if he had met Mrs Hatt after those two years, he would have discovered that he and she had grown quite different and new persons. This, theoretically, he ought to have done. He spent the night after the English Mail came in rather severe pain.

Next morning, Dicky Hatt felt disinclined to work. He argued that he had missed the pleasure of youth. He was tired, and he had tasted all the sorrow in life before three-and-twenty. His honour was gone – that was the man; and now he, too, would go to the Devil – that was the boy in him. So he put his head down on the green oil-cloth table-cover, and wept before resigning his post and all it offered.

But the reward of his services came. He was given three days to reconsider himself, and the Head of the establishment, after some telegraphings, said that it was a most unusual step, but, in view of the ability that Mr Hatt had displayed at such-and-such a time, at such-and-such junctures, he was in a position to offer him an infinitely superior post – first on probation and later, in the natural course of things, on confirmation. 'And how much does the post carry?' said Dicky. 'Six hundred and fifty rupees,' said the Head slowly, expecting to see the young man sink with gratitude and joy.

And it came then! The seven-hundred-rupee passage, and enough to have saved the wife and the little son, and to have allowed of assured and open marriage, came then. Dicky burst into a roar of laughter – laughter he could not check – nasty, jangling merriment that seemed as if it would go on for ever. When he had recovered himself he said, quite seriously, 'I'm tired of work. I'm an old man now. It's about time I retired. And I will.'

'The boy's mad!' said the Head.

I think he was right; but Dicky Hatt never reappeared to settle the question.

⁅ Pig ⁆

Go, stalk the red deer o'er the heather,
　Ride, follow the fox if you can!
But, for pleasure and profit together,
　Allow me the hunting of Man –
The chase of the Human, the search for the Soul
　To its ruin – the hunting of Man.

The Old Shikarri

I believe the difference began in the matter of a horse, with a twist in his temper, whom Pinecoffin sold to Nafferton, and by whom Nafferton was nearly slain. There may have been other causes of offence; the horse was the official stalking-horse. Nafferton was very angry; but Pinecoffin laughed, and said that he had never guaranteed the beast's manners. Nafferton laughed too, though he vowed that he would write off his fall against Pinecoffin if he waited five years. Now, a Dalesman from beyond Skipton will forgive an injury when the Strid lets a man live; but a South Devon man is as soft as a Dartmoor bog. You can see from their names that Nafferton had the race-advantage of Pinecoffin. He was a peculiar man, and his notions of humour were cruel. He taught me a new and fascinating form of *shikar*. He hounded Pinecoffin from Mithankot to Jagadri, and from Gurgaon to Abbottabad – up and across the Punjab, a large Province, and in places remarkably dry. He said that he had no intention of allowing Assistant Commissioners to 'sell him pups', in the shape of ramping, screaming countrybreds, without making their lives a burden to them.

Most Assistant Commissioners develop a bent for some special work after their first hot weather in the country. The boys with digestions hope to write their names large on the Frontier, and struggle for dreary places like Bannu and Kohat. The bilious ones climb into the Secretariat; which is very bad for the liver. Others are bitten with a mania for District work, Ghaznevid[1] coins or Persian poetry; while some, who come of farmers' stock, find that the smell of the earth after the Rains gets into their blood, and calls them to 'develop the resources of the Province'. These men are enthusiasts. Pinecoffin belonged to their class. He knew a great many facts bearing on the cost of bullocks, and temporary wells, and opium-scrapers, and what happens if you burn too much rubbish on a field in the hope of enriching used-up soil. All the Pinecoffins come of a landholding breed, and so the land only took back her own again. Unfortunately – most unfortunately for Pinecoffin – he was a Civilian as well as a farmer. Nafferton watched him, and thought about the horse. Nafferton said, 'See me chase that boy till he drops!' I said, 'You can't get your knife into an Assistant Commissioner.' Nafferton told me that I did not understand the administration of the Province.

Our Government is rather peculiar. It gushes on the agricultural and general information side, and will supply a moderately respectable man with all sorts of 'economic statistics', if he speaks to it prettily. For instance, you are interested in gold-washing in the sands of the Sutlej. You pull the string, and find that it wakes up half-a-dozen Departments, and finally communicates, say, with a friend of yours in the Telegraph, who once wrote some notes on the customs of the gold-washers when he was on construction work in their part of the Empire. He may or may not be pleased at being ordered to write out everything he knows for your benefit. This depends on his temperament. The bigger man you are, the more information and the greater trouble can you raise.

Nafferton was not a big man; but he had the reputation of being very 'earnest'. An 'earnest' man can do much with a Government. There was an earnest man once who nearly wrecked ... But all India knows *that* story. I am not sure what real 'earnestness' is. A very fair imitation can be manufactured by neglecting to dress decently, by mooning about in a dreamy, misty sort of way, by taking office work home, after staying in office till seven, and by receiving crowds of native gentlemen on Sundays. That is one sort of 'earnestness'.

Pig

Nafferton cast about for a peg whereon to hang his earnestness, and for a string that would communicate with Pinecoffin. He found both. They were Pig. Nafferton became an earnest inquirer after Pig. He informed the Government that he had a scheme whereby a very large percentage of the British Army in India could be fed, at a very large saving, on Pig. Then he hinted that Pinecoffin might supply him with the 'varied information necessary to the proper inception of the scheme'. So the Government wrote on the back of the letter, 'Instruct Mr Pinecoffin to furnish Mr Nafferton with any information in his power.' Government is very prone to writing things on the backs of letters which, later, lead to trouble and confusion.

Nafferton had not the faintest interest in Pig, but he knew that Pinecoffin would flounce into the trap. Pinecoffin was delighted at being consulted about Pig. The Indian Pig is not exactly an important factor in agricultural life; but Nafferton explained to Pinecoffin that there was room for improvement, and corresponded direct with that young man.

You may think that there is not much to be evolved from Pig. It all depends how you set to work. Pinecoffin being a Civilian and wishing to do things thoroughly, began with an essay on the Primitive Pig, the Mythology of the Pig, and the Dravidian Pig, Nafferton filed that information – twenty-seven foolscap sheets – and wanted to know about the distribution of the Pig in the Punjab, and how it stood the Plains in the hot weather. From this point onwards remember that I am giving you only the barest outlines of the affair – the guy-ropes, as it were, of the web that Nafferton spun round Pinecoffin.

Pinecoffin made a coloured Pig-population map, and collected observations on the comparative longevity of Pig (*a*) in the sub-montane tracts of the Himalayas, and (*b*) in the Rechna Doab. Nafferton filed that, and asked what sort of people looked after Pig. This started an ethnological excursus on swineherds, and drew from Pinecoffin long tables showing the proportion per thousand of the caste in the Derajat. Nafferton filed that bundle, and explained that the figures which he wanted referred to the Cis-Sutlej states, where he understood that Pigs were very fine and large, and where he proposed to start a Piggery. By this time Government had quite forgotten their instructions to Mr Pinecoffin. They were like the gentlemen in Keats' poem,[2] who turned well-oiled wheels to skin other people. But Pinecoffin was just entering into the spirit of the Pig-hunt, as Nafferton well knew he would do. He had a fair amount of work of his own to clear away; but he sat up of nights reducing Pig to five places of decimals for the honour of his Service. He was not going to appear ignorant of so easy a subject as Pig.

Then Government sent him on special duty to Kohat, to 'inquire into' the big, seven-foot, iron-shod spades of that District. People had been killing each other with those peaceful tools; and Government wished to know 'whether a modified form of agricultural implement could not, tentatively and as a temporary measure, be introduced among the agricultural population without needlessly or unduly exacerbating the existing religious sentiments of the peasantry'.

Between those spades and Nafferton's Pig, Pinecoffin was rather heavily burdened.

Nafferton now began to take up '(a) The food-supply of the indigenous Pig, with a view to the improvement of its capacities as a flesh-former. (b) The acclimatization of the exotic Pig, maintaining its distinctive peculiarities.' Pinecoffin replied exhaustively that the exotic Pig would become merged in the indigenous type; and quoted horse-breeding statistics to prove this. The side-issue was debated at great length on Pinecoffin's side, till Nafferton owned that he had been in the wrong, and moved the previous question. When Pinecoffin had quite written himself out about flesh-formers, and fibrins, and glucose, and the nitrogenous constituents of maize and lucerne, Nafferton raised the question of expense. By this time Pinecoffin, who had been transferred from Kohat, had developed a Pig theory of his own, which he stated in thirty-three folio pages – all carefully filed by Nafferton; who asked for more.

These things took ten months, and Pinecoffin's interest in the potential Piggery seemed to die down after he had stated his own views. But Nafferton bombarded him with letters on 'the Imperial aspect of the scheme, as tending to officialize the sale of pork, and thereby calculated to give offence to the Mahommedan population of Upper India'. He guessed that Pinecoffin would want some broad, free-hand work after his niggling, stippling, decimal details. Pinecoffin handled the latest development of the case in masterly style, and proved that no 'popular ebullition of excitement was to be apprehended'. Nafferton said that there was nothing like Civilian insight in matters of this kind, and lured him up a by-path – 'the possible profits to accrue to the Government from the sale of hog-bristles'. There is an extensive literature of hog-bristles, and the shoe, brush, and colourman's trades recognize more varieties of bristles than you would think possible. After Pinecoffin had wondered a little at Nafferton's rage for information, he sent back a monograph, fifty-one pages, on 'Products of the Pig'. This led him, under Nafferton's tender handling, straight to the Cawnpore factories, the trade in hog-skin for saddles – and thence to the tanners. Pinecoffin wrote that pomegranate-seed was the best cure for hog-skin, and suggested – the past fourteen months had wearied him – that Nafferton should 'raise his pigs before he tanned them'.

Nafferton went back to the second section of his fifth question. How could the exotic Pig be brought to give as much pork as it did in the West and yet 'assume the essentially hirsute characteristics of its Oriental congener'? Pinecoffin felt dazed, for he had forgotten what he had written sixteen months before, and fancied that he was about to reopen the entire question. He was too far involved in the hideous tangle to retreat, and, in a weak moment, he wrote, 'Consult my first letter'; which related to the Dravidian Pig. As a matter of fact, Pinecoffin had still to reach the acclimatization stage; having gone off on a side-issue on the merging of types.

Then Nafferton really unmasked his batteries! He complained to the Government, in stately language, of 'the paucity of help accorded to me in my earnest attempts to start a potentially remunerative industry, and the flippancy with which my requests for information are treated by a gentleman whose pseudo-scholarly attainments should at least have taught him the primary differences between the Dravidian and the Berkshire variety of the genus *Sus*. If I am to understand that the letter to which he refers me contains his serious views on the acclimatization of a valuable, though possibly uncleanly, animal, I am reluctantly compelled to believe', etc. etc.

There was a new man at the head of the Department of Castigation. The wretched Pinecoffin was told that the Service was made for the Country, and not the Country for the Service, and that he had better begin to supply information about Pig.

Pinecoffin answered insanely that he had written everything that could be written about Pig, and that some furlough was due to him.

Nafferton got a copy of that letter, and sent it, with the essay on the Dravidian Pig, to a down-country paper which printed both in full. The essay was rather high-flown; but if the Editor had seen the stacks of paper, in Pinecoffin's handwriting, on Nafferton's table, he would not have been so sarcastic about the 'nebulous discursiveness and blatant self-sufficiency of the modern Competition-wallah,³ and his utter inability to grasp the practical issues of a practical question'. Many friends cut out these remarks and sent them to Pinecoffin.

I have already stated that Pinecoffin came of a soft stock. This last stroke frightened and shook him. He could not understand it; but he felt that he had been, somehow, shamelessly betrayed by Nafferton. He realized that he had wrapped himself up in the Pigskin without need, and that he could not well set himself right with his Government. All his acquaintances asked after his 'nebulous discursiveness' or his 'blatant self-sufficiency', and this made him miserable.

He took a train and went to Nafferton, whom he had not seen since the Pig business began. He also took the cutting from the paper, and blustered feebly and called Nafferton names, and then died down to a watery, weak protest of the 'I-say-it's-too-bad-you-know' order.

Nafferton was very sympathetic.

'I'm afraid I've given you a good deal of trouble, haven't I?' said he.

'Trouble!' whimpered Pinecoffin; 'I don't mind the trouble so much, though that was bad enough; but what I resent is this showing up in print. It will stick to me like a burr all through my service. And I *did* do my best for your interminable swine. It's too bad of you – on my soul it is!'

'I don't know,' said Nafferton. 'Have you ever been stuck with a horse? It isn't the money I mind, though that is bad enough; but what I resent is the chaff that follows, especially from the boy who stuck me. But I think we'll cry quits now.'

Pinecoffin found nothing to say save bad words; and Nafferton smiled ever so sweetly, and asked him to dinner.

⟨ The Rout of the White Hussars ⟩

It was not in the open fight
  We threw away the sword,
But in the lonely watching
  In the darkness by the ford.
The waters lapped, the night-wind blew,
Full-armed the Fear was born and grew,
And we were flying ere we knew
  From panic in the night.

Beoni Bar

Some people hold that an English Cavalry regiment cannot run. This is a mistake. I have seen four hundred and thirty-seven sabres flying over the face of the country in abject terror – have seen the best Regiment that ever drew rein wiped off the Army List for the space of two hours. If you repeat this tale to the White Hussars they will, in all probability, treat you severely. They are not proud of the incident.

You may know the White Hussars by their 'side',[1] which is greater than that of all the Cavalry regiments on the roster. If this is not a sufficient mark, you may know them by their old brandy. It has been sixty years in the Mess, and is worth going far to taste. Ask for the 'McGaire' old brandy, and see that you get it. If the Mess-Sergeant thinks that you are uneducated, and that the genuine article will be lost on you, he will treat you accordingly. He is a good man. But, when you are at Mess, you must never talk to your hosts about forced marches or long-distance rides. The Mess are very sensitive; and, if they think that you are laughing at them, will tell you so.

As the White Hussars say, it was all the Colonel's fault. He was a new man, and he ought never to have taken the Command. He said that the Regiment was not smart enough. This to the White Hussars, who knew that they could walk round any Horse,

204

and through any Guns, and over any Foot on the face of the earth! That insult was the first cause of offence.

Then the Colonel cast[2] the Drum-Horse – the Drum-Horse of the White Hussars! Perhaps you do not see what an unspeakable crime he had committed. I will try to make it clear. The soul of the Regiment lives in the Drum-Horse who carries the silver kettle-drums. He is nearly always a big piebald Waler. That is a point of honour; and a Regiment will spend anything you please on a piebald. He is beyond the ordinary laws of casting. His work is very light, and he only manoeuvres at a foot-pace. Wherefore, so long as he can step out and look handsome, his well-being is assured. He knows more about the Regiment than the Adjutant, and could not make a mistake if he tried.

The Drum-Horse of the White Hussars was only eighteen years old, and perfectly equal to his duties. He had at least six years' more work in him, and carried himself with all the pomp and dignity of a Drum-Major of the Guards. The Regiment had paid twelve hundred rupees for him.

But the Colonel said that he must go, and he was cast in due form and replaced by a washy, bay beast, as ugly as a mule, with a ewe-neck, rat-tail, and cow-hocks. The Drummer detested that animal, and the rest of the Band-horses put back their ears and showed the whites of their eyes at the very sight of him. They knew him for an upstart and no gentleman. I fancy that the Colonel's ideas of smartness extended to the Band, and that he wanted to make it take part in the regular parade movements. A Cavalry Band is a sacred thing. It only turns out for Commanding Officer's parades, and the Bandmaster is one degree more important than the Colonel. He is a High Priest, and the 'Keel Row'[3] is his holy song. The 'Keel Row' is the Cavalry Trot; and the man who has never heard that tune rising, high and shrill, above the rattle of the Regiment going past the saluting-base, has something yet to hear and understand.

When the Colonel cast the Drum-Horse of the White Hussars there was nearly a mutiny.

The officers were angry, the Regiment were furious, and the Bandsmen swore – like troopers. The Drum-Horse was going to be put up to auction – public auction – to be bought, perhaps, by a Parsee and put into a cart! It was worse than exposing the inner life of the Regiment to the whole world, or selling the Mess Plate to a Jew – a Black Jew.

The Colonel was a mean man and a bully. He knew what the Regiment thought about his action; and, when the troopers offered to buy the Drum-Horse, he said that their offer was mutinous and forbidden by the Regulations.

But one of the subalterns – Hogan-Yale, an Irishman – bought the Drum-Horse for a hundred and sixty rupees at the sale; and the Colonel was wroth. Yale professed repentance – he was unnaturally submissive – and said that, as he had only made the purchase to save the horse from possible ill-treatment and starvation, he would now shoot him and end the business. This appeared to soothe the Colonel, for he wanted the Drum-Horse disposed of. He felt that he had made a mistake, and could not, of course, acknowledge it. Meantime, the presence of the Drum-Horse was an annoyance to him.

Yale took to himself a glass of the old brandy, three cheroots, and his friend Martyn; and they all left the Mess together. Yale and Martyn conferred for two hours in Yale's quarters; but only the bull-terrier who keeps watch over Yale's boot-trees knows what they said. A horse, hooded and sheeted to his ears, left Yale's stables and was taken, very unwillingly, into the Civil Lines. Yale's groom went with him. Two men broke into the Regimental Theatre and took several paint-pots and some large scenery-brushes. Then night fell over the cantonments, and there was a noise as of a horse kicking his loose-box to pieces in Yale's stables. Yale had a big, old, white Waler trap-horse.

The next day was a Thursday, and the men, hearing that Yale was going to shoot the Drum-Horse in the evening, determined to give the beast a regular Regimental funeral – a finer one than they would have given the Colonel had he died just then. They got a bullock-cart and some sacking, and mounds and mounds of roses, and the body, under sacking, was carried out to the place where the anthrax cases were cremated; two-thirds of the Regiment following. There was no Band, but they all sang 'The Place where the old Horse died'[4] as something respectful and appropriate to the occasion. When the corpse was dumped into the grave and the men began throwing down armfuls of roses to cover it, the Farrier-Sergeant ripped out an oath and said aloud, 'Why, it ain't the Drum-Horse any more than it's me!' The Troop-Sergeant-Majors asked him whether he had left his head in the Canteen. The Farrier-Sergeant said that he knew the Drum-Horse's feet as well as he knew his own; but he was silenced when he saw the regimental number burnt in on the poor, stiff, upturned nearfoot.

Thus was the Drum-Horse of the White Hussars buried; the Farrier-Sergeant grumbling. The sacking that covered the corpse was smeared in places with black paint; and the Farrier-Sergeant drew attention to this fact. But a Troop-Sergeant-Major kicked him severely on the shin, and told him that he was undoubtedly drunk.

On the Monday following the burial, the Colonel sought revenge on the White Hussars. Unfortunately, being at that time temporarily in command of the station, he ordered a Brigade field-day. He said that he wished to make the Regiment 'sweat for their damned insolence', and he carried out his notion thoroughly. That Monday was one of the hardest days in the memory of the White Hussars. They were thrown against a skeleton-enemy, and pushed forward, and withdrawn, and dismounted, and 'scientifically handled' in every possible fashion over dusty country, till they sweated profusely. Their only amusement came late in the day when they fell upon the battery of Horse Artillery and chased it for two miles. This was a personal question, and most of the troopers had money on the event; the Gunners saying openly that they had the legs of the White Hussars. They were wrong. A march-past concluded the campaign, and when the Regiment got back to their Lines the men were coated with dirt from spur to chin-strap.

The White Hussars have one great and peculiar privilege. They won it at Fontenoy,[5] I think.

Many regiments possess special rights, such as wearing collars with undress uniform, or a bow of riband between the shoulders, or red and white roses in their helmets on certain days of the year. Some rights are connected with regimental Saints, and some with regimental successes. All are valued highly; but none so highly as the right of the White Hussars to have the Band playing when their horses are being watered in the lines. Only one tune is played, and that tune never varies. I don't know its real name, but the White Hussars call it 'Take me to London again'. It sounds very pretty. The Regiment would sooner be struck off the roster than forgo their distinction.

After the 'dismiss' was sounded, the officers rode off home to prepare for stables; and the men filed into the lines riding easy. That is to say, they opened their tight buttons, shifted their helmets, and began to joke or to swear as the humour took them; the more careful slipping off and easing girths and curbs. A good trooper values his mount exactly as much as he values himself, and believes, or should believe, that the two together are irresistible where women or men, girls or guns, are concerned.

Then the Orderly-Officer gave the order, 'Water horses,' and the Regiment loafed off to the squadron-troughs which were in rear of the stables, and between these and the barracks. There were four huge troughs, one for each squadron, arranged *en échelon*, so that the whole Regiment could water in ten minutes if it liked. But it lingered for seventeen, as a rule, while the Band played.

The Band struck up as the squadrons filed off to the troughs, and the men slipped their feet out of the stirrups and chaffed each other. The sun was just setting in a big, hot bed of red cloud, and the road to the Civil Lines seemed to run straight into the sun's eye. There was a little dot on the road. It grew and grew till it showed as a horse, with a sort of gridiron-thing on his back. The red cloud glared through the bars of the gridiron. Some of the troopers shaded their eyes with their hands and said, 'What the mischief 'as that there 'orse got on 'im?'

In another minute they heard a neigh that every soul – horse and man – in the Regiment knew, and saw, heading straight towards the Band, the dead Drum-Horse of the White Hussars!

On his withers banged and bumped the kettle-drums draped in crape, and on his back, very stiff and soldierly, sat a bareheaded skeleton.

The Band stopped playing, and, for a moment, there was a hush.

Then some one in E Troop — men said it was the Troop-Sergeant-Major — swung his horse round and yelled. No one can account exactly for what happened afterwards; but it seems that at least one man in each troop set an example of panic, and the rest followed like sheep. The horses that had barely put their muzzles into the troughs reared and capered; but as soon as the Band broke, which it did when the ghost of the Drum-Horse was about a furlong distant, all hooves followed suit, and the clatter of the stampede — quite different from the orderly throb and roar of a movement on parade, or the rough horse-play of watering in camp — made them only more terrified. They felt that the men on their backs were afraid of something. When horses once know that, all is over except the butchery.

Troop after troop turned from the troughs and ran — anywhere and everywhere — like spilt quick-silver. It was a most extraordinary spectacle, for men and horses were in all stages of easiness, and their gear flopping against their sides urged the horses on. Men were shouting and cursing, and trying to pull clear of the Band, which was being chased by the Drum-Horse, whose rider had fallen forward and seemed to be spurring for a wager.

The Colonel had gone over to the Mess for a drink. Most of the officers were with him, and the Subaltern of the Day was preparing to go down to the lines, and receive the watering reports from the Troop-Sergeant-Majors. When 'Take me to London again' stopped, after twenty bars, everyone in the Mess said, 'What on earth has happened?' A minute later, they heard unmilitary noises, and saw, far across the plain, the White Hussars scattered, and broken, and flying.

The Colonel was speechless with rage, for he thought that the Regiment had risen against him or was unanimously drunk. The Band, a disorganized mob, tore past, and at its heels laboured the Drum-Horse — the dead and buried Drum-Horse — with the jolting, clattering skeleton. Hogan-Yale whispered softly to Martyn, 'No wire will stand that treatment,' and the Band, which had doubled like a hare, came back again. But the rest of the Regiment was gone, was rioting all over the Province, for the dusk had shut in, and each man was howling to his neighbour that the Drum-Horse was on his flank. Troop-horses are far too tenderly treated as a rule. They can, in emergencies, do a great deal, even with seventeen stone on their backs; as the troopers found out.

How long this panic lasted I cannot say. I believe that when the moon rose the men saw they had nothing to fear, and, by twos and threes and half-troops, crept back into cantonments very much ashamed of themselves. Meantime, the Drum-Horse, disgusted at his treatment by old friends, pulled up, wheeled round, and trotted up to the Mess veranda-steps for bread. No one liked to run; but no one cared to go forward till the Colonel made a movement and laid hold of the skeleton's foot. The Band had halted some distance away, and now came back slowly. The Colonel called it, individually and collectively, every evil name that occurred to him at the time; for he had set his hand on the bosom of the Drum-Horse and found flesh and blood. Then he beat the kettle-drums with his clenched fist, and discovered that they were but made of silvered paper and bamboo. Next, still swearing, he tried to drag the skeleton out of the saddle, but found that it had been wired into the cantle. The sight of the Colonel, with his arms round the skeleton's pelvis and his knee in the old Drum-Horse's stomach, was striking; not to say amusing. He worried the thing off in a minute or two, and threw it down on the ground, saying to the Band, 'Here, you curs, that's what you're afraid of.' The skeleton did not look pretty in the twilight. The Band-Sergeant seemed to recognize it, for he began to chuckle and choke. 'Shall I take it away, sir?' said the Band-Sergeant. 'Yes,' said the Colonel, 'take it to Hell, and ride there yourselves!'

The Band-Sergeant saluted, hoisted the skeleton across his saddle-bow, and led off to the stables. Then the Colonel began to make inquiries for the rest of the Regiment, and the language he used was wonderful. He would disband the Regiment – he would court-martial every soul in it – he would not command such a set of rabble, and so on, and so on. As the men dropped in, his language grew wilder, until at last it exceeded the utmost limits of free speech allowed even to a Colonel of Horse.

Martyn took Hogan-Yale aside and suggested compulsory retirement from the Service as a necessity when all was discovered. Martyn was the weaker man of the two. Hogan-Yale put up his eyebrows and remarked, firstly, that he was the son of a Lord, and, secondly, that he was as innocent as the babe unborn of the theatrical resurrection of the Drum-Horse.

'My instructions,' said Hogan-Yale, with a singularly sweet smile, 'were that the Drum-Horse should be sent back as impressively as possible. I ask you, *am* I responsible if a mule-headed friend sends him back in such a manner as to disturb the peace of mind of a Regiment of Her Majesty's Cavalry?'

Martyn said, 'You are a great man, and will in time become a General; but I'd give my chance of a troop to be safe out of this affair.'

Providence saved Martyn and Hogan-Yale. The Second-in-Command led the Colonel away to the little curtained alcove wherein the subalterns of the White Hussars were accustomed to play poker of nights; and there, after many oaths on the Colonel's part, they talked together in low tones. I fancy that the Second-in-Command must have represented the scare as the work of some trooper whom it would be hopeless to detect; and I know that he dwelt upon the sin and the shame of making a public laughing-stock of the scare.

'They will call us,' said the Second-in-Command, who had really a fine imagination – 'they will call us the "Fly-by-Nights"; they will call us the "Ghost-Hunters"; they will nickname us from one end of the Army List to the other. All the explanation in the world won't make outsiders understand that the officers were away when the panic began. For the honour of the Regiment and for your own sake keep this thing quiet.'

The Colonel was so exhausted with anger that soothing him down was not so difficult as might be imagined. He was made to see, gently and by degrees, that it was obviously impossible to court-martial the whole Regiment, and equally impossible to proceed against any subaltern who, in his belief, had any concern in the hoax.

'But the beast's alive! He's never been shot at all!' shouted the Colonel. 'It's flat, flagrant disobedience! I've known a man broke for less – dam' sight less. They're mocking me, I tell you, Mutman! They're mocking me!'

Once more the Second-in-Command set himself to soothe the

Colonel, and wrestled with him for half an hour. At the end of that time the Regimental Sergeant-Major reported himself. The situation was rather novel to him; but he was not a man to be put out by circumstances. He saluted and said, 'Regiment all come back, sir.' Then, to propitiate the Colonel, 'An' none of the 'orses any the worse, sir.'

The Colonel only snorted and answered, 'You'd better tuck the men into their cots, then, and see that they don't wake up and cry in the night.' The Sergeant-Major withdrew.

His little stroke of humour pleased the Colonel, and, further, he felt slightly ashamed of the language he had been using. The Second-in-Command worried him again, and the two sat talking far into the night.

Next day but one there was a Commanding Officer's parade, and the Colonel harangued the White Hussars vigorously. The pith of his speech was that, since the Drum-Horse in his old age had proved himself capable of cutting up the whole Regiment, he should return to his post of pride at the head of the Band, *but* the Regiment were a set of ruffians with bad consciences.

The White Hussars shouted, and threw everything movable about them into the air, and when the parade was over they cheered the Colonel till they couldn't speak. No cheers were put up for Lieutenant Hogan-Yale, who smiled very sweetly in the background.

Said the Second-in-Command to the Colonel, unofficially:

'These little things ensure popularity, and do not the least affect discipline.'

'But I went back on my word,' said the Colonel.

'Never mind,' said the Second-in-Command. 'The White Hussars will follow you anywhere from to-day. Regiments are just like women. They will do anything for trinketry.'

A week later, Hogan-Yale received an extraordinary letter from some one who signed himself 'Secretary, *Charity and Zeal*,[6] 3709, E. C.', and asked for 'the return of our skeleton which we have reason to believe is in your possession'.

'Who the deuce is this lunatic who trades in bones?' said Hogan-Yale.

'Beg your pardon, sir,' said the Band-Sergeant, 'but the

skeleton is with me, an' I'll return it if you'll pay the carriage into the Civil Lines. There's a coffin with it, sir.'

Hogan-Yale smiled and handed two rupees to the Band-Sergeant, saying, 'Write the date on the skull, will you?'

If you doubt this story, and know where to go, you can see the date on the skeleton. But don't mention the matter to the White Hussars.

I happen to know something about it, because I helped to prepare the Drum-Horse for his resurrection. He did not take kindly to the skeleton at all.

The Bronckhorst Divorce-Case

In the daytime, when she moved about me,
　　In the night, when she was sleeping at my side –
I was wearied, I was wearied of her presence,
　　Day by day and night by night I grew to hate her –
　　Would God that she or I had died!

Confessions

There was a man called Bronckhorst – a three-cornered, middle-aged man in the Army – grey as a badger, and, some people said, with a touch of country-blood in him. That, however, cannot be proved. Mrs Bronckhorst was not exactly young, though fifteen years younger than her husband. She was a large, pale, quiet woman, with heavy eyelids over weak eyes, and hair that turned red or yellow as the lights fell on it.

Bronckhorst was not nice in any way. He had no respect for the pretty public and private lies that make life a little less nasty than it is. His manner towards his wife was coarse. There are many things – including actual assault with the clenched fist – that a wife will endure; but seldom a wife can bear – as Mrs Bronckhorst bore – with a long course of brutal, hard chaff, making light of her weaknesses, her headaches, her small fits of gaiety, her dresses, her queer little attempts to make herself attractive to her husband when she knows that she is not what she has been, and – worst of all – the love that she spends on her children. That particular sort of heavy-handed jest was specially dear to Bronckhorst. I suppose that he had first slipped into it, meaning no harm, in the honeymoon, when folk find their ordinary stock of endearments run short, and so go to the other extreme to express their feelings. A similar impulse makes a man say, '*Hutt*,[1] you old beast!' when a favourite horse nuzzles his coat-front. Unluckily, when the reaction of marriage sets in, the form of speech remains, and, the tenderness having died out,

214

hurts the wife more than she cares to say. But Mrs Bronckhorst was devoted to her 'Teddy' as she called him. Perhaps that was why he objected to her. Perhaps – this is only a theory to account for his infamous behaviour later on – he gave way to the queer, savage feeling that sometimes takes by the throat a husband twenty years married, when he sees, across the table, the same, same face of his wedded wife, and knows that, as he has sat facing it, so must he continue to sit until the day of its death or his own. Most men and all women know the spasm. It only lasts for three breaths as a rule, must be a 'throw-back' to times when men and women were rather worse than they are now, and is too unpleasant to be discussed.

Dinner at the Bronckhorsts' was an infliction few men cared to undergo. Bronckhorst took a pleasure in saying things that made his wife wince. When their little boy came in at dessert, Bronckhorst used to give him half a glass of wine, and, naturally enough, the poor little mite got first riotous, next miserable, and was removed screaming. Bronckhorst asked if that was the way Teddy usually behaved, and whether Mrs Bronckhorst could not spare some of her time 'to teach the little beggar decency'. Mrs Bronckhorst, who loved the boy more than her own life, tried not to cry – her spirit seemed to have been broken by her marriage. Lastly, Bronckhorst used to say, 'There! That'll do, that'll do. For God's sake try to behave like a rational woman. Go into the drawing-room.' Mrs Bronckhorst would go, trying to carry it all off with a smile; and the guest of the evening would feel angry and uncomfortable.

After three years of this cheerful life – for Mrs Bronckhorst had no women-friends to talk to – the station was startled by the news that Bronckhorst had instituted proceedings *on the criminal count*,[2] against a man called Biel, who certainly had been rather attentive to Mrs Bronckhorst whenever she had appeared in public. The utter want of reserve with which Bronckhorst treated his own dishonour helped us to know that the evidence against Biel would be entirely circumstantial and native. There were no letters; but Bronckhorst said openly that he would rack Heaven and Earth until he saw Biel superintending the manufacture of carpets in the Central Jail. Mrs Bronckhorst kept entirely to her house, and let charitable folks say what they pleased. Opinions were divided. Some two-thirds of the station jumped at once to the conclusion that Biel was guilty; but a dozen men who knew and liked him held by him. Biel was furious and surprised. He denied the whole thing, and vowed that he would thrash Bronckhorst within an inch of his life. No jury, we knew, would convict a man on the criminal count on native evidence in a land where you can buy a murder-charge, including the corpse, all complete for fifty-four rupees; but Biel did not care to scrape through by the benefit of a doubt. He wanted the whole thing cleared; but, as he said one night, 'He can prove anything with servants' evidence, and I've only my bare word.' This was almost a month before the case came on; and beyond agreeing with Biel, we could do little. All that we could be sure of was that the native evidence would be bad enough to blast Biel's character for the rest of his service; for when a native begins perjury he perjures himself thoroughly. He does not boggle over details.

Some genius at the end of the table whereat the affair was being talked over, said, 'Look here! I don't believe lawyers are any good. Get a man to wire to Strickland, and beg him to come down and pull us through.'

Strickland was about a hundred and eighty miles up the line. He had not long been married to Miss Youghal, but he scented in the telegram a chance of return to the old detective work that his soul lusted after, and next night he came in and heard our story. He finished his pipe and said oracularly, 'We must get at the evidence. Oorya³ bearer, Mussulman *khit* and sweeper *ayah*, I suppose, are the pillars of the charge. I am on in this piece; but I'm afraid I'm getting rusty in my talk.'

He rose and went into Biel's bedroom, where his trunk had been put, and shut the door. An hour later, we heard him say, 'I hadn't the heart to part with my old make-ups when I married. Will this do?' There was a loathly *fakir* salaaming in the doorway.

'Now lend me fifty rupees,' said Strickland, 'and give me your Words of Honour that you won't tell my wife.'

He got all that he asked for, and left the house while the table drank his health. What he did only he himself knows. A *fakir* hung about Bronckhorst's compound for twelve days. Then a

sweeper appeared, and when Biel heard of *him*, he said that
Strickland was an angel full-fledged. Whether the sweeper made
love to Janki, Mrs Bronckhorst's *ayah*, is a question which
concerns Strickland exclusively.

He came back at the end of three weeks, and said quietly, 'You
spoke the truth, Biel. The whole business is put up from beginning
to end. 'Jove! It almost astonishes *me*! That Bronckhorst beast
isn't fit to live.'

There was uproar and shouting, and Biel said, 'How are you
going to prove it? You can't say that you've been trespassing on
Bronckhorst's compound in disguise!'

'No,' said Strickland. 'Tell your lawyer-fool, whoever he is, to
get up something strong about "inherent improbabilities" and
"discrepancies of evidence". He won't have to speak, but it will
make him happy. *I'm* going to run this business.'

Biel held his tongue, and the other men waited to see what
would happen. They trusted Strickland as men trust quiet men.
When the case came off the Court was crowded. Strickland hung
about in the veranda of the Court, till he met the Mahommedan
khitmutgar. Then he murmured a *fakir*'s blessing in his ear, and
asked him how his second wife did. The man spun round, and,
as he looked into the eyes of 'Estreekin Sahib', his jaw dropped.
You must remember that before Strickland was married, he was,
as I have told you already, a power among natives. Strickland
whispered a rather coarse vernacular proverb to the effect that
he was abreast of all that was going on, and went into the Court
armed with a gut trainer's-whip.

The Mahommedan was the first witness, and Strickland
beamed upon him from the back of the Court. The man moist-
ened his lips with his tongue and, in his abject fear of 'Estreekin
Sahib' the *fakir*, went back on every detail of his evidence –
said he was a poor man, and God was his witness that he had
forgotten everything that Bronckhorst Sahib had told him to
say. Between his terror of Strickland, the Judge, and Bronckhorst he collapsed weeping.

Then began the panic among the witnesses. Janki, the *ayah*,
leering chastely behind her veil, turned grey, and the bearer left
the Court. He said that his Mamma was dying, and that it was

not wholesome for any man to lie unthriftily in the presence of 'Estreekin Sahib'.

Biel said politely to Bronckhorst, 'Your witnesses don't seem to work. Haven't you any forged letters to produce?' But Bronckhorst was swaying to and fro in his chair, and there was a dead pause after Biel had been called to order.

Bronckhorst's Counsel saw the look on his client's face, and without more ado pitched his papers on the little green baize table, and mumbled something about having been misinformed. The whole court applauded wildly, like soldiers at a theatre, and the Judge began to say what he thought.

Biel came out of the Court, and Strickland dropped a gut trainer's-whip in the veranda. Ten minutes later, Biel was cutting Bronckhorst into ribbons behind the old Court cells, quietly and without scandal. What was left of Bronckhorst was sent home in a carriage; and his wife wept over it and nursed it into a man again.

Later on, after Biel had managed to hush up the counter-charge against Bronckhorst of fabricating false evidence, Mrs Bronckhorst, with her faint, watery smile, said that there had been a mistake, but it wasn't her Teddy's fault altogether. She would wait till her Teddy came back to her. Perhaps he had grown tired of her, or she had tried his patience, and perhaps we wouldn't cut her any more, and perhaps the mothers would let their children play with 'little Teddy' again. He was so lonely. Then the station invited Mrs Bronckhorst everywhere, until Bronckhorst was fit to appear in public, when he went Home and took his wife with him. According to latest advices, her Teddy did come back to her, and they are moderately happy. Though, of course, he can never forgive her the thrashing that she was the indirect means of getting for him.

What Biel wants to know is, 'Why didn't I press home the charge against the Bronckhorst brute, and have him run in?'

What Mrs Strickland wants to know is, 'How *did* my husband bring such a lovely, lovely Waler from your station? I know *all* his money-affairs; and I'm *certain* he didn't *buy* it.'

The Bronckhorst Divorce-Case

What I want to know is, 'How do women like Mrs Bronckhorst come to marry men like Bronckhorst?'

And my conundrum is the most unanswerable of the three.

Venus Annodomini [1]

And the years went on, as the years must do;
But our great Diana was always new –
Fresh, and blooming, and blonde, and fair,
With azure eyes, and with aureate hair;
And all the folk, as they came or went,
Offered her praise to her heart's content.

Diana of Ephesus

She had nothing to do with Number Eighteen in the Braccio
Nuovo of the Vatican, between Visconti's Ceres and the God of
the Nile. She was purely an Indian deity – an Anglo-Indian deity,
that is to say – and we called her *the* Venus Annodomini, to
distinguish her from other Annodominis of the same everlasting
order. There was a legend among the Hills that she had once been
young; but no living man was prepared to come forward and say
boldly that the legend was true. Men rode up to Simla, and
stayed, and went away and made their name and did their life's
work, and returned again to find the Venus Annodomini exactly
as they had left her. She was as immutable as the Hills. But not
quite so green. All that a girl of eighteen could do in the way of
riding, walking, dancing, picnicking, and over-exertion generally,
the Venus Annodomini did, and showed no sign of fatigue or
trace of weariness. Besides perpetual youth, she had discovered,
men said, the secret of perpetual health; and her fame spread
about the land. From a mere woman, she grew to be an Institution,
insomuch that no young man could be said to be properly formed,
who had not, at some time or another, worshipped at the shrine
of the Venus Annodomini. There was no one like her, though
there were many imitations. Six years in her eyes were no more
than six months to ordinary women; and ten made less visible
impression on her than does a week's fever on an ordinary woman.
Every one adored her, and in return she was pleasant and

220

courteous to nearly every one. Youth had been a habit of hers for so long that she could not part with it – never realized, in fact, the necessity of parting with it – and took for her more chosen associates young people.

Among the worshippers of the Venus Annodomini was young Gayerson. 'Very Young Gayerson' he was called to distinguish him from his father 'Young' Gayerson, a Bengal Civilian, who affected the customs – as he had the heart – of youth. 'Very Young' Gayerson was not content to worship placidly and for form's sake, as the other young men did, or to accept a ride or a dance or a talk from the Venus Annodomini in a properly humble and thankful spirit. He was exacting, and, therefore, the Venus Annodomini repressed him. He worried himself nearly sick in a futile sort of way over her; and his devotion and earnestness made him appear either shy or boisterous or rude, as his mood might vary, by the side of the older men who, with him, bowed before the Venus Annodomini. She was sorry for him. He reminded her of a lad who, three-and-twenty years ago, had professed a boundless devotion for her, and for whom in return she had felt something more than a week's weakness. But that lad had fallen away and married another woman less than a year after he had worshipped her; and the Venus Annodomini had almost – not quite – forgotten his name. 'Very Young' Gayerson had the same big blue eyes and the same way of pouting his underlip when he was excited or troubled. But the Venus Annodomini checked him sternly none the less. Too much zeal was a thing that she did not approve of; preferring instead a tempered and sober tenderness.

'Very Young' Gayerson was miserable, and took no trouble to conceal his wretchedness. He was in the Army – a Line regiment, I think, but am not certain – and, since his face was a looking-glass and his forehead an open book, by reason of his innocence, his brothers-in-arms made his life a burden to him and embittered his naturally sweet disposition. No one except 'Very Young' Gayerson, and he never told his views, knew how old 'Very Young' Gayerson believed the Venus Annodomini to be. Perhaps he thought her five-and-twenty, or perhaps she told him that she was this age. 'Very Young' Gayerson would have forded the

Indus in flood to carry her lightest word, and had implicit faith in her. Every one liked him, and everyone was sorry when they saw him so bound a slave of the Venus Annodomini. Every one, too, admitted that it was not her fault; for the Venus Annodomini differed from Mrs Hauksbee and Mrs Reiver in this particular – she never moved a finger to attract any one; but, like Ninon de L'Enclos,² all men were attracted to her. One could admire and respect Mrs Hauksbee, despise and avoid Mrs Reiver, but one was forced to adore the Venus Annodomini.

'Very Young' Gayerson's Papa held a Division, or a Collectorate, or something administrative, in a particularly unpleasant part of Bengal – full of Babus³ who edited newspapers proving that 'Young' Gayerson was a 'Nero' and a 'Scylla' and a 'Charybdis'; and, in addition to the Babus, there was a good deal of dysentery and cholera abroad for nine months of the year. 'Young' Gayerson – he was about five-and-forty – rather liked Babus, they amused him, but he objected to dysentery, and when he could get away, went to Darjeeling for the most part. This particular season he fancied that he would come up to Simla and see his boy. The boy was not altogether pleased. He told the Venus Annodomini that his father was coming up, and she flushed a little and said that she should be delighted to make his acquaintance. Then she looked long and thoughtfully at 'Very Young' Gayerson, because she was very, very sorry for him, and he was a very, very big idiot.

'My daughter is coming out in a fortnight, Mr Gayerson,' she said.

'Your *what*?' said he.

'Daughter,' said the Venus Annodomini. 'She's been out for a year at Home already, and I want her to see a little of India. She is nineteen, and a very sensible nice girl, I believe.'

'Very Young' Gayerson, who was a short twenty-two years old, nearly fell out of his chair with astonishment; for he had persisted in believing, against all belief, in the youth of the Venus Annodomini. She, with her back to the curtained window, watched the effect of her sentences and smiled.

'Very Young' Gayerson's Papa came up twelve days later, and had not been in Simla four-and-twenty hours before two men, old acquaintances of his, had told him how 'Very Young' Gayerson had been conducting himself.

'Young' Gayerson laughed a good deal, and inquired who the Venus Annodomini might be. Which proves that he had been living in Bengal where nobody knows anything except the rate of Exchange. Then he said boys would be boys, and spoke to his son about the matter. 'Very Young' Gayerson said that he felt wretched and unhappy; and 'Young' Gayerson said that he repented of having helped to bring a fool into the world. He suggested that his son had better cut his leave short and go down to his duties. This led to an unfilial answer, and relations were strained until 'Young' Gayerson demanded that they should call on the Venus Annodomini. 'Very Young' Gayerson went with his papa, feeling, somehow, uncomfortable and small.

The Venus Annodomini received them graciously, and 'Young' Gayerson said, 'By Jove! It's Kitty!' 'Very Young' Gayerson would have listened for an explanation, if his time had not been taken up with trying to talk to a large, handsome, quiet, well-dressed girl – introduced to him by the Venus Annodomini as her daughter. She was far older in manner, style, and repose than 'Very Young' Gayerson; and, as he realized this thing, he felt sick.

Presently he heard the Venus Annodomini saying, 'Do you know that your son is one of my most devoted admirers?'

'I don't wonder,' said 'Young' Gayerson. Here he raised his voice. 'He follows his father's footsteps. Didn't I worship the ground you trod on, ever so long ago, Kitty? – and you haven't changed since then. How strange it all seems!'

'Very Young' Gayerson said nothing. His conversation with the daughter of the Venus Annodomini was, through the rest of the call, fragmentary and disjointed.

'At five to-morrow, then,' said the Venus Annodomini. 'And mind you are punctual.'

'At five punctually,' said 'Young' Gayerson. 'You can lend your old father a horse, I daresay, youngster, can't you? I'm going for a ride to-morrow afternoon.'

'Certainly,' said 'Very Young' Gayerson. 'I am going down to-morrow morning. My ponies are at your service, sir.'

The Venus Annodomini looked at him across the half-light of the room, and her big grey eyes filled with moisture. She rose and shook hands with him.

'Good-bye, Tom,' whispered the Venus Annodomini.

The Bisara of Pooree

Little Blind Fish, thou art marvellous wise,
Little Blind Fish, who put out thy eyes?
Open thy ears while I whisper my wish –
Bring me a lover, thou little Blind Fish.
The Charm of the Bisara

Some natives say that it came from the other side of Kulu, where the eleven-inch Temple Sapphire is. Others that it was made at the Devil-Shrine of Ao-Chung in Tibet, was stolen by a Kafir,[1] from him by a Gurkha, from him again by a Lahouli, from him by a *khitmutgar*, and by this latter sold to an Englishman, so all its virtue was lost; because, to work properly, the Bisara of Pooree must be stolen – with bloodshed if possible, but, at any rate, stolen.

These stories of the coming into India are all false. It was made at Pooree ages since – the manner of its making would fill a small book – was stolen by one of the Temple dancing-girls there, for her own purposes, and then passed on from hand to hand, steadily northward, till it reached Hanlé; always bearing the same name – the Bisara of Pooree. In shape it is a tiny square box of silver, studded outside with eight small balas-rubies.[2] Inside the box, which opens with a spring, is a little eyeless fish, carved from some sort of dark, shiny nut and wrapped in a shred of faded gold cloth. That is the Bisara of Pooree, and it were better for a man to take a king-cobra in his hand than to touch the Bisara of Pooree.

All kinds of magic are out of date and done away with, except in India, where nothing changes in spite of the shiny, top-scum stuff that people call 'civilization'. Any man who knows about the Bisara of Pooree will tell you what its powers are – always supposing that it has been honestly stolen. It is the only regularly working, trust-worthy love-charm in the country, with one excep-

225

tion. (The other charm is in the hands of a trooper of the Nizam's Horse,[3] at a place called Tuprani, due north of Hyderabad.) This can be depended upon for a fact. Someone else may explain it.

If the Bisara be not stolen, but given or bought or found, it turns against its owner in three years, and leads to ruin or death. This is another fact which you may explain when you have time. Meanwhile, you can laugh at it. At present the Bisara is safe on a hack-pony's neck, inside the blue bead-necklace that keeps off the Evil Eye. If the pony-driver ever finds it, and wears it, or gives it to his wife, I am sorry for him.

A very dirty Hill-coolie woman, with goitre, owned it at Theog in 1884. It came into Simla from the North before Churton's *khitmutgar* bought it, and sold it, for three times its silver-value, to Churton, who collected curiosities. The servant knew no more what he had bought than the master; but a man looking over Churton's collection of curiosities – Churton was an Assistant Commissioner, by the way – saw, and held his tongue. He was an Englishman, but knew how to believe. Which shows that he was different from most Englishmen. He knew that it was dangerous to have any share in the little box when working or dormant; for Love unsought is a terrible gift.

Pack – 'Grubby' Pack, as we used to call him – was, in every way, a nasty little man who must have crawled into the Army by mistake. He was three inches taller than his sword, but not half so strong. And the sword was a fifty-shilling, tailor-made one. Nobody liked him, and, I suppose, it was his wizenedness and worthlessness that made him fall so hopelessly in love with Miss Hollis, who was good and sweet, and five feet seven in her tennis-shoes. He was not content with falling in love quietly, but brought all the strength of his miserable little nature into the business. If he had not been so objectionable, one might have pitied him. He vapoured, and fretted, and fumed, and trotted up and down, and tried to make himself pleasing in Miss Hollis's big, quiet, grey eyes, and failed. It was one of the cases that you sometimes meet, even in our country, where we marry by Code, of a really blind attachment all on one side, without the faintest possibility of return. Miss Hollis looked on Pack as some sort of vermin running about the road. He had no prospects beyond Captain's pay, and no wits to help that out by one penny. In a large-sized man love like his would have been touching. In a good man it would have been grand. He being what he was, it was only a nuisance.

You will believe this much. What you will not believe is what follows: Churton, and The Man who Knew what the Bisara was, were lunching at the Simla Club together. Churton was complaining of life in general. His best mare had rolled out of stable down the cliff and had broken her back; his decisions were being reversed by the upper Courts more than an Assistant Commissioner of eight years' standing has a right to expect; he knew liver and fever, and for weeks past had felt out of sorts. Altogether, he was disgusted and disheartened.

Simla Club dining-room is built, as all the world knows, in two sections, with an arch-arrangement dividing them. Come in, turn to your own left, take the table under the window, and you cannot see any one who has come in, turned to the right, and taken a table on the right side of the arch. Curiously enough, every word that you say can be heard, not only by the other diner, but by the servants beyond the screen through which they bring dinner. This is worth knowing. An echoing-room is a trap to be forewarned against.

Half in fun, and half hoping to be believed, The Man who Knew told Churton the story of the Bisara of Pooree at rather greater length than I have told it to you in this place; winding up with a suggestion that Churton might as well throw the little box down the hill and see whether all his troubles would go with it. In ordinary ears, English ears, the tale was only an interesting bit of folklore. Churton laughed, said that he felt better for his tiffin, and went out. Pack had been tiffining by himself to the right of the arch, and had heard everything. He was nearly mad with his absurd infatuation for Miss Hollis, that all Simla had been laughing about.

It is a curious thing that, when a man hates or loves beyond reason, he is ready to go beyond reason to gratify his feelings; which he would not do for money or power merely. Depend upon it, Solomon would never have built altars to Ashtaroth and all those ladies with queer names, if there had not been trouble of some kind in his zenana,⁴ and nowhere else. But this is beside the story. The facts of the case are these: Pack called on Churton next day when Churton was out, left his card, and stole the Bisara of Pooree from its place under the clock on the mantelpiece! Stole it like the thief he was by nature! Three days later, all Simla was electrified by the news that Miss Hollis had accepted Pack – the shrivelled rat, Pack! Do you desire clearer evidence than this? The Bisara of Pooree had been stolen, and it worked as it had always done when won by foul means.

There are three or four times in a man's life when he is justified in meddling with other people's affairs to play Providence.

The Man who Knew felt that he was justified; but believing and acting on a belief are quite different things. The insolent satisfaction of Pack as he ambled by the side of Miss Hollis, and Churton's striking release from liver, as soon as the Bisara of Pooree had gone, decided The Man. He explained to Churton, and Churton laughed, because he was not brought up to believe that men on the Government House List steal – at least little things. But the miraculous acceptance by Miss Hollis of that tailor, Pack, decided him to take steps on suspicion. He vowed that he only wanted to find out where his ruby-studded silver box had vanished to. You cannot accuse a man on the Government House List of stealing; and if you rifle his room, you are a thief yourself. Churton, prompted by The Man who Knew, decided on burglary. If he found nothing in Pack's room . . . But it is not nice to think of what would have happened in that case.

Pack went to a dance at Benmore – Benmore was Benmore in those days, and not an office – and danced fifteen waltzes out of twenty-two with Miss Hollis. Churton and The Man took all the keys that they could lay hands on, and went to Pack's room in the hotel, certain that his servants would be away. Pack was a cheap soul. He had not purchased a decent cash-box to keep his papers in, but one of those native imitations that you buy for ten rupees. It opened to any sort of key, and there at the bottom, under Pack's Insurance Policy, lay the Bisara of Pooree!

Churton called Pack names, put the Bisara of Pooree in his pocket, and went to the dance with The Man. At least, he came in time for supper, and saw the beginning of the end in Miss

Hollis's eyes. She was hysterical after supper, and was taken away by her Mamma.

At the dance, with the abominable Bisara in his pocket, Churton twisted his foot on one of the steps leading down to the old Rink, and had to be sent home in a 'rickshaw, grumbling. He did not believe in the Bisara of Pooree any the more for this manifestation, but he sought out Pack and called him some ugly names; and 'thief' was the mildest of them. Pack took the names with the nervous smile of a little man who wants both soul and body to resent an insult, and went his way. There was no public scandal.

A week later Pack got his definite dismissal from Miss Hollis. There had been a mistake in the placing of her affections, she said. So he went away to Madras, where he can do no great harm even if he lives to be a Colonel.[5]

Churton insisted upon The Man who Knew taking the Bisara of Pooree as a gift. The Man took it, went down to the Cart-Road at once, found a cart-pony with a blue bead-necklace, fastened the Bisara of Pooree inside the necklace with a piece of shoe-string and thanked Heaven that he was rid of a danger.[6] Remember, in case you ever find it, that you must not destroy the Bisara of Pooree. I have not time to explain why just now, but the power lies in the little wooden fish. Mr Gubernatis or Max Müller[7] could tell you more about it than I.

You will say that all this story is made up. Very well. If ever you come across a little, silver, ruby-studded box, seven-eighths of an inch long by three-quarters wide, with a dark-brown wooden fish, wrapped in gold cloth, inside it, keep it. Keep it for three years, and then you will discover for yourself whether my story is true or false.

Better still, steal it as Pack did, and you will be sorry that you had not killed yourself in the beginning.

﴾ A Friend's Friend ﴿

Wherefore slew I the stranger? He brought me dishonour.
I saddled my mare Bijli. I set him upon her.
I gave him rice and goat's flesh. He bared me to laughter.
When he was gone from my tent, swift I followed after,
Taking a sword in my hand. The hot wine had filled him:
Under the stars he mocked me. Therefore I killed him.

Hadramauti[1]

This tale must be told in the first person for many reasons. The man whom I want to expose is Tranter of the Bombay side. I want Tranter black-balled at his Club, divorced from his wife, turned out of the Service, and cast into prison, until I get an apology from him in writing. I wish to warn the world against Tranter of the Bombay side.

You know the casual way in which men pass on acquaintances in India? It is a great convenience, because you can get rid of a man you don't like by writing a letter of introduction and putting him, with it, into the train. Globe-Trotters[2] are best treated thus. If you keep them moving, they have no time to say insulting and offensive things about 'Anglo–Indian Society'.

One day, late in the cold weather, I got a letter of preparation from Tranter of the Bombay side, advising me of the advent of a G.T., a man called Jevon; and saying, as usual, that any kindness shown to Jevon would be a kindness to Tranter. Every one knows the regular form of these communications.

Two days afterwards, Jevon turned up with his letter of introduction, and I did what I could for him. He was lint-haired, fresh-coloured, and very English. But he held no views about the Government of India. Nor did he insist on shooting tigers on the Station Mall, as some G.T.s do. Nor did he call us 'colonists', and dine in a flannel shirt and tweeds, under that delusion, as other G.T.s do. He was well behaved and very grateful for the little I won for him – most grateful of all when I secured him an invitation for the Afghan Ball, and introduced him to a Mrs Deemes, a lady for whom I had a great respect and admiration, who danced like the shadow of a leaf in a light wind. I set great store by the friendship of Mrs Deemes; but, had I known what was coming, I would have broken Jevon's neck with a curtain-pole before getting him that invitation.

But I did not know, and he dined at the Club, I think, on the night of the ball. I dined at home. When I went to the dance, the first man I met asked me whether I had seen Jevon. 'No,' said I. 'He's at the Club. Hasn't he come?' – 'Come!' said the man. 'Yes, he's very much come. You'd better look at him.'

I sought for Jevon. I found him sitting on a bench and smiling to himself and a programme. Half a look was enough for me. On that one night, of all others, he had begun a long and thirsty evening by taking too much! He was breathing heavily through his nose, his eyes were rather red, and he appeared very satisfied with all the earth. I put up a little prayer that the waltzing would work off the wine, and went about programme-filling, feeling uncomfortable. But I saw Jevon walk up to Mrs Deemes for the first dance, and I knew that all the waltzing on the card was not enough to keep Jevon's rebellious legs steady. That couple went round six times. I counted. Mrs Deemes dropped Jevon's arm and came across to me.

I am not going to repeat what Mrs Deemes said to me, because she was very angry indeed. I am not going to write what I said to Mrs Deemes, because I didn't say anything. I only wished that I had killed Jevon first and been hanged for it. Mrs Deemes drew her pencil through all the dances that I had booked with her, and went away, leaving me to remember that what I ought to have said was that Mrs Deemes had asked to be introduced to Jevon because he danced well; and that I really had not carefully worked out a plot to get her insulted. But I felt that argument was no good, and that I had better try to stop Jevon from waltzing me into more trouble. He, however, was gone, and about every third dance I set off to hunt for him. This ruined what little pleasure I expected from the entertainment.

Just before supper I caught Jevon at the buffet with his legs wide apart, talking to a very fat and indignant chaperon. 'If this person is a friend of yours, as I understand he is, I would recommend you to take him home,' said she. 'He is unfit for decent society.' Then I knew that goodness only knew what Jevon had been doing, and I tried to get him away.

But Jevon wasn't going; not he. He knew what was good for him, he did; and he wasn't going to be dictated to by any loconial nigger-driver, he wasn't; and I was the friend who had formed his infant mind, and brought him up to buy Benares brassware and fear God, so I was; and we would have many more blazing good drunks together, so we would; and all the she-camels in black silk in the world shouldn't make him withdraw his opinion that there was nothing better than Benedictine to give one an appetite. And then . . . But he was my guest.

I set him in a quiet corner of the supper-room, and went to find a wall-prop that I could trust. There was a good and kindly Subaltern – may Heaven bless that Subaltern, and make him a Commander-in-Chief! – who heard of my trouble. He was not dancing himself, and he owned a head like five-year-old teak-baulks. He said that he would look after Jevon till the end of the ball.

'Don't suppose you much mind what I do with him?' said he.

'Mind!' said I. 'No! You can murder the beast if you like.'

But the Subaltern did not murder him. He trotted off to the supper-room, and sat down by Jevon, drinking peg for peg with him. I saw the two fairly established, and went away, feeling more easy.

When 'The Roast Beef of Old England' sounded, I heard of Jevon's performances between the first dance and my meeting with him at the buffet. After Mrs Deemes had cast him off, it seems that he had found his way into the gallery, and offered to conduct the Band or to play any instrument in it, just as the Bandmaster pleased.

When the Bandmaster refused, Jevon said that he wasn't appreciated, and he yearned for sympathy. So he trundled down-stairs and sat out four dances with four girls, and proposed to three of them. One of the girls was a married woman, by the way. Then he went into the whist-room, and fell face-down and wept on the hearth-rug in front of the fire, because he had fallen into a den of card-sharpers, and his Mamma had always warned him against bad company. He had done a lot of other things, too, and had taken about three quarts of mixed liquors. Besides speaking of me in the most scandalous fashion!

All the women wanted him turned out, and all the men wanted him kicked. The worst of it was that every one said it was my fault. Now, I put it to you, how on earth could I have known that this innocent, fluffy G.T. would break out in this disgusting manner? You see, he had gone round the world nearly, and his vocabulary of abuse was cosmopolitan, though mainly Japanese, which he had picked up in a low tea-house at Hakodate.[3] It sounded like whistling.

While I was listening to first one man and then another telling me of Jevon's shameless behaviour and asking me for his blood, I wondered where he was. I was prepared to sacrifice him to Society on the spot.

But Jevon was gone, and, far away in the corner of the supper-room, sat my dear, good Subaltern, a little flushed, eating salad. I went over and said, 'Where's Jevon?' – 'In the cloakroom,' said the Subaltern. 'He'll keep till the women have gone. Don't you interfere with my prisoner.' I didn't want to interfere, but I peeped into the cloakroom, and found my guest put to bed on some rolled-up carpets, all comfy, his collar free, and a wet swab on his head.

The rest of the evening I spent in making timid attempts to explain things to Mrs Deemes and three or four other ladies, and trying to clear my character – for I am a respectable man – from the shameful slurs that my guest had cast upon it. Libel was no word for what he had said.

When I wasn't trying to explain, I was running off to the cloakroom to see that Jevon wasn't dead of apoplexy. I didn't want him to die on my hands. He had eaten my salt.

At last that ghastly ball ended, though I was not in the least restored to Mrs Deemes' favour. When the ladies had gone, and some one was calling for songs at the second supper, that angelic Subaltern told the servants to bring in the Sahib who was in the cloakroom, and clear away one end of the supper-table. While this was being done we formed ourselves into a Board of Punishment with the Doctor for President.

Jevon came in on four men's shoulders, and was put down on the table like a corpse in a dissecting-room, while the Doctor lectured on the evils of intemperance, and Jevon snored. Then we set to work.

We corked the whole of his face. We filled his hair with meringue-cream till it looked like a white wig. To protect everything till it dried, a man in the Ordnance Department, who understood the work, luted[4] a big blue paper cap from a cracker, with meringue-cream, low down on Jevon's forehead. This was punishment, not play, remember. We took gelatine off crackers, and stuck blue gelatine on his nose, and yellow gelatine on his chin, and green and red gelatine on his cheeks, pressing each dab down till it held as firm as gold-beaters' skin.[5]

We put a ham-frill round his neck, and tied it in a bow in front. He nodded like a mandarin.

We fixed gelatine on the back of his hands, and burnt-corked them inside, and put small cutlet-frills round his wrists, and tied both wrists together with string. We waxed up the ends of his moustache with isinglass.[6] He looked very martial.

We turned him over, pinned up his coat-tails between his shoulders, and put a rosette of cutlet-frills there. We took up the red cloth from the ball-room to the supper-room, and wound him up in it. There were sixty feet of red cloth, six feet broad; and he rolled up into a big fat bundle, with only that amazing head sticking out.

Lastly, we tied up the surplus of the cloth beyond his feet with coconut-fibre string as tightly as we knew how. We were so angry that we hardly laughed at all.

Just as we finished, we heard the rumble of bullock-carts taking away some chairs and things that the General's wife had lent for the ball. So we hoisted Jevon, like a roll of carpets, into one of the carts, and the carts went away.

Now the most extraordinary part of this tale is that never again did I see or hear anything of Jevon, G.T. He vanished utterly. He was not delivered at the General's house with the carpets. He just went into the black darkness of the end of the night, and was swallowed up. Perhaps he died and was thrown into the river.

But, alive or dead, I have often wondered how he got rid of the red cloth and the meringue-cream. I wonder still whether Mrs Deemes will ever take any notice of me again, and whether I shall live down the infamous stories that Jevon set afloat about my manners and customs between the first and the ninth waltz of the Afghan Ball. They stick closer than cream.

Wherefore, I want Tranter of the Bombay side, dead or alive. But dead for preference.

⟨ The Gate of the Hundred Sorrows ⟩

If I can attain Heaven for a pice,[1] why should you be envious?
Opium Smoker's Proverb

This is no work of mine. My friend, Gabral Misquitta, the half-caste, spoke it all, between moonset and morning, six weeks before he died; and I took it down from his mouth as he answered my questions. So:–

It lies between the Coppersmith's Gully and the pipe-stem sellers' quarter, within a hundred yards, too, as the crow flies, of the Mosque of Wazir Khan. I don't mind telling any one this much, but I defy him to find the Gate, however well he may think he knows the City. You might even go through the very gully it stands in a hundred times, and be none the wiser. We used to call the gully 'The Gully of the Black Smoke', but its native name is altogether different, of course. A loaded donkey couldn't pass between the walls; and, at one point, just before you reach the Gate, a bulged house-front makes people go along all sideways.[2]

It isn't really a gate, though. It's a house. Old Fung-Tching had it first five years ago. He was a boot-maker in Calcutta. They say that he murdered his wife there when he was drunk. That was why he dropped bazar-rum and took to the Black Smoke instead. Later on, he came up north and opened the Gate as a house where you could get your smoke in peace and quiet. Mind you, it was a *pukka*, respectable opium-house, and not one of those stifling, sweltering *chandoo-khanas* that you can find all over the City. No; the old man knew his business thoroughly, and he was most clean for a Chinaman. He was a one-eyed little chap, not much more than five feet high, and both his middle fingers were gone. All the same, he was the handiest man at rolling black pills I have ever seen. Never seemed to be touched by the Smoke, either; and what he took day and night, night and day, was a caution. I've been at it five years, and I can do my fair share of the Smoke with any one; but I was a child to Fung-Tching that way. All the same, the old man was keen on his money; very keen; and that's what I can't understand. I heard he saved a good deal before he died, but his nephew has got all that now; and the old man's gone back to China to be buried.

He kept the big upper room, where his best customers gathered, as neat as a new pin. In one corner used to stand Fung-Tching's Joss [3] – almost as ugly as Fung-Tching – and there were always sticks burning under his nose; but you never smelt 'em when the pipes were going thick. Opposite the Joss was Fung-Tching's coffin. He had spent a good deal of his savings on that, and whenever a new man came to the Gate he was always introduced to it. It was lacquered black, with red and gold writings on it, and I've heard that Fung-Tching brought it out all the way from China. I don't know whether that's true or not, but I know that, if I came first in the evening, I used to spread my mat just at the foot of it. It was a quiet corner, you see, and a sort of breeze from the gully came in at the window now and then. Besides the mats, there was no other furniture in the room – only the coffin, and the old Joss all green and blue and purple with age and polish.

Fung-Tching never told us why he called the place 'The Gate of the Hundred Sorrows'. (He was the only Chinaman I know who used bad-sounding fancy names. Most of them are flowery. As you'll see in Calcutta.) We used to find that out for ourselves. Nothing grows on you so much, if you're white, as the Black Smoke. A yellow man is made different. Opium doesn't tell on him scarcely at all; but white and black suffer a good deal. Of course, there are some people that the Smoke doesn't touch any more than tobacco would at first. They just doze a bit, as one would fall asleep naturally, and next morning they are almost fit for work. Now, I was one of that sort when I began, but I've been at it for five years pretty steadily, and it's different now. There was an old aunt of mine, down Agra way, and she left me a little at her death. About sixty rupees a month secured. Sixty isn't much. I can recollect a time, seems hundreds and hundreds of years ago, that I was getting my three hundred a month, and pickings, when I was working on a big timber-contract in Calcutta.

I didn't stick to that work for long. The Black Smoke does not allow of much other business; and even though I am very little affected by it, as men go, I couldn't do a day's work now to save my life. After all, sixty rupees is what I want. When old Fung-Tching was alive he used to draw the money for me, give me about half of it to live on (I eat very little), and the rest he kept himself. I was free of the Gate at any time of the day and night, and could smoke and sleep there when I liked; so I didn't care. I know the old man made a good thing out of it; but that's no matter. Nothing matters much to me; and besides, the money always came fresh and fresh each month.

There was ten of us met at the Gate when the place was first opened. Me, and two Babus from a Government Office somewhere in Anarkulli, but they got the sack and couldn't pay (no man who has to work in the daylight can do the Black Smoke for any length of time straight on); a Chinaman that was Fung-Tching's nephew; a bazar-woman that had got a lot of money somehow; an English loafer – MacSomebody,[4] I think, but I have forgotten, – that smoked heaps, but never seemed to pay anything (they said he had saved Fung-Tching's life at some trial in Calcutta when he was a barrister); another Eurasian, like myself, from Madras; a half-caste woman, and a couple of men who said they had come from the North. I think they must have been Persians or Afghans or something. There are not more than five of us living now, but we come regular. I don't know what happened to the Babus; but the bazar-woman, she died after six months of the Gate, and I think Fung-Tching took her bangles and nose-ring for himself. But I'm not certain. The Englishman, he drank as well as smoked, and he dropped off. One of the Persians got killed in a row at night by the big well near the mosque a long time ago, and the Police shut up the well, because they said it was full of foul air. They found him dead at the bottom of it. So, you see, there is only me, the Chinaman, the half-caste woman that we call the Memsahib (she used to live with Fung-Tching), the other Eurasian, and one of the Persians. The Memsahib looks very old now. I think she was a young woman when the Gate was opened; but we are all old for the matter of that. Hundreds and hundreds of years old. It's very hard to keep count of time in the Gate, and, besides, time doesn't matter to me. I draw my sixty rupees fresh and fresh every month. A very, very long while ago, when I used to be getting three hundred and fifty rupees a month, and pickings, on a big timber-contract at Calcutta, I had a wife of sorts. But she's dead now. People said that I killed her by taking to the Black Smoke. Perhaps I did, but it's so long since that it doesn't matter. Sometimes, when I first came to the Gate, I used to feel sorry for it; but that's all over and done with long ago, and I draw my sixty rupees fresh and fresh every month, and am quite happy. Not *drunk* happy, you know, but always quiet and soothed and contented.

How did I take to it? It began at Calcutta. I used to try it in my own house, just to see what it was like. I never went very far, but I think my wife must have died then. Anyhow, I found myself here, and got to know Fung-Tching. I don't remember rightly how that came about; but he told me of the Gate and I used to go there, and, somehow, I have never got away from it since. Mind you, though, the Gate was a respectable place in Fung-Tching's time, where you could be comfortable, and not at all like the *chandoo-khanas* where the niggers go. No; it was clean, and quiet, and not crowded. Of course, there were others besides us ten and the man; but we always had a mat apiece, with a wadded woollen headpiece, all covered with black and red dragons and things, just like the coffin in the corner.

At the end of one's third pipe the dragons used to move about and fight. I've watched 'em many and many a night through. I used to regulate my Smoke that way, and now it takes a dozen pipes to make 'em stir. Besides, they are all torn and dirty, like the mats, and old Fung-Tching is dead. He died a couple of years ago, and gave me the pipe I always use now – a silver one, with queer beasts crawling up and down the receiver-bottle below the cup. Before that, I think, I used a big bamboo stem with a copper cup, a very small one, and a green jade mouthpiece. It was a little thicker than a walking-stick stem, and smoked sweet, very sweet. The bamboo seemed to suck up the smoke. Silver doesn't, and I've got to clean it out now and then; that's a great deal of trouble, but I smoke it for the old man's sake. He must have made a good thing out of me, but he always gave me clean mats and pillows, and the best stuff you could get anywhere.

When he died, his nephew Tsin-ling took up the Gate, and he called it the 'Temple of the Three Possessions', but we old ones speak of it as the 'Hundred Sorrows', all the same. The nephew does things very shabbily, and I think the Memsahib must help him. She lives with him; same as she used to do with the old man. The two let in all sorts of low people, niggers and all, and the Black Smoke isn't as good as it used to be. I've found burnt bran in my pipe over and over again. The old man would have died if that had happened in his time. Besides, the room is never cleaned, and all the mats are torn and cut at the edges. The coffin is gone – gone to China again – with the old man and two ounces of Smoke inside it, in case he should want 'em on the way.

The Joss doesn't get so many sticks burnt under his nose as he used to. That's a sign of ill-luck, as sure as death. He's all brown, too, and no one ever attends to him. That's the Memsahib's work, I know; because, when Tsin-ling tried to burn gilt paper before him, she said it was waste of money, and, if he kept a stick burning very slowly, the Joss wouldn't know the difference. So now we've got the sticks mixed with a lot of glue, and they take half an hour longer to burn, and smell stinky. Let alone the smell of the room by itself. No business can get on if they try that sort of thing. The Joss doesn't like it. I can see that. Late at night, sometimes, he turns all sorts of queer colours – blue and green and red – just as he used to do when old Fung-Tching was alive; and he rolls his eyes and stamps his feet like a devil.

I don't know why I don't leave the place and smoke quietly in a little room of my own in the bazar. Most like, Tsin-ling would kill me if I went away – he draws my sixty rupees now – and besides, it's too much trouble, and I've grown to be very fond of the Gate. It's not much to look at. Not what it was in the old man's time, but I couldn't leave it. I've seen so many come in and out. And I've seen so many die here on the mats that I should be afraid of dying in the open now. I've seen some things that people would call strange enough; but nothing is strange when you're on the Black Smoke, except the Black Smoke. And if it was, it wouldn't matter.

Fung-Tching used to be very particular about his people, and never got in any one who'd give trouble by dying messy and such. But the nephew isn't half so careful. He tells everywhere that he keeps a 'first-chop' house. Never tries to get men in quietly, and make them comfortable like Fung-Tching did. That's why the Gate is getting a little bit more known than it used to be. Among the niggers of course. The nephew daren't get a white, or, for matter of that, a mixed skin into the place. He has to keep us three, of course – me and the Memsahib and the other Eurasian. We're fixtures. But he wouldn't give us credit for a pipeful – not for anything. [5]

One of these days, I hope, I shall die in the Gate. The Persian and the Madras man are terribly shaky now. They've got a boy to light their pipes for them. I always do that myself. Most like, I shall see them carried out before me. I don't think I shall ever outlive the Memsahib or Tsin-ling. Women last longer than men at the Black Smoke, and Tsin-ling has a deal of the old man's blood in him, though he does smoke cheap stuff. The bazar-woman knew when she was going two days before her time; and she died on a clean mat with a nicely-wadded pillow, and the old man hung up her pipe just above the Joss. He was always fond of her, I fancy. But he took her bangles just the same.

I should like to die like the bazar-woman – on a clean, cool mat with a pipe of good stuff between my lips. When I feel I'm going, I shall ask Tsin-ling for them, and he can draw my sixty rupees a month, fresh and fresh, as long as he pleases. Then I shall lie back, quiet and comfortable, and watch the black and red dragons have their last big fight together; and then ... [6]

Well, it doesn't matter. Nothing matters much to me – only I wish Tsin-ling wouldn't put bran into the Black Smoke.

⟨ The Madness of Private Ortheris ⟩

Oh! Where would I be when my froat was dry?
Oh! Where would I be when the bullets fly?
Oh! Where would I be when I come to die?
        Why,
Somewheres anigh my chum.
        If 'e's liquor 'e'll give me some,
        If I'm dyin' 'e'll 'old my 'ead,
An' 'e'll write 'em 'Ome when I'm dead.
Gawd send us a trusty chum!

Barrack-Room Ballad

My friends Mulvaney and Ortheris had gone on a shooting-expedition for one day. Learoyd was still in hospital, recovering from fever picked up in Burma. They sent me an invitation to join them, and were genuinely pained when I brought beer – almost enough beer to satisfy two Privates of the Line ... and Me.

"Twasn't for that we bid you welkim, sorr,' said Mulvaney sulkily. ''Twas for the pleasure av your comp'ny.'

Ortheris came to the rescue with – 'Well, 'e won't be none the worse for bringin' liquor with 'im. We ain't a file o' Dooks. We're bloomin' Tommies, ye cantankris Hirishman; an' 'ere's your very good 'ealth!'

We shot all the forenoon, and killed two pariah-dogs, four green parrots, sitting, one kite by the burning-ghat,[1] one snake flying, one mud-turtle, and eight crows. Game was plentiful. Then we sat down to tiffin–'bull-mate an' bran-bread', Mulvaney called it – by the side of the river, and took pot shots at the crocodiles in the intervals of cutting up the food with our only pocket-knife. Then we drank up all the beer, and threw the bottles into the water and fired at them. After that, we eased belts and stretched ourselves on the warm sand and smoked. We were too lazy to continue shooting.

Ortheris heaved a big sigh, as he lay on his stomach with his head between his fists. Then he swore quietly into the blue sky.

'Fwhat's that for?' said Mulvaney. 'Have ye not dhrunk enough?'

'Tott'nim Court Road, an' a gal I fancied there. Wot's the good o' sodgerin'?'

'Orth'ris, me son,' said Mulvaney hastily, ''tis more than likely you've got throuble in your inside wid the beer. I feel that way mesilf whin my liver gets rusty.'

Ortheris went on slowly, not heeding the interruption:

'I'm a Tommy – a bloomin', eight-anna, dog-stealin' Tommy, with a number instead of a decent name. Wot's the good o' me? If I 'ad a stayed at 'Ome, I might a married that gal and kep' a little shorp in the 'Ammersmith 'Igh – "S. Orth'ris, Prac-ti-cal Taxi-der-mist". With a stuff' fox, like they 'as in the Haylesbury Dairies, in the winder, an' a little case of blue and yaller glass-heyes, an' a little wife to call "shorp!" "shorp!" when the doorbell rung. As it *his*, I'm on'y a Tommy – a Bloomin', Gawd-forsaken, Beer-swillin' Tommy. "Rest on your harms – '*versed*; Stan' at – *hease*; 'Shun. 'Verse – *harms*. Right an' lef' – *tarrn*. Slow – *march*. 'Alt – *front*. Rest on your harms – '*versed*. With blank-cartridge – *load*." An' that's the end o' me.' He was quoting fragments from Funeral Parties' Orders.

'Stop ut!' shouted Mulvaney. 'Whin ye've fired into nothin' as often as me, over a better man than yoursilf, ye will not make a mock av thim ordhers. 'Tis worse than whistlin' the *Dead March* in barracks. An' you full as a tick, an' the sun cool, an' all an' all! I take shame for you. Ye're no better than a Pagin – you an' your firin'-parties an' your glass-eyes. Won't *you* stop ut, sorr?'

What could I do? Could I tell Ortheris anything that he did not know of the pleasures of his life? I was not a Chaplain nor a Subaltern, and Ortheris had a right to speak as he thought fit.

'Let him run, Mulvaney,' I said. 'It's the beer.'

'No! 'Tisn't the beer,' said Mulvaney. 'I know fwhat's comin'. He's tuk this way now an' agin, an' ut's bad – ut's bad – for I'm fond av the bhoy.'

Indeed, Mulvaney seemed needlessly anxious; but I knew that he looked after Ortheris in a fatherly way.

'Let me talk, let me talk,' said Ortheris dreamily. 'D'you stop your parrit screamin' of a 'ot day, when the cage is a-cookin' 'is pore little pink toes orf, Mulvaney?'

'Pink toes! D'ye mane to say you've pink toes undher your bullswools, ye blandandherin',' – Mulvaney gathered himself together for a terrific denunciation – 'school-misthress? Pink toes! How much Bass wid the label did that ravin' choild dhrink?'

''Tain't Bass,' said Ortheris. 'It's a bitterer beer nor that. It's 'ome-sickness!'

'Hark to him! An' he goin' Home in the *Sherapis* in the inside av four months!'

'I don't care. It's all one to me. 'Ow d' you know I ain't 'fraid o' dyin' 'fore I gets my discharge paipers?' He recommenced, in a sing-song voice, the Orders.

I had never seen this side of Ortheris' character before, but evidently Mulvaney had, and attached serious importance to it. While Ortheris babbled, with his head on his arms, Mulvaney whispered to me:

'He's always tuk this way whin he's been checked overmuch by the childher they make Sargints nowadays. That an' havin' nothin' to do. I can't make ut out anyways.'

'Well, what does it matter? Let him talk himself through.'

Ortheris began singing a parody of 'The Ramrod Corps', full of cheerful allusions to battle, murder, and sudden death. He looked out across the river as he sang; and his face was quite strange to me. Mulvaney caught me by the elbow to ensure attention.

'Matther? It matthers everything! 'Tis some sort av fit that's on him. I've seen ut. 'Twill hould him all this night, an' in the middle av ut he'll get out av his cot an' go rakin' in the rack for his 'coutremints. Thin he'll come over to me an' say, "I'm goin' to Bombay. Answer for me in the mornin'." Thin me an' him will fight as we've done before – him to go, an' me to hould him – an' so we'll both come on the books for disturbin' in barracks. I've belted him, an' I've bruk his head, an' I've talked to him, but 'tis no manner av use whin the fit's on him. He's as good a bhoy as ever stepped whin his mind's clear. I know fwhat's comin', though, this night in barracks. Lord send he doesn't loose on me whin I rise to knock him down. 'Tis *that* that's in my mind day an' night.'

This put the case in a much less pleasant light, and fully accounted for Mulvaney's anxiety. He seemed to be trying to coax Ortheris out of the fit; for he shouted down the bank where the boy was lying:

'Listen now, you wid the "pore pink toes" an' the glass-eyes! Did you shwim the Irriwaddy at night, behin' me, as a bhoy shud; or were you hidin' undher a bed, as you was at Ahmid Kheyl?'

This was at once a gross insult and a direct lie, and Mulvaney meant it to bring on a fight. But Ortheris seemed shut up in some sort of trance. He answered slowly, without a sign of irritation, in the same cadenced voice as he had used for his firing-party orders:

'*Hi* swum the Irriwaddy in the night, as you know, for to take the town of Lungtungpen, nakid an' without fear. *Hand* where I was at Ahmed Kheyl you know, and four bloomin' Paythans know too. But that was summat to do, an' I didn't think o' dyin'. Now I'm sick to go 'Ome – go 'Ome – go 'Ome! No, I ain't mammysick, because my uncle brung me up, but I'm sick for London again; sick for the sounds of 'er, an' the sights of 'er, and the stinks of 'er; orange-peel and hasphalt an' gas comin' in over Vaux'all Bridge. Sick for the rail goin' down to Box 'Ill, with your gal on your knee an' a new clay pipe in your face. That, an' the Stran' lights where you knows ev'ry one, an' the Copper that takes you up is a old friend that tuk you up before, when you was a little, smitchy boy lying loose 'tween the Temple an' the Dark Harches. No bloomin' guard-mountin', no bloomin' rotten-stone, nor khaki, an' yourself your own master with a gal to take an' see the Humaners practisin' a-hookin' dead corpses out of the Serpentine o' Sundays. An' I lef' all that for to serve the Widder[2] beyond the seas, where there ain't no women and there ain't no liquor worth 'avin', and there ain't nothin' to see, nor do, nor say, nor feel, nor think. Lord love you, Stanley Orth'ris, but you're a bigger bloomin' fool than the rest o' the Reg'ment and Mulvaney wired together! There's the Widder sittin' at 'Ome with a gold crownd on 'er 'ead; and 'ere am Hi, Stanley Orth'ris, the Widder's property, a rottin' FOOL!'

His voice rose at the end of the sentence, and he wound up with a six-shot Anglo-Vernacular oath. Mulvaney said nothing, but looked at me as if he expected that I could bring peace to poor Ortheris' troubled brain.

I remembered once at Rawal Pindi having seen a man, nearly mad with drink, sobered by being made a fool of. Some regiments may know what I mean. I hoped that we might slake off Ortheris in the same way, though he was perfectly sober. So I said:

'What's the use of grousing there, and speaking against The Widow?'

'I didn't!' said Ortheris. 'S'elp me Gawd, I never said a word agin 'er, an' I wouldn't – not if I was to desert this minute!'

Here was my opening. 'Well, you meant to, anyhow. What's the use of cracking-on for nothing? Would you slip it now if you got the chance?'

'On'y try me!' said Ortheris, jumping to his feet as if he had been stung.

Mulvaney jumped too. 'Fwhat are you going to do?' said he.

'Help Ortheris down to Bombay or Karachi, whichever he likes. You can report that he separated from you before tiffin, and left his gun on the bank here!'

'I'm to report that – am I?' said Mulvaney slowly. 'Very well. If Orth'ris manes to desert now, and will desert now, an' you, sorr, who have been a frind to me an' to him, will help him to ut, I, Terence Mulvaney, on my oath which I've niver bruk yet, will report as you say. But —' here he stepped up to Ortheris, and shook the stock of the fowling-piece in his face – 'your fistes help you, Stanley Orth'ris, if iver I come across you agin!'

'I don't care!' said Ortheris. 'I'm sick o' this dorg's life. Give me a chanst. Don't play with me. Le' me go!'

'Strip,' said I, 'and change with me, and then I'll tell you what to do.'

I hoped that the absurdity of this would check Ortheris; but he had kicked off his ammunition-boots and got rid of his tunic almost before I had loosed my shirt-collar. Mulvaney gripped me by the arm.

'The fit's on him: the fit's workin' on him still! By my Honour and Sowl, we shall be accessiry to a desartion yet. Only twenty-

eight days, as you say, sorr, or fifty-six, but think o' the shame –
the black shame to him an' me!' I had never seen Mulvaney so
excited.

But Ortheris was quite calm, and, as soon as he had exchanged
clothes with me, and I stood up a Private of the Line, he said
shortly, 'Now! Come on. What nex'? D'ye mean fair. What must
I do to get out o' this 'ere a-Hell?'

I told him that, if he would wait for two or three hours near
the river, I would ride into the station and come back with one
hundred rupees. He would, with that money in his pocket, walk
to the nearest side-station on the line, about five miles away, and
would there take a first-class ticket for Karachi. Knowing that he
had no money on him when he went out shooting, his Regiment
would not immediately wire to the seaports, but would hunt for
him in the native villages near the river. Further, no one would
think of seeking a deserter in a first-class carriage. At Karachi he
was to buy white clothes and ship, if he could, on a cargo-steamer.

Here he broke in. If I helped him to Karachi, he would arrange
all the rest. Then I ordered him to wait where he was until it was
dark enough for me to ride into the station without my dress
being noticed. Now, God in His wisdom has made the heart of
the British Soldier, who is very often an unlicked ruffian, as soft
as the heart of a little child, in order that he may believe in and
follow his officers into tight and nasty places. He does not so
readily come to believe in a 'civilian', but, when he does, he
believes implicitly and like a dog. I had had the honour of the
friendship of Private Ortheris, at intervals, for more than three
years, and we had dealt with each other as man by man. Consequently, he considered that all my words were true, and not
spoken lightly.

Mulvaney and I left him in the high grass near the river-bank,
and went away, still keeping to the high grass, towards my horse.
The shirt scratched me horribly.

We waited nearly two hours for the dusk to fall and allow me
to ride off. We spoke of Ortheris in whispers, and strained our
ears to catch any sound from the spot where we had left him. But
we heard nothing except the wind in the plume-grass.

'I've bruk his head,' said Mulvaney earnestly, 'time an' agin.

I've nearly kilt him wid the belt, an' *yet* I can't knock thim fits out av his soft head. No! An' he's not soft, for he's reasonable an' likely by natur'. Fwhat is ut? Is ut his breedin' which is nothin', or his edukashin which he niver got? You that think ye know things, answer me thot.'

But I found no answer. I was wondering how long Ortheris, on the bank of the river, would hold out, and whether I should be forced to help him to desert, as I had given my word.

Just as the dusk shut down and, with a very heavy heart, I was beginning to saddle up my horse, we heard wild shouts from the river.

The devils had departed from Private Stanley Ortheris, No. 22639, B Company. The loneliness, the dusk, and the waiting had driven them out as I had hoped. We set off at the double and found him plunging about wildly through the grass, with his coat off – my coat off, I mean. He was calling for us like a madman.

When we reached him he was dripping with perspiration, and trembling like a startled horse. We had great difficulty in soothing him. He complained that he was in civilian kit, and wanted to tear my clothes off his body. I ordered him to strip, and we made a second exchange as quickly as possible.

The rasp of his own 'greyback' shirt and the squeak of his boots seemed to bring him to himself. He put his hands before his eyes and said:

'Wot was it? I ain't mad, I ain't sunstrook, an' I've bin an' gone an' said, an' bin an' gone an' done ... *Wot* 'ave I bin an' done?'

'Fwhat have you done?' said Mulvaney. 'You've dishgraced yoursilf – though that's no matther. You've dishgraced B Comp'ny, an' worst av all, you've dishgraced *Me*! Me that taught you how for to walk abroad like a man – whin you was a dhirty little, fish-backed little, whimperin' little recruity. As you are now, Stanley Orth'ris!'

Ortheris said nothing for a while. Then he unslung his belt, heavy with the badges of half-a-dozen regiments that his own had lain with, and handed it over to Mulvaney.

'I'm too little for to mill with you, Mulvaney,' said he, 'an' you've strook me before; but you can take an' cut me in two with this 'ere if you like.'

Mulvaney turned to me.

'Lave me to talk to him, sorr,' said Mulvaney.

I left, and on my way home thought a good deal over Ortheris in particular, and my friend Private Thomas Atkins whom I love, in general.

But I could not come to any conclusion of any kind whatever.

⚡ The Story of Muhammad Din ⚡

Who is the happy man? He that sees, in his own house at home, little
children crowned with dust, leaping and falling and crying.

Munichandra,[1] translated by Professor Peterson

The polo-ball was an old one, scarred, chipped, and dinted. It
stood on the mantelpiece among the pipe-stems which Imam
Din, *khitmutgar*, was cleaning for me.

'Does the Heaven-born want this ball?' said Imam Din deferen-
tially.

The Heaven-born set no particular store by it; but of what use
was a polo-ball to a *khitmutgar*?

'By Your Honour's favour, I have a little son. He has seen
this ball, and desires it to play with. I do not want it for
myself.'

No one would for an instant accuse portly old Imam Din of
wanting to play with polo-balls. He carried out the battered thing
into the veranda; and there followed a hurricane of joyful squeaks,
a patter of small feet, and the *thud-thud-thud* of the ball rolling
along the ground. Evidently the little son had been waiting outside
the door to secure his treasure. But how had he managed to see
that polo-ball?

Next day, coming back from office half an hour earlier than
usual, I was aware of a small figure in the dining-room – a tiny,
plump figure in a ridiculously inadequate shirt which came,
perhaps, half-way down the tubby stomach. It wandered round
the room, thumb in mouth, crooning to itself as it took stock of
the pictures. Undoubtedly this was the 'little son'.

He had no business in my room, of course; but was so deeply
absorbed in his discoveries that he never noticed me in the
doorway. I stepped into the room and startled him nearly into a
fit. He sat down on the ground with a gasp. His eyes opened, and

250

his mouth followed suit. I knew what was coming, and fled, followed by a long, dry howl which reached the servants' quarters far more quickly than any command of mine had ever done. In ten seconds Imam Din was in the dining-room. Then despairing sobs arose, and I returned to find Imam Din admonishing the small sinner, who was using most of his shirt as a handkerchief.

'This boy,' said Imam Din judicially, 'is a *budmash* – a big *budmash*. He will, without doubt, go to the *jail-khana* for his behaviour.' Renewed yells from the penitent, and an elaborate apology to myself from Imam Din.

'Tell the baby,' said I, 'that the Sahib is not angry, and take him away.' Imam Din conveyed my forgiveness to the offender, who had now gathered all his shirt round his neck, stringwise, and the yell subsided into a sob. The two set off for the door. 'His name,' said Imam Din, as though the name were part of the crime, 'is Muhammad Din, and he is a *budmash*.' Freed from present danger, Muhammad Din turned round in his father's arms, and said gravely, 'It is true that my name is Muhammad Din, Tahib, but I am not a *budmash*. I am a *man*!'

From that day dated my acquaintance with Muhammad Din. Never again did he come into my dining-room, but on the neutral ground of the garden we greeted each other with much state, though our conversation was confined to 'Talaam, Tahib' from his side, and 'Salaam, Muhammad Din' from mine. Daily on my return from office, the little white shirt and the fat little body used to rise from the shade of the creeper-covered trellis where they had been hid; and daily I checked my horse here, that my salutation might not be slurred over or given unseemly.

Muhammad Din never had any companions. He used to trot about the compound, in and out of the castor-oil bushes, on mysterious errands of his own. One day I stumbled upon some of his handiwork far down the grounds. He had half buried the polo-ball in dust, and stuck six shrivelled old marigold flowers in a circle round it. Outside that circle again was a rude square, traced out in bits of red brick alternating with fragments of broken china; the whole bounded by a little bank of dust. The waterman from the well-curb put in a plea for the small architect, saying that it was only the play of a baby and did not much disfigure my garden.

Heaven knows that I had no intention of touching the child's work then or later; but, that evening, a stroll through the garden brought me unawares full on it; so that I trampled, before I knew, marigold-heads, dust-bank, and fragments of broken soap-dish into confusion past all hope of mending. Next morning, I came upon Muhammad Din crying softly to himself over the ruin I had wrought. Some one had cruelly told him that the Sahib was very angry with him for spoiling the garden, and had scattered his rubbish, using bad language the while. Muhammad Din laboured for an hour at effacing every trace of the dust-bank and pottery fragments, and it was with a tearful and apologetic face that he said, 'Talaam, Tahib,' when I came home from office. A hasty inquiry resulted in Imam Din informing Muhammad Din that, by my singular favour, he was permitted to disport himself as he pleased. Whereat the child took heart and fell to tracing the ground-plan of an edifice which was to eclipse the marigold-polo-ball creation.

For some months the chubby little eccentricity revolved in his humble orbit among the castor-oil bushes and in the dust; always fashioning magnificent palaces from stale flowers thrown away by the bearer, smooth water-worn pebbles, bits of broken glass, and feathers pulled, I fancy, from my fowls – always alone, and always crooning to himself.

A gaily-spotted sea-shell was dropped one day close to the last of his little buildings; and I looked that Muhammad Din should build something more than ordinarily splendid on the strength of it. Nor was I disappointed. He meditated for the better part of an hour, and his crooning rose to a jubilant song. Then he began tracing in the dust. It would certainly be a wondrous palace, this one, for it was two yards long and a yard broad in ground-plan. But the palace was never completed.

Next day there was no Muhammad Din at the head of the carriage-drive, and no 'Talaam, Tahib' to welcome my return. I had grown accustomed to the greeting, and its omission troubled me. Next day Imam Din told me that the child was suffering slightly from fever and needed quinine. He got the medicine, and an English Doctor.

'They have no stamina, these brats,' said the Doctor, as he left Imam Din's quarters.

A week later, though I would have given much to have avoided it, I met on the road to the Mussulman burying-ground Imam Din, accompanied by one other friend, carrying in his arms, wrapped in a white cloth, all that was left of little Muhammad Din.

On the Strength of a Likeness

If your mirror be broken, look into still water; but have a care that you do not fall in.

Hindu Proverb

Next to a requited attachment, one of the most convenient things that a young man can carry about with him at the beginning of his career is an unrequited attachment. It makes him feel important and business-like, and *blasé*, and cynical; and whenever he has a touch of liver, or suffers from want of exercise, he can mourn over his lost love, and be very happy in a tender, twilight fashion.

Hannasyde's affair of the heart had been a godsend to him. It was four years old, and the girl had long since given up thinking of it. She had married and had many cares of her own. In the beginning, she had told Hannasyde that, 'while she could never be anything more than a sister to him, she would always take the deepest interest in his welfare'. This startlingly new and original remark gave Hannasyde something to think over for two years; and his own vanity filled in the other twenty-four months. Hannasyde was quite different from Phil Garron, but, none the less, had several points in common with that far too lucky man.

He kept his unrequited attachment by him as men keep a well-smoked pipe – for comfort's sake, and because it had grown dear in the using. It brought him happily through one Simla season. Hannasyde was not lovely. There was a crudity in his manners, and a roughness in the way in which he helped a lady on to her horse, that did not attract the other sex to him; even if he had cast about for their favour, which he did not. He kept his wounded heart all to himself for a while.

Then trouble came to him. All who go to Simla know the slope from the Telegraph to the Public Works Office. Hannasyde was loafing up the hill, one September morning between calling-hours, when a 'rickshaw came down in a hurry, and in the 'rickshaw sat the living, breathing image of the girl who had made him so happily unhappy. Hannasyde leaned against the railings and gasped. He wanted to run downhill after the 'rickshaw, but that was impossible; so he went forward with most of his blood in his temples. It was impossible, for many reasons, that the woman in the 'rickshaw could be the girl he had known. She was, he discovered later, the wife of a man from Dindigul, or Coimbatore, or some out-of-the-way[1] place, and she had come up to Simla early in the season for the good of her health. She was going back to Dindigul, or wherever it was, at the end of the season; and in all likelihood would never return to Simla again, her proper Hill-station being Ootacamund. That night Hannasyde, raw and savage from the raking up of all old feelings, took counsel with himself for one measured hour. What he decided upon was this; and you must decide for yourself how much genuine affection for the old love, and how much a very natural inclination to go abroad and enjoy himself, affected the decision. Mrs Landys-Haggert would never in all human likelihood cross his path again. So whatever he did didn't much matter. She was marvellously like the girl who 'took a deep interest' and the rest of the formula. All things considered, it would be pleasant to make the acquaintance of Mrs Landys-Haggert, and for a little time – only a very little time – to make believe that he was with Alice Chisane again. Every one is more or less mad on one point. Hannasyde's particular monomania was his old love, Alice Chisane.

He made it his business to get introduced to Mrs Haggert, and the introduction prospered. He also made it his business to see as much as he could of that lady. When a man is in earnest as to interviews, the facilities which Simla offers are startling. There are garden-parties, and tennis-parties, and picnics, and luncheons at Annandale, and rifle-matches, and dinners and balls; besides rides and walks, which are matters of private arrangement. Hannasyde had started with the intention of seeing a likeness, and he ended by doing much more. He wanted to be deceived, he meant to be deceived, and he deceived himself very thoroughly. Not only were the face and figure the face and figure of Alice

Chisane, but the voice and lower tones were exactly the same, and so were the turns of speech; and the little mannerisms, that every woman has, of gait and gesticulation, were absolutely and identically the same. The turn of the head was the same; the tired look in the eyes at the end of a long walk was the same; the stoop-and-wrench over the saddle to hold in a pulling horse was the same; and once, most marvellous of all, Mrs Landys-Haggert singing to herself in the next room, while Hannasyde was waiting to take her for a ride, hummed, note for note, with a throaty quiver of the voice in the second line, 'Poor Wandering One!'[2] exactly as Alice Chisane had hummed it for Hannasyde in the dusk of an English drawing-room. In the actual woman herself – in the soul of her – there was not the least likeness, she and Alice Chisane being cast in different moulds. But all that Hannasyde wanted to know and see and think about, was this maddening and perplexing likeness of face and voice and manner. He was bent on making a fool of himself that way; and he was in no sort disappointed.

Open and obvious devotion from any sort of man is always pleasant to any sort of woman; but Mrs Landys-Haggert, being a woman of the world, could make nothing of Hannasyde's admiration.

He would take any amount of trouble – he was a selfish man habitually – to meet and forestall, if possible, her wishes. Anything she told him to do was law; and he was, there could be no doubting it, fond of her company so long as she talked to him, and kept on talking about trivialities. But when she launched into expression of her personal views and her wrongs, those small social differences that make the spice of Simla life, Hannasyde was neither pleased nor interested. He didn't want to know anything about Mrs Landys-Haggert, or her experiences in the past – she had travelled nearly all over the world, and could talk cleverly – he wanted the likeness of Alice Chisane before his eyes and her voice in his ears. Anything outside that, reminding him of another personality, jarred, and he showed that it did.

Under the new Post Office, one evening, Mrs Landys-Haggert turned on him, and spoke her mind shortly and without warning. 'Mr Hannasyde,' said she, 'will you be good enough to explain why you have appointed yourself my special *cavalier servente*? I don't understand it. But I am perfectly certain, somehow or other, that you don't care the least little bit in the world for *me*.' This seems to support, by the way, the theory that no man can act or tell lies to a woman without being found out. Hannasyde was taken off his guard. His defence never was a strong one, because he was always thinking of himself, and he blurted out, before he knew what he was saying, this inexpedient answer, 'No more I do.'

The queerness of the situation and the reply made Mrs Landys-Haggert laugh. Then it all came out; and at the end of Hannasyde's lucid explanation Mrs Haggert said, with the least little touch of scorn in her voice, 'So I'm to act as the lay-figure for you to hang the rags of your tattered affections on, am I?'

Hannasyde didn't see what answer was required, and he devoted himself generally and vaguely to the praise of Alice Chisane, which was unsatisfactory. Now it is to be thoroughly made clear that Mrs Haggert had not the shadow of a ghost of an interest in Hannasyde. Only . . . only no woman likes being made love through instead of to – specially on behalf of a musty divinity of four years' standing.

Hannasyde did not see that he had made any very particular exhibition of himself. He was glad to find a sympathetic soul in the arid wastes of Simla.

When the season ended, Hannasyde went down to his own place and Mrs Haggert to hers. 'It was like making love to a ghost,' said Hannasyde to himself, 'and it doesn't matter; and now I'll get to my work.' But he found himself thinking steadily of the Haggert–Chisane ghost; and he could not be certain whether it was Haggert or Chisane that made up the greater part of the pretty phantom.

He got understanding a month later.

A peculiar point of this peculiar country is the way in which a heartless Government transfers men from one end of the Empire to the other. You can never be sure of getting rid of a friend or an enemy till he or she dies. There was a case once . . . but that's another story.

Haggert's Department ordered him up from Dindigul to the Frontier at two days' notice, and he went through, losing money at every step, from Dindigul to his station. He dropped Mrs Haggert at Lucknow, to stay with some friends there, to take part in a big ball at the Chutter Munzil,[3] and to come on when he had made the new home a little comfortable. Lucknow was Hannasyde's station, and Mrs Haggert stayed a week there. Hannasyde went to meet her. As the train came in, he discovered what he had been thinking of for the past month. The unwisdom of his conduct also struck him. The Lucknow week, with two dances, and an unlimited quantity of rides together, clinched matters; and Hannasyde found himself pacing this circle of thought:[4] he adored Alice Chisane, at least he *had* adored her. *And* he admired Mrs Landys-Haggert because she was like Alice Chisane. *But* Mrs Landys-Haggert was not in the least like Alice Chisane, being a thousand times more adorable. *Now* Alice Chisane was 'the bride of another', and so was Mrs Landys-Haggert, and a good and honest wife too. *Therefore* he, Hannasyde, was ... Here he called himself several hard names, and wished that he had been wise in the beginning.

Whether Mrs Landys-Haggert saw what was going on in his mind she alone knows. He seemed to take an unqualified interest in everything connected with herself, as distinguished from the Alice Chisane likeness, and he said one or two things which, if Alice Chisane had been still betrothed to him, could scarcely have been excused, even on the grounds of the likeness. But Mrs Haggert turned the remarks aside, and spent a long time in making Hannasyde see what a comfort and a pleasure she had been to him because of her strange resemblance to his old love. Hannasyde groaned in his saddle and said, 'Yes, indeed,' and busied himself with preparations for her departure to the Frontier, feeling very small and miserable.

The last day of her stay at Lucknow came, and Hannasyde saw her off at the Railway Station. She was very grateful for his kindness and the trouble he had taken, and smiled pleasantly and sympathetically as one who knew the Alice-Chisane reason of that kindness. And Hannasyde abused the coolies with the luggage, and hustled the people on the platform, and prayed that the roof might fall in and slay him.

As the train went out slowly, Mrs Landys-Haggert leaned out of the window to say good-bye. 'On second thoughts, *au revoir*, Mr Hannasyde. I go Home in the spring, and perhaps I may meet you in Town.'

Hannasyde shook hands, and said very earnestly and adoringly, 'I hope to Heaven I shall never see your face again!'

And Mrs Haggert understood.

Wressley of the Foreign Office

> I closed and drew for my Love's sake,
>   That now is false to me,
> And I slew the Riever of Tarrant Moss,[1]
>   And set Dumeny free.
>
> And ever they give me praise and gold,
>   And ever I moan my loss;
> For I struck the blow for my false Love's sake,
>   And not for the men of the Moss!
>
> *Tarrant Moss*

One of the many curses of our life in India is the want of atmosphere in the painter's sense. There are no half-tints worth noticing. Men stand out all crude and raw, with nothing to tone them down, and nothing to scale them against. They do their work, and grow to think that there is nothing but their work, and nothing like their work, and that they are the real pivots on which the Administration turns. Here is an instance of this feeling. A half-caste clerk was ruling forms in a Pay Office. He said to me, 'Do you know what would happen if I added or took away one single line on this sheet?' Then, with the air of a conspirator, 'It would disorganize the whole of the Treasury payments throughout the whole of the Presidency Circle! Think of that!'

If men had not this delusion as to the ultra-importance of their own particular employments, I suppose that they would sit down and kill themselves. But their weakness is wearisome, particularly when the listener knows that he himself commits exactly the same sin.

Even the Secretariat believes that it does good when it asks an over-driven Executive Officer to take a census of wheat-weevils through a District of five thousand square miles.

There was a man once in the Foreign Office – a man who had grown middle-aged in the Department, and was commonly said, by irreverent juniors, to be able to repeat Aitchison's *Treaties and Sunnuds*[2] backwards in his sleep. What he did with his stored knowledge only the Secretary knew; and he, naturally, would not publish the news abroad. This man's name was Wressley, and it was the Shibboleth, in those days, to say, 'Wressley knows more about the Central Indian States than any living man.' If you did not say this, you were considered one of mean understanding.

Nowadays, the man who says that he knows the ravel of the inter-tribal complications across the Border is of more use; but, in Wressley's time, much attention was paid to the Central Indian States. They were called 'foci' and 'factors', and all manner of imposing names.

And here the curse of Anglo-Indian life fell heavily. When Wressley lifted up his voice, and spoke about such-and-such a succession to such-and-such a throne, the Foreign Office were silent, and Heads of Departments repeated the last two or three words of Wressley's sentences, and tacked 'Yes, yes', on to them, and knew that they were assisting the Empire to grapple with serious political contingencies. In most big undertakings one or two men do the work, while the rest sit near and talk till the ripe decorations begin to fall.

Wressley was the working member of the Foreign Office firm, and, to keep him up to his duties when he showed signs of flagging, he was made much of by his superiors and told what a fine fellow he was. He did not require coaxing, because he was of tough build, but what he received confirmed him in the belief that there was no one quite so absolutely and imperatively necessary to the stability of India as Wressley of the Foreign Office. There might be other good men, but the known, honoured, and trusted man among men was Wressley of the Foreign Office. We had a Viceroy in those days who knew exactly when to 'gentle' a fractious big man, and to hearten-up a collar-galled little one, and so keep all his team level. He conveyed to Wressley the impression which I have just set down; and even tough men are apt to be disorganized by a Viceroy's praise. There was a case once . . . But that is another story.[3]

All India knew Wressley's name and office – it was in Thacker and Spink's[4] Directory – but who he was personally, or what he did, or what his special merits were, not fifty men knew or cared. His work filled all his time, and he found no leisure to cultivate acquaintances beyond those of dead Rajput chiefs[5] with *Ahir* blots in their scutcheons. Wressley would have made a very good Clerk in the Herald's College had he not been a Bengal Civilian.

Upon a day, between office and office,[6] great trouble came to Wressley – overwhelmed him, knocked him down, and left him gasping as though he had been a little schoolboy. Without reason, against prudence, and at a moment's notice, he fell in love with a frivolous, golden-haired girl who used to tear about Simla Mall on a high, rough Waler, with a blue velvet jockey-cap crammed over her eyes. Her name was Venner – Tillie Venner – and she was delightful. She took Wressley's heart at a hand-gallop, and Wressley found that it was not good for man to live alone; even with half the Foreign Office Records in his presses.[7]

Then Simla laughed, for Wressley in love was slightly ridiculous. He did his best to interest the girl in himself – that is to say, his work – and she, after the manner of women, did her best to appear interested in what, behind his back, she called 'Mr W'essley's Wajahs'; for she lisped very prettily. She did not understand one little thing about them, but she acted as if she did. Men have married on that sort of error before now.

Providence, however, had care of Wressley. He was immensely struck with Miss Venner's intelligence. He would have been more impressed had he heard her private and confidential accounts of his calls. He held peculiar notions as to the wooing of girls. He said that the best work of a man's career should be laid reverently at their feet. Ruskin writes something like this somewhere,[8] I think; but in ordinary life a few kisses are better and save time.

About a month after he had lost his heart to Miss Venner, and had been doing his work vilely in consequence, the first idea of his *Native Rule in Central India* struck Wressley and filled him with joy. It was, as he sketched it, a great thing – the work of his life – a really comprehensive survey of a most fascinating subject – to be written with all the special and laboriously acquired knowledge of Wressley of the Foreign Office – a gift fit for an Empress.

He told Miss Venner that he was going to take leave, and hoped, on his return, to bring her a present worthy of her acceptance. Would she wait? Certainly she would. Wressley drew seventeen hundred rupees a month. She would wait a year for that. Her Mamma would help her to wait.

So Wressley took one year's leave and all the available documents, about a truck-load, that he could lay hands on, and went down to Central India with his notion hot in his head. He began his book in the land he was writing of. Too much official correspondence had made him a frigid workman, and he must have guessed that he needed the white light of local colour on his palette. This is a dangerous paint for amateurs to play with.[9]

Heavens, how that man worked! He caught his Rajahs, analysed his Rajahs, and traced them up into the mists of Time and beyond, with their queens and their concubines. He dated and cross-dated, pedigreed and triple-pedigreed, compared, noted, connoted, wove, strung, sorted, selected, inferred, calendared and counter-calendared[10] for ten hours a day. And, because this sudden and new light of Love was upon him, he turned those dry bones of history and dirty records of misdeeds into things to weep or to laugh over as he pleased. His heart and soul were at the end of his pen, and they got into the ink. He was dowered with sympathy, insight, humour, and style for two hundred and thirty days and nights; and his book was a Book. He had his vast special knowledge with him, so to speak; but the spirit, the woven-in human Touch, the poetry and the power of the output, were beyond all special knowledge. But I doubt whether he knew the gift that was in him then, and thus he may have lost some happiness. He was toiling for Tillie Venner, not for himself. Men often do their best work blind, for some one else's sake.

Also, though this has nothing to do with the story, in India, where every one knows every one else, you can watch men being driven, by the women who govern them, out of the rank-and-file and sent to take up points alone. A good man, once started, goes forward; but an average man, so soon as the woman loses interest in his success as a tribute to her power, comes back to the battalion and is no more heard of.[11]

Wressley bore the first copy of his book to Simla, and, blushing and stammering, presented it to Miss Venner. She read a little of it. I give her review *verbatim* – 'Oh, your book? It's all about those howwid Wajahs. I didn't understand it.'

Wressley of the Foreign Office was broken, smashed – I am not exaggerating – by this one frivolous little girl. All that he could say feebly was: 'But – but it's my *magnum opus*! The work of my life.' Miss Venner did not know what *magnum opus* meant; but she knew that Captain Kerrington had won three races at the last Gymkhana. Wressley didn't press her to wait for him any longer. He had sense enough for that.

Then came the reaction after the year's strain, and Wressley went back to the Foreign Office and his 'Wajahs', a compiling, gazetteering, report-writing hack, who would have been dear at three hundred rupees a month. He abided by Miss Venner's review; which proves that the inspiration in the book was purely temporary and unconnected with himself. Nevertheless, he had no right to sink, in a hill-tarn, five packing-cases, brought up at enormous expense from Bombay, of the best book of Indian history ever written.

When he sold off before retiring, some years later, I was turning over his shelves, and came across the only existing copy of *Native Rule in Central India* – the copy that Miss Venner could not understand. I read it, sitting on his mule-trunks, as long as the light lasted, and offered him his own price for it. He looked over my shoulder for a few pages and said to himself drearily:

'Now, how in the world did I come to write such damned good stuff as that?'

Then to me:

'Take it and keep it. Write one of your penny-farthing yarns about its birth. Perhaps – perhaps – the whole business may have been ordained to that end.'

Which, knowing what Wressley of the Foreign Office was once, struck me as about the bitterest thing that I had ever heard a man say of his own work.

⟨ By Word of Mouth ⟩

Not though you die to-night, O Sweet, and wail,
    A spectre at my door,
Shall mortal Fear make Love immortal fail –
    I shall but love you more,
Who, from Death's house returning, give me still
One moment's comfort in my matchless ill.

Shadow Houses

This tale may be explained by those who know how souls are made, and where the bounds of the Possible are put down. I have lived long enough in this India to know that it is best to know nothing, and can only write the story as it happened.

Dumoise was our Civil Surgeon at Meridki,[1] and we called him 'Dormouse', because he was a round little, sleepy little man. He was a good Doctor and never quarrelled with any one, not even with our Deputy-Commissioner who had the manners of a bargee and the tact of a horse. He married a girl as round and as sleepy-looking as himself. She was a Miss Hillardyce, daughter of 'Squash' Hillardyce of the Berars, who married his Chief's daughter by mistake ... But that is another story.

A honeymoon in India is seldom more than a week long; but there is nothing to hinder a couple from extending it over two or three years. India is a delightful country for married folk who are wrapped up in one another. They can live absolutely alone and without interruption – just as the Dormice did. Those two little people retired from the world after their marriage, and were very happy. They were forced, of course, to give occasional dinners, but they made no friends thereby, and the station went its own way and forgot them: only saying, occasionally, that Dormouse was the best of good fellows though dull. A Civil Surgeon who never quarrels is a rarity, appreciated as such.

Few people can afford to play Robinson Crusoe anywhere –

least of all in India, where we are few in the land and very much dependent on each other's kind offices. Dumoise was wrong in shutting himself from the world for a year, and he discovered his mistake when an epidemic of typhoid broke out in the station in the heart of the cold weather, and his wife went down. He was a shy little man, and five days were wasted before he realized that Mrs Dumoise was burning with something worse than simple fever, and three days more passed before he ventured to call on Mrs Shute, the Engineer's wife, and timidly speak about his trouble. Nearly every household in India knows that Doctors are very helpless in typhoid. The battle must be fought out between Death and the Nurses minute by minute and degree by degree. Mrs Shute almost boxed Dumoise's ears for what she called his 'criminal delay', and went off at once to look after the poor girl. We had seven cases of typhoid in the station that winter, and, as the average of death is about one in every five cases, we felt certain that we should have to lose somebody. But all did their best. The women sat up nursing the women, and the men turned to and tended the bachelors who were down, and we wrestled with those typhoid cases for fifty-six days, and brought them through the Valley of the Shadow[2] in triumph. But, just when we thought all was over, and were going to give a dance to celebrate the victory, little Mrs Dumoise got a relapse and died in a week, and the station went to the funeral. Dumoise broke down utterly at the brink of the grave, and had to be taken away.

After the death Dumoise crept into his own house and refused to be comforted. He did his duties perfectly, but we all felt that he should go on leave, and the other men of his own Service told him so. Dumoise was very thankful for the suggestion – he was thankful for anything in those days – and went to Chini on a walking-tour. Chini is some twenty marches from Simla, in the heart of the Hills, and the scenery is good if you are in trouble. You pass through big, still deodar forests, and under big, still cliffs, and over big, still grass-downs swelling like a woman's breasts; and the wind across the grass, and the rain among the deodars say – 'Hush – hush – hush.' So little Dumoise was packed off to Chini, to wear down his grief with a full-plate camera and a rifle. He took also a useless bearer, because the man had been his wife's favourite servant. He was idle and a thief, but Dumoise trusted everything to him.

On his way back from Chini, Dumoise turned aside to Bagi, through the Forest Reserve which is on the spur of Mount Huttoo. Some men who have travelled more than a little say that the march from Kotgarh to Bagi is one of the finest in creation. It runs through dark, wet forest, and ends suddenly in bleak, nipped hillside and black rocks. Bagi *dâk*-bungalow³ is open to all the winds and is bitterly cold. Few people go to Bagi. Perhaps that was the reason why Dumoise went there. He halted at seven in the evening, and his bearer went down the hillside to the village to engage coolies for the next day's march. The sun had set, and the night-winds were beginning to croon among the rocks. Dumoise leaned on the railing of the veranda, waiting for his bearer to return. The man came back almost immediately after he had disappeared, and at such a rate that Dumoise fancied he must have crossed a bear. He was running as hard as he could up the face of the hill.

But there was no bear to account for his terror. He raced to the veranda and fell down, the blood spurting from his nose and his face iron-grey. Then he gurgled, 'I have seen the Memsahib! I have seen the Memsahib!'

'Where?' said Dumoise.

'Down there, walking on the road to the village. She was in a blue dress, and she lifted the veil of her bonnet and said, "Ram Dass, give my salaams to the Sahib, and tell him that I shall meet him next month at Nuddea." Then I ran away, because I was afraid.'

What Dumoise said or did I do not know. Ram Dass declares that he said nothing, but walked up and down the veranda all the cold night, waiting for the Memsahib to come up the hill, and stretching out his arms into the dark like a madman. But no Memsahib came, and, next day, he went on to Simla, cross-questioning the bearer every hour.

Ram Dass could only say that he had met Mrs Dumoise, and that she had lifted up her veil and given him the message which he had faithfully repeated to Dumoise. To this statement Ram Dass adhered. He did not know where Nuddea was, had no friends at Nuddea, and would most certainly never go to Nuddea, even though his pay were doubled.

Nuddea is in Bengal, and has nothing whatever to do with a Doctor serving in the Punjab. It must be more than twelve hundred miles south of Meridki.

Dumoise went through Simla without halting, and returned to Meridki, there to take over charge from the man who had been officiating for him during his tour. There were some Dispensary accounts to be explained, and some recent orders of the Surgeon-General to be noted, and, altogether, the taking-over was a full day's work. In the evening Dumoise told his *locum tenens*,[4] who was an old friend of his bachelor days, what had happened at Bagi; and the man said that Ram Dass might as well have chosen Tuticorin[5] while he was about it.

At that moment a telegraph-peon came in with a telegram from Simla, ordering Dumoise not to take over charge at Meridki, but to go at once to Nuddea on special duty. There was a nasty outbreak of cholera at Nuddea, and the Bengal Government being short-handed, as usual, had borrowed a Surgeon from the Punjab.

Dumoise threw the telegram across the table and said, 'Well?'

The other Doctor said nothing. It was all that he could say.

Then he remembered that Dumoise had passed through Simla on his way from Bagi; and thus might, possibly, have heard first news of the impending transfer.

He tried to put the question and the implied suspicion into words, but Dumoise stopped him with: 'If I had desired *that*, I should never have come back from Chini. I was shooting there. I wish to live, for I have things to do ... but I shall not be sorry.'

The other man bowed his head, and helped, in the twilight, to pack up Dumoise's just-opened trunks. Ram Dass entered with the lamps.

'Where is the Sahib going?' he asked.

'To Nuddea,' said Dumoise softly.

Ram Dass clawed Dumoise's knees and boots and begged him not to go. Ram Dass wept and howled till he was turned out of the room. Then he wrapped up all his belongings and came back to ask for a character. He was not going to Nuddea to see his Sahib die and, perhaps, to die himself.

So Dumoise gave the man his wages and went down to Nuddea alone, the other Doctor bidding him good-bye as one under sentence of death.

Eleven days later he had joined his Memsahib; and the Bengal Government had to borrow a fresh Doctor to cope with that epidemic at Nuddea. The first importation lay dead in Choo-adanga *dâk*-bungalow.[6]

To be Filed for Reference

By the hoof of the Wild Goat uptossed
From the Cliff where she lay in the Sun,
    Fell the Stone
To the Tarn where the daylight is lost;
So She fell from the light of the Sun,
    And alone.

Now the fall was ordained from the first,
With the Goat and the Cliff and the Tarn.
    But the Stone
Knows only her life is accursed
As she sinks from the light of the Sun,
    And alone.

Oh, Thou Who hast builded the World!
Oh, Thou Who hast lighted the Sun!
Oh, Thou Who hast darkened the Tarn!
    Judge Thou
The sin of the Stone that was hurled
By the Goat from the light of the Sun,
As she sinks in the mire of the Tarn,
        Even now – even now – even now!
                        From the Unpublished Papers of McIntosh Jellaludin

'Say, is it dawn, is it dusk in thy Bower,
Thou whom I long for, who longest for me?
Oh, be it night – be it –'[1]

Here he fell over a little camel–colt that was sleeping in the Serai[2]
where the horse-traders and the best of the blackguards from
Central Asia live; and, because he was very drunk indeed and the
night was dark, he could not rise again till I helped him. That
was the beginning of my acquaintance with McIntosh Jellaludin.
When a loafer, and drunk, sings 'The Song of the Bower,' he
must be worth cultivating. He got off the camel's back and said,
rather thickly, 'I – I – I'm a bit screwed, but a dip in Loggerhead

will put me right again; and, I say, have you spoken to Symonds about the mare's knees?'

Now Loggerhead was six thousand weary miles away from us, close to Mesopotamia, where you mustn't fish and poaching is impossible, and Charley Symonds' stable a half-mile farther across the paddocks. It was strange to hear all the old names,[3] on a May night, among the horses and camels of the Sultan Caravanserai. Then the man seemed to remember himself and sober down at the same time. He leaned against the camel and pointed to a corner of the Serai where a lamp was burning.

'I live there,' said he, 'and I should be extremely obliged if you would be good enough to help my mutinous feet thither; for I am more than usually drunk – most – most phenomenally tight. But not in respect to my head. "My brain cries out against" – how does it go? But my head rides on the – rolls on the dunghill, I should have said, and controls the qualm.'

I helped him through the gangs of tethered horses, and he collapsed on the edge of the veranda in front of the line of native quarters.

'Thanks – a thousand thanks! O Moon and little, little Stars! To think that a man should so shamelessly ... Infamous liquor too. Ovid in exile drank no worse. Better. It was frozen. Alas! I had no ice. Good-night. I would introduce you to my wife were I sober – or she civilized.'

A native woman came out of the darkness of the room and began calling the man names, so I went away. He was the most interesting loafer that I had had the pleasure of knowing for a long time; and later on, he became a friend of mine. He was a tall, well-built, fair man, fearfully shaken with drink, and he looked nearer fifty than the thirty-five which, he said, was his real age. When a man begins to sink in India, and is not sent Home by his friends as soon as may be, he falls very low from a respectable point of view. By the time that he changes his creed, as did McIntosh, he is past redemption.

In most big cities natives will tell you of two or three Sahibs, generally low-caste, who have turned Hindu or Mussulman, and who live more or less as such. But it is not often that you can get to know them. As McIntosh himself used to say, 'If I change my religion for my stomach's sake, I do not seek to become a martyr to missionaries, nor am I anxious for notoriety.'

At the outset of acquaintance McIntosh warned me. 'Remember this. I am not an object for charity. I require neither your money, your food, nor your cast-off raiment. I am that rare animal, a self-supporting drunkard. If you choose, I will smoke with you, for the tobacco of the bazars does not, I admit, suit my palate; and I will borrow any books which you may not specially value. It is more than likely that I shall sell them for bottles of excessively filthy country-liquors. In return, you shall share such hospitality as my house affords. Here is a charpoy⁴ on which two can sit, and it is possible that there may, from time to time, be food in that platter. Drink, unfortunately, you will find on the premises at any hour; and thus I make you welcome to all my poor establishment.'

I was admitted to the McIntosh household – I and my good tobacco. But nothing else. Unluckily, one cannot visit a loafer in the Serai by day. Friends buying horses would not understand it. Consequently, I was obliged to see McIntosh after dark. He laughed at this, and said simply, 'You are perfectly right. When I enjoyed a position in society, rather higher than yours, I should have done exactly the same thing. Good Heavens! I was once' – he spoke as though he had fallen from the Command of a Regiment – 'an Oxford Man!' This accounted for the reference to Charley Symonds' stable.

'You,' said McIntosh slowly, 'have not had that advantage; but, to outward appearance, you do not seem possessed of a craving for strong drinks. On the whole, I fancy that you are the luckier of the two. Yet I am not certain. You are – forgive my saying so even while I am smoking your excellent tobacco – painfully ignorant of many things.'

We were sitting together on the edge of his bedstead, for he owned no chairs, watching the horses being watered for the night, while the native woman was preparing dinner. I did not like being patronized by a loafer, but I was his guest for the time being, though he owned only one very torn alpaca coat and a pair of trousers made out of gunny-bags.⁵ He took the pipe out of his mouth, and went on judicially, 'All things considered, I doubt whether you are the luckier. I do not refer to your extremely limited classical attainments, or your excruciating quantities, but to your gross ignorance of matters more immediately under your notice. That, for instance.' He pointed to a woman cleaning a samovar near the well in the centre of the Serai. She was flicking the water out of the spout in regular cadenced jerks.

'There are ways and ways of cleaning samovars. If you knew why she was doing her work in that particular fashion, you would know what the Spanish Monk meant when he said:

> I the Trinity illustrate,
>   Drinking watered orange-pulp –
> In three sips the Arian frustrate,
>   While he drains his at one gulp –[6]

and many other things which now are hidden from your eyes. However, Mrs McIntosh has prepared dinner. Let us come and eat after the fashion of the people of the country – of whom, by the way, you know nothing.'

The native woman dipped her hand in the dish with us. This was wrong. The wife should always wait until the husband has eaten. McIntosh Jellaludin apologized, saying:

'It is an English prejudice which I have not been able to overcome; and she loves me. Why, I have never been able to understand. I forgathered with her at Jullundur, three years ago, and she has remained with me ever since. I believe her to be moral, and know her to be skilled in cookery.'

He patted the woman's head as he spoke, and she cooed softly. She was not pretty to look at.

McIntosh never told me what position he had held before his fall. He was, when sober, a scholar and a gentleman. When drunk, he was rather more of the first than the second. He used to get drunk about once a week for two days. On those occasions the native woman tended him while he raved in all tongues except his own. One day, indeed, he began reciting *Atalanta in Calydon*,[7] and went through it to the end, beating time to the swing of the verse with a bedstead-leg. But he did most of his ravings in Greek or German. The man's mind was a perfect rag-bag of useless things. Once, when he was beginning to get sober, he told me that I was the only rational being in the Inferno into which he had descended – a Virgil in the Shades, he said – and that, in return for my tobacco, he would, before he died, give me the materials of a new *Inferno* that should make me greater than Dante. Then he fell asleep on a horse-blanket and woke up quite calm.

'Man,' said he, 'when you have reached the uttermost depths of degradation, little incidents which would vex a higher life are to you of no consequence. Last night my soul was among the Gods; but I make no doubt that my bestial body was writhing down here in the garbage.'

'You were abominably drunk, if that's what you mean,' I said.

'I *was* drunk – filthily drunk. I who am the son of a man with whom you have no concern – I who was once Fellow of a College whose buttery-hatch you have not seen – I was loathsomely drunk. But consider how lightly I am touched. It is nothing to me – less than nothing; for I do not even feel the headache which should be my portion. Now, in a higher life, how ghastly would have been my punishment, how bitter my repentance! Believe me, my friend with the neglected education, the highest is as the lowest – always supposing each degree extreme.'

He turned round on the blanket, put his head between his fists and continued:

'On the Soul which I have lost and on the Conscience which I have killed, I tell you that I cannot feel! I am as the Gods, knowing good and evil, but untouched by either. Is this enviable or is it not?'

When a man has lost the warning of 'next morning's head' he must be in a bad state. I answered, looking at McIntosh on the blanket, with his hair over his eyes and his lips blue-white, that I did not think the insensibility good enough.

'For pity's sake, don't say that! I tell you it *is* good and most enviable. Think of my consolations!'

'Have you so many, then, McIntosh?'

'Certainly. Your attempts at sarcasm, which is essentially the weapon of a cultured man, are crude. First, my attainments, my classical and literary knowledge, blurred, perhaps, by immoderate drinking – which reminds me that before my soul went to the Gods last night I sold the Pickering Horace[8] you so kindly lent me. Ditta Mull the clothes-man has it. It fetched ten annas, and may be redeemed for a rupee – but still infinitely superior to yours. Secondly, the abiding affection of Mrs McIntosh, best of wives. Thirdly, a monument, more enduring than brass, which I have built up in the seven years of my degradation.'

He stopped here, and crawled across the room for a drink of water. He was very shaky and sick.

He referred several times to his 'treasure' – some great possession that he owned – but I held this to be the raving of drink. He was as poor and as proud as he could be. His manner was not pleasant, but he knew enough about the natives, among whom seven years of his life had been spent, to make his acquaintance worth having. He used actually to laugh at Strickland as an ignorant man – 'ignorant West and East' – he said. His boast was, first, that he was an Oxford Man of rare and shining parts, which may or may not have been true – I did not know enough to check his statements; and, secondly, that he 'had his hand on the pulse of native life' – which was a fact. As an Oxford man, he struck me as a prig: he was always throwing his education about. As a Mahommedan *fakir* – as McIntosh Jellaludin – he was all that I wanted for my own ends. He smoked several pounds of my tobacco, and taught me several ounces of things worth knowing; but he would never accept any gifts, not even when the cold weather came, and gripped the poor thin chest under the poor thin alpaca coat. He grew very angry, and said that I had insulted him, and that he was not going into hospital. He had lived like a beast and he would die rationally, like a man.

As a matter of fact, he died of pneumonia; and on the night of his death sent over a grubby note asking me to come and help him to die.

The native woman was weeping by the side of the bed. McIntosh, wrapped in a cotton cloth, was too weak to resent a fur coat being thrown over him. He was very active as far as his mind was concerned, and his eyes were blazing. When he had abused the Doctor who came with me so foully that the indignant old fellow left, he cursed me for a few minutes and calmed down.

Then he told his wife to fetch out 'The Book' from a hole in the wall. She brought out a big bundle, wrapped in the tail of a petticoat, of old sheets of miscellaneous notepaper, all numbered and covered with fine cramped writing. McIntosh ploughed his hand through the rubbish and stirred it up lovingly.

'This,' he said, 'is my work – the Book of McIntosh Jellaludin, showing what he saw and how he lived, and what befell him and others; being also an account of the life and sins and death of Mother Maturin.⁹ What Mirza Murad Ali Beg's book ¹⁰ is to all other books on native life, will my work be to Mirza Murad Ali Beg's!'

This, as will be conceded by any one who knows Mirza Murad Ali Beg's book, was a sweeping statement. The papers did not look specially valuable; but McIntosh handled them as if they were currency-notes. Then said he slowly:

'In despite the many weaknesses of your education, you have been good to me. I will speak of your tobacco when I reach the Gods. I owe you much thanks for many kindnesses. But I abominate indebtedness. For this reason I bequeath to you now the monument more enduring than brass – my one book – rude and imperfect in parts, but oh, how rare in others! I wonder if you will understand it. It is a gift more honourable than . . . Bah! where is my brain rambling to? You will mutilate it horribly. You will knock out the gems you call Latin quotations, you Philistine, and you will butcher the style to carve into your own jerky jargon; but you cannot destroy the whole of it. I bequeath it to you. Ethel¹¹ . . . My brain again! . . . Mrs McIntosh, bear witness that I give the Sahib all these papers. They would be of no use to you, Heart of my Heart; and I lay it upon you,' he turned to me here, 'that you do not let my book die in its present form. It is yours unconditionally – the story of McIntosh Jellaludin, which is *not* the story of McIntosh Jellaludin, but of a greater man than he, and of a far greater woman. Listen now! I am neither mad nor drunk! That book will make you famous.'

I said, 'Thank you,' as the native woman put the bundle into my arms.

'My only baby!' said McIntosh, with a smile. He was sinking fast, but he continued to talk as long as breath remained. I waited for the end; knowing that, in six cases out of ten, a dying man calls for his mother. He turned on his side and said:

'Say how it came into your possession. No one will believe you, but my name, at least, will live. You will treat it brutally, I know you will. Some of it must go; the public are fools and prudish fools. I was their servant once. But do your mangling gently – very gently. It is a great work, and I have paid for it in seven years' damnation.'

His voice stopped for ten or twelve breaths, and then he began mumbling a prayer of some kind in Greek. The native woman cried very bitterly. Lastly, he rose in bed and said, as loudly as slowly, 'Not guilty, my Lord!'

Then he fell back, and the stupor held him till he died. The native woman ran into the Serai among the horses, and screamed and beat her breasts; for she had loved him.

Perhaps his last sentence in life told what McIntosh had once gone through; but, saving the big bundle of old sheets in the cloth, there was nothing in his room to say who or what he had been.

The papers were in a hopeless muddle.

Strickland helped me to sort them, and he said that the writer was either an extreme liar or a most wonderful person. He thought the former. One of these days you may be able to judge for yourselves. The bundle needed much expurgation, and was full of Greek nonsense at the head of the chapters, which has all been cut out.

If the thing is ever published, some one may perhaps remember this story, now printed as a safeguard to prove that McIntosh Jellaludin and not I myself wrote the Book of Mother Maturin.

I don't want *The Giant's Robe*[12] to come true in my case!

Notes

Most of the verse epigraphs to the stories are original, and have been reprinted in the Definitive Edition of *Kipling's Verse* (Hodder & Stoughton, London, 1940), pp. 503–8. I have only identified places if their position seems of particular importance to the story. In compiling these notes I have drawn heavily upon Roger Lancelyn Green and Alec Mason (eds.), *The Reader's Guide to Kipling's Works*, Volume 1, prepared for Mr R. E. Harbord (1961).

Lispeth

First published as No. 8, *CMG*, 29 November 1886.

1. *Moravian missionaries*: Protestant sect founded in Saxony in the eighteenth century.
2. *Diana*: goddess of hunting and virginity.
3. *'globe-trotters'*: tourists. The P. & O. (Peninsular and Orient) fleet sailed regularly between India and Britain.
4. *Tarka Devi*: goddess of the dawn, a local deity.

Three and – an Extra

First published as No. 4, *CMG*, 17 November 1886.

1. *gram*: a pulse crop, usually chick-peas.
2. *'the Stormy Petrel'*: sea-bird, often sighted before storms.
3. *went off at score*: behaved impetuously, like a horse breaking away from the starting line.
4. *July 26*: revision from 'July 6'. Peterhof was the Viceroy's residence in Simla from 1862 to 1888.
5. *spoke the thing which was not*: in Swift's *Gulliver's Travels*, the entirely rational Houyhnhnms cannot conceive of untruth, and

therefore refer to 'the thing which is not'. Kipling inserted the phrase into the 1888 edition.

6. *The Queen*: a London magazine specializing in fashion. In the *CMG* version, Kipling attributed the remark to a less specific 'they'.

7. '*The Roast Beef of Old England*': song played as a sign that the meal is ready. From Henry Fielding's *Grub Street Opera* (1731).

8. *dandy*: 'carrying-chair' (Kipling's note in the Sussex edition).

Thrown Away

First printed in 1888.

1. *lunge*: drive round in a circle on a long rein. The breaking-yard is a paddock where horses are trained.

2. *to him*: the 1888 edition reinforced the narrator's knowingness by adding 'and he lost his head over the drink because that was new to him too.'

3. *hogged*: clipped to the neck. The race is for rickshaw-ponies under fourteen hands high which have never won a race. The entrance fee is two Indian sovereigns (goldmohurs). *Ekka*: a one-horse, two-wheeled vehicle.

4. '*Colonel's wigging*': reprimand.

5. *shikar-kit*: shooting-clothes, with puttees and cartridge belt.

6. *ring*: in the 1889 and 1890 editions, Kipling wrote 'rings', perhaps to hint at effeminacy.

7. *Valley of the Shadow*: Psalm 23, verse 4.

Miss Youghal's *Sais*

First published as No. 30, *CMG*, 25 April 1887.

1. *Sais*: groom.

2. *Kazi*: Mahommedan judge.

3. *Jamma Musjid*: the largest mosque in Delhi. The Ghor Kathri is a Hindu temple in Peshawar.

4. *But . . . Government*: in the *CMG* version, the tone of the complaint was sharper: 'But what good this has done him with the Government. None in the world. He has never got Simla; and his name is almost unknown to Englishmen.'

5. *Nasiban Murder Case*: the description of Strickland's activities is intended to mystify (and impress). I have not been able to identify the Nasiban Murder Case or the *Hálli-Hukk* dance. A fantee is a negro from the Gold Coast. The *Sat Bhai* (seven brothers) is a secret society. The Sansis are gypsies. *Changars* are gangs of women employed by earthwork contractors. The Yusufzai are a Pathan tribe.

6. *Jemadar*: Indian foreman. *Jhampanis*: rickshaw-coolies.

7. *Benmore*: large house on the Mall in Simla.

8. *Rachel*: Genesis 29, 18.

9. *purple and fine linen*: Luke 14, 19.

Bitters Neat

First published as No. 29, *CMG*, 19 April 1887.

1. *A.D.C.'s . . . Civilian*: *A.D.C.'s end of the table*: where the junior guests were seated. *P.W.D.*: Public Works Department. *Civilian*: member of the Civil Service.

2. *jawabed*: 'refused' (Kipling's note in the Sussex edition).

3. *from Colombo to Dadar*: i.e., from one end of the country to the other.

4. The *CMG* version continues: 'Mrs Hauksbee was quite right when she said, *apropos* of a business something like this but worse, where the man was a jilt: – "You men may be blundering idiots, but we women are mincing fiends!".'

5. *bones*: grilled bones, apparently a favourite dish in the Officer's Mess.

'Yoked with an Unbeliever'

First published as No. 11, *CMG*, 7 December 1886.

1. *Yoked with an Unbeliever*': 2 Corinthians 6, 14.

2. *Subadar-Major*: the highest rank open to an Indian in the British army.

False Dawn

First printed in 1888.

1. *a Civilian*: a member of the Civil Service, and therefore expected to behave correctly, and with detachment.
2. *we moved off*: the 1888 edition adds a further military touch: 'we fell in and moved off'.
3. *pagri*: light turban or head-covering.

The Rescue of Pluffles

First published as No. 5, *CMG*, 19 November 1886.

1. *Captain Hayes*: expert horse-trainer. Kipling wrote two articles about him for the *CMG*, on 14 and 19 April 1886. See *Kipling's India*, pp. 154–8 and 160–63.
2. *Elysium*: hill to the north of Simla.
3. *does it*: in the *CMG*, Kipling added, for good measure: 'and a man who has had anything to do with deep-sea fishing, knows exactly how his boat means to behave.'
4. *snaffle*: bridle-bit without curb, not likely to hurt the pony.
5. *curse of Reuben*: inclination to adultery. Genesis 35, 22.

Cupid's Arrows

First printed in 1888. Perhaps based on an incident in George Eliot's *Daniel Deronda* (1876), Chapters 10 and 11.

1. *lawn-tennis*: reached India in the early 1880s.
2. *self-yew*: made of one piece of wood. *Stele*: arrow without feathers. *Backed*: compound.

The Three Musketeers

First published as No. 21, *CMG*, 11 March 1887. Kipling has borrowed the title of the famous romance by Alexandre Dumas, about a poor Gascon gentleman, d'Artagnan, and his three companions, Athos, Porthos and Aramis.

1. *Balar 'Issar*: citadel of Kabul, where the British Embassy was housed at the time of the massacre of September 1879.

2. *a Peer*: originally, Trig was an MP rather than a peer, and described as 'useless' rather than 'unofficial'.

3. *Helanthami*: perhaps a nickname: 'hell-an'-the-army'.

4. *decoity*: dacoity: gang-robbery.

5. *Bote achee!*: Very good. *Mallum his bat*: understand what he was saying. *Thruck*: parcels. *B'roosh*: barouche. *Jildi*: fast. *Padsahi Jhil*: lake in Lahore. *Jehannum ke marfik*: like hell. *Bukkin'*: talking. *Samjao*: understand. *Bolos*: says. *Choop*: be silent. *Chel*: go on. *Dekker?*: do you understand? *Arsty*: slowly. *Arder*: half. *Thin . . . be*: then drive on, like the devil, and the less you say and the faster you go, the more pleased the Sahib will be.

6. *a tat an' a lookri*: a pony and a stick.

7. *you can*: in the *CMG*, Kipling had added: 'I can't give dialects properly.' The dialects in the Mulvaney stories clearly gave him a lot of trouble, since he made many minor revisions.

8. *Victoria*: Victoria Theatre, in London, famous for its melodramas.

9. *budmash*: rogue.

10. *Ahmid Kheyl wid Maiwand*: Mainwund and Ahmed Khel were battles in the second Afghan War, 1880.

11. *Bobs Bahadur*: Lord Roberts, Commander-in-Chief of the British Army in India, Commander of the Expeditionary Force in the second Afghan War. *Bahadur* means hero or champion, and was a title often given to European officers in Indian documents.

12. *the Sherapis*: a troop-ship.

His Chance in Life

First published as No. 24, *CMG*, 2 April 1887.

1. *Derozio*: Henry Louis Derozio, author of *Poems* (1827) and *The Fakir of Jungheera* (1828).

2. *tussore*: coarse, fawn-coloured.

3. *Backergunge*: district 120 miles to the east of Calcutta.

4. *Mohurrum*: festival commemorating the deaths of the Imams Hassan and Hussein, often the occasion for fighting between Muslim and Hindu. Kipling described a Mohurrum festival in Lahore for the *CMG* on 1 October 1887 (*Kipling's India*, pp. 266–9). 'Donnybrook' was a riotous Irish fair.

Watches of the Night

First published as No. 23, *CMG*, 25 March 1887.

1. *lip-strap*: the lip-strap prevents the curb-chain from chafing a horse's lip.
2. *Kismet*: Fate.
3. *territs*: loops through which the reins pass.
4. *feu-de-joie*: rolling volley which starts at one end of a parade-line and ends at the other.
5. *Vessel of Wrath*: Romans 9, 22.
6. *little body*: in the *CMG*, Kipling had added: 'and it would have been an unwholesome day for any man who valued his teeth, when he spoke lightly of Mrs Larkyn'.
7. *babies' hearts*: Proverbs 22, 15.
8. *Shakespeare alludes*: *Hamlet*, III, iv, 205–7.

The Other Man

First published as No. 3, *CMG*, 13 November 1886, where it begins: 'Everyone who was mixed up in this story is dead now – all except one man and he does not matter – but it's a nasty tale to tell all the same.

1. *P.W.D.*: Public Works Department.
2. *terai*: broad-brimmed hat with special ventilation.
3. *bukshish*: a tip.
4. *Tonga Babu*: a clerk who books tongas (small two-wheeled vehicles).

Haunted Subalterns

First published as No. 37, *CMG*, 27 May 1887.

1. *ulta-pulta*: upside-down.
2. *banquette*: raised platform running along the inside of a rampart.
3. *'seven other Devils'*: Matthew 12: 45.
4. *budnamed*: in bad reputation [Kipling's note].

Consequences

First published as No. 12, *CMG*, 9 December 1886.

1. *Paracelsus . . . Flood*: Paracelsus (1493–1541), Robert Fludd (1574–1637), alchemists.
2. *Pachmari*: hill-station 300 miles south of Agra.
3. *Dufferin . . . Ripon*: Ripon, whose conversion to Roman Catholicism in 1874 caused something of a stir, became Viceroy in 1880; Dufferin, previously Governor-General of Canada, in 1884.
4. *or filling . . . red pepper*: the detail of the red pepper was added in 1888. Vakils and Motamids were diplomatic representatives.
5. *chlorodyne*: drug prescribed for diarrhoea.
6. *blocked*: arranged. Kipling had originally written 'to see how it was to be done'.
7. *What the Viceroy said*: the final three paragraphs imitate the game of Consequences, in which a story is relayed from one participant to the next, according to a prescribed formula: What she said was . . . What they said was . . . What the world said was . . .

The Conversion of Aurelian McGoggin

First published as No. 31, *CMG*, 28 April 1887.

1. *Comte . . . Spencer*: Auguste Comte (1798–1857), French sociologist who founded Positivism. Herbert Spencer (1820–1903), Utilitarian sociologist and psychologist. In the *CMG* version, Kipling added 'and a Professor Clifford': probably William Clifford (1845–79), Professor of Applied Mathematics at University College London, a disciple of Spencer and popularizer of scientific thought.
2. *'Blastoderm'*: The germinal skin or membrane surrounding the yolk in the impregnated living ovum, and constituting the superficial layer of the embryo in its earliest condition) (*OED*). Possibly not what McGoggin's friends have in mind.

The Taking of Lungtungpen

First published as No. 26, *CMG*, 11 April 1887.

1. *Dagshai*: small military station near Kasauli on the Kalka–Simla railway.

2. *scutt*: rogue.
3. *Wolseley*: Field-Marshal Garnet Joseph Wolseley (1833–1913), who had a great reputation as an administrator.
4. *ramps*: can hardly contain themselves. *Bull-mate*: beef.
5. *Snider*: rifle. *Dah*: Burmese knife.
6. *puckarowed*: caught.
7. *jingles*: long guns fired from rests.
8. *nullah*: watercourse.
9. *Diarmid*: Celtic hero.

A Germ-Destroyer

First published as No. 35, *CMG*, 17 May 1887.

1. tiffin: lunch.
2. *Seepee*: picnic-spot nine miles from Simla.
3. *Wonder understood*: the original version had 'Wonder grasped', and so missed the facetious assonance.

Kidnapped

First published as No. 22, *CMG*, 21 March 1887.

1. *girl's fancies*: the *CMG* version added, knowingly: 'Ask a child of four to order the clothes it would like to dress in all its life; and the dear little innocent will point out a sailor's suit with lots of brass buttons, a lanyard and a shiny hat. Very few grown men care for brass buttons and low, turn-down collars.'
2. *K.C.I.E.*: Knight Commander of the Indian Empire: an order instituted by Queen Victoria in 1878, when she assumed the title of Empress of India.
3. *innocent people at Home*: in the *CMG* version, just 'they'. See Introduction, p. 21.
4. *opal-tinted onyx . . . finger-nails*: supposedly a sign of 'mixed-blood'. See Introduction, p. 20.
5. *wisdom of the Serpent*: Matthew 10, 16.
6. *Solon . . . Summer Hill*: places in vicinity of Simla.
7. *'peg'*: a drink of spirits.

The Arrest of Lieutenant Golightly

First published as No. 6, *C M G*, 23 November 1886.

1. *post*: changing horses every ten miles or so. A *solah* helmet is very light, made of pith.
2. *khitmutgar*: servant.
3. *D.T.*: delirium tremens.

In the House of Suddhoo

First published as 'Section 420, I.P.C.', *C M G*, 30 April 1886.

1. *Djinn*: spirit capable of assuming human shape. A *Churel* is a witch.
2. *Taksali Gate*: in the west wall of Lahore.
3. *Huzuri Bagh*: garden not far to the north of the city.
4. *Sirkar*: Government of India.
5. *thermantidote-paddle*: machine fitted to the window which drives currents of cool air through the house.
6. *Poe's account*: in 'The Facts in the Case of M. Valdemar'.
7. *Egyptian teraphim*: household gods.
8. *'Asli nahin! Fareib!'*: 'Not real. A trick' (Kipling's note in the Sussex edition).
9. *bunnia*: shopkeeper.
10. *purdahnashin*: woman of position who observes the rules of seclusion. 'Under coverture' (Kipling's note in the Sussex edition).

His Wedded Wife

First published as No. 19, *C M G*, 25 February 1887.

1. *Shakespeare says something*: *Measure for Measure*, III, i, 76–8.
2. *'Shikarris'*: 'Hunters'. In the *C M G*, Kipling underlined his knowledge of the fine distinctions between regiments: 'The "Shikarris" are not to be confused with the "Inextinguishables", though they hold the same views on polo and dances and all the serious business of life. Both Regiments are high caste, and . . .'

The Broken-Link Handicap

First published as No. 25, *CMG*, 6 April 1887

1. *G.R.*: gentleman rider. A 'ten-three' is a horse carrying the official weight for a four-year-old over a three-mile steeplechase (10 stone, 3 lbs).
2. *immoral . . . worse*: Kipling originally wrote 'skittles, and mean skittles at that.'
3. *But if . . . shoeing-bills*: In the *CMG*, Kipling was less expansively ironic: 'But my business is to describe the Broken-Link Handicap – not to pretend to be virtuous because the fun of one particular vice does not appeal to me.' A *larrikin* is a yob; a *brumby* a half-trained horse; a *shroff* a money-lender; *chumars* low-caste Indian saddlers.
4. *b.w.g.*: bay waler gelding. A 'waler' is a horse imported from New South Wales, or from Australia in general.
5. *jarrah*: an Australian timber.

Beyond the Pale

First printed in 1888.

1. *bustee*: inhabited quarter, village.
2. *cardamons*: seed-capsules. The *dhak* is a small bushy tree found in the jungles of the Punjab.
3. *boortka*: grown.

In Error

First published as No. 17, *CMG*, 24 January 1887.

1. *L.L.L. and Christopher*: Kinahan's L.L.L., Christopher and Grant's Morella Cherry Brandy.

A Bank Fraud

First published as No, 27, *CMG*, 14 April 1887.

1. *hoondi*: bills of exchange.
2. *burked*: suppressed. The *CMG* has 'burnt', forgoing the pun.

3. *a Gilbarte or a Hardie*: James William Gilbart (1794–1863), author of *The History and Principles of Banking* (1834). According to the *Reader's Guide*, Hardie was the author of *Simple and Compound Interest* (1839).

Tods' Amendment

First published as No. 28, *CMG*, 16 April 1887.

1. *Bhagat*: Hindu holy man.
2. *find out what*: in the *CMG*, Kipling added 'find out how horses were made, and what . . .'. An *ayah* is a nurse.
3. *khit, khitmutgar*: servant. A *jhampani* is a rickshaw-coolie; a *sais* a groom; a *dhobi* a washerman.
4. *chotee bolee*: speech used by women when speaking to children.
5. *Sub-Montane Tracts*: area at foot of mountains.
6. *chaprassis*: uniformed government messengers. *Durbaris*: executive members of native governments who attended the Viceroy's Courts and Audiences.
7. *Lat*: Lord.
8. *Ryotwari*: system whereby land revenue is settled directly between the Government and the individual cultivator, without reference to a landlord or village community.
9. *lakhs*: a *lakh* is 100,000.
10. *bundobust*: arrangement; *Jehannum*: hell; *takkus*: tax; *vakils*: lawyers.

The Daughter of the Regiment

First published as No. 34, *CMG*, 11 May 1887.

2. *Circassian Circle*: dance which the whole company could take part in.
2. *Pummeloe*: large Indian lime.
3. *Saint Lawrence*: suffered martyrdom by fire.
4. *tope*: copse.
5. *lotah*: small brass pot.

In the Pride of His Youth

First published as No. 33, *CMG*, 5 May 1887.

2. *at 1–6⅞*: at the rate of exchange of 6⅞ rupees to the pound.
2. *chummery*: accommodation shared by bachelors.
3. *Parsee*: well-to-do Persian.
4. *'gone with a handsomer man than you'*: popular ballad by William Carleton (1784–1869).
5. *he left Gravesend*: in the *CMG*, the narrator interjects: 'Curious. Some women rake up a small error or omission long ago, generally in the honeymoon by way of excusing premeditated sin on their own part.'
6. *when the dawn . . . in the bed*: added in 1888 to heighten the pathos.

Pig

First published as No. 38, *CMG*, 3 June 1887.

1. *Ghaznevid*: twelfth-century work from Ghazni, in Afghanistan.
2. *Keats' poem*: 'Isabella'. The gentlemen are her brothers.
3. *Competition-wallah*: member of the Indian Civil Service who has entered under the competitive system first introduced in 1856.

The Rout of the White Hussars

First printed in 1888.

1. *'side'*: style.
2. *cast*: decided to get rid of.
3. *'Keel Row'*: a quick-step.
4. *'The Place where the old Horse died'*: song by G. J. Whyte-Melville (1821–78).
5. *Fontenoy*: battle in which the French defeated the Allies, on 11 May 1745.
6. *Charity and Zeal*: masonic lodge. Kipling was Secretary of Hope and Perseverance, 782, E.C.

The Bronckhorst Divorce-Case

First printed in 1888.

1. *Hutt*: go away.
2. *on the criminal count*: Section 497 of the Indian Penal Code provided for the punishment of adultery by fines or imprisonment.
3. *Oorya*: from the district of Orissa, between Bengal and the Coromandel Coast.

Venus Annodomini

First published as No. 10, *CMG*, 4 December 1886.

1. *Venus Annodomini*: a modern (A.D.) Venus Anadyomene (rising from the waves). The Braccio Nuovo was the sculpture gallery of the Vatican.
2. *Ninon de L'Enclos*: seventeenth-century beauty and wit.
3. *Babus*: educated Bengalis.

The Bisara of Pooree

First published as No. 20, *CMG*, 4 March 1887.

1. *Kafir*: tribesman from the Hindu-Kush.
2. *balas-rubies*: rose-red stones from north-east Afghanistan.
3. *Nizam's Horse*: cavalry of the largest native state in South India.
4. *zenana*: women's quarters. Ashtaroth was the Phoenician goddess of fertility (1 Kings 11, 5).
5. *where he can do ... Colonel*: originally and rather more brutally: 'where there is a fine hope of his drinking himself to death. He is no good alive any way.'
6. *a danger*: in the *CMG*, 'the disgusting thing'.
7. *Mr Gubernatis or Max Muller*: Angelo de Gubernatis (1840–1913), Professor of Sanskrit at the University of Florence. Max Müller (1823–1900), Professor of Comparative Philology at Oxford.

A Friend's Friend

First published as No. 32, *CMG*, 2 May 1887.

1. *Hadramauti*: inhabitant of a district in southern Arabia.
2. *Globe-Trotters*: tourists. In the *CMG*, and in the first three editions of *Plain Tales*, Kipling identified Jevon as a T.G. – a Travelling Gent, or commercial traveller – and thus associated his bad behaviour with social status. In the eyes of the Anglo-Indian elite, trade was rather vulgar.
3. *Hakodate*: port on the north island of Japan.
4. *luted*: cemented.
5. *gold-beaters' skin*: animal membrane used to separate pieces of gold leaf.
6. *isinglass*: transparent glue.

The Gate of the Hundred Sorrows

First published as 'By the Janitor', *CMG*, 26 September 1884; signed E.M.

1. *pice*: small coin.
2. *sideways*: in the *CMG*, Kipling added: 'One of these days that house-front will come down, and the Municipality will send some one to inspect, and a lot of men to clear away the rubbish, and will go away not knowing how near they've been to the Gate.'
3. *Joss*: household god.
4. *MacSomebody*: McIntosh Jellaludin, who appears in 'To be Filed for Reference'. Kipling introduced him here in 1888. *Anarkulli* is a district in Lahore.
5. *anything*: in the *CMG*, the narrator had been more garrulous: 'In Fung-Tching's time we used to have all sorts of strange people – white, that's to say – to visit us. Somehow, they never told of what they'd seen, and it would be a hard business for any one to find the Gate even now. But I knew one youngster once (he was a Eurasian) that used to visit us regular. Fung-Tching put him up to it. He came first to see what things were like; then he found it pleasant, and as he paid well, the Old Man kept him on. No one of his own people could have dreamt of the thing. He used to slip a white *chudder* over his night-clothes, and stroll over into the City about one or two in the morning; stay for an hour or so, and then get home

quiet and comfortable. One pipe was enough for him, and he died of it.' A *chudder* is a square piece of cloth worn as a mantle.
6. *and then . . .*: followed in the *CMG* by a further sentence: 'Well, I'm trying to recollect something I heard a long, long time ago, when I was a little boy in Mangoe Lane – but I'm too sleepy to make head or tail of it.'

The Madness of Private Ortheris

First printed in 1888.

1. *burning-ghat*: where the dead were cremated.
2. *the Widder*: Queen Victoria. *Rotten-stone* is a powder used to polish metal. The *Humaners* are the Royal Humane Society, who had a station on the north side of the Serpentine, in Hyde Park.

The Story of Muhammad Din

First published as 'Mahommed Din', *CMG*, 8 September 1886.

1. *Munichandra*: 'Hymns of the Saints'. Peter Peterson (1847–99), a Sanskrit scholar, had discovered a number of rare manuscripts in 1882.

On the Strength of a Likeness

First published as No. 16, *CMG*, 10 January 1887.

1. *out-of-the-way*: in the *CMG*: 'utterly heathenish'.
2. '*Poor Wandering One*': soprano solo from Gilbert and Sullivan's *Pirates of Penzance*.
3. *Chutter Munzil*: literally, Umbrella Mansion.
4. *pacing this circle of thought*: in the *CMG*, the allusion to Dante is more explicit: 'in the lowest circle of the Inferno reserved for idiots on this earth.'

Wressley of the Foreign Office

First published as No. 26, *CMG*, 20 May 1887.

1. *Moss*: bog; a *reiver* is a raider.
2. *Treaties and Sunnuds*: *A Collection of Treaties and Sunnuds*, ed. Sir Charles Aitchison, eleven volumes, 1862–92. Aitchison (1832–96) was Lieutenant-Governor of the Punjab. *Sunnud*: official document.
3. *and even . . . another story*: in the *CMG*, 'and the consideration which Wressley received from his few friends at Simla confirmed his delusion.'
4. *Thacker and Spink*: publishers and booksellers.
5. *Rajput chiefs*: rulers of native states; *Ahir* is the caste of herdsmen.
6. *between office and office*: between office-hours, at lunchtime.
7. *presses*: wardrobe.
8. *Ruskin writes . . . somewhere*: 'Of Queens' Gardens', in *Sesame and Lilies* (1865).
9. *in the land . . . play with*: not in the *CMG* version. Probably added in order to emphasize the professionalism of the narrator, who handles the white light of local colour expertly.
10. *counter-calendared*: double-listed.
11. *Also, though . . . heard of*: not in the *CMG* version.

By Word of Mouth

First published as No. 39, *CMG*, 10 June 1887.

1. *Meridki*: eighteen miles north of Lahore.
2. *Valley of the Shadow*: Psalm 23, verse 4.
3. *dâk-bungalow*: resthouse.
4. *locum tenens*: temporary replacement.
5. *Tuticorin*: 1600 miles from Meridki.
6. *dâk-bungalow*: in the *CMG*, Kipling added: 'Now this is the last of the Plain Tales, because there are no more to follow.'

To be Filed for Reference

First printed in 1888.

1. '*Say is it dawn . . . be it*': from D. G. Rossetti (1828–1882), 'The Song of the Bower'.

2. *Serai*: courtyard.

3. *all the old names*: of places at Oxford. *Loggerhead*: bathing-place. *Mesopotamia*: a walk on the River Cherwell. *Charley Symonds' stable*: in Holywell Street.

4. *charpoy*: bed.

5. *gunny-bags*: jute sacks. *Alpaca*: a thin wool.

6. *I the Trinity . . . one gulp*: from Robert Browning (1812–1889), 'Soliloquy of the Spanish Cloister'.

7. *Atalanta in Calydon*: by A. C. Swinburne (1837–1909).

8. *the Pickering Horace*: William Pickering (1796–1854) produced his Diamond Classics edition of the works of Horace in 1825. The very high quality of the printing made it a valuable book.

9. *Mother Maturin*: during the 1880s, Kipling planned and partly wrote a novel called *Mother Maturin*, about an old Irish woman who owns an opium den in Lahore.

10. *Mirza Murad Ali Beg's book*: *Lalun the Bergun* (1884), a novel about the seamier side of native life.

11. *Ethel*: Ethel Stronnard, a character in *Mother Maturin*.

12. *The Giant's Robe*: *The Giant's Robe* (1884), by F. Anstey. A man publishes a novel written by a friend under his own name, and wins a great reputation, but cannot write another book to equal it.

MORE ABOUT PENGUINS, PELICANS,
PEREGRINES AND PUFFINS

For further information about books available from Penguins please write
to Dept EP, Penguin Books Ltd, Harmondsworth, Middlesex UB7 0DA.

In the U.S.A.: For a complete list of books available from Penguins in
the United States write to Dept DG, Penguin Books, 299 Murray Hill
Parkway, East Rutherford, New Jersey 07073.

In Canada: For a complete list of books available from Penguins in
Canada write to Penguin Books Canada Ltd, 2801 John Street,
Markham, Ontario L3R 1B4.

In Australia: For a complete list of books available from Penguins in
Australia write to the Marketing Department, Penguin Books Australia
Ltd, P.O. Box 257, Ringwood, Victoria 3134.

In New Zealand: For a complete list of books available from Penguins in
New Zealand write to the Marketing Department, Penguin Books (N.Z.)
Ltd, Private Bag, Takapuna, Auckland 9.

In India: For a complete list of books available from Penguins in India
write to Penguin Overseas Ltd, 706 Eros Apartments, 56 Nehru Place,
New Delhi 110019.

ENGLISH AND AMERICAN LITERATURE IN PENGUINS

☐ *Emma* **Jane Austen**

'I am going to take a heroine whom no one but myself will much like,' declared Jane Austen of Emma, her most spirited and controversial heroine in a comedy of self-deceit and self-discovery.

☐ *Tender is the Night* **F. Scott Fitzgerald**

Fitzgerald worked on seventeen different versions of this novel, and its obsessions – idealism, beauty, dissipation, alcohol and insanity – were those that consumed his own marriage and his life.

☐ *The Life of Johnson* **James Boswell**

Full of gusto, imagination, conversation and wit, Boswell's immortal portrait of Johnson is as near a novel as a true biography can be, and still regarded by many as the finest 'life' ever written. This shortened version is based on the 1799 edition.

☐ *A House and its Head* **Ivy Compton-Burnett**

In a novel 'as trim and tidy as a hand-grenade' (as Pamela Hansford Johnson put it), Ivy Compton-Burnett penetrates the facade of a conventional, upper-class Victorian family to uncover a chasm of violent emotions – jealousy, pain, frustration and sexual passion.

☐ *The Trumpet Major* **Thomas Hardy**

Although a vein of unhappy unrequited love runs through this novel, Hardy also draws on his warmest sense of humour to portray Wessex village life at the time of the Napoleonic wars.

☐ *The Complete Poems of Hugh MacDiarmid*

☐ Volume One
☐ Volume Two

The definitive edition of work by the greatest Scottish poet since Robert Burns, edited by his son Michael Grieve, and W. R. Aitken.

ENGLISH AND AMERICAN LITERATURE IN PENGUINS

☐ *Main Street* **Sinclair Lewis**

The novel that added an immortal chapter to the literature of America's Mid-West, *Main Street* contains the comic essence of Main Streets everywhere.

☐ *The Compleat Angler* **Izaak Walton**

A celebration of the countryside, and the superiority of those in 1653, as now, who love *quietnesse, vertue* and, above all, *Angling*. 'No fish, however coarse, could wish for a doughtier champion than Izaak Walton' – Lord Home

☐ *The Portrait of a Lady* **Henry James**

'One of the two most brilliant novels in the language', according to F. R. Leavis, James's masterpiece tells the story of a young American heiress, prey to fortune-hunters but not without a will of her own.

☐ *Hangover Square* **Patrick Hamilton**

Part love story, part thriller, and set in the publands of London's Earls Court, this novel caught the conversational tone of a whole generation in the uneasy months before the Second World War.

☐ *The Rainbow* **D. H. Lawrence**

Written between *Sons and Lovers* and *Women in Love*, *The Rainbow* covers three generations of Brangwens, a yeoman family living on the borders of Nottinghamshire.

☐ *Vindication of the Rights of Woman*
   Mary Wollstonecraft

Although Walpole once called her 'a hyena in petticoats', Mary Wollstonecraft's vision was such that modern feminists continue to go back and debate the arguments so powerfully set down here.

CLASSICS IN TRANSLATION
IN PENGUINS

☐ *Remembrance of Things Past* **Marcel Proust**
☐ Volume One: *Swann's Way, Within a Budding Grove*
☐ Volume Two: *The Guermantes Way, Cities of the Plain*
☐ Volume Three: *The Captive, The Fugitive, Time Regained*

Terence Kilmartin's acclaimed revised version of C. K. Scott Moncrieff's original translation, published in paperback for the first time.

☐ *The Canterbury Tales* **Geoffrey Chaucer**

'Every age is a Canterbury Pilgrimage . . . nor can a child be born who is not one of these characters of Chaucer' – William Blake

☐ *Gargantua & Pantagruel* **Rabelais**

The fantastic adventures of two giants through which Rabelais (1495–1553) caricatured his life and times in a masterpiece of exuberance and glorious exaggeration.

☐ *The Brothers Karamazov* **Fyodor Dostoevsky**

A detective story on many levels, profoundly involving the question of the existence of God, Dostoevsky's great drama of parricide and fraternal jealousy triumphantly fulfilled his aim: 'to find the man in man . . . [to] depict all the depths of the human soul.'

☐ *Fables of Aesop*

This translation recovers all the old magic of fables in which, too often, the fox steps forward as the cynical hero and a lamb is an ass to lie down with a lion.

☐ *The Three Theban Plays* **Sophocles**

A new translation, by Robert Fagles, of *Antigone, Oedipus the King* and *Oedipus at Colonus*, plays all based on the legend of the royal house of Thebes.

CLASSICS IN TRANSLATION
IN PENGUINS

☐ *The Treasure of the City of Ladies*
Christine de Pisan

This practical survival handbook for women (whether royal courtiers or prostitutes) paints a vivid picture of their lives and preoccupations in France, *c.* 1405. First English translation.

☐ *La Regenta* **Leopoldo Alas**

This first English translation of this Spanish masterpiece has been acclaimed as 'a major literary event' – *Observer*. 'Among the select band of "world novels" ... outstandingly well translated' – John Bayley in the *Listener*

☐ *Metamorphoses* **Ovid**

The whole of Western literature has found inspiration in Ovid's poem, a golden treasury of myths and legends that are linked by the theme of transformation.

☐ *Darkness at Noon* **Arthur Koestler**

'Koestler approaches the problem of ends and means, of love and truth and social organization, through the thoughts of an Old Bolshevik, Rubashov, as he awaits death in a G.P.U. prison' – *New Statesman*

☐ *War and Peace* **Leo Tolstoy**

'A complete picture of human life;' wrote one critic, 'a complete picture of the Russia of that day; a complete picture of everything in which people place their happiness and greatness, their grief and humiliation.'

☐ *The Divine Comedy: 1 Hell* **Dante**

A new translation by Mark Musa, in which the poet is conducted by the spirit of Virgil down through the twenty-four closely described circles of hell.

PENGUIN TRAVEL BOOKS

☐ *Arabian Sands* **Wilfred Thesiger**

'In the tradition of Burton, Doughty, Lawrence, Philby and Thomas, it is, very likely, the book about Arabia to end all books about Arabia' – *Daily Telegraph*

☐ *The Flight of Ikaros* **Kevin Andrews**

'He also is in love with the country . . . but he sees the other side of that dazzling medal or moon . . . If you want some truth about Greece, here it is' – Louis MacNeice in the *Observer*

☐ *D. H. Lawrence and Italy*

In *Twilight in Italy, Sea and Sardinia* and *Etruscan Places,* Lawrence recorded his impressions while living, writing and travelling in 'one of the most beautiful countries in the world'.

☐ *Maiden Voyage* **Denton Welch**

Opening during his last term at public school, from which the author absconded, *Maiden Voyage* turns into a brilliantly idiosyncratic account of China in the 1930s.

☐ *The Grand Irish Tour* **Peter Somerville-Large**

The account of a year's journey round Ireland. 'Marvellous . . . describes to me afresh a landscape I thought I knew' – Edna O'Brien in the *Observer*

☐ *Slow Boats to China* **Gavin Young**

On an ancient steamer, a cargo dhow, a Filipino kumpit and twenty more agreeably cranky boats, Gavin Young sailed from Piraeus to Canton in seven crowded and colourful months. 'A pleasure to read' – Paul Theroux

PENGUIN TRAVEL BOOKS

☐ *The Kingdom by the Sea* **Paul Theroux**

1982, the year of the Falklands War and the Royal Baby, was the ideal time, Theroux found, to travel round the coast of Britain and surprise the British into talking about themselves. 'He describes it all brilliantly and honestly' – Anthony Burgess

☐ *One's Company* **Peter Fleming**

His journey to China as special correspondent to *The Times* in 1933. 'One reads him for literary delight . . . But, he is also an observer of penetrating intellect' – Vita Sackville West

☐ *The Traveller's Tree* **Patrick Leigh Fermor**

'A picture of the Indies more penetrating and original than any that has been presented before' – *Observer*

☐ *The Path to Rome* **Hilaire Belloc**

'The only book I ever wrote for love,' is how Belloc described the wonderful blend of anecdote, humour and reflection that makes up the story of his pilgrimage to Rome.

☐ *The Light Garden of the Angel King* **Peter Levi**

Afghanistan has been a wild rocky highway for nomads and merchants, Alexander the Great, Buddhist monks, great Moghul conquerors and the armies of the Raj. Here, quite brilliantly, Levi writes about their journeys and his own.

☐ *Among the Russians* **Colin Thubron**

'The Thubron approach to travelling has an integrity that belongs to another age' – Dervla Murphy in the *Irish Times*. 'A magnificent achievement' – Nikolai Tolstoy

PENGUIN REFERENCE BOOKS

☐ *The Penguin Map of the World*

Clear, colourful, crammed with information and fully up-to-date, this is a useful map to stick on your wall at home, at school or in the office.

☐ *The Penguin Map of Europe*

Covers all land eastwards to the Urals, southwards to North Africa and up to Syria, Iraq and Iran * Scale = 1:5,500,000 * 4-colour artwork * Features main roads, railways, oil and gas pipelines, plus extra information including national flags, currencies and populations.

☐ *The Penguin Map of the British Isles*

Including the Orkneys, the Shetlands, the Channel Islands and much of Normandy, this excellent map is ideal for planning routes and touring holidays, or as a study aid.

☐ *The Penguin Dictionary of Quotations*

A treasure-trove of over 12,000 new gems and old favourites, from Aesop and Matthew Arnold to Xenophon and Zola.

☐ *The Penguin Dictionary of Art and Artists*

Fifth Edition. 'A vast amount of information intelligently presented, carefully detailed, abreast of current thought and scholarship and easy to read' – *The Times Literary Supplement*

☐ *The Penguin Pocket Thesaurus*

A pocket-sized version of Roget's classic, and an essential companion for all commuters, crossword addicts, students, journalists and the stuck-for-words.